Blindfold: The Complete Series Box Set

By Cassie Wild and M.S. Parker

This book is a work of fiction. The names, characters, places and incidents are products of the writer's imagination or have been used fictitiously and are not to be construed as real. Any resemblance to persons, living or dead, actual events, locales or organizations is entirely coincidental.

Copyright © 2015 Belmonte Publishing

Published by Belmonte Publishing.

All rights reserved. Without limiting the rights under copyright reserved above, no part of this publication may be reproduced, stored in or introduced into a retrieval system, or transmitted, in any form, or by any means (electronic, mechanical, photocopying, recording, or otherwise) without the prior written permission of the copyright owner.

The author acknowledges the trademarked status and trademark owners of various products referenced in this work of fiction, which have been used without permission. The publication/use of these trademarks is not authorized, associated with, or sponsored by the trademark owners.

ISBN-13: 978-1519234421
ISBN-10: 1519234422

Table of Contents

Blindfold Vol. I 9
Chapter 1 9
Chapter 2 21
Chapter 3 29
Chapter 4 37
Chapter 5 47
Chapter 6 53
Chapter 7 61
Chapter 8 67
Chapter 9 75
Chapter 10 87
Blindfold Vol. II 101
Chapter 1 101
Chapter 2 113
Chapter 3 125
Chapter 4 135
Chapter 5 143

Chapter 6	151
Chapter 7	153
Chapter 8	165
Chapter 9	171
Chapter 10	181
Blindfold Vol. III	191
Chapter 1	191
Chapter 2	201
Chapter 3	211
Chapter 4	221
Chapter 5	235
Chapter 6	241
Chapter 7	247
Chapter 8	255
Chapter 9	265
Chapter 10	275
Chapter 11	279
Chapter 12	285
Chapter 13	291
Chapter 14	295
Blindfold Vol. IV	299
Chapter 1	299
Chapter 2	309
Chapter 3	317
Chapter 4	327
Chapter 5	331

Chapter 6 343
Chapter 7 349
Chapter 8 355
Chapter 9 361
Chapter 10 369
Chapter 11 381
Chapter 12 393
Blindfold Vol. V 403
Chapter 1 403
Chapter 2 413
Chapter 3 425
Chapter 4 433
Chapter 5 443
Chapter 6 451
Chapter 7 455
Chapter 8 459
Chapter 9 463
Chapter 10 467
Chapter 11 477
Chapter 12 489
Chapter 13 495
Chapter 14 503
Chapter 15 507
Blindfold Epilogue 513
Acknowledgement 531
About The Authors 532

MS Parker 532
Cassie Wild 532

Blindfold Vol. I

Chapter 1

Toni

"Six months."

I stared at the check Dr. Willis Schumacher had given me when I visited him in the hospital, trying to understand how this could have happened. All right, I understood how it happened. On an intellectual level anyway.

A hand reached out and tugged my hair, successfully getting my attention. Victor, my pain-in-the-ass older brother was grinning at me. He'd always pissed me off when he pulled my hair as a kid, but it had always been impossible not to smile at least a little.

Only a little, though.

It would take quite a bit more to make me smile as much as I normally did. I didn't get down often, but the past week had managed to shoot my mood straight down to the level of toxic.

"Aw, come on, Sis." Vic braced his elbows on the table and leaned down, trying to catch my gaze. His dark red hair was the exact same shade as mine and the wind blew it back from his face. "It's going to work out."

The brisk April breeze had managed to rip my hair from its loose knot, so I glared at him through a tangle of hair. "Six fucking months!"

He sighed and leaned back in his chair. "Toni..."

"Stop it, Vic."

Aggravated, I surged up from the wrought iron chair and started to pace. We'd met for coffee in Bryant Park, which showed how well Vic knew me. At twenty-seven, he was three years older than me and we'd always been close. It had been Vic and me against our three older brothers more times than I could count. And he knew that what I needed right now was to vent.

"Doc Schumacher had a heart attack, Toni."

Sometimes, I needed somebody to yell at since I couldn't yell at life.

"Really?" I practically snarled at him. "So that's why I spent ten minutes pounding on his chest?"

Ribs had cracked. I'd never forget the sound of it. Rubbing the heel of my hand over my chest, I swallowed back the bile that rose there even as I thought of it now, days later.

Vic lapsed into silence. Doc Schumacher, my boss – former boss now – was one of my oldest friends. One of my family's oldest friends. I'd known him since I was a little girl. He was part of the reason I decided I wanted to help people. I'd had a kitten when I was four, and she'd somehow managed to break her leg. He'd found me bawling in the alley next to my family's house, the house where my parents still lived.

He'd helped calm the kitten – and me – down, then he'd

stabilized her leg and taken me to my parents. Her name had been Reeses. Like the candy. She died a few years ago. I'd never forgotten how kind he'd been. That was one of the reasons I'd wanted to work for him while I put myself through college.

I guess that's why I wasn't prepared for the fact that the heart attack that almost killed him would also terminate my employment earlier than I'd planned. Willis had always seemed invincible to me. Even at seventy-two, I'd only seen him as strong and capable. I'd seen him that way up until the moment he collapsed. When he told me that his doctor told him he had to make major changes, I hadn't truly realized what that would mean.

I was trying to be logical about this. Logical and not selfish, but the job that had paid my tuition, my living expenses, for my books, for *everything* these past few years was just…gone.

I was six months shy of being done with my Ph.D in psychology. I could have been done two years ago, but balancing the course load with my finances…well. It was basically impossible.

Feeling Vic's gaze on me, I looked over at him. "Where am I going to find another job that will pay what I make and let me have the days off I need to finish up?"

"I might have an idea," he said.

His dark eyes shifted away from mine, and I knew whatever he was thinking was probably a bad idea. I loved my big brother, but he wasn't exactly known for his good ideas. I lifted my face to sky and blew out a breath.

Six damn months. The luck I had sometimes was just ridiculous. Although, looking at it logically, I wasn't the one who'd technically died for six minutes, so I supposed I was being a bit petty.

"Talk about putting things in perspective," I muttered.

"If you're done talking to yourself..."

Glaring at him, I shoved my hair out of my face as the wind snatched at it again. I swore as it whipped across my face. Going to sit back by my brother, I dug through the messenger bag that doubled as a purse and book bag.

"Whatever idea you have probably isn't the sort of job I want, Vic."

I ran a brush quickly through the snarls and then separated my heavy hair into two sections. The braided pigtails might look juvenile to some, but it was a style that had been popular for a reason – it *worked*. Especially for pain-in-the-ass hair like mine.

"Fine." Vic shrugged. "Don't listen to me. I guess you can always go to work for the family business."

I made a face at him, refusing to let the idea even settle in my brain. My family was close, as close as a family could be, really. But there was still tension between Vic and the rest of our brothers. And with Dad.

Vic had gotten into trouble as a teenager, and it still rubbed him wrong that Dad had left him to deal with his mess rather than bail him out even though Vic and I both knew it had been good for him.

But knowing it and liking it were two different things.

"All right, big brother, what exactly do you have to offer me?" I asked, cocking my eyebrow at him. "Dealing cards in some back alley game? Mixing drinks until two a.m.?"

He grimaced at the last one. "Well..."

"I can't."

I secured one braid and got to work on the other. Without saying anything else, I finished the second braid, and then dropped down onto the metal chair across from him and took his hand in both of mine. His big paw dwarfed my smaller ones. He was the tallest of all my brothers, towering over me by a foot.

"Vic, I love you, and thanks for trying, but I can't pull those hours, finish up with school, and stay sane enough to help other people with their problems." I knew it had only been because of Doc Schumacher's kindness that I was able to get this far this fast. If I'd needed to get a different job, it would've taken me even longer to make it to this point.

Vic looked away, his face going a dull, ruddy red. He wanted to help so bad and I knew why.

Everybody had expected me to go off to Yale on a full ride.

I had expected it.

Then Vic had gotten into trouble, right as I'd been applying for scholarships. He'd gotten in trouble in the worst kind of way – hitting national news and everything.

What he'd done shouldn't have affected me.

I was smart. No bones about it, I was fricking brilliant. I had graduated from high school at sixteen and, thanks to advanced placement courses, already had a good portion of pre-requisites under my belt. I'd already been accepted to Stanford to pursue my BA, and then on to my Masters before pursuing my Ph.D. But then the deadline for financial aid had passed and ... nothing.

So I stayed home.

At first, I told everyone that it just made more sense for me to stay and finish up my BA rather than worrying about transferring credits. I needed to be around my family during the trial anyway. Mom had needed me too. When I'd started on my Masters, no one bothered asking why I hadn't moved away.

The sound of my phone whistling at me interrupted my heavy brood marathon. I jolted and looked down to see that yet another brother was calling to check up on me. The oldest this time.

I blew out a breath.

Six months. That's all I had needed.

"Hey, Deacon."

Deacon was the opposite of Vic in every way. Grounded and steady, my oldest brother was following in my dad's footsteps and he took the job seriously. Too seriously, and I didn't just mean he was a damn good electrician. He also seemed to think he was there to watch out for me, like I was still some skinny, brainy little eleven year-old, heading into middle school without him there to look out for me.

"I think I might have a line on a job for you," Deacon said without preamble.

Rolling my eyes, I said, "It's *sooooo* wonderful to hear from you too. Yeah, I'm here with Vic, but it's a *great* time to talk and tell me how to live my life."

Across from me, Vic was laughing and I glared at him. Vic may have been the screw-up, but I was the baby...and none of my brothers ever let me forget it.

I could practically hear him smirking.

"Okay, brat. How are you?"

"Lousy," I countered. "How's the family?"

Deacon had married the girl he'd fallen for in tenth grade. They'd gotten engaged after she graduated from high school and had gotten married six months after that. Their fifteenth anniversary loomed in front of them, as well as the first birthday of their fifth, and last, child. Beth had made it very clear that this one would be the last or she'd be giving Deacon a vasectomy herself. Without anesthetic.

"Let's not discuss that." Some strain came through my brother's voice.

"What's wrong?"

I could practically hear the mental debate and finally, he sighed. "Hell, we think Emma has chicken pox. There's a girl at the daycare...I don't know the whole story, but somehow she got in without getting vaccinated, and now Emma has it."

"Oh, no." Mentally, I was crossing my fingers and

hoping, but Beth was a nurse. She knew what chicken pox looked like. I wanted to tell my brother not to worry, but I remembered what it had been like to have chicken pox as a kid and two year-old Emma was going to be climbing the walls. "Keep me updated."

"I will. Anyway…the job."

I couldn't even talk my way out of whatever he had to say now. He was stubborn like that. "Okay, what is it?"

I behaved myself while he was talking and waited until he fell silent before I spoke. "This *is* Deacon Gallagher, right? Old man? Dark brown hair?" I glanced at Vic, who appeared to be waiting for me to share. "What the hell are you thinking?"

"Toni, be reasonable."

At least he didn't scold me for swearing like he'd done when I was younger. Eleven years older than me, he'd taken it upon himself to be another parent pretty much since moment one.

"It's a job and your hours are negotiable with your boss. You're matched by hours available and your personality." He paused and then added, "Okay, keeping that in mind, you're in trouble."

"Very funny, asshat," I said darkly. "You're screwing with me. A personal assistant? I'm going to school to be a psychiatrist, not a secretary."

Deacon's voice hardened. "Our mom's a secretary, Toni. Remember?"

He didn't have to point that out for me to feel bad. I wanted to kick myself the second the words left my mouth. "I know that." Self-conscious, I glanced over at Vic. He gave me a sympathetic look, but it didn't help.

"Look, Toni. You know what Mom and Dad always told us. There's no shame in any kind of honest work. And it's not like it'd be forever. Just until you finish your degree. That does still matter to you, right?"

Nothing else he said could have made me go. Absolutely nothing.

The gleaming of Winter Enterprises made me think of a penis. I couldn't help it. I was the youngest of four brothers and they were guys to the nth degree. Everything was a penis metaphor to them, even if it wasn't. They'd been overprotective, but that hadn't kept them from talking like typical guys around me.

I actually felt a little bad about thinking that way about Winter Enterprises. While they'd been involved in charities since they were founded by Dominic Snow a few years ago, he'd recently announced that he'd founded In From the Cold to help find people who'd been victims of, or involved with, human trafficking. The foundation had gotten a lot of extra press recently due to the scandal of some high society woman who'd gotten arrested for conspiring to blackmail Snow and his fiancé. Considering his fiancé was a small town girl who'd become his assistant and was now wearing his ring, it had been like Christmas for the media.

Shaking my head in an attempt to clear it, I moved forward. All the people milling around made my nerves jack up even more and that just irritated me even more. I didn't like being nervous. Ask me to organize and keep track of the workings of an entire doctor's office, I'm fine. Put me in the middle of my brothers and their crazy friends, no problem. Professionally and with my family, I was a rock, but this crowded job fair was turning me into a five foot, twenty-four year-old ball of nerves.

Taking a deep breath, I made my way inside and looked around, taking a minute to acclimate. Early in life, I'd learned to deal with being thrown into situations where I wasn't comfortable. One of the many joys of having always been smart.

Lines for registering, lines to get sorted…

What a fucking mess.

I took another look over some of the groups clustered around, and had the sinking sensation I'd have to tell my brother that this just wasn't going to work out. These were so not my kind of people.

Many of them were dressed to the nines in designer names and expensive haircuts. And then there was me, with my cute sundress and chic little shrug draped over my arm. I had a file and my iPad, while others carried giant briefcases and padfolios likely stuffed with impressive resumes.

"Something of a zoo, isn't it?"

The quiet voice came from next to me and I glanced up to see a stocky, pleasant-looking man standing next to me. With his salt-and-pepper hair, I put his age in the early forties. "I'd say that sums it up." I couldn't help but add, "I see mostly herd animals, very few standing out from the pack."

That elicited a chuckle, his dark blue eyes sparkling.

"If you don't mind my asking, what position are you applying for?"

I took a closer look at him and realized with a start that he was an employee here. Not that he wore a nametag. This place probably stopped with the nametags outside the lobby.

"Personal assistant," I said slowly. I shifted toward him, using the movement to tuck my single file folder behind my back. I was really starting to think this was a bad idea.

"*Exclusive.*"

I didn't know what to say, so I just nodded. *Exclusive* was the name Winter Enterprises had given to the new service offering to match up personal assistants with the New York elite. Again, I told myself I was an idiot. This so wasn't the job for me. What did I know about helping out the jet set?

What did I *care* about the jet set?

"May I?" He held out a hand, clearly waiting for the file I'd stowed behind me.

Reluctant, I turned over the file. He opened and skimmed it, but I had the feeling he was more interested in me than in what a couple of papers had to say. "What would you do if your employer received a call that they were being investigated by the IRS for tax fraud?"

"Call their accountant," I responded without even thinking. What did I know about their taxes? "And probably whatever lawyer they have on retainer for that sort of thing," I added after a moment. If they were rich enough to use a service like this, then they probably had a lawyer.

He flicked me a look over the edge of the file, but I couldn't read it.

"Your client asks you to pick up someone at the airport and to make sure that their luggage bypasses security. Would you ask questions?"

Frowning, I held his gaze. This was a loaded question. I could already tell. Finally, I shrugged and said, "I would tell my client that, while I don't need to know what's in the luggage, I wouldn't be comfortable bending the law. If the client insisted, I would hand in my notice. I don't want to work for criminals."

He nodded and held out a hand. "I'm Robson Findley. Come on. I'll finish your interview myself."

It was the quickest and weirdest interview of my life. Instead of asking me about my previous experience, he hammered me with more odd questions.

It's your off night and you get called to order some flowers and candy sent to an unknown address. What do you do?

You're meeting a friend for your employer and the friend hits on you. Do you tell your employer?

You're visiting your employer and you hear some unusual noises coming from one of the rooms. What do you do?

It didn't take me long to realize that this wasn't going to work. I didn't interrupt though. I wanted to be able to tell Deacon I at least gave it a fair shot. I waited until there was a gap and then rose. "Mr. Findlay, I really appreciate the opportunity, but I don't think this job would be right for me."

"Yes?" He cocked his head, eyes shrewd, but not annoyed. "Just why is that?"

I didn't have an exact reason I could give, and in a moment of utter desperation and stupidity, I blurted out, "I don't like rich people."

It sounded offensive enough that I assumed I'd be thrown out on my ass as soon as he called security. I lifted my chin, crossed my arms over my chest, and waited.

To my surprise, Findlay laughed. He dropped down into the chair behind his desk, tipped back his head and actually laughed. A few moments passed before he stopped, but when he looked at me, his eyes were still glinting with mirth. "Can I be blunt with you for a moment?"

I stared at him.

"Sometimes, I don't like them much either."

The moment he said it, he blinked, almost as if startled he'd actually said it.

It was a look I was familiar with. I was always having people tell me things they wouldn't have told anyone else. I'd been told I have one of those faces. It's not really all that great.

He cleared his throat and began shuffling papers on his desk. "As I was saying…"

He hadn't been saying anything, but I didn't call him on the lie, just watched as he regained his composure.

"I think you're going to work out rather well, Ms. Gallagher. Assuming we find you the right match. And while I still need you to fill out the forms, I already have a couple of ideas for good matches."

Hesitant, I eyed the forms. I still had some serious misgivings about this.

"Perhaps you should have an idea what it pays," he said with a smile.

The figure he named made my jaw drop.

Hello college tuition.

Chapter 2

Toni

Fifth Avenue.

What the hell was I doing on Fifth Avenue?

Especially this part of Fifth Avenue.

Smoothing a hand down the trim black pants I'd selected to wear, I approached the door and tried not to look like I was hesitating. There was no doorman. That might have struck me as odd, except this massive building wasn't some collection of ultra-cool, ultra-expensive condos.

It was one, ginormous family home.

I couldn't even fathom how many millions of dollars a family home on Fifth Avenue must have cost. The buzz of traffic around here was noticeably less, and as I drew closer to the house, some lady decked all in white sailed by with her dog on a pink leash. There was a sparkle at its neck and I had the insane idea that the sparkle might be from diamonds. Real diamonds. But that couldn't be possible, could it?

My skin started to prickle. I looked up at the ditz who put the diamonds on a dog and found her sending me a sidelong look. When she caught me eying her, her nostrils flared as if she'd smelled something bad, and she whipped her head around.

Wow.

Mentally bracing myself, I marched up the steps between two stately lion statues and knocked.

I'd been paired with a woman by the name of Isadora Lang. I supposed if I paid more attention to the society pages, I would've known the name, but all I had was what Mr. Findley sent me yesterday afternoon.

Isadora was twenty years old and needing help a few days a week – my choice of days – to help her keep her life organized. She hadn't requested any off-hours availability or included a list of crazy demands. It really sounded like a dream job.

But I had a sinking feeling I was about to endure the same sort of treatment I'd received from the ditzy dog owner.

The door swung open and I flashed the suit-clad gentleman my best smile. He was wearing a suit that probably cost more than two months' rent and looked to be in his mid to late fifties.

"Hello. I'm Toni—"

A woman's voice interrupted me.

"Please tell me that's her, Doug! I can't figure out this damn newsletter!" She sounded nearly frantic, but not obnoxious.

The suited man gave me a pained look. "Are you with *Exclusive*?"

"I am."

A moment later, a tall, curvy woman came bursting out from somewhere behind him. She had stylish black curls, large olive green eyes, porcelain skin, and an elegant, beautiful face. Absolutely gorgeous.

"In, now," she said as she reached around the man and grabbed my wrist. I stared at her, shocked into silence as she pulled me into the house. "Thank God you're here. If I don't get this straightened out, I'm doomed."

Once I was inside, she let my hand go and turned to beam

at the man in the black suit. "You can shut the door now, Doug," she said, giving him the sweetest genuine smile I'd ever seen. "My new assistant and I have a lot of work to do."

My head was spinning. I didn't think I'd ever seen anybody smile that brilliantly and mean it. When she turned that megawatt smile on me, I felt almost a little dazzled. Heaven help any man who found themselves in her sights.

"Ma'am – uh, I mean, Miss?"

"Call me Isadora, please. Just as Doug here. I don't like the whole 'Miss' thing."

"All right." I nodded, starting to find my footing. "Now, what seems to be the problem?"

Her smile turned a little sheepish and she bit her lower lip. "I have to admit, Toni…it is Toni, right? I'm hopeless. I thought I could figure out this whole newsletter thing, but…" She spread her hands out wide and shrugged, her expression making her look less like a beautiful young woman and more like a wide-eyed, innocent child.

"You want a newsletter."

"No," she said, rolling her eyes. "I don't *want* it. I need it. I told the committee I could do it. I'm good on computers, and I didn't think it would be that hard."

Despite myself, I was starting to like her. Sure, I couldn't imagine what was so difficult about making a newsletter, but she didn't seem like she was above it. Just clueless.

"So what's the newsletter for?" I asked with a smile.

"Rich assholes."

She delivered the answer without blinking an eye.

Behind me, Doug, in his perfect black suit, smothered a laugh and pretended it was a cough before hurrying away.

"You know what?" I gave her my own version of a brilliant smile. "I think we should start from the top."

She'd led me into a large, airy sitting room.

There was no way I could call it a living room. It was too elegant, too posh, for that. The walls were a pale, soft yellow with the trim painted a gleaming white. In the middle of the room stood a low, round table that gleamed like gold. In the precise middle of that table, there was a vase of the most beautiful white roses I'd ever seen in my life, each petal perfection.

I'd always had a weakness for white roses.

There were any number of small chairs and couches scattered throughout the large, airy room, but Isadora had guided me to a round, fat chair, practically the size of a small pond, and big enough for both of us. Probably two more. A fifth if we wanted to snuggle.

That had been two hours ago and I was still sitting in that chair, comparing the list she'd given me with the newsletter I was compiling. The last one had indeed been for rich assholes. Even I'd recognized those names.

This one seemed to be geared toward the opposite. Wary single moms loathe to accept anything from anybody.

I finished that one up just as she managed to compile a somewhat neat stack of information. I looked at it with a combination of trepidation and chagrin.

"I think what you need," I said suddenly. "Is to learn how to say no."

Immediately, I realized I probably shouldn't have said it. What if she was touchy and took it as judgmental? What if she was whiny?

But Isadora threw back her head and laughed. "I know, right? It's always *somebody needs to do it and nobody else wants to say yes.*"

Looking away from that engaging smile, I focused on the notes in front of me. Handwritten notes, printed interviews, discs with yet more information, graphs, articles, pictures and a dozen other things that needed to be included in a dozen other newsletters.

Over the past few hours, I'd learned enough to realize I needed to stop making snap judgments. It was a flaw of mine. A flaw I hated in others, but there I was, doing it far too often.

It was sad.

I generally only did it with people like Isadora, the privileged and wealthy. My own kind of people, I gave the benefit of the doubt.

Isadora spoke up, interrupting my mental reverie. "What time did you say the first newsletter would go out?"

"About one this afternoon."

All in all, that one had been the easiest to do. Cleverly and cleanly written, the author poked fun at more than a few of the well-known families here in the city.

Arching an eyebrow at her, I smiled. "You afraid we're going to get mobbed? These streets are quiet. You'll hear them coming long before they get here."

She rolled her eyes. "Well, *one* of them lives here."

"Oh?" I gave her a questioning look. Mr. Findley hadn't said anything about a husband.

"Yep. My brother."

She slid her legs off her side of the chair and rose, arching her arms back high over her head and stretching. It brought her shirt up over her belly, revealing a flat stomach with skin the right kind of pale. I was the other kind of pale, the kind that came with my red hair. My brothers used to say I could cause traffic accidents if I left too much skin exposed. I didn't even freckle in the sun. I just went all lobster crispy.

Then I processed what she said. "That could get...interesting." If her brother was anything like mine, I could only imagine how he'd take it. "What do your folks think about this?"

For the first time, her bright smile dimmed. "They're gone," she said softly.

She moved from the couch to stand in front of the fireplace with its candle-scape insert in the hearth and the pictures that dotted the mantle. She took one down and turned, displaying it in front of her. It revealed a pretty little girl, a handsome young man who looked to be in his late teens. There were two adults, each of them looking to be in their mid-forties. All of them looked happy.

"They died in a car wreck when I was seven. This picture was taken just a couple of months before it happened." She turned it back to her, lifting it to trace their faces with her hand. "My brother raised me. I barely remember them."

I went to apologize, to say something. I didn't even know what. I couldn't imagine my life without either of my parents, much less having lost both of them at the same time, and as a child.

Before I could figure out what I should say, she put the picture down and clapped her hands. "Hey, you know what? I'm starving. You wanna order some pizza?"

I'd decided this job could work.

I also thought I might even grow to like the somewhat ditzy, but decidedly adorable Isadora.

She was smart as hell, but couldn't focus worth a damn. I found myself psychoanalyzing her all the time and asking strange little questions that were just a little too nosy, but I couldn't stop myself. She was fascinating.

She didn't seem to notice or care, and I was trying to work up the courage to ask yet more questions when we heard a door slam and loud male voices followed.

"Mr. Lang!"

"Okay, Doug. Who the *fuck* is this Toni person my sister hired? I thought I hired you all to watch over her, not let her bring strange guys into the house."

"Guys?" I mouthed to Isadora.

But she didn't notice. She had her face buried in her hands and was shaking her head, though I couldn't tell if she was upset or trying not to laugh.

A shadow appeared in the doorway and I instinctively stood. She caught my hand and looked up at me with a pleading expression on her face.

"Please don't let him scare you off."

Scare me off? I snorted. As if. I squeezed Isadora's hand.

"I'm fine," I assured her.

Then I turned towards the door and met the hard green eyes of a man who was seriously, *seriously* beautiful. His hair was the sort of black that would almost look blue in some light, and he had the sort of features that made heads turn.

He was also staring at me as though I was something he'd found on the bottom of his shoe. No amount of good looks could make up for that.

"Who the fuck are you?" he demanded.

I almost snapped back at him, but, instead, I decided to go a different route and make him feel like the asshole he appeared to be.

"Hi." I gave him a winning, but fake, smile. "I'm Toni. And you are?"

Chapter 3

Ash

I'm not a patient man.

I wasn't one by nature, and my life didn't allow for the time or luxury of patience. It didn't allow for time for much of anything.

So when I demanded to know who in the fuck Tony was, I wanted a damn answer right then.

I got one, too.

Granted, it wasn't the answer I was expecting.

I'm Toni. And you are?

Bemused, I looked down at the small hand held out to me, and then lifted my eyes to stare into a pair of smoky blue eyes so gorgeous that I imagined I could lose myself in them. I let myself entertain that fanciful thought for maybe ten seconds, and then I cut it off. No point in going there.

"Again." Crossing my arms over my chest, I narrowed my eyes at her. "Who the fuck are you?"

Nobody was supposed to be allowed inside, especially allowed inside with my little sister, unless I cleared it. Everyone on my staff knew that.

Some people were going to find themselves without a job today.

"I'm Toni," she repeated.

She blinked at me, somehow managing to look completely innocent and confused, but I had the damnedest feeling she was laughing at me and that pissed me off even more.

"Toni Gallagher." She offered with another smile that I was sure was fake. "*Exclusive* sent me. Isadora wanted an assistant, and I was the one best suited to her and the position."

"I'm the one who decides who is best suited to work for my sister," I said, walking towards her until we were only inches apart.

I waited.

I had a good fifteen inches on her, and I knew how to use my height – hell, my everything – to intimidate anyone.

She just peered up at me, raised an eyebrow and came back with the last thing I'd expected. "Do you really think you're the best person to decide who should work for your sister? She is an adult."

I gaped.

And Toni Gallagher just stared at me, head cocked to the side as she tapped a finger against lips slicked the color of merlot. I hated that shit, but I found myself craving a taste just then. And I didn't want it from a glass.

She continued, "I mean, do you even know what's going on in her life?"

"I...what?"

Thrown off track, and still thinking about that damn intriguing mouth, I planted my hands on my hips and glared down at her. She shifted her weight, and braced her own hand on her hip.

"She needs somebody who knows what's going on in her life now. What foundations and organizations does she belong to? What she's interested in. Do you know any of that?"

"Again," I said, biting the word off as I glared at the tiny, irritating woman in front of me. She looked like the kind of person who'd break in a stiff wind, but I was quickly seeing that her appearance was deceiving. "I'm the one who decides who gets hired in this household."

That tone of voice usually had only one of two responses – abject terror or abject humility. Often it was both. I was the heir to two of the oldest families in the country, and one of the richest bastards in said country. And I was a bastard in the figurative sense. I made no bones about it. I pushed until I got my way, but more often than not, I didn't have to push, because people gave me what I wanted.

I was a Lang.

So it shocked the hell out of me when Toni pursed her lips and gave me a slow, thorough study, her eyes going from my head to my feet and back again. It took more self-control than I liked to keep from fidgeting under that intense gaze.

"Does this..." She waved her hand at me. "...really work?"

The question was so unexpected, I answered honestly, "Yes."

"I thought so." She shrugged. "It won't work on me. I grew up with four older brothers who always thought I should do what they told me. It doesn't work with them and it won't work with you."

I had the strange and sudden thought that this had to be some sort of joke. People didn't talk to me like that. Certainly not people who wanted to be employed.

Then, without so much as a dismissive glance, she turned to Isadora. "I was thinking about how we can get all the information up at the top of your newsletter. Half the time, people only skim..."

I shot a look at Isadora.

My sister was grinning at me. "Before we go any further," she deftly cut into what Toni was saying. "I should make formal introductions. Ash, this is my amazing new assistant,

Toni Gallagher. Who, as you can see, is not a man. Toni, I'd like you to meet my big brother, Ashford Lang. You can call him Ash."

I scowled. No, she most certainly could not. "Employees address me as Mr. Lang."

Isadora ignored my comment and continued, her smile tightening the way it did when she was upset. "She's right, by the way. You can't possibly decide who'd be best for me to work with because you're more interested in having people hover over me than talk to me."

There was a hint of displeasure, maybe even hurt, in her voice, but she looked away before I could figure out just what I'd seen. Scowling, I went to jam my hands into my pockets before I stopped myself. I wasn't in the jeans I preferred to wear when I wasn't working. I was still in the suit I'd put on that morning, and tailored suits weren't exactly designed for men to shove their hands into the pockets. Ruined the lines.

Focusing back on what Isadora said, I slid Toni a look.

No, she definitely wasn't a man.

I gave myself a mental shake. I didn't think she was amazing either. People around my sister needed to be scared of me, not dismiss me like I didn't matter.

"We've talked about this," I told Isadora as she turned her attention back to Toni.

Neither of them said anything to me as Toni went back to explaining whatever idea it was that she'd had. I waited a few more moments, expecting them to draw me into their conversation. People did that. People wanted my involvement. They wanted my input. They wanted my approval, and more often than not, my money.

Isadora didn't need the money, but she usually sought my approval. I'd raised her since our parents died and we had an odd combination of a brother-sister, father-daughter relationship. In some ways, I was the only parent she'd ever know. But she didn't even look my way.

After a few more moments of being ignored, I turned on my heel and stalked out of the room. I was going to have to dig into this woman's background. Since I hadn't hired her, I had no idea what kind of person she was or what kind of skeletons she was hiding.

As I came out of the parlor, I caught Doug's eyes and indicated with a jerk of my head that he was to follow me. He gave me a differential bob of his head, but it didn't do shit to cool my temper. Once we were inside the large office that took up much of the southeast corner of the family home, I turned on him, needing to take my frustration out on someone.

"You've got less than five minutes to convince me why I shouldn't fire you."

He didn't even flinch. "Miss Isadora gave me the name of her new assistant just this morning." His gaze flicked to my desk. "Once she told me she'd hired somebody without speaking with you first, I started the background check. I sent you an email as well, but you must not have received it."

Feeling a little deflated, I skirted around my desk and saw the file folder sitting in front of my computer. I flipped the file open and saw the answers to the same routine background check I did on all my employees. Well, maybe not exactly routine. It was a bit more thorough than average, but for good reason.

I hadn't allowed anybody near my little sister without an extensive background check since she was ten. I'd always been protective, but an incident during her birthday party had made me realize that I hadn't done enough to keep her safe. When she'd been coming downstairs before the guests had begun arriving, a new employee – one of the grounds crew – had approached her and started talking to her. Later, she'd told me that it had been innocent at first, but then he'd become crude and vulgar. Then he'd exposed himself, and grabbed her hand, tried to make her touch him. I'd beaten the shit out of him and then called the cops, but the damage had already been done.

Isadora hadn't talked for a month after that.

She'd been so outgoing and happy as a child up until our parents died. Then, just as she'd started to come out of her shell, that sick fuck had twisted her up again.

I'd gotten her the best help money could buy and I'd promised her that I'd never let anyone hurt her again.

Since then, I'd made sure I knew the dirt on anybody and everybody coming in contact with her. And I made sure all of them were intimidated by me, if not terrified.

The file on Toni wasn't complete, but if Doug had just started it, there would be more coming. I reached up and pinched the bridge of my nose, trying to calm myself.

"Okay," I said tiredly. "I should know you'd be on top of things."

"Mr. Lang, if I may…" Doug's words were solicitous. His tone was blunt. He'd been my father's right-hand man for several years before my parents died, and he'd stayed on to help the overwhelmed and grieving nineteen year-old I'd been. He was the closest thing to family Isadora and I had. I trusted him more than I trusted myself sometimes.

"You may."

He was quiet for a moment, and then his eyes met mine. His voice was soft as he spoke, "At some point, you will have to let Isadora live her life."

"She is living it." I flipped the folder closed. He was the only person I'd let make such an observation.

"No," he countered. "She's existing. She goes to parties only after you've approved the guest lists. She has dates only once you've made sure you're aware of the itinerary, and only with a driver you've vetted."

"I'm protecting her."

"Ashford."

I started at his use of my first name. He'd been allowed to use it for years, but he rarely ever did. Usually it was when he wanted to make a point.

"When you found out she'd left the house to see a man she'd recently met, you made her feel like she isn't smart enough to know her own mind. That you don't trust her or her judgement. She feels like you treat her like a child."

I ignored the majority of his statements and focused on the one I had a response for. "That idiot doesn't deserve her."

"He makes her happy." Doug inclined his head. "Is that worth so little? Where he comes from matters more than Isadora's happiness?"

If it had been anyone but Doug making these observations, he would have been on his ass as soon as he'd opened his mouth. As it was, I turned away and braced my hands on the flat surface of the file cabinets that ran along the wall behind my desk. I couldn't quite put a name to the emotions surging inside me. It stung, I realized. It stung a lot, and the worst part was, I knew he was right.

"She's dated a lot of men who've made her happy." The words sounded hollow.

"Not like this." I heard the weariness in Doug's voice.

I heard it, and understood it. We'd had this sort of argument more than once. We'd have it again, because I couldn't stop trying to protect my sister. We'd lost our parents. All we had was each other. I knew he wanted to protect her too, but it was different. He was like family, but he had his own. Isadora was all I had.

"Finish the check on the Gallagher woman. As long as she's clean, she can stay." I shoved away from the cabinets and headed toward the door.

Toni made Isadora happy.

Doug wasn't wrong. That should count for something.

It didn't mean that I had to like her.

Chapter 4

Toni

He was entirely too pretty and entirely too bossy.

He was also an asshole.

That pretty much summed up my opinion of Ashford Lang.

Ashford. The name itself made me smirk. I could see why Isadora called him Ash. Ashford made me think of snooty men in striped coats with boater hats who walked around twirling canes as they talked about their trophy wives, Muffin and Cupcake, or whatever random pastry they were named after.

He'd brought Isadora to our lunch meeting instead of letting her take a cab or town car. Not that it was much of a meeting. We'd talked for maybe two minutes about a party she was thinking of having, and she asked if I'd ever planned a party. I told her I had planned a surprise party for my parent's fortieth anniversary just last month, and if I could wrangle my family, I could do almost anything.

She laughed, then asked me about my family and the conversation had devolved from there.

And Ash – no, I wasn't allowed to call him that – Mr. Lang had watched us from the elegance of the bar. He didn't even have the decency to pretend he wasn't watching, either.

A few times, I glanced up and he'd been checking his

email on his phone. Or maybe he'd been watching internet porn or checking the stocks. I couldn't tell from the arrogant and slightly bored expression on his face. But for the most part, all he did was stare at me.

Determined not to let it get to me, I kept my attention focused on Isadora.

She ate some sort of fish entrée that looked more like art than food, while I nibbled on pasta that hadn't had a price on the menu. I was secretly thankful she'd told me it was her treat. I was smart enough to know that if there wasn't a price, then I couldn't afford it. Not even on what she was paying me. Since I had only three weeks between finals and the start of my summer session, I had to save everything I had to buy more books.

"Four brothers…" Isadora blew out a breath.

I'd just finished telling her how I'd brought home my first date to find all of them strategically waiting in front of the house. My date hadn't even tried to kiss me, he'd been so nervous. He hadn't called me after that either.

I wished I could say it had been an isolated incident, but it had been more like a regular occurrence. My brothers, except Vic, were all under six feet tall, but that never seemed to make them any less scary to the few guys I'd dated over the years.

And the few that had managed to get past my brothers hadn't lasted long either. In one way or another, I ended up overshadowing them. I didn't know how else to put it. I was too smart. Too straight forward. Too...something.

I hadn't had a serious boyfriend since I was nineteen, and I'd dumped that shit when I'd found out he was sleeping with me just to copy my schoolwork.

My experience had made me somewhat leery of guys in general. I still held out hope that, at some point, I could find a man who was strong enough to handle someone like me. At the moment, I wasn't looking though. I had enough on my plate to worry about without having to deal with some asshole who felt like his manhood was threatened because I was smart and didn't back down from a fight.

"It made for an experience." I grinned at Isadora before glancing at Ash – Mr. Lang. I didn't want to think of him as Ash, even if Isadora had said that it was okay. A nickname was too sexy, too casual. Too intimate. It made him sound too...normal. I preferred for him to sound like the snooty asshole I knew him to be. Even if he was a sexy snooty asshole.

"Oh! I needed to get you something…" Isadora clapped a hand to her forehead. "I know you need to go soon, but you have to have this. It was the whole reason I wanted to see you today, really."

Sipping from my soda, I watched Isadora dig around in her purse. When she still couldn't find a pen, I turned over one of mine. I had to move if I was going to make it to my class today. I was just grateful I had finals next week, and then three weeks off before I had to talk to her about adjusting my schedule for my summer classes.

She scrawled something on a piece of paper and shoved it at me. "Here."

I blinked at the number, trying to understand what I was reading. She shoved a phone across the table at me and beamed.

"It's the newest version. Doug picked it up yesterday. You need a better phone," she said.

She couldn't be serious.

"You can just use this one for work, if you want." Isadora leaned forward and touched my hand. "But if you want it for personal use, you can use it for that too. It's just…" She shrugged. "I saw you grumbling at your other one yesterday and...and, well, I'll make you work a lot and a better phone will help."

I was still staring at it. Everything that wasn't vital fell to the wayside while I was paying for school. A new phone wasn't vital. As long as my old one worked, then I'd stick with it, even if the battery sucked, the browser was outdated, and few apps worked on it anymore...

"And it has unlimited data so you can even use it for school stuff while you're waiting on stuff for me."

I jerked my head up. "What?"

Isadora bit her lip and looked away, her pale skin flushing pink.

"What did you say about school?" I demanded.

"Ah…" She shrugged and looked sheepish. "I kind of know you're finishing up your Ph.D in psychology."

"How do you know that?" I managed to keep the question calm. I hadn't mentioned it on my application and I'd only told Robson Findley that I was finishing up school. I'd never mentioned which degree I was pursuing.

"My…" Isadora hesitated, and then finally heaved out a sigh. "Ash did a background check on you. Like a work-for-the-president kind of check. He does it on everybody who works for us. Especially anybody coming in close contact with me. I'm sorry, Toni."

The look in her eyes was so forlorn, I had to force myself to smile. I didn't want her feeling bad. It seemed like she'd had to deal with the repercussions of her brother's behavior quite a bit.

As for her brother...I absolutely wanted him to feel bad. Guilty for putting his sister in this position. And guilty for sticking his nose where it didn't belong.

Shifting my attention toward him, I gave him my best glare, the kind that had always let my brothers know they'd crossed the line.

He simply cocked his eyebrow and met my gaze head on.

Asshole.

There was nothing like family dinners with my folks.

Exhausted after a week of running from home to school, and then all the way uptown to work with Isadora, I practically collapsed into my customary seat, ready to eat until I popped and then fall asleep. I just kept telling myself that I had to get through finals and then I could rest before the insanity started up again.

"How's the new job going?" My mother stood at the stove, her face pink from the heat, her eyes glowing and bright.

Mom was fifty-eight years old, but she looked like she was in her early forties. People were always surprised to hear her actual age. She was beautiful, her hair cut to chin length and her eyes just as blue as mine. She'd been eighteen when she'd married my father, and he still looked at her the same way. I'd often wondered if that was the reason I'd never found someone I could settled down with. I wanted what they had.

"It's…" I opened the refrigerator, rummaging through for the condiments I knew we'd need as I searched for the right word. "Interesting. We'll go with interesting for now."

"Working for somebody rich, and all you can say is interesting?" Vic asked as he came striding into the room. "Heard you were working for the Langs. Damn, Toni. That's some serious money there."

I rolled my eyes. "Yeah, and none of it's mine."

"Boo-hoo."

Franky, my middle brother at thirty-one, flung himself down into the chair next to Vic's while his wife came in and immediately went to my mom for a hug. Yvette and Franky had been married for seven years and had three kids. I could hear them all out in the living room, chattering away to my dad. The table squeaked as Franky settled his elbows on the surface and leaned forward, drawing my eyes back to his light brown ones. Out of all of us kids, he looked the most like dad, even with the slight auburn tint to his hair.

"I heard where the house was. Working at some swank joint on Fifth Avenue for a rich, pampered little princess. What's her husband do? Sit around and sip martinis all day?" He grinned at me.

"No." Irritated for reasons I didn't understand, I set the butter dish down with more force than necessary. "She's not married. She's this twenty year-old, cute little darling." I looked over at Mom then, my heart aching with the realization that Isadora didn't have this. "She lost both of her parents when she was seven. Her older brother raised her."

I remembered, then, how she told me that everyone had assumed she'd be sent away to England to live with some distant cousins of her mother. Strangers she'd never met. How Ash had been only nineteen and away at school getting his MBA when their parents died, but he'd come back and transferred to NYU so he could have custody of her and she wouldn't have to leave their home. Ash had gone from being a carefree teenager enjoying the college life and its freedom, to being a single dad to a grief-stricken little girl.

And he'd never complained.

Dammit.

He wasn't Mr. Lang in my head any longer.

All because he'd pushed to take care of his little sister.

Family mattered.

Unaware of my distraction, my mother sighed at the stove, shaking her head. "How awful. Those poor kids."

"I don't think *poor* is the right word, Mom," Vic said as he got a beer from the fridge and went back to his chair.

My dad passed behind Vic at the worst possible moment for my brother. The crack to the back of my brother's head was hard enough to sting, but not hard enough to actually hurt.

42

"There's more to life than money, Vic," Dad said, shaking his head.

At sixty, my father was still as strong and broad as he'd been in his twenties, although his brown hair had long since gone to gray. He claimed that we were responsible for scaring the life out of it. We probably were. Vic more than any of us.

I smiled at my dad and he winked at me before moving up behind my mom and grabbing her around the waist, planting a loud kiss on her neck.

She laughed and leaned into him for a minute before elbowing him back gently. "Come on, Thomas. If you keep that up, it'll be midnight before we eat."

"Good things come to those who wait, my beautiful Margie." He nuzzled her for a moment longer, and then moved away, sneaking a scoop of the potatoes she was mashing. He fired a look at me, his brows arching. "So, the Langs. Deacon told me. They okay with you leaving in six months?"

I looked down at the table, tracing my fingers over the wood grain. "I didn't exactly tell them."

Silence filled the room. Or as much as it could with my nieces and nephew wrestling around in the other room.

Dad broke it with a heavy sigh. "Antoinette Gallagher..."

"Please don't." My face burned. My parents rarely ever used my full name. "I felt bad doing it and I did tell the guy at Winter Enterprises that I was finishing up my degree. He said that Isadora thrives on change and he doesn't think it will be an issue when I leave. And..."

I got up then, moving away from the table and my brothers and my father – and my mother. They weren't going to like this next part, but they had the right to know, especially if Isadora was right and Ash's background check was insanely thorough.

"So, I mentioned that Isadora was raised by her brother. He's like...well, crazy overprotective of her. I mean, like worse than all of you guys put together. Even though *Exclusive* did my background check, he doesn't think theirs is good enough."

I stared out the back window over the postage stamp that made up our backyard. Dad had inherited this house from his parents. We were lucky that we actually *had* a house. If Mom and Dad ever decided to sell it and retire somewhere, they might make some serious cash. Real estate in New York was insane.

"Toni." My dad's voice was level, but I recognized the tone well enough. It was the same one he'd used on me when he caught me trying to sneak out when I was fifteen and had wanted to go to a party.

Slowly, I turned to face him. "He's digging deep. I mean, not just like if I have a police record or anything like that. He's looking into everything. Where I live. School. Family and friends. Everything and everyone." I didn't want to add the last part, but they needed to know. "He's even had someone following me the last couple days to make sure that I'm not hiding anything."

Then I waited for the explosion.

"Well. That went well." I gave my mom a bright smile as she sat down next to me on the swing. I'd retreated to the back porch while Deacon and Vic cleaned up. It was their turn and a damn good thing. If I had to stay inside much longer, things might have gotten ugly.

Mom reached over and patted my thigh, concern on her

face. "Are you sure you want to work for somebody who goes digging into your background like that? Who has someone following you?"

"Mom, he's just protective of his sister." Gesturing to the house, I managed a partial smile. "Come on, you should understand that. Remember how it was when I first started dating?"

To my surprise, she laughed. "Do I ever. I kept thinking I'd have to bail one of them out of jail. Or worse…sit through a trial." The humor faded from her eyes and she looked over at me. "But it's not really the same thing, is it? The young woman…she's twenty and he still hovers like she's a fifteen year-old kid going out with the captain of the high school football team. You've never been in any trouble. You're going to school to help people. He didn't need to have you followed."

"I shouldn't have said anything." I sighed. "But I didn't want one of the boys to see someone lurking around and freak out." I gave her a weak smile. "You might not have gotten out of bail after all."

"That just seems...extreme."

"I know, Mom." I shoved my hair back and lifted my face to the sky. "I...look, I get the feeling there are things that made him this way. But I can handle it. It's not like the PI he has looking into me has done anything or even gotten too close. Besides, Ash – Mr. Lang – isn't my employer. Isadora is." Abruptly, I started to laugh. "You should have seen the look on his face when I stood up to him. I don't think he's ever had anybody get in his face and go toe-to-toe with him before. You'd think somebody had stuck a lemon in his mouth. A rotten lemon."

"Maybe you'll be good for both of them, then." She wrapped an arm around my shoulders and squeezed. "But remember, Toni, if it comes down to it, you don't have to stay someplace where you're miserable. Your father and I can give

45

you the money for school. The business is doing better than it was last year..." I started to shake my head, but she lifted a hand. "Don't argue with me. You've done so well, taking care of everything on your own, but I'm not going to see you give up on a dream when you're so close."

She stood up, but before she could walk away, I caught her hand. Squeezing it, I said, "Thanks, Mom. I love you."

Her smile said everything.

Chapter 5

Toni

Friday evenings were for my family, but Friday nights were for me. I spent most of my time working, going to school and/or studying, so by the end of the week, I needed to unwind. Sometimes wine, a hot bath, and a good book were enough. Sometimes, I needed something more.

My favorite club was close to my minuscule apartment – and I do mean miniscule. There'd been a TV show on a few years back that had featured making the most out of some of the efficiency apartments in New York. I knew some people thought that show had exaggerated, but it hadn't.

My entire apartment could have fit in my parents' bedroom and bathroom. There was enough room for my murphy bed and a small kitchenette. My desk was the tiny little breakfast nook at the end of the kitchen counter. Clever use of vertical space gave me bookshelves and places to store my clothing, although reaching them required a step-stool since I was so damn short.

After dinner, I swung by my place to change. I couldn't exactly wear the sort of clothes I'd wear to go dancing over to my parents, and I wasn't going dancing in jeans and t-shirt.

The smoky blue, spaghetti strap dress went a few inches past my butt and clung to what little curves I had. It highlighted my assets and played up the fact that while my legs weren't long, they were a damn good pair anyway.

The dress, combined with a pair of shoes that wouldn't kill me in a matter of minutes, took all of ten minutes to change into. I swept my hair up into a loose knot, dusted on light make-up, and was out the door.

There were a few whistles and catcalls, but I ignored them all. A woman in New York had to learn how to handle ignorance, and generally, pretending the nuisance didn't exist was the best thing to do.

The club was already packed by the time I managed to make my way inside. I went straight for the dance floor, waving at a few familiar faces, but before I managed to reach them, I bumped into a broad, muscular chest.

"I'm sorry." I had to shout over the pounding music.

A pair of deep, dark eyes met mine, and a slow, sexy smile spread across a face so sinfully handsome, my heart did a slow roll in my chest. "Please, don't be."

I grinned up at him. Damn, he was fine.

His dark eyes went nearly black, and that shiver of heat inside me turned into something a little more. He moved in closer and dipped his head so we didn't have to yell. At the same time, he held out a hand. "Dance with me?"

He didn't have to ask twice.

I'd seen him around more than once and he was almost always with a different woman. That didn't bother me. I wasn't looking for a relationship, just some fun. And the man could dance like nobody's business.

One dance turned into two, and I could feel the stress of the past few weeks sliding away, dissolving until there was nothing but music and rhythm and a hard, strong body that matched mine beat for beat.

The fast pace slid into a slower one, and instead of assuming, my partner gave me a questioning look. I appreciated the courtesy and moved in closer, bringing my hands up to loop around his neck. He rested his hand on my hip, his eyes still on me, and I moved in closer. The hand on my hip settled more firmly, and I rested my head on his chest.

He smelled like soap and bourbon, two scents I could appreciate on a man, and when he spun me around in a lazy twirl, I started to laugh. My feet tangled in the next moment, and I almost tripped as my eyes landed on a figure standing in a pool of light near the bar.

Half of his face was in shadow, but the rest of him...all hollows and angles and brooding eyes. He was looking right at me, and there was no mistaking that face.

Ash.

My partner steadied me, and I jerked my head around to meet his concerned gaze.

"Are you okay?" he asked, lowering his head to speak directly into my ear.

I nodded, looking back to where I thought I'd seen Ash.

But he wasn't there.

I was imagining things. I had to be. There was no way someone like Ashford Lang would be somewhere like this. This was a club for people like me. People who actually had to work for a living.

Forcing my mouth into a smile, I moved closer to him, trying to settle back into the rhythm we'd found. "I couldn't be better."

I didn't know if he heard me, but judging by the glint in his eyes, he caught my meaning just fine. He slid one hand down my spine until he reached the small of my back, guiding my hips until we were moving in tandem.

The dance was slowly becoming more intimate, and it wasn't very hard to stop thinking about what – *who* – I'd thought I'd seen.

Right up until I saw him again about ten minutes later.

I managed not to trip this time, instead, ducking my head and spinning myself around to press my back up against my partner's chest. He wrapped his arm around my waist, and even as I searched for Ash, I had to appreciate the solid length of the man at my back. And one part of him was getting even more solid as I ground back against him...

Ash had disappeared.

Again.

Was he here?

Or was I imagining things?

Why would I be imagining him though? That was a question I really didn't want to think about.

Hard, calloused hands stroked down my shoulders, and I shivered a little as he moved me back around. The music changed, but I was sweating and in need of a break. My partner must have either sensed it or needed a break as much as I did, because he started to lead me off the dance floor towards the bar where I'd seen Ash. Or, at least, where I thought I'd seen Ash.

"Can I buy you a drink?" he asked, his breath hot against my ear.

"I buy my own." I gave him a quick smile. This wasn't a date and I didn't want him to mistake it for one.

He nodded, unfazed, and flagged down the bartender.

Once we had our drinks, he bent over me so he could talk without having to actually shout. "You got a guy watching you. You know that?"

I almost spilled my drink.

Again, he steadied me, his hand curling over my elbow and staying there. "Don't look over there yet, he'll just get lost in the crowd."

"You sound like you're a pro at this."

"I'm a cop." He grinned at me and shrugged, taking a sip from his beer.

A cop. I studied him thoughtfully for a moment, and then shook my head. "I wouldn't have guessed that." Throat dry, I looked down at my vodka martini, and then took a healthy swallow.

"It's my pretty face." He winked and then nodded off to the side—the right side. "Glance over to my left, casual, like you're looking for the ladies room or something," he advised, reaching out and stroking a hand down my shoulder.

I did, trying not to think about the way his skin felt against mine. It had been a while since I'd gotten laid. Far too long.

My gaze collided with Ashford Lang.

This time, he didn't look away.

For a beat of maybe five seconds, we stared at each other, and my heart pounded harder with each moment that ticked by. I suddenly didn't feel my dance partner's hand anymore.

Furious now, I tossed back the rest of the vodka martini, and practically slammed my glass down on the surface of the bar.

"I take it you know him."

I looked at the sexy cop I'd been dancing with, but I wasn't really seeing him. "You could say that. I'll be back."

I shot up and began to make my way through the crowd.

Chapter 6

Ash

Fuck me.

She moved like sex personified. Calm, self-assured sensuality. Someone with that much fire and intensity shouldn't be allowed to move like that on top of everything else.

I still wasn't sure why I'd followed her into the club. It definitely wasn't my kind of scene. When I went out, it was for a specific reason, and it wasn't to make friends.

That seemed to be the main reason she was here, although I wasn't sure I liked the kind of friends she wanted to make.

The guy she was dancing with had some issues keeping his eyes – and hands – off of her, but she didn't seem to mind. Hell, for all I knew, she'd come here to find a guy to take home and fuck him six different ways from Sunday.

The idea irritated me more than I was comfortable with. But it wasn't because I was bothered by the idea of a woman who was comfortable with her sexuality and wanted to have sex. I was bothered because when I pictured Toni spread out and naked, I was picturing her with me.

And there was no way in hell that was going to happen.

But I couldn't stop watching her. Hell, I hadn't been able to stop thinking about her from the moment she'd sized me up and told me off. At first, I'd chalked it up to me being pissed, but the first time I let myself remember my sudden urge to kiss her, I hadn't been able to put it out of my mind. I'd found myself watching her whenever she was around, making excuses to spend time with Isadora when I'd known Toni would be there. It had only been a week, but I couldn't quit thinking about her and it was driving me crazy.

She spun around and pressed back up against her partner. I watched as he caught her hips, pulled her ass snug against him. The narrow blue skirt wasn't insanely short, but as she bent and swayed and twisted to the music, it rode up a little higher, and I could imagine how easy it would be to push it all the way up, strip away whatever fussy, frilly bit of panties she wore and drive myself inside her.

She was so petite, she'd have to fight to take me all at once.

I would fist one hand in her hair, force her to hold still as her body worked to take my cock. As her tight pussy squeezed me...

I blew out a slow, controlled breath and shoved the image out of my head.

It wasn't going to happen.

She was Isadora's employee.

And there was some shit in her background that didn't exactly thrill me. It wasn't even that she'd taken this job knowing it was only short term, although I sure as hell wasn't please about that. Isadora had been crestfallen when I'd told her that the woman she was bubbling over about was only working for her to pay for her last six months of school.

I was still sort of stunned by the fact that the girl was going to be a psychiatrist.

She just didn't seem…well, I couldn't say she didn't seem smart enough or determined enough – or ballsy enough.

The private investigator I'd retained – a quiet, soft-spoken former cop by the name of Stanley Kowalski – had turned over a veritable mountain of information on her. It had taken me some time to page through it and I was still puzzled by some of it. She'd graduated high school at sixteen, even with taking advanced placement courses so that she'd been a good part of her way through a BA in psychiatry when she'd gotten her diploma. She'd also been on her way to Stanford once she'd gotten approved for all of the scholarships she'd been a shoe-in for.

And then...nothing.

She'd gone nowhere. She'd still gone to school, but she hadn't had any scholarships. Hence the reason she was working for my sister.

Kowalski postulated that her sudden change in plans was related to the mess one of her brothers had been tied up in.

That was the real reason I was pissed off.

Three of her four brothers were clean. The fourth was a felon. A felon with a record. A felon who'd done a whopping six months, and had then been let off with a slap on the wrist after he'd turned over evidence that led to the conviction of some of his 'friends.' Even after that, coming so close to getting his ass thrown behind bars for who knew how long, he still kept fucking up. More than a few minor brushes with the law.

I didn't want somebody with that kind of history even tangentially connected to my sister.

I wanted...

My gaze flicked back to Toni and I just about shattered the glass in my hand.

She had turned her head and was staring up at her partner. I could read her desire from where I was standing. He had one arm wrapped around her waist and his expression was just as hungry as hers. The heat between the two of them should have been enough to make the room spontaneously combust.

I wanted to tear her away from him.

I wanted to pull her up against me, and feel her body

move against mine.

They left the dance floor and I blew out a breath. I needed to leave. I didn't know what I expected to find, following her like this. It wasn't solving anything. Wasn't providing me with any easy answers.

All it was doing was make me think even more about what it would be like to have her naked and submissive...

I couldn't resist though. I stopped and risked another look. It wasn't hard to find her, even among the tightly packed bodies. It was like she was a beacon, and my gaze was drawn straight to her. She was at the bar with the guy she'd been dancing with, but I didn't think they were here on a date. She'd bumped into him and he'd led her onto the dance floor. Still, that had been nearly an hour ago and she hadn't left his side since.

Her gaze swung to mine, pinning me in place.

Shit.

Even though she was too far away for me to see her eye color, I knew that precise shade of blue so well I could still see it. She was staring straight at me and for a span of maybe five seconds, I couldn't look away.

I knew the very moment when her speculation gave way to irritation, then anger.

Fuck.

She surged upright and started toward me.

Shit.

The crowd shifted and I shifted with it.

If I stayed, I had a feeling I'd do something I'd regret…like put my hands on her.

And then my mouth...

The cool elegance of Olympus wrapped around me, a startling contrast to the hot, pulsing place I'd left behind.

Part of me wished I hadn't left.

Part of me was playing out exactly what would have happened if I'd stayed there and waited for Toni to fight her way through the bodies toward me. I was a good judge of character and I'd spent enough time observing her over the last week to have a pretty good idea of what would've happened when she'd reached me.

She would have told me off, her pale skin flushing, eyes sparking. I would have listened, and it would have amused me and pissed me off at the same time. Right up until she pushed too far, and then I would have snapped at her. Then she would have shouted back, and I would have grabbed her, wrapping my hand in that glorious hair as I finally shut her up the way I'd wanted to since almost the first moment I'd seen her.

Would she moan when I kissed her? Shiver?

Would she freak out and back away? Slap me?

I didn't know, but I was guessing that last one was the most likely option.

The light in the club changed as I settled down at a table near the railing on the upper level and I looked down at the stage below. A show was getting ready to start.

Bored already despite the fact that I'd just arrived, I looked around.

I didn't want to watch some Dom spank or whip his – or her – chosen pet into submission. Nor was I in the mood for a public orgy or any of the exhibitionism that I usually found entertaining.

I wasn't even sure why I'd come here, but then a familiar form caught my eye. Contessa Reyes, with her sleek cap of black hair and pale gold eyes, was one of the loveliest women I'd ever seen. She was also one of my preferred subs because she knew exactly how to behave.

She saw me and bowed her head, looking up at me from beneath her thick lashes. The perfect submissive pose. My body automatically responded.

I nodded at the empty seat in front of me and a few moments later, she sat down, crossing one leg over the other. Unlike most of the subs here, she wasn't dressed in leather, nor was she wearing a skirt so short I didn't have to guess if she'd gone for a Brazilian. I liked my women submissive, but there were some styles that the bdsm set went for that I didn't find particularly attractive.

To each their own though.

Contessa wore a long, sleek skirt that went all the way down to her ankles but there was a slit in it that went halfway up her left thigh. The slit allowed me to see the vicious red of her boots, a red that echoed the corset she wore. Her dynamite curves practically poured out of the device, although I knew from experience, those curves were all natural. Large breasts, round, lush hips and the kind of ass that filled a man's hands, Contessa looked like a pin-up from the forties.

And she was the complete opposite of Toni, which was exactly what I needed to get the tiny redhead out of my mind.

"I haven't seen you here in a while," she said, her words tinged with her Dominican accent.

"I've been busy."

She reached out, her eyes seeking permission before she touched me. I gave it with a single nod.

Her fingers brushed across my knee. "You look tense, Sir. May I help with that?"

Instead of answering, I stood up and held out my hand.

In less than five minutes, we were in a private room and Contessa was on her knees in front of me.

It wasn't her I was seeing though.

It was a diminutive redhead with a mouth I was dying to

taste.

Chapter 7

Toni

"So...are you really a cop?"

My dance partner's name was Luke McCoy, and we'd left the club ten minutes ago.

Before we'd gone, I'd traded out my heels for the little fold-up shoes I kept tucked inside my palm-sized purse. Whoever thought those up needed to be nominated for sainthood. Luke had taken my shoes as I traded them out and was still carrying them for me. Not only did he dance like a dream, he had to be one of the sweetest, sexiest guys I'd come across in a long time.

If I'd been looking for a relationship, he'd be a catch. He was a catch for just one night as it was.

"Really." His eyes gleamed in the darkness and he grinned at me, a nice, easy smile. "Want to see my badge?" He wiggled his eyebrows. "Handcuffs?"

I laughed. "No. I don't think that's necessary. Although, I guess I could shoot your name off to my brothers. They know half the cops in the city."

"I imagine." He shifted his gaze to stare straight ahead, his posture stiffening slightly. "I...ah. Well, I've had a few run-ins with your older brother, Vic."

I tensed, waiting for what inevitably came next.

Luke glanced over at me and shrugged. "What he's done

is his business, his problem. None of yours. But I'd seen you around before, and when you told me your name, I figured out why you looked familiar." He paused, then added, "If you'd rather me just drop you off..."

"No." Tugging him to a halt, I smiled at him. "I've...well, I've gotten use to people making snap judgements about me based off him. It's nice to not have to put up with it."

Luke stared down at me, and when he lifted a hand to cup my face, my heart started to race. When he lowered his head to brush his lips against mine, my breath caught, then squeezed inside my lungs.

Damn.

We ended up backing into one of the doorways of a nearby business, dark now, the *closed* sign telling us when we could find them open again. His hands held my face as he came back for another taste, and then another, his tongue slowly exploring my mouth even as I slid mine into his. I caught his tongue between my teeth and bit him gently, whimpering as he growled in his throat and pressed his body closer.

His cock was hard against my belly and I moaned as he rocked his hips.

He lifted his head, staring down at me and I licked my lips, enjoying the taste he'd left there. Scotch...and him.

"Luke." My voice was breathless and I could feel my pulse pounding in my chest.

He pressed his mouth to my neck and I arched my head to the side, shivering as stubble rasped against sensitive skin.

"Do you want to come back to my place?"

At first, he didn't reply, but then he straightened, looking at me with eyes that seemed to burn. "I can't think of anything I'd like more. But..."

He stroked a hand down and gripped my hip. Through the material of my dress, his thumb stroked, around and around, stoking the heat inside me.

"I'm going to be upfront about this. I won't call you. You won't see me again, except maybe on the dance floor. I don't do repeats."

"That sounds about perfect."

We practically stumbled inside my apartment, hands and mouths all over each other. He was still kicking the door closed when I turned on him and grabbed the hem of his shirt, yanking upward. I wanted to see if he looked as good without it as he did with it.

Damn. He did.

His mouth closed over mine the second the shirt cleared his head, and I found myself pinned between him and the door. That suited me just fine. It was even better when he caught my hips and lifted me, bracing my weight using only his body. My dress rucked up around my waist as his hand worked its way between us. I heard his zipper, then felt his finger brush over the crotch of my panties before pulling it aside.

Foil tore and I whimpered as I felt the head of his cock pressing against me.

"Yes, please," I gasped out.

His mouth gentled on mine and I tangled my hands in his hair.

He eased into me, one hand stroking up my thigh as he lifted his head, staring into my eyes. He was big and thick and I winced a little as I worked to accommodate him. It was a delicious kind of pain and it only made me wetter. And that made it easier to take him.

I hadn't expected him to take it easy. Most guys who wanted one-night stands weren't the slow and sweet type. Especially not guys who I fully expected to be fucking me against the door.

Fuck that.

If I'd wanted tender, I'd have picked up a guy at an art gallery or wherever the hell guys like that hung out.

I twisted myself on the thick length stretching me, forcing him into me faster. He tensed, air hissing between his teeth as I used the arms around his neck as leverage to ride him. He moved harder when I started to whimper every time I dropped my body onto him, driving him deeper.

When I sank my nails into his shoulder, he made a rough noise, his hips jerking up. I cried out and Luke growled. I felt it click for him and he began to slam into me, driving me back against the door until I knew I was going to have bruises.

Just before I was ready to come, he stumbled us backwards towards the bed. It was too small for both of us, but I solved that problem by using my weight to drop us backwards so I landed on top of him. I wailed as it drove the tip of him into the end of me.

"You're going to kill me," Luke gasped, his teeth flashing in the darkness.

"You'll die a happy man." I could barely get the words out. Every nerve in my body felt like it was on fire.

He reached up and plucked at my nipples, the pressure light, gentle, using me to move. Watching him through slitted eyes, I started to ride him faster, a burning ache inside me spreading and widening until it was a void.

As if sensing my frustration, Luke twisted and flipped me over. He pulled back and I groaned, but all he did was pull me onto my hands and knees. When he drove into me this time, he wasn't gentle and I shuddered.

Eyes closed, I braced myself for another thrust and this one was hard enough to make me cry out.

My mind slid away and sensation took over.

Need took over.

I found myself thinking…dreaming…*needing* as I pushed back against him.

It wasn't Luke's hands on me now.

It was Ash's.

He'd come up to me in the club. Touched me.

And now he was in bed with me.

Wrong, wrong, wrong.

A part of me was protesting, but it was a small part of me.

But it felt so right. I climaxed with a hoarse cry and Luke continued to pound away at me, fingers digging into my hips. I was still convulsing from my first climax when another started and sent me flying, all thoughts of Luke and Ash disappearing as I focused only on the pleasure.

Chapter 8

Ash

Contessa knelt over the table in front of me.

Her hands were bound, her face averted. I didn't want her looking at me. I'd told her not to come, not to speak, not to even whimper.

These weren't unusual commands for a Dom to give a Sub, but I had an asshole reason behind it. I supposed it was a sign of good self-insight that I acknowledged it was an asshole reason and not just me wanting to dominate her.

I didn't want to think about Contessa, her pleasure, her submission.

I was thinking about *my* pleasure. What I wanted. I knew it made me not only an asshole, but a bad Dom. Contrary to what most people thought, being a Dominant wasn't about using a Sub for personal pleasure. Even if there was no emotional connection between a Dom and a Sub, a certain element of trust and understanding was involved. Even Subs who were into more pain than I understood were taken care of by their Dom.

I didn't want to take care of Contessa. Not like I should have. I was doing something I'd never imagined myself capable of doing.

I was pretending she was somebody else. A petite redhead

with snapping blue eyes and a mouth that drove me insane.

At the thought, I surged inside Contessa and her pussy contracted, tightening around me until I groaned. She wasn't naturally as tight as some others I'd been with – as tight as I imagined that little redhead would be – but Contessa knew how to work those muscles.

I thrust into her again, not even attempting to be gentle, and I felt her convulse beneath me. She wasn't necessarily into pain, but she did like it rough. I didn't have to hold back with her. The issue was going to be her ability to hold back, I thought, as I drove into her again, hard and deep.

"Don't come," I reminded her, bringing my hand down on the satiny smooth skin of her rump. It wasn't much of a smack, barely turning her skin pink, but it served its purpose.

She nodded frantically. Her hands, bound at the small of her back, knotted into fists, the only indication of her struggle to push back an impending orgasm. She was the sort of Sub made for any type of orgasm play, whether it was making her come so many times that she passed out, or forcing her to hold back until she was sobbing for release. I'd never met anyone who got off as easily as she did.

Of course, that made me wonder how Toni came. Would she be the sort who could climax almost at will? Could she come from penetration alone? Would I be able to coax an orgasm from her in public with just a few simple touches or would I have to work at it? The thought of needing to take hours to get her to come wasn't as disappointing as it would have been with any other partner.

I pounded into Contessa, barely aware of her presence, my mind swept up in images of Toni. Of how it would feel to have her bent over, or spread out before me. If I told her not to come, I knew she wouldn't comply with a bowed head and consent. She'd snarl at me. She'd dare me. She would do what no Sub should ever do. She'd push back.

That feeling in the pit of my stomach tightened, and I knew I was close. I wasn't so far gone that I'd completely forgotten the woman beneath me. She deserved at least a release. I wasn't a complete bastard.

I barked at Contessa, "Come. Do it now, or don't do it at all."

She wailed as the climax she'd been fighting to hold back erupted, her pussy milking and contracting my cock. A shudder ran the entire length of her body.

"Can I…" she started to speak.

I yanked her up and covered her mouth with my hand, driving inside her without breaking the rhythm. I hadn't told her she could speak. I didn't want to hear her as she came.

I didn't look at her, still focused on the mental image of Toni, bent over, snarling at me for daring to withhold a climax from her. Of how she would look when I finally let her come. How I could make her scream with pleasure.

It was the most erotic image I'd ever had in my life.

I came so hard, it was a miracle I didn't blow through the damn condom.

Contessa shrieked against my hand as another orgasm slammed into her, her body convulsing.

It was...intense.

And it wasn't enough.

She was still shaking when I pulled out, stripped off the condom and grabbed another. She let out a half-strangled sound as I drove into her again. I was determined to fuck the thought of Toni out of my mind.

"Who is she?"

Contessa slid onto the couch next to me nearly two hours later.

We'd both showered – separately, of course – and we were now waiting on a meal. Several hours of rough sex would drain anyone. Normally, I would've just left after my shower without a word, but I'd come down enough now to feel like an ass for the way I'd been with her and figured dinner was the least I could do. Besides, it wasn't as if I disliked her company.

Lifting my head, I studied her pretty face. "Excuse me?"

"I know when I'm being fucked, Ashford." She managed a slight smile before she lowered her eyes.

She wasn't being submissive. Even outside of the bedroom, she was the sort of woman who avoided eye contact. I didn't know why. I'd never cared enough to ask.

Her tone was cordial enough as she continued, "I also know when I'm being used as a replacement for someone else. Are you involved with her?"

"I…" Scowling, I looked away. I didn't want to think about her. Not after...I shook my head. "No."

Contessa ran her fingers over the arm of the couch. "Maybe you should be."

Rising from the couch, I paced over to the window that faced out over the city. It was treated with tinted glass, allowing me to see out, but nobody could see in. I'd fucked more than one woman up against that glass.

"Maybe you shouldn't worry about it," I said tightly. I didn't look back at her. "It's my life, after all. We're good at fucking, Contessa. Don't mistake it for something more."

"Oh." She laughed. It was all amusement and no bitterness. "Trust me, Ashford. I wouldn't make that mistake. That'd be like keeping a lion for a house pet because you like cats. I'm not stupid."

Suddenly, she stood. I still didn't look at her, but I watched her reflection in the window as she started for the door.

"I'm not terribly hungry tonight, I don't think." Before she slid out of the room, she met my eyes in the reflection. Her voice softened. "Don't deprive yourself of everything that's good in life. You've missed out on so much already."

The drive home was grim, which completely negated the entire point of me going to the club.

Contessa and I rarely talked about personal things although we had enough in common. It was always about sex, or at least leading up to it. Outside of Olympus, we occasionally saw each other at various social functions, but we never spoke at them. It wasn't that either of us went out of the way to avoid each other. There were plenty of other people who went to Olympus who ran in our social circles, and I occasionally talked to them.

No, I amended. I didn't talk to them. I sometimes talked to the men, or the women I didn't fuck. I never talked to any of the Subs I'd had sex with, and they never tried to initiate conversation. The one thing I made sure all of my Subs knew up front was that I didn't want any contact outside of fucking. I wasn't looking for a Sub to be a part of my life.

I blew out a breath as I punched the accelerator, sending the Bugatti blasting through the light just as it turned to red.

"Asshole," I muttered.

I wasn't talking about any of the other drivers.

Even though she'd Subbed for me more than any other woman, I had no desire to talk to Contessa outside of sex. I didn't think I'd care for her outside of playroom. Or at least no more than one human being cared about another. I didn't care for much of anybody, save for Isadora, and I preferred it that way.

There wasn't anything wrong with Contessa, or any of the other women for that matter. I just didn't care about them outside of that relatively short time span we spent together. I didn't want to care about them.

What bothered me wasn't my way of thinking, however. It was how easily she'd read me tonight. I didn't like anyone but Isadora, and maybe Doug, to be able to see me at all. I didn't want anyone to read me about this though. The fact that Contessa had been able to meant that this thing with Toni was worse than I'd thought.

Maybe you should be.

Those four words, so simple, echoed around in my head for the rest of the drive home, but it wasn't just those that were bothering me. If it had only been her suggestion, it wouldn't have made much of an impact. I just couldn't stop thinking about the rest of what she'd said.

Don't deprive yourself of everything that's good in life. You've missed out on so much already.

I was in a foul mood by the time I pulled into the multi-car garage attached to the side of the house. Climbing out, I stared at cars that had belonged to my father, and to his father, then looked over at the three I owned. The cars alone were worth a mint, and I took care to make sure they were all driven and stayed in working order. They were a connection to the family I no longer had.

What I did have was more money than I'd ever spend in my lifetime.

I had two family businesses that weren't just surviving in tough financial times – they were thriving. And I wasn't being arrogant when I said a lot of that was because of me. I hadn't grown up fearing change the way a lot of business types did. I welcomed it and adapted to it, so my companies were doing more than fine.

I had a healthy, albeit unusual, sex life, and a place where my appetites weren't just tolerated but supported.

I had a sister I loved and adored, and who loved me back, even when I was being an ass.

Just what had I missed out on?

Yeah, my parents were dead, but I wasn't the only orphan in the world. Kids sometimes grew up without parents. And I'd been nineteen, so I'd had them through a lot of important years.

Okay, I had to move back here to raise my little sister, but that had been a choice and one I'd never regretted. Besides, it hadn't been like I'd done it completely alone. I might not have had family around to help me, but I'd had the money to have a full staff of housekeepers and chefs and security guards.

Maybe you should...

"Should what?" I muttered to myself as I headed towards the house. "Get involved with Toni?"

I'd tried "normal" relationships with women who weren't in my kind of lifestyle, and they'd all been disasters. I could get aroused enough for sex, but I never enjoyed it, and the women always knew. After one complete disaster, I never told any of the others why I didn't seem to enjoy myself. They might've suspected, but none asked. The relationships just fizzled away, and I'd realized that I could never do "normal." Any attempt with Toni would have the same end result. I had no doubt.

Yet, even as I had the thought, I found myself thinking about what it would be like to take her the way I'd taken Contessa.

Bent over, tied. Waiting for me to fill her with my cock. Waiting to give her permission to come.

She'd never wait, though. She'd take and demand.

I'd have to punish her.

Spanking that sweet, lush ass...

Even though I'd already come so many times tonight that my cock almost felt raw, the thought of bringing my hand down on that pale skin made it jerk and pulse.

"Dammit."

It took all my self-control not to slam the door as I came into the house. I went straight towards my wing of the house, not wanting to see anyone. I was a frustrated wreck as I stripped out of my clothes and threw myself down on the bed.

My cock pulsed, bobbed against my belly, half-hard and promising to be more. I reached down, grasped it, hissing out a breath at the contact. It was almost too sensitive.

This morning, I wrapped my fist around my dick and pictured Toni while I'd gotten myself off. Then Contessa had sucked me off, and I'd fucked her three times. Not the most I'd ever come in a day, but definitely close. Now, I was already burning for relief, all over again.

I felt like a boy who'd just found his first skin mag.

And it was all because of that smart-mouthed, tiny, pain-in-the-ass redhead.

I had to do something about this.

My cock throbbed beneath my fingers.

I really, really had to do something about it or I was going to explode.

Chapter 9

Ash

Monday morning didn't bring a better mood.

It actually brought a much worse one, and I made damn sure to get my lousy ass out of the house before Isadora came downstairs. I loved my sister and I didn't like avoiding her, but when I felt like this, the less human interaction I had, the better. And if I was going to end up taking out my bad mood on someone, I'd rather it wasn't someone I actually cared about.

Since it was Monday, I had to get up at the ass crack of dawn to miss her. She was always up and moving early on Mondays. She had classes at the beginning and the end of the week, something that still stuck in my gut.

After she'd graduated from the best private school in the city, I'd told her that she could do whatever she wanted and had given her control of her trust fund. To my annoyance, she said she wanted to go to college, to get a degree in fine arts. At first, I'd refused point-blank, but she hadn't let it go. She'd pushed and pushed and pushed until I finally relented. Mostly because if I hadn't, she'd threatened to move out and I wasn't about to have that.

I needed to keep her safe, and it was hard enough doing that when she was going into NYU two days a week. I wasn't going to try to do it from a distance. She was too important to me to risk losing her the way we'd lost our parents.

I didn't understand. I'd told her she didn't need to worry about college or anything like that. She could just take it easy and have fun.

Have fun…is that what I'm to do with my life? Have fun?

I'd known the moment I'd said it that I'd messed up.

So I hadn't argued when she'd said she needed more.

I guess on some level I could understand. I wouldn't have wanted to sit around watching TV or reading or go shopping...or sitting on endless committees for charities that wanted our money. The sweet little girl who'd come crying to me night after night with nightmares about our parents' deaths just didn't exist anymore.

A heavy rain started to fall during the drive into the office building where I spent most of my days. After my parents married, they'd taken all of their families' money and the businesses they'd created, and merged them all into Phenicie-Lang. I kept my mother's real estate conglomerate and my father's hotel dynasty, building them both into even more. I also added to the family business, dabbling in dozens of different areas. Art, theater, technology, education, the environment...

Phenicie-Lang was a sparkling spiral in the sky. Normally the sight of it filled me with a burst of pride, but not today. In fact, the ugly gray clouds reflecting off the mirrored surface seemed the perfect echo of my toxic mental state. I strode in and everybody seemed to realize in an instant that I wasn't in the mood for small talk or even the standard greeting.

The express elevator, reserved for my use alone, had never seemed so far away, and when the doors finally closed around me, I leaned against the wall and breathed a sigh of relief. I'd never been so glad to be alone.

"Get your head out of your ass." I ran my hand over my

face.

I had a board meeting at ten, and I had a potential takeover I needed to look into. My top hand man was coming in later to brief me with the details and walk me through the specifics so I could decide if I wanted to proceed. Technically, I was supposed to take it to the board, but in the end, if I said I wanted to proceed, they would do what I wanted.

Likewise, if I thought it was a bad fit, they would agree.

Everybody fucking agreed with me.

All the time.

A pair of smoky blue eyes flashed through my mind and I clenched my jaw.

I wasn't going to think about her.

Mind made up, I strode out of the elevator the second the doors slid open, giving a short nod to my assistant, Melody Strum, as I walked by. She returned the nod and went back to whatever she was working on. She'd been with me almost as long as I'd been in charge, and if anybody understood my moods, it was her.

I could count on not being disturbed unless if was vital. She wouldn't want to put up with my temper unless she had no choice.

My decision to not think about Toni lasted through the board meeting, and even most of the way through the lunch that followed. It was a tradition my father had started and I'd kept it up, partially because it was a good business practice, but also because it reminded me of Dad and the type of man he was. So even though I didn't have anything in common with the rest of the members of the board, I stayed and did the small talk thing.

Regardless of how tense a meeting was, it seemed that we all functioned better – and were less likely to be at odds – if we knew we would have some time to socialize and relax afterwards. I wasn't much for socializing, but my father had worked hard to keep Phenicie-Lang not just a successful company, but a good one.

Time after time, the company my parents had created together came up on one of the best places to work, and that didn't happen because I gave out bonuses or sent people home with a coffee cup at Christmas. It was because I made sure to keep one very important priority. I would always make sure Phenicie-Lang was a company my parents would've been proud of.

I was in the middle of a particularly banal conversation about golf when I saw a waitress who bore a slight resemblance to one Toni Gallagher.

She wasn't as slim, wasn't as pretty.

But her hair was almost the same shade of dark red, and her laugh was just as easy, just as quick and open. Not that Toni had ever laughed with me like that. I'd only been fortunate enough to hear her second-hand, when she and Isadora were discussing something amusing.

And there I was again, trapped and thinking about a woman who was so completely wrong for me.

Robert Townsend was only ten years older than me, but he was already completely bald.

He weighed exactly what I weighed, but he was several inches shorter and built like the broad side of a barn, solid and heavy.

We boxed sometimes at the gym, and I knew for a fact that he had a jaw like a concrete wall. And a right hook that felt like a sledgehammer wrapped in human skin. He was also one of the most brilliant men I'd ever known.

He sat across from me, sipping on a glass of bourbon as I studied the printouts he'd just finished spreading across the space in front of me.

"At this point, it's an either/or situation."

I nodded and continued to read the fine print, looking at Robert's estimates for five and ten years down the road. Then I looked at how much it would cost to bail these people out if we decided to do the buy out. The hotel line used to be one of the best, but bad management and some lousy customer service, complicated by the fact that they hadn't done any major upgrades in over a decade...I whistled and rubbed at my forehead.

"This is more of a mess than I'd anticipated."

"I told you it wouldn't be pretty."

I shot him a dark look. "I'm not looking for *I told you so*'s." And I sure as fuck wasn't in the mood for them.

Unrepentant, Robert shrugged. We'd met my first week as the new CEO. He'd come in to try to get me to hire him and I'd been...well, unpleasant. He'd simply smiled, apologized and said he'd come back. A month later, he had, and he'd accepted my apology without being condescending. Then he'd shown me what he could do for me and I hired him on the spot.

As an independent consultant, Robert wasn't part of the company, which meant he had no problem telling me where things stood. As a friend, he wasn't afraid to be honest. That made him invaluable.

As if sensing the direction my thoughts had gone, Robert grinned at me. "If you didn't want an honest opinion, you should have had one of your *yes-men* do the job, rich boy."

I snorted at him and plucked up the closest report.

"Look at it this way...if you pick up the project, when you're done, you'll own the lion's share in the market."

"I know."

"Yeah. But if you don't..." He tossed something down in front of me.

I barely glanced at it at first. Then I looked again, eyes narrowing. "What's that?"

Robert slid a hand back along his naked scalp, an innocent look on his face. A look I didn't believe for a single moment.

"It's a picture, smart guy. You know him, of course...Huey Rossiter."

My lip curled. Yeah, I knew who he was. I just didn't know why Robert was showing me the picture.

"He had lunch with two of the board members from the chain."

"Shit."

That decided it. I nodded and reached for the phone on the table. A moment later, Melody came in, barely sparing Robert a glance although he made no attempt to hide the fact that he was studying her. They'd had a whole back-and-forth thing going for years. Sort of like that couple from that Shakespeare play. Not *Romeo and Juliet* but the other one. *Much Ado About Nothing*.

"Call the board. Emergency meeting. Offer my apologies, but I need their approval to move forward on a takeover and we don't have time to wait." I passed the information over to Melody.

"Of course, Mr. Lang." She didn't even glance over at

Robert.

"Damn." He sighed as she closed the door behind her. "If I ask her out, think she'll say yes this time?"

"She didn't say yes the first two hundred times."

"Two hundred and one's the charm." He grinned at me as he stood.

We made a bit of small talk, then said our goodbyes. I was Robert's biggest client, but I wasn't his only one. I waited until he had enough time to leave and then I followed.

With one of the biggest business decisions of my life breathing down my neck, what I should have been doing was sitting in my office, running the numbers. Instead, what I was doing was sitting in my car at a red light, wanting it to turn faster.

My gaze strayed to the clock built into the dashboard and I pressed harder on the gas.

I couldn't think.

I couldn't get jackshit done.

I hadn't been able to all week.

"It's because of this mess with Toni," I muttered. Actually, it was because of my dick and how it wanted to be *in* Toni, but logic didn't need to enter into this. Logic, as far as I was concerned, could take a flying leap.

Toni was the root of my problems, and we were going to have it out. I wanted answers and I hoped that those answers would finally clear my head.

For starters, I wanted to know why in the hell she hadn't come clean about the problems with her brother. When they did background checks, just what did she think people were asking about? Whether or not she'd ever stolen a candy bar as a kid? No one fucking cared about stuff like that. Especially not for something like this. When trusting someone to work in your home, you needed to know if there was anything that might put your loved ones at risk.

I was good and worked up by the time I got home. Once I parked, however, I took a moment to pull it all back in. I didn't want to blow up around Isadora. I hadn't seen her that morning, and I was almost positive she had some sort of paper due this week. I wanted to ask how she'd done. Then maybe I could talk her into going out. While she was getting ready, Toni and I could...talk.

My stomach clenched at the thought.

But Isadora wasn't in the sitting parlor where she preferred to spend much of her time.

Toni was, though.

Toni was stretched out on one of the long, low couches and she looked completely bitable.

Standing in the shadows of the hall, I watched as she got up, frowned at a note she had on a pad of paper, and then tossed it down before she walked over to a bag and bent down. The narrow black skirt she wore pulled tight over her ass and again, the image from the other night at the club slammed into me.

Pushing that skirt up over her hips.

Dragging down her panties.

Wrapping that hair around my fist and holding her steady as I forced her to take my cock. I'd get her wet, so wet, and so ready –

She jerked upright and turned around, her eyes unerringly seeking me out.

I didn't realize it, but I'd moved forward until I stood in the doorway.

Her eyes met mine and I saw something flash across them, then disappear. "Back to lurking in the shadows, are we, Mr. Lang?" she asked, giving me a saccharine smile that I was pretty sure was fake.

"Ash."

Shit. Why had I told her to call me that? I'd made it clear

when I first met her that she wasn't going to be calling me that.

I knew the answer, no matter how much I hated it.

I wanted to hear my name on her lips. I wanted to hear her moaning it, then sobbing it as she begged me to let her come.

She wouldn't beg.

I knew she wouldn't. Wouldn't beg. Wouldn't submit. She wasn't a part of my world, and the separation had nothing to do with money or society.

"I'm sorry." She moved back to where she'd dropped her notepad and sat down.

I heard the whisper of skin against skin, and my gaze dropped as she crossed her legs. Shit. I wanted to uncross them, push them wide, press my mouth against her...

I forced myself to pull my gaze back up.

She wasn't even looking at me.

"Sorry?" I prodded, remembering what she'd said.

"Yes." She gave me a distracted smile.

Her eyes were snapping, though. Snapping and hot. Fuck. It drove me out of my mind.

"I seem to remember you telling me that employees were supposed to call you Mr. Lang."

"You work for Isadora, not me."

Dammit. Why had I pointed that out?

Toni arched her eyebrows, a bemused look on her face. "You're right, I do. And Isadora doesn't seem to think it's a problem for me to call you Mr. Lang. And until she tells me otherwise, it's not going to happen. And I don't see why she would change her mind."

Her eyes laughed at me. "Do you?"

I wanted to bite her. I wanted to haul her out of the chair, turn her around and make every fantasy I'd had over the past week come true. Instead, I deliberately strode forward and put my briefcase down. As she watched, I gave her a cool smile.

"Very well, Ms. Gallagher." She wanted to play it that

way? Fine. "I tried being friendly. But that's apparently not what you want."

I took a file out of the briefcase and moved closer, sitting down on the heavy mahogany coffee table that was just a few feet in front of her. To her credit, she didn't lean away when I crowded into her personal space. She held firm and steady. Again, I was overcome with the need to see just how far I could push her – how far I could take her – how far she could take me.

"I've done some research into your background."

"I'm aware." A smile cold as the arctic curved her lips. "But having someone follow me? Really? Wasn't the background check done by Winter Enterprises enough?"

I was a bit surprised that she knew. Stanley Kowalski was good. He wouldn't have slipped up. Unless he'd hired someone else to follow her and they'd messed up. But I kept my surprise hidden.

"Nothing is good enough when it comes to my sister." Tapping the file against my thigh, I leaned in closer until she was just an inch away. Still, she didn't flinch. "I've got to admit, I'm not overly happy to have somebody who was arrested on felony drug charges so closely connected to my sister...Ms. Gallagher."

Her face was blank for a moment.

Then her face went red and she surged upright. I moved with her, but the narrow space behind the coffee table didn't provide for a lot of movement.

Shit. I probably just made a tactical error.

"You *ass!*" She planted her hands on my chest and shoved.

Hard.

She was a lot stronger than she looked, and I'd had more than a few looks at that tight body. I half-stumbled, and while I struggled to regain my balance, she darted away, placing herself in the middle of the room and staring at me with sheer loathing, as if she couldn't stand to be in the same room as me.

My head was spinning.

She'd just *pushed* me.

People didn't put their hands on me. No one ever put their hands on me. Not even when I'd been a scrawny little rich kid who preferred to play on his computer instead of joining the other boys outside.

A woman more than half my size had just pushed me.

"You are an *asshole*!" she said, her voice low and raw.

"I'm voicing valid concerns–"

"Fuck your concerns." She jabbed a finger at me. "My brother was arrested on felony drug charges when he was eighteen. That was nearly ten years ago."

Her lip curled as she stared at me and I almost wanted to take a step back. I'd never been looked at like that by anyone. I'd had admiration. Jealousy. Mostly admiration. Never that look of disgust.

"You…" She shook her head. "Fuck, Lang. You're a piece of work. Although, all things considered, I guess I can see why you think everybody is scum. After all, *you* are."

"Now, that's enough." I took a step toward her, my temper stretched to the snapping point.

"No, it's not enough! He was a kid. A stupid kid, and he came clean. He testified." Her hands clenched into fists as she glared at me. "It all but tore our family apart, and I'm not going to stand here while some pretty boy born with a silver spoon in his mouth judges *me* for something my brother did as a kid."

I gaped at her, trying to figure out just where I'd lost ground here.

She took a step toward me. The light in her eyes should have warned me.

"Now if you want to talk about questionable actions, we

could talk about you following me to the club the other night," she said, her voice silky. "You do realize stalking is illegal, right, Mr. Lang?"

I swallowed hard and tried not to look like I'd done it at all. "It was hardly stalking."

Except it sort of was.

"Really?" She cocked her eyebrow, a derisive smile tugging up the corner of her mouth.

Damn her. I wanted to take that lower lip between my teeth, suck on it. Bite it. Nibble on it. Make her moan.

She sidled a little closer, and now she was near enough that I could have fisted my hand in her hair – exactly the way I'd fantasized.

"Then what would you call it, Mr. Lang? You just happened to be going the same way I was? Visiting the same club? Staring at me numerous times because you...what? Mistook me for somebody else?"

"Ash," I corrected her, ignoring the rest. If she called me *Mr. Lang* one more time...

She clucked her tongue. "I've already explained that, Mr. Lang–"

I snapped.

Without thinking, I grabbed her upper arms and pulled her to me.

The slight weight of her crashed into my chest and I let go of one arm, shoved my freed hand into her long, silken strands of hair. Still staring at her, I twisted the heavy strands around my hand and wrist, cranking her head back until she had no choice but to look up at me.

There was a look in her eyes, expectant. Waiting.

Challenging.

"Ash," I said again, my voice rough.

Then I lowered my head and kissed her, exactly as I'd wanted to almost from the first second I'd seen her.

Chapter 10

Toni

Oh. Shit.

Those two words circled around in my head as his mouth closed over mine.

He didn't kiss me though.

Not exactly.

And a hell of a not exactly.

His tongue slid across my lower lip.

Then he caught it between his teeth and bit down, lightly. When he sucked it between his teeth, I felt my legs go a little weak. I moaned, and he wrapped his other arm around my waist. I was in trouble.

I was in so much trouble.

His knee pushed between my thighs as he lifted his head a little. "Open your mouth," he whispered. It didn't matter how soft he'd spoken. There was no doubt it was a command.

With a slow blink, I tilted my head back and studied him.

Was he serious?

When his mouth came back to mine, I didn't open. At least not right away. When his tongue probed my lips, I resisted long enough to let him know I wasn't going to just do what he said. Then he started to tease me, taunt me, into relaxing, and that was when I opened. But it wasn't because he told me to, and I intended for him to know it. I caught his tongue between my teeth and bit him, then sucked on him.

It drew a harsh, ragged moan from him, and he jerked me up into his arms, lifting me off my feet.

Blazing green eyes met mine as he half-staggered, half-walked to the nearest chair. He fell backward on to it while his hands slid over the narrow skirt I'd worn that morning. There was no fumbling, no hesitation, in his touch.

And I was doing touching of my own. Through his dress pants, he felt thick and hard, making my stomach tighten. I slid my hand up, then back down his chest to his crotch, closing my fingers around him as best as I could.

He arched into my touch, and then grabbed my hand, curling my fingers tighter around him until I knew it had to be just this edge of painful. Still, I tightened them even more, and leaned down to bite his chin, run the tip of my tongue along his bottom lip.

He growled and yanked my head up, kissing me again.

It was a rough, hungry kiss, and it filled every empty, aching spot inside me.

Shit.

His hands went to my hips, and he hauled me closer. It threw me off balance and I grabbed his shoulders, steadying myself. His eyes gleamed with satisfaction, and I shivered as he caught my hips, dragging me up and down over his cock. My skirt had ridden up, and my panties were no protection from how wet he was making me.

The slacks he wore, something pricey and elegant, were starting to show my arousal. I thought maybe I should get embarrassed about that. Isadora would be coming in soon.

But I didn't care.

I didn't care about anything except the way he felt, the way his body felt beneath me, against me.

And his mouth –

I cried out when he sat up and closed his mouth over my breast. Through the material of my bra and blouse, I could feel him. Wet tongue, the sharp edge of his teeth.

There was nothing subtle, nothing hesitant or reluctant.

He didn't even slow to ask permission.

He just *took*.

I should have been appalled.

But when he flipped me over onto my back and pressed me into the couch, I wasn't appalled.

I was...turned on.

So fucking turned on.

He moved between my thighs and started to rock his hips against me.

I shuddered.

One big hand cupped my ass, and I couldn't stop the startled whimper when he moved his fingers, partially exposing the crevice between my cheeks.

"I want to feel you, hot and wet, and wrapped around my dick," Ash said against my lips. "I want to hear you, begging and desperate, screaming my name as you come."

I bit his lower lip.

He jerked his head up, staring down at me, eyes glittering.

I stared into his eyes. "I don't beg."

Curling my legs around his hips, I arched up.

Through my lashes, I could see his eyes narrow. He drove his cock against me, and I felt a shudder go through his body.

"I make men beg," I said, smiling at him tauntingly.

A look of challenge came across his face and he caught my wrists.

I didn't resist as he dragged them over my head. It sent a hot, delicious little thrill through me as he stretched them higher, almost to the point of discomfort. It arched my back, lifted my breasts to him. He lowered his head until he could nuzzle the delicate skin of my breastbone.

"I don't beg either, Toni."

"Then I guess it's a stalemate." My voice was breathless.

"No." He licked me. I felt the blazing heated path of his touch all the way up to my neck. Then he stopped and whispered in my ear, "For it to be a stalemate, we'd have to start the game." He ground his hips against me. "I haven't started yet. Are you sure you're ready to play?"

Hell, yes.

I rolled my hips against him and he growled.

"Are you?"

His mouth came down on mine and this time, there was a savage intensity that hadn't been there before. His hand slid down to grab my thigh while the free one now pinned both of my wrists. He started to move between my thighs with deliberate slowness and my breath caught.

I knew in an instant I was in trouble.

He rocked against me until he had me hovering on the edge of orgasm and we hadn't even taken any clothes off.

Then he stopped, his lips leaving mine to feather teasing little kisses over my face until I lost the edge.

Oh...he was evil.

He settled between my legs again, but this time, instead of kissing me, he raked his teeth down my neck and began to work his way down, down, down...

"Tiger cubs need milk!" I blurted out.

He stilled, then lifted his head, looking at me with confusion.

I closed my eyes and started the mnemonic I'd learned in my anatomy elective two semesters ago.

"Tiger cubs need MILC. Ankle bones of the foot are talus, calcaneus, navicular, medial cuneiform, intermediate cuneiform, lateral cuneiform, cuboid." I finished it and opened my eyes.

Ash was staring at me, flabbergasted. I'd actually made him speechless, which I suspected didn't happen often.

Narrowing my eyes, I started on the muscles of respiration. "Don't exercise in quicksand. Diaphragm, external intercostals, internal intercostals, quadratus."

"What the hell are you doing?" he demanded.

It was hard to shrug with your hands stretched out over your head, but I tried. "I'm...amusing myself."

He surged up over me, and pushed his face into mine, his eyes burning. "I'll fucking amuse you."

"Oh, honey." I kissed his nose, mostly because I knew it would piss him off.

He growled at me before letting go of my hands to shove his fingers into my hair. I watched his control slipping, and I loved it.

Hands freed, I slid mine down his chest and cupped him through his pants. "Sex organs..." I traced my thumb over the faint ridge at the head of his cock. "The glans."

Ash shuddered and shoved himself into my hand.

I squeezed my hand around the width of him and stroked down, wondering if he was really as big as he felt. "The shaft."

"What, no cute little word puzzle?" he muttered, his voice hoarse.

"Who needs one?" I smiled up at him, having fun despite the heat that felt like it was going to swallow me whole. I was determined to show him that I wasn't his toy. "Everybody knows what a cock is. Sadly, not everybody knows how to use one. Do you?"

He pressed his mouth to my ear. "Get naked. I'll show you."

I was so tempted.

He slid his hand up my thigh and then between, cupping me. "I know something about female anatomy, Miss

Gallagher. Shall I demonstrate?"

My eyes almost crossed when he ground the heel of his hand against me, but I still managed to keep myself coherent enough to speak. "By all means. I appreciate the educated lay person."

"This is your clitoris." He flicked it lightly through my panties and I shivered.

"Sometimes called the clit. Stroking it, biting it, can bring one hell of a response." He gave me a wicked smile. "Allow me to demonstrate."

My wail was cut off by his kiss, his tongue thrusting into my mouth, plundering every inch as he stroked me through my soaked panties. I was going to die if he didn't bring me to climax.

And he didn't.

He raised his head to look at me. He slid inside the leg of my panties. He didn't touch me where I ached to feel him, not yet. "Your mons."

I shuddered and arched before I could stop myself.

A grin canted his lips up. "Your labia." He stroked my folds, separating the larger, fuller lips from the smaller to demonstrate that he knew the difference there. Not that I was doubting his knowledge of anatomy. Not anymore.

"And here..." He circled my entrance, dipped the tip of one finger inside. "Your vagina. I prefer *cunt* or *pussy*, but I would assume someone as educated as you would want to be technical."

"We're not in class." My voice came out breathy and rough.

"True."

He dipped his head and bit my nipple through my clothes. To my chagrin, I let out a sound that was very much a squeak.

"That being the case..." Ash thrust two fingers inside me and my body jerked, arching up to ride him. "I want to feel your pussy wrapped around my dick, Toni. And I will. As soon as you beg me."

I might have, in that moment, with my body throbbing and aching.

But I couldn't breathe. The need was too much and I couldn't form the words. Shooting my hand down, I caught his wrist and moved against him, harder, faster.

Fuck him and his demands.

He stared at me. "You think you can just..."

I flicked my thumb against my clit and came in a rush, the pleasure coursing through my body as I shuddered beneath him.

For a moment, Ash just stared at me.

Then he started to laugh, a slow, throaty chuckle that made things low in my body throb.

I lay there panting as he sat back on his knees. A look of amused incredulity settled over his face, and I started to snicker. It bloomed into a whoop of laughter when he shook his head, his eyes still hot as he stared at me.

But my amusement faded, fizzled, and then died as he lifted his hand and lazily licked his fingers.

I gulped, heat exploding through me like a series of mini-fireworks. *Pop-pop-pop.*

"I think next time, I'll tie you up…"

Next time? I wanted to sneer at him, laugh at him, show him that he had no power over me. But all I could see was myself stretched out underneath hum, my hands tied up, bound to something over my head. My body stripped bare under that hot gaze. I wondered if he'd even ask before slipping the first rope around my wrist.

"Mr. Lang!"

The voice from the hall had us both bolting upright.

Ash was on his feet and moving while I half-rolled, half-fell to the floor.

I fumbled my skirt back into place while Ash strode across the room and yanked the doors closed.

Fuck.

He turned his head to stare at me, and the look in his eyes almost sent me to my knees. It was pure naked lust.

I'd never felt so wanted in my life.

Then there was a fist pounding on the door, breaking the spell. Someone tried to open it. "Mr. Lang!"

"I need a few minutes," he said, his voice remarkably calm as he kept one hand on the door without looking away from me.

Nice that he could be calm. I couldn't. Reality had just slammed into me, and as blood rushed to stain my face red, I thought I might be sick.

What had I been thinking?

He was practically my employer! He was Isadora's brother. An obscenely wealthy man who moved in circles I could never even dream of breaking into.

Fuck!

"I..." I swallowed and looked around, feeling strangely lost. "I need a restroom."

He jerked his head off to the right and I nodded, feeling foolish. I'd known there was a bathroom in there. I'd even used it before. My face was on fire, and my legs were stiff and awkward. They didn't want to move at all.

I just had to make it to the bathroom. It was only a few feet away, but after what seemed like an age, I finally reached it and ducked inside. Yet when I tried to close the door, a hand stopped me.

I shoved against it and he pushed back.

Gently, but inexorably, he pushed. I was strong – damn strong for a woman who's five foot nothing – but I didn't have a chance against a guy his size. Not when it came to strength anyway.

He came inside, his eyes intent on my face.

I drew myself up to my full height. In my heels, it was all of five foot three. But I could cut a man off at the knees with my glare, or so I'd been told. "Excuse me, Mr. Lang. I need to use the restroom."

"Don't start that shit again." He jabbed a finger at me.

"I'm sorry?" Widening my eyes in mock innocence, I pressed a hand to my chest.

That was a bad move.

His eyes immediately fell to my breasts, and in response, my nipples hardened. Fortunately, I'd discovered the beauty of lined bras years ago, yet I still had a feeling he knew exactly what sort of reaction he'd caused.

"Don't do that," he said, his voice a rough growl. "I had you all but purring my name. Don't you dare go back to calling me *Mr. Lang* in that haughty voice again."

"Mr. Lang—"

"Don't!"

The snapping fury in his voice ignited my own temper, and I shoved myself up onto my toes, snapping at him. "Excuse me? You don't get to talk to me in that tone of voice." I jabbed him in the chest and had the pleasure of watching his eyes widen. "I'm not your doting baby sister who hasn't figured out yet that you're a total ass. I'm not your employee to boss around. I'm not your *anything*."

"Yeah?" He shot out an arm and yanked me against him.

A startled *oomph* escaped me as I crashed into his chest. His hard, muscled chest.

Fuck.

I shoved my hands between us and wedged as much distance between us as I could.

"Two minutes ago, you were the woman I was getting ready to have wrapped around my cock, sweetheart."

The smoky heat in his voice made my heart race.

The potent desire in his eyes made my knees weak.

And the arrogance on his face made me want to punch him in the head.

Curling a hand into a fist, I was seriously considering the last option. Out in the parlor, I heard a woman's voice and I froze.

It wasn't Isadora.

It was somebody older – and she sounded scared.

"Mr. Lang?"

Ash shot a fulminating glare at the door, but his voice was level as he said, "Just a couple of minutes, Beth."

"How about now?" I smiled sweetly and pointed towards the door. I needed him away from me.

"Because we're not done, Princess."

I gaped at him. *Princess?* Had he seriously just called me *Princess*?

He chuckled, apparently amused by the look he'd seen on my face.

"Did you just call me Princess?"

"Yes." He scraped the tips of his fingers down his jaw, rasping them over the light growth of stubble. Stubble I'd felt scraping against my skin. "I think it suits you. All damn high and mighty, staring down your nose at me."

"Oh, really?" I sniffed and raked him up and down with a telling look. "I'm not the one who thinks I can snap my fingers and everybody will come rushing to do my bidding."

There was a flicker in his eyes.

Out in the parlor, I heard Beth again and she sounded really upset. "Mr. Lang, *please...*"

I started to move toward the door, but he shoved an arm up, blocking me.

"Beth, two minutes isn't going to hurt!" He all but shouted it.

Then he bent down, placing his lips next to mine. "What

do you think, Princess? If I snap my fingers, will you do my bidding?" The hand he'd curved over my hip slid up, up, up until it was right under my breast. "Because I'm tempted to try. See, I've been having these fantasies ever since I first saw you."

I sucked in a breath.

He lifted a hand, snapped his fingers right between our faces.

I jolted and heat exploded through me. My face burned red.

And my pussy...oh, man. I was so wet and so empty, I ached.

"I want to see you on your knees, Toni," he said, his voice low and rough and raw. "I want you on your knees with your mouth wrapped around my cock."

I had to swallow my whimper to keep it from escaping. I wasn't going to give him the satisfaction. I just had to keep remembering that he wasn't the kind of guy I wanted. He was an asshole.

I could see it, me on my knees doing exactly what he'd just described. My mouth was practically watering, and I had to fight to keep myself from reaching out and freeing him from his trousers. Running my fingers up, then down his length. Taking him between my lips. Tasting him...

I jumped as a fist pounded on the bathroom door. "Mr. Lang," Beth said, her voice plaintive. "Please, this is urgent."

He snarled and spun away, yanking open the door.

The sight of the ugly snarl on his face froze something in me.

But not as much as the sound of the woman's voice.

Something was wrong.

I'd heard enough bad news in my life to know that.

Before he could yell at her, I cut between them.

She still stared at him. "Mr. Lang—"

"It couldn't wait two minutes?" he bellowed.

"It's probably been five," I snapped, smacking a hand against his chest when he would have advanced. Then I looked back at the woman. Her pale eyes were overly wide, her breath coming too raggedly. And she was swaying.

Hell.

"Come on," I said gently, slipping my arm around her waist.

She was only a couple of inches taller than me so it wasn't hard to guide her over to the closet sofa and she practically poured onto it like water.

"If it's that damn important–"

"Would you stop?" I hissed as I spun around and glared at him. "She's terrified. She's about to pass out, you asshat."

I don't know if he finally looked at her or if I'd just startled him into shutting up with the asshat insult, but he blinked and scowled, focusing on the woman who sat, weaving back and forth, on the couch. I crouched in front of her and reached out to take her hands. They were cold and clammy and when I checked, her pulse was racing.

"Beth?"

Her eyes focused on mine. They were a startling shade of light blue. "You're Toni. Isadora's assistant." She smiled weakly. "She likes you."

"Yeah." The fact that she'd immediately swung to Isadora had my gut turning to ice. I squeezed her hands. "You said something was wrong. What is it, Beth? What's wrong?"

She swallowed and her gaze tracked up until she was staring at Ashford.

"She's..." Beth swallowed. She stopped and squeezed her eyes closed.

I tightened my grasp on her fingers. "Beth, tell us." I put a hard edge into my voice.

It worked.

She steadied and nodded, looking back
know what happened, ma'am. She was there.
She wanted me to bring her a pitcher..." She
look at Ash – at Mr. Lang.

"Oh, for fuck's sake. Isadora likes a pitch
every now and then," he snapped. "I gave her
few months ago. I'd rather she drink here than anywhere else.
What, did she pass out? Is that all that's wrong?"

I could have told him that wasn't it.

Beth started to cry. "No, sir. She's...sir, I can't find her!"

He had been standing behind me, apparently content to let me handle the weeping female.

Suddenly though, he was the one in front of Beth. I had somehow been moved aside. I hadn't been shoved or jostled or even rudely pushed. I was just...*moved*. He had his hands on the older woman's shoulders and I could see him almost shaking with the effort of restraining himself.

"What did you say?" he demanded, his voice low.

Beth sniffed. "Sir, I tried to tell you it was urgent. Miss Isadora...she's *gone*."

Blindfold Vol. II

Chapter 1

Toni

"Sir. I understand that you're upset." The officer spoke in a voice that managed to be soothing and calm without being condescending.

It was a nice voice and I had to admit, if he had been talking to me, it might have done something to penetrate whatever emotions were trying to drown me. As it was, it helped to ease the near-panic I was feeling. A little bit.

It had absolutely no effect on the man standing next to me.

Maybe it shouldn't have.

We had no idea what happened to his sister.

She was just…gone.

Twenty year-old Isadora Lang, wealthy and beautiful heiress – and my boss – was nowhere to be found.

Slowly, he turned away from the window and approached the officer.

I had to give the cop some credit. Even though thirty-two year-old Ashford Lang stood a good eight inches taller, and was probably a good fifty pounds heavier, the boy in blue didn't back down or even blink. As someone who knew what it felt like to go toe-to-toe with the wealthy CEO of Phenicie-Lang, I could appreciate the courage that took.

Ash stared down at him, green eyes blazing. "You understand?" he echoed, his voice cutting. "My sister is missing. But you *understand*? Do you think *upset* even comes close to what I'm feeling?"

I'd seen how he behaved when he'd believed I was a man his sister had hired as an assistant, and calling that upset would've been a stretch. No. I was pretty sure *upset* didn't even come close to how he was feeling at the moment.

"Gentlemen."

A new voice rang out, cutting through the rapidly growing tension. Reluctantly, Ash pulled his eyes from the cop. He and I both turned. The cop didn't. From the corner of my eye, I thought I saw him take a deep breath and I wondered if he truly understood how close he'd been to having his ass handed to him.

The newcomer turned out to be a woman, dressed in a sharp suit, her hair cut in a neat, pixie-like cut that framed a face that could have been twenty-five or fifty. I pegged her at somewhere in between, but only because of the age I saw in her eyes. Those eyes were an incisive shade of brown and she looked like she'd seen it all, done it all, and probably invented a few things while she was at it.

Her smile was polite and professional.

The badge she displayed wasn't needed. I could spot a cop a mile away, and her entire demeanor practically screamed it.

"Officer Raleigh, why don't you join the other officers?"

She glanced past us to look at the cop. "I'll take over here."

The uniformed cop gave her a nod, then tipped his head in our direction before leaving the room. I had to give him credit for the polite exit. I wouldn't have blamed him if he'd simply left without a glance.

Once we were alone with her, she focused on Ash.

"Mr. Lang, I'm Lieutenant Green." She held out a hand and Ash shook it, his expression still dark and angry. She continued, "My superiors thought it might be better if I came down here." She paused, gave me an acknowledging glance, and then added, "I've worked with abduction cases in the past."

Next to me, Ash tensed and it was all I could do not to put a hand on his arm to try to comfort him, soothe him. No matter what had happened between us in the moments before we'd learned of Isadora's disappearance, he and I didn't have that kind of relationship. I was here because I was Isadora's assistant and I'd been in the house when she'd disappeared. Nothing more.

Nerves and anger pulsed under his voice. "Abduction. Is there a ransom demand I don't know about? I'll pay whatever's asked."

"No." Green shook her head. "It's far too early to be making assumptions. And in all honesty, your sister has probably gone out to a club or to visit some friends. Maybe she decided to take a few days to herself." She glanced at the furniture and arched one dark eyebrow. "Perhaps we could sit?"

Ash looked like he was going to explode.

Quickly, I moved forward and touched his arm, acting before I could think better of it. "This will probably take some time, Ash."

It was probably my use of his nickname more than anything that got through to him. Brilliant green eyes glinted almost feverishly as he studied me. After a moment, he gave a short, terse nod. I was slightly surprised when he took my elbow and led me to a couch, gesturing to the lieutenant to have a seat as well. Fortunately, it wasn't the couch we'd been on earlier. That could've been...awkward.

Green sat down and smoothed her skirt, folding her hands in her lap, taking an almost deliberate amount of time to do it. If she was waiting for hors d' oeuvres, she was wasting her time. Finally, she spoke, her attention still focused on Ash. "It's my understanding that you employ several bodyguards for your sister?"

Lieutenant Green studied Ash the same way I would have looked at bacteria under a microscope in one of my biology classes.

I didn't like it.

Ash gave her a cool look that said he didn't like it either. "Yes, though they're used for when Isadora goes out. I rely on my home security staff to keep her safe while she's at home. You should know that each security member who was on duty today will be fired, so you might want to get their contact information in case you need to see them again."

"That seems a bit harsh."

"Harsh?" His body stiffened. "My sister was taken on their watch."

"That is still undetermined."

"Really?" Ash's sarcasm was so thick, I was surprised nothing viscous dropped from the air to stain the thick, expensive carpet. "Oh, maybe I missed her while I was going over the security footage, or when I was tearing the house up, bellowing her name."

"She could have left." Green sighed and glanced at me.

I recognized the look well enough, but she was looking the wrong way for backup. I might not have known Isadora that well, but I didn't think it was likely that she just stepped out without telling anyone where she was going, especially since she hadn't told me that we were done for the day. She was disorganized, but never thoughtless. I wasn't a mind reader, but I was a good judge of character on top of studying to be a psychiatrist.

I returned Green's steady look, but didn't say anything. If she wanted my opinion, she was going to have to ask for it. And I doubted she'd like it when she did. Her gaze lingered for a moment and then she turned back to Ash.

"Here are my concerns, Mr. Lang. Your sister is twenty years-old. I've got a fourteen year-old. I all but raised my two younger sisters. And although it was quite some time ago, I recall how it felt to be twenty. You want privacy. You want some independence. Does your sister have any of that?"

"She has safety," Ash snapped.

"Safety." Green nodded as she said the word slowly, as if weighing it on her tongue.

"Look," he said. "My sister wouldn't leave without telling me where she was going or taking her bodyguards with her."

I was torn between hugging him and rolling my eyes. He was smart. He'd managed to get his MBA while raising Isadora and taking over the family's numerous companies, even though he'd only been nineteen when his parents had died. But smart didn't always produce insight. And insight into a loved one was always the hardest.

I knew that from experience. I'd had common sense drilled into me by my older brothers, but I'd known plenty of kids through the accelerated learning programs I'd been in who were practically as dumb as a stump when it came to practical things.

When it came to his sister, I had a feeling Ash was clueless.

Actually, when it came to twenty year-old females in general, Ash was probably clueless.

That wasn't to say he didn't have a clue about women. Or

at least a certain type of woman. But Isadora wasn't that type of woman, and she was at the weird stage where she was still figuring out who she was. Ash, on the other hand, probably looked at her and saw a girl in pigtails and a Catholic school girl skirt – or whatever flavor of private school she'd attended. Had he actually thought she was more interested in being safe than having a life?

I would've felt bad for him if I hadn't been so worried about Isadora.

When I was twenty, I'd at least kept my parents advised of my whereabouts in general. I still lived at home even though I'd been in college. I'd respected them enough to know that they just wanted to make sure I was safe.

My brothers, however, were a different matter entirely. If they'd tried to dictate my every move after I'd become an adult? I probably would have filled their shampoo bottles with Nair. Again. Their overprotectiveness and over-helpfulness was bad enough.

Even though I loved my family, the freedom from all of that had been one of the reasons I'd chosen to move out shortly before my twenty-first birthday, even though it cut into my college funds.

It was a different sort of vibe here. Ash had raised Isadora since she was seven, so she'd had to have some respect for his authority. But still, he was her brother, not her father, and even if her memories of their parents were dim, she still had them. It had to irk her that she had so little freedom to come and go as she pleased. The question was, was her annoyance enough that she would've just taken off without a word to anyone, even if it was just to cover for her?

Sighing, I rubbed my temples with my fingers, a headache settling in nice and tight.

The sad thing was, I did understand why he was so determined to look after her. Aside from the fact that he'd been responsible for her for the past thirteen years, she was all the family he had left. Also, for all intents and purposes, Isadora was an adult, but she was sweet and naïve, not the best combination to have when roaming the city streets alone. Granted, she could probably thank her brother for that, since Ash had sheltered her to the point that she had no idea what real life was like.

Caught up in my thoughts, I startled slightly when the lieutenant said my name.

"I'm sorry?"

Green arched a brow. "I was wondering if you might have any idea where Isadora might have gone."

Blinking at the unexpected question, I shook my head. "No, I'm sorry. I've only been working for her for a week."

"What is it you do exactly?" Green asked as she pulled a notebook from inside her bag.

A deep pulse of envy went through me at the sight of that bag. It was a rich shade of purple, a Michael Kors bag, so out of my price range for now. I would have thought it would be too pricey for a cop, too, but what did I know?

"I'm her assistant." Dragging my gaze away from the bag, I looked back at Lieutenant Green.

"And you assist with…?"

"Everything?" I offered her a half-hearted smile and shrugged.

"And when did you last see Miss Lang?"

"About an hour before we were told she was missing. I was working with her and she said she needed a bit of a break, so she left the room."

"Did she do that often?"

I shrugged. "I've only been with her for a week and she's done it twice. She leaves for a bit and then comes back. I had no reason to believe she wasn't going to do the same thing, so I waited. Mr. Lang came home and the two of us were…talking when we got the news." If Green noticed my slight hesitation on the word, she didn't say anything.

"What sort of person is she?" Green asked.

From the corner of my eye, I glanced toward Ash, but he had risen and walked back to his position at the window. It was like he expected her to just come walking up Fifth Avenue, even though it was coming up on eleven o'clock. I hadn't realized it was that late.

Ash was probably going to throw me out of here soon enough, and when he heard what I had to say, it would probably be sooner rather than later, but I knew the best thing to do with cops was be honest.

That settled it in my mind.

"I love working with Isadora. She's a sweet girl. She's bright, determined, and she's got a good heart. But I have to be honest."

I saw Ash turning towards me, but I didn't let myself look over at him. What was the point?

"The girl could get distracted on her way to the bathroom, even if her bladder was about to bust." I knew Ash was staring at me and I felt a blush start in my cheeks, but I kept going. "She starts projects and stops two minutes later. She'll look for her phone while it's in her hand. She'll look for her jacket while she's wearing it. She composes emails and half-way through, she forgets what she's writing about. The girl is like the energizer bunny on speed."

Both Ash and Green were staring at me now.

I twisted my fingers together. "The fact of the matter is, I'm surprised she can make it down the stairs without somebody reminding her that she needs to eat breakfast. She's so focused on what she *wants* to do she forgets about what she *needs* to do."

Ash was glaring at me.

I ignored him.

"And what does she want to do?" Green asked curiously.

"Save the world." I smiled now, a strange little lurch of protectiveness settling inside me. "Isadora Lang is probably the most flighty woman I have ever met in my life, but she hired me because she knows it, and she wants big things. With her passion, the world better look out. Because she just might change it. Whether the world wants it or not."

I heard a sharp intake of air and dared to glance over at Ash.

I was prepared for his fury.

But the look he was giving me was something I couldn't quite place, but that made me more nervous than I liked.

Flushing, I shoved myself to my feet. "I'm sorry I can't tell you much."

Green gave me a strange look. "Oh, you told me quite a bit."

Forcing a smile, I excused myself and left the room. I needed some water and some air.

When I came back nearly thirty minutes later, it was to find Ash shouting at Green.

Green didn't look concerned.

She stood there listening with her hands crossed in front of her, her head cocked to one side as she listened. There was an expression on her face that seemed to say she found this whole thing terribly fascinating. But not compelling – as in, she wasn't compelled to go and investigate anything just yet.

"I'm very sorry, Mr. Lang. But the fact he's a meat packer doesn't give credence to anything."

Ash's eyes narrowed and he shoved a finger into Green's face. His entire face was flushed. "If anything happens to my sister because of your lack of action–"

Shit.

Pasting a smile on my face, I shoved between them and put my hands on Ash's chest. I had a feeling that if I tried to touch Green, I'd end up in handcuffs. "This isn't going to help find Isadora." I kept my voice soft, even.

A muscle jumped in his cheek, but he let me ease him back a couple steps.

"I'll look into it," Green said. "That's all I can promise. Now, if you'll excuse me, Mr. Lang, Miss Gallagher."

I had the feeling the lieutenant decided to take advantage of my showing up to vacate the room.

Once she did, Ash's eyes narrowed in on me.

My heart lurched and I had to fight the urge to back up a pace. I had no reason to. I hadn't done anything.

"How could you let this happen?"

"I…" I sucked in a breath and then let the question go through my head once more. Yes, he had just said what I thought. I managed to keep my voice even. "How could I let what happen?"

"You were supposed to take care of her!"

"I'm supposed to help her!" I countered, the statement coming out from between clenched teeth. I had to remind myself that he was worried about his sister.

"And you show it by letting her get kidnapped!" His roar echoed around the room and I couldn't control my flinch.

I jerked my spine straight as he came close enough to loom over me. He might've been worried, but it didn't give him the right to yell at me like that.

I glared up at him. "I was hired to be an assistant, you dumb ass. I wasn't hired to be a prison guard or a babysitter. Maybe if you'd loosen the reins a bit, the cops wouldn't be so quick to say that she wanted to get away."

Harsh flags of color appeared on his cheeks and he caught my wrist, jerking me forward. "Are you saying this is my fault?"

I twisted my wrist against his thumb, breaking his grip before stepping back and putting several feet between us. My voice was calm. "No. I'm not. But it sure as hell isn't mine, so why don't you back the fuck off."

He opened his mouth, but before he could say anything else, I held up a hand.

I doubted anybody had ever dared to do that to him before and the shock of it stopped him.

"I'm going home," I said coolly. "I hope Isadora comes home and this is all a misunderstanding, but I'm not going to stay here and let you yell at me for something that isn't my fault. If the cops want to talk to me again, they can contact me there. And you?" I gave him a tight smile. "You can kiss my ass."

Chapter 2

Ash

The silence in the house was deafening.

I was still staring at the empty doorway a few minutes later when Beth appeared, shaking her hands, her lips compressed into a line so tight, they almost disappeared. The police had been talking to her in the hallway. She worked with Doug to run the household and had been with the family for nearly eight years. She'd also been the last person to see Isadora.

"Mr. Lang, I am so sorry–"

"Don't." Weary, I dropped down onto the couch and stared at nothing.

The sound of the door slamming was still echoing in my ears. I clenched my teeth, and not just because it was something that annoyed the hell out of me on my best days.

Isadora might've gotten away with slamming doors in the house because she didn't do it out of pique, but she was always in such a hurry to do everything. It was like it never occurred her that she didn't get anywhere faster by not slamming a door.

Toni…she was just unprofessional, irritating, annoying…

And right.

That realization slammed into me with the force of a sledgehammer, and it was the only thing that stopped me from storming out the door and catching up with her. I already knew she wouldn't have made it to the subway yet. It wasn't like we had a stop right in front of the house and I knew she hadn't driven.

I could catch up with her, and I was tempted.

But only because I wanted to yell at her some more.

Yell, because that was the one thing that would take my mind of my worry.

"Maybe not the one thing," I muttered.

Shit. I ran my hand through my hair.

What happened earlier had been a mistake, and not just because I'd been too distracted to pay attention to Isadora.

Maybe if you'd loosened the reins...

Toni's voice was like an echo in the back of my head, but I brushed it off. She didn't know shit about my family, didn't know shit about me or my sister. She had no idea some of the things the two of us had dealt with growing up, or what it was like having so much money, that people saw dollar signs instead of people. What it was like to always have to question everyone's motives, wondering if they were only after money.

Although that didn't seem to be the case with her.

"Mr. Lang."

I turned at the sound of my name and saw Doug, the head of my household staff. His pale eyes were grim, and he looked behind him before moving deeper into the room. "Nothing."

It wasn't a question. Doug had been with my family for years, since before my parents died. I had vague memories of him taking me out to go Christmas shopping for my parents as a young teenager. That seemed a lifetime ago. He knew me well enough to know that if I'd learned something, the staff would have been made aware. They all adored my sister. Most of them barely tolerated me anymore.

Except Doug. He'd been the one to call me at college and tell me about the accident. It had been his voice consoling me when I started to cry in my dorm room, miles away. He'd been the one who'd watched Isadora the time it had taken me to drive home. He was the closest thing to extended family that Isadora and I had.

"Nothing." I turned to the window and stared outside. "How did this happen?"

The question wasn't rhetorical and I wasn't asking some existential, meaning-of-life bullshit. I wanted to know the facts. How the hell had someone gotten into my house and taken my sister? Because that was the only logical explanation, no matter what Lieutenant Green thought.

"I'm working on it, Sir." His voice was hard and flat and when I shot him a look, the troubled expression in his eyes was enough to make me glad I hadn't snapped at him. If anyone was feeling Isadora's loss almost as much as I was, it was Doug.

"I want a list of all staff who was here today, even if they left before..." I paused for a moment, and then continued, "And call Ricin. I want him in here first thing in the morning. Whoever was on security today is getting fired."

"I took the liberty of calling him already to inform him of what happened," Doug said. "I told him I wasn't sure if you would want to do the firing yourself. He said that if you wanted him to do it, it wouldn't be a problem."

That was good, at least. The last thing I wanted was my head of security trying to argue me out of firing his men. There was something else on my mind at the moment though and I needed to get it out there.

"The cops think she might have gone out to a club or taken a trip – tried to get away from me for a while." It was hard to even get the words out.

To my surprise, Doug's eyes slid away from mine.

I turned slowly and took a step toward him. "Doug?" There was a warning in the word.

"Sir." He inclined his head. "Please keep in mind, you

turned the running of the household over to Miss Isadora six months ago. That being the case, there have been a few times when she has…asked our help in taking some time away."

I clenched my hands into fists and tried to control my temper. "And the bodyguards?" I asked.

"They were told that Miss Isadora would be staying in for the evening."

"And my security team?" I had a feeling I was going to be firing a lot of people tomorrow.

"They saw only me leaving." Doug met my eyes dead on, and I could see he was prepared for whatever I planned to do or say.

"You realize I'm likely to fire you over this."

"Yes, Sir." A faint smile curled his lips. "However, I consider it odd that you would fire me when she was always safe on the excursions I arranged, but on an evening when she was home with both you and your security team present…"

It was a blow I hadn't expected, and I realized in that moment that Doug was angry.

He'd hidden it, but he was angry.

"You want to tell me what the problem is?" The question came out more harshly than I'd intended, but I didn't apologize for it. My sister was missing and he was pissed at me.

He hesitated a moment and then rocked back on his heels, linking his hands behind his back. He served time in the military – security details, my father had told me. Old habits died…never.

"Permission to speak freely, Mr. Lang?"

"That's not what you've been doing?"

His lips twitched in what might have been a smile. He inclined his head slightly. "I've considered how lucky you are on a number of occasions, you know. Had Isadora been any less of a sweet child, or if she'd decided at any point in her life that she didn't want to always make you proud of her…things could have been very different. I've thought, often, about how easily you could have lost her too."

"Why do you think I want her safe?" I demanded. Of all people, I'd have thought he would understand.

The anger in his eyes faded away to something else. Sadness. "If I may, Sir. There are other ways to lose somebody than by burying them. Isadora is a sweet young woman...and an insightful one. Many people, including you, often don't realize just how insightful she is. She always knew why you fought to protect her and why you treated her as though she were made of glass. It's why she's tolerated it for so long. But her patience was...is...growing thin. I don't know if this has anything to do with her disappearance, but there's more to your sister than you know."

I drew in a slow breath. "What's been going on that I don't know about?"

"Perhaps..." He gestured to the couch. "We should sit down."

It had been nearly an hour since Doug had finished talking to me.

Fifty minutes had passed since I'd torn out of the underground garage in the Bugatti, the need to tear something up burning hot and fast in my gut. The road happened to be available, so the road it was.

It was Monday night, which meant fewer people would be out late in general, so it hadn't taken me long to get to roads with enough room for me to actually move.

It wasn't doing anything to help my state of mind, though.

A light in front of me turned red, and I would have blasted through, but at the last minute, I saw lights pooling on the road and I hit my brakes. A car on the cross street came through and I stopped, shoving the heels of my hands against my eyes.

Shit!

I was being stupid.

Anger did that to me.

But it didn't always make me careless. And what just happened was fucking careless. My parents died because someone hadn't been paying attention when they were driving.

I had to slow down and I had to think.

No. What I had to do was find Isadora. Maybe she had just left, taken off for the night like Lieutenant Green said. I didn't want to believe it, but I supposed it was better than the alternative.

If she really had slipped out voluntarily, then I just had to figure out where she would've gone. After a minute, I knew. She would've gone to see that lousy boyfriend of hers. So…

"I'll go see that lousy boyfriend."

I whipped the wheel to the right at the next available chance and headed for Brooklyn. It hadn't escaped my notice that Toni only lived about a mile away from Isadora's boyfriend.

For all I knew, Isadora had slipped out and Toni was covering for her. Toni liked my sister. Everybody liked my sister. I scowled. I loved my sister too. I just put her safety before her happiness. How did I know Toni hadn't decided that Isadora's happiness should come first?

But I wasn't going to think along those lines yet.

I'd see Colton first.

I'd talk to him.

We'd be calm and rational.

I was partially right.

Colton Stevens, although clearly freaked out by my sudden and angry appearance, had managed to be calm and rational.

I, on the other hand, had listened to him for all of thirty seconds before I grabbed him by the front of a wrinkled Star Wars T-shirt and hauled him up until we were nose to nose.

"Where the fuck is my sister?" I snarled.

"She's not here."

"The hell she's not."

He pushed away from me. He might've been lean, but he was still strong. He fell back a few steps. "She's not here." His eyes widened suddenly. "What happened?"

"Like you don't know." I swung at him, my knuckles cracking against his nose as he took the hit.

He came to his feet in a fast, easy bounce, blood dripping down from his nose. He wiped it on the back of his wrist, flinging the drops away without even looking at them.

Either he'd taken a few punches before or I'd hadn't broken it. Maybe both. I had to admit, the fact that he came back up so fast was pretty impressive. Even more impressive was how level his voice was, despite the nasal twang.

"I'll give you that one," Colton said. "Now tell me what the hell is going on."

Shit. He was either an extraordinary liar or he really didn't know. As pissed as I was at the guy, I tended to believe it was the latter…but I wasn't going to give him any details. Just in case I was wrong.

"She's not at home and she's not picking up her phone. I figured she was here." I hoped he'd think I was just being an asshole brother and not that I was freaking out because I didn't know where Isadora was.

Blood continued to drip and he muttered something under his breath, then turned. I stared at his back, feeling a little sick as he turned away and strode down a small, cramped hall. He had an efficiency apartment. Since it wasn't right smack dab in downtown, it had more room than some, but the entire place would've fit inside my home office. It was clean, though, and judging by the décor – heavy on the geek – he'd put his stamp on it.

When he came back in, he had a rag shoved up against his nose and his eyes were snapping.

I tucked my hands into my pockets and studied him, hoping to figure out what it was about this twenty-six year-old meat packer with the messy bronze hair that had entranced my baby sister so much that she'd been sneaking out for six months to see him.

His face was grim, or what I could see of it.

After a minute, he lowered the rag. The blood had slowed to a trickle.

"I gave you that one, rich boy, and only that one, because I understand. I got a sister too, and I'd be upset if I was in your shoes. But you come at me again and it won't be free."

Rich boy?

I ran my tongue along the inside of my teeth. He wasn't making me like him any better. I gave him a longer, harder look. He might've been thinner than me, but I could see the corded muscles in his arms. He wasn't a pushover.

"If you're looking for a piece of me," Colton offered. "I wouldn't mind blowing off steam."

It was like he was reading my mind.

Then he grinned, and the smile had a hard slant. "And since you've already thrown the first punch, I don't have to worry about Dory getting pissed off at me when she sees that I marked up that pretty boy face of yours."

"Dory?" I echoed.

He cocked a brow at me. "What of it?"

"That's the name of a fish."

"I know." He grinned. "It suits her. She's adorable and ditzy. She cussed me out and smacked me when I told her that."

I was tempted to do the same – maybe not a smack – but I could punch him again.

Except I had a lousy feeling in my gut. It was one I'd experienced a few too many times today. The one I got when I was wrong. And I'd been wrong a lot today. I had a feeling I'd been wrong about this guy too.

"You really care about my sister, don't you?" I kept my eyes on his face as I asked the question.

"You just now figuring that out, rich boy?" He said it with a bit of a sneer. It was only mildly softened by the light of sympathy in his eyes. "Don't worry. I don't expect you to invite me for Christmas or anything. I'll keep my dirty, blue-collar germs to myself."

I could feel heat climbing up my neck, but I didn't bother to try and correct him. It had nothing to do with the fact that he worked for living.

But at the same time, it had everything to do with it. Especially now.

He'd already told me he didn't know where Isadora was, and from what I'd recently learned, if anybody would know, it was him. But if that was the case, then it was looking more and more like she'd been taken.

So I didn't give a damn if Colton worked with his hands for a living, but wasn't it possible that someone with only a little money would be the kind of person who might want to find a way to make some easy money. Like a ransom.

I should've felt bad suspecting something like that about

someone who cared for my sister, but if I didn't have him as a suspect, who did I have?

Nobody.

After a couple of drinks, I could admit, to myself at least, that I'd handled the night badly.

Of course, this was the first time I'd ever had my sister kidnapped, so it wasn't like I'd had a lot of experience in dealing with the proper way to handle it. Still, I'd always liked to think I was one of those guys who could maintain his composure even under pressure.

Now, I knew the truth. Under pressure, I was exactly what I was at any other time in my life.

An ass.

I'd lashed out at anybody and everybody but the persons responsible – the sons of bitches who'd grabbed my sister…and myself for failing to protect her.

That was the honesty yielded by a couple of drinks.

Of course, I also sucked when it came to any kind of self-reflection.

So I had a few more drinks.

That's where things got fuzzy.

At some point between brooding and having my keys taken away by the nice but firm bartender – admittedly, I wasn't so far gone to know that I needed to give them up – my brain started to spin in and out of focus.

I think I tumbled into one cab, and then out.

I should have gone home.

But something else I sucked at too many times was doing

what I should do.

Things got *really* fuzzy after that.

Which was probably how I ended up staggering up a set of stairs that I didn't recognize.

What I did know was that I'd asked the cabbie to drop me off somewhere around here.

Why?

That was the fuzzy…

The door opened, and everything snapped into focus.

Toni.

Toni Gallagher stood there glaring at me. Her dark red hair piled on her head. She was wearing an old t-shirt that hit her mid-thigh.

Her eyes, dark and blue, raked over me from head to toe, and the look on her face was one of vague disgust.

For reasons I couldn't recall, that pissed me off.

I lifted a hand and pointed my finger at her.

Both of her.

"You…"

I swallowed and realized I was slurring my words. Damn. I was drunker than I realized.

She finished for me, an elegant eyebrow arching over her pretty eyes. "You're drunk."

"Are you?"

Toni rolled her eyes. "Go home, Ash."

"Home." I nodded. That made sense. I guess. Then I remembered and my face fell. "Iz…she's gone."

Toni's face softened and she moved closer.

That made it okay, right?

Chapter 3

Toni

The last thing I expected at nearly three a.m. was to have somebody banging on my door.

No. Correction.

The last thing I expected at nearly three a.m. was to have Ashford Lang knocking on my door, drunk off his ass. Once I managed to get his drunk ass over to my couch, I saw that his knuckles were busted up.

At some point, he'd hit somebody. I really hoped it wasn't someone who was going to press charges. That was the last thing he needed at the moment.

Sighing, I pushed his hair back from his face. "What in the hell am I supposed to do with you?" I murmured. It was a rhetorical question. He wasn't even close to coherent enough to answer.

Besides, common sense already told me what I should do.

I should call a cab and send Mr. Lang back home. At the most generous, I should call the emergency number for Doug that Isadora gave me and have him come get his boss.

I didn't listen.

Forty minutes later, I was practically drowning him in water, tomato juice and a little extra something I learned helped replace the lost electrolytes and helped beat a hangover. Well, I hadn't technically learned it. Aside from all of the tips pre-med and psych students exchanged, I'd had years of watching my four older brothers come home drunk and not wanting our parents to know. I'd paid attention.

The good news was that Ash was getting my expertise before he reached the hangover stage.

The bad news was that I didn't think he appreciated it.

When I started to lift his head to take another glass of water, he caught my wrist and opened a pair of eyes so green, they shouldn't have been permitted by nature. The fact that they were blood-shot just made the green stand out more.

"You need the water," I told him, using my best stern sister voice.

In a surprisingly clear voice, he said, "Haven't you shoved a swimming pool full of it down my throat already?"

I smiled sweetly. "No. Only a wading pool. Now drink."

To my surprise, he obliged, and then accepted the ibuprofen I gave him.

But the second he sat up, it was damn clear he still wasn't sober. He swayed a little and I braced myself. If I had to catch him, we'd both go down. I was strong, but there was no way I could handle that much dead weight.

"Just how much have you had to drink?" I asked him.

He squinted at me.

I was almost amused. "Do I need to rephrase the question?"

"No." He spoke with the clear, careful enunciation of a man who was drunk enough to know he was drunk, but was trying to pretend otherwise. "I'm trying to remember the exact amount. I lost count after the second bar."

I sighed. "You idiot." I nodded at his hand. "You hit somebody."

"Those keen powers of observation will serve you well when you're shrinking people."

He flexed his hand, frowning down at his scraped

knuckles as if he'd never seen his own hand before. In that moment, he looked so lost that I reached out, unable to stop myself, and stroked his hair.

At the exact same moment, he looked up and caught my wrist, our gazes connecting. His thumb stroked over the inside and my pulse leaped in response. Heavy, thick lashes drooped, but not before I saw his pupils flare with desire.

Memories of the heated moments we'd shared surged to life, and I could feel that fire arcing between us. He tugged me closer, reaching up with his free hand to cup my cheek. He stroked his thumb over my lip.

Echoing his movement, I caught his wrist.

"No." Shaking my head, I turned my face away. "That isn't a good idea."

"Why not?"

He sounded like a petulant child, and if the circumstances had been different, I might've found it endearing.

"You're drunk. You're upset."

He made a frustrated sound. "I was five seconds away from fucking you a few hours ago. I wasn't drunk or upset then. Safe to say, that's not why I want you."

He tugged on my wrist and I looked down at him. His expression changed, the atmosphere shifting. There was a sadness to him now, dangerously close to vulnerability.

"Toni...I don't want to think anymore. It's not solving anything and I keep doing stupid things...yelling at you..." He was almost pleading.

He tugged me into his lap, and I was helpless to resist. I groaned as he buried his face between my breasts. Through the material of my shirt, I felt the heat of his breath and an ache pulsed between my thighs. But logic was still in control.

For now.

"This isn't..."

He gripped my thigh, squeezing. His voice was rough. "I

think right now, fucking you is the one thing that will keep me from flying apart."

Shit. My heart nearly stuttered to a stop. Logic continued to scream inside my head, and I cupped his face. I had to take control of the situation.

"This won't solve anything," I said, my voice shaking. "You'll wake up and Isadora will still be missing. You'll be half-wondering if you can stand me again."

"I can stand you just fine." He wrapped my braid around his hand, using it to hold me so that I couldn't look away. "It's just hard to look at you and not want to bury my cock in you the second I see you."

It was like my blood had turned into a river of fire.

This time, when he tugged me closer, I couldn't resist anymore. And, logic be damned, I didn't want to.

I gasped as his mouth closed over mine, and when his tongue stabbed between my lips, my pussy throbbed in demanding envy.

He was still wearing the thin, dressy trousers from earlier, and I sucked in a breath at how easily I could feel him hardening beneath me.

I wore an old, threadbare T-shirt from college and nothing else, not even panties. Nothing, save what he wore, separated us and it definitely wasn't enough material. His fingers were nearly frantic in my hair, pulling apart my braid so that my still-damp hair fell in waves down my back. With that accomplished, he caught my hips and dragged me up, then down, rubbing me against him.

I whimpered.

The sound broke through the haze of arousal and some semblance of sanity tried to assert itself. I braced my hands against his shoulders, putting some distance between us. "Ash…"

"Toni," he said, mimicking my inflection.

He dipped his head, raked his teeth along my neck. When he closed his mouth on the fleshy area where neck met shoulder and started to suck, hunger gathered and pulsed between my thighs. I could feel myself growing wetter. I knew I shouldn't have been so turned on, especially not by this man who made me so angry, but my body had other ideas.

As if he sensed the winning battle, he arched up and started to rock against me.

When he lifted me up and pulled at his trousers, all I did was brace my weight on his shoulders and my knees. I'd made my decision and I wasn't going anywhere. I looked at him, our gazes caught, tangled. Our breaths came in ragged pants and in no time, he had freed himself and he caught my hand, guided it to his cock.

I groaned when I closed my fingers around him. He was just as big and hard as I'd imagined he would be.

"Tell me again how stupid this is," he said against my lips just before he stole another deep, hungry kiss.

My hair turned into a veil around us, blocking out the world. "It's so stupid. And I don't care."

He lifted me up, and I braced myself. I was wet, but there'd been no other foreplay and he was big. This was going to be intense. With a groan, I sank down on him.

I think I'd been preparing for this almost from the moment I'd seen him at my door, and although I had to fight to take him, it was the sweetest damn battle. But he wasn't going to let me win it, not my way. I was only half-way down when he took over, lifting me back up. I groaned and flexed, trying to take control back from him. Even like this, it was a fight between us.

He responded to my attempt by twisting and shifting in a movement so smooth, it took my brain a moment to process it. And, even still half-drunk, a moment was all he needed.

I was on my back a second later, half-leaning over the arm

of the couch, and he was crouched between my thighs. His gaze bore into mine as he withdrew, almost completely leaving me. Then, slowly, he dragged his gaze down, as if he could see through the T-shirt neither of us had bothered to discard. I followed his gaze, down over the hard points of my nipples that were clearly visible through the thin cotton. When I saw what he was looking at, my belly contracted, the muscles in my pussy clamping tighter.

He was staring at where we joined, where I was stretched around him, his cock mostly outside of my body, only the swollen head still inside me. I groaned and shuddered, rolled my hips, desperate to draw him inside.

He simply tightened his grip on my hips, making it impossible to move.

"I knew you'd be like this," Ash said, his voice harsh and hungry.

There was no trace of a slur to his words now. Whether it was the lust or the drinks that I've given him, it didn't matter. He wasn't too drunk to know what he was doing.

"You want to take control."

He fed me one slow inch, and then retreated. He smiled when I made a sound of protest.

"I control things," Ash said, staring down at me in challenge.

Nothing had ever made me hotter in my life. Still, I wasn't one to let a challenge go unmet. I hadn't survived twenty-four years of being a baby sister to four brothers in New York City by having a weak personality.

"You can't control me." Keeping my eyes locked on his, I slid a hand down the middle of my torso, stopping only to lightly tease my nipples. When I reached the place where we were joined, he caught my hand. I grinned up at him and used my other one.

He caught that one too. That freed my hips and I arched

up, sucking in a breath as he sank a few inches deeper. So good.

A hot light came into his eyes, and he flipped me over onto my knees, driving into me deep and hard before I could catch my breath. It tore a cry from me, one that was as much victory as it was pleasure. But it was a victory I tried to celebrate too soon, because in the next moment, he grabbed my wrists and pulled my arms behind me, securing them at the base of my spine with one large hand.

"Now what are you going to do, Toni?" he demanded, slowing to shallow, short thrusts that only fanned the fire inside me.

It was doing the same to him too, I knew. It was little comfort though, since my entire body was screaming for him to take me. There were times when I enjoyed a little slow and tender love-making.

This wasn't one of them.

I drove myself back against him, making a sound in the back of my throat as he started to fill me.

He grabbed my hip, immobilizing me. He was only halfway inside, but he was still as big as some other lovers I'd had in the past.

"Do you want to come?" he asked.

"You think you can make me beg?"

He laughed and the sound was ragged. "Yes. I can make you beg."

He surged deep again, hard and fast, three times – *almost* –

Then he stopped. I was still panting and on the edge of climax when he settled back into that shallow, teasing pattern. I swore and twisted my hips as best I could. If he would only–

He drove into me again, hard, fast. Three thrusts.

Then again, slow, teasing.

"You son of a bitch," I snarled. Damn bastard.

"Beg." This time, when he said it, he let go of my hands and grabbed my hair, hauling me up so that my spine pressed against his chest. The pressure on my scalp was electric. Upright now, being so much shorter than him, I was all but impaled on his cock, my knees barely touching the cushion beneath me. I undulated and gasped as the motion had the head of his cock rubbing in almost the right spot. He was so close. A little more to the–

There.

"Toni..."

But I didn't hear anything else. Lost in the most powerful climax of my life, I was deaf to everything, even the sound of my own ragged moans.

Morning came.

I'd kind of figured it would, since the clock had kept ticking away during the night. After the gut-wrenchingly raw sex on the couch, Ash had scooped me up into his arms and staggered his way the few short steps to my tiny bed.

He'd collapsed on the bed, me on top of him...and then he was inside me and it had started all over again. A few minutes after it ended, he staggered upright and went to the bathroom.

When he came out, he dropped beside me and didn't move again. After a few minutes, I'd gotten up and gone into the bathroom to shower. It was only then that I realized we hadn't used any protection. Fortunately, I'd been on the pill since college – well, since I was sixteen anyway. I could only hope that Ash had been smarter with his other partners than he had been with me. I'd get tested just in case. I hadn't let myself brood on it though. I'd showered and gone back to bed.

That had been five hours ago.

I'd left him alone in the bedroom a few minutes ago and had come out to the living room to, of course, brood.

I'd just made one of the biggest mistakes of my life and I knew it.

Ashford Lang might not have been my boss, per se, but he was damn close.

I wasn't worried so much about any kind of power imbalance there since he didn't technically have any control over me. Well, maybe he could tell Isadora, but if she ended up firing me because I'd had sex with her brother, I didn't want to work with her anyway. I was still trying to figure out if I'd stay on even if –

"No *if*," I muttered into my coffee. "When. *When*."

I'd carve it in concrete if I had to. *When* she was found, the question was, could I keep working with her? Part of me didn't want to think about walking away. I'd only known her a week, but I already cared about her. I totally understood that she had to be feeling somewhat smothered, but at the same time, the girl I knew was so…sweet, she'd let herself suffer. She'd deal with her own unhappiness to make others happy and she'd somehow *be* happy because of it. She'd let me go with some amazing severance package and a smile even if it left her in the lurch.

It was part of what just made her…sweet.

It was also part of what made me determined to think *when*.

She'd be found.

And when she was…

I gripped my coffee cup and lifted it to my lips.

Could I keep working for her? Knowing that I'd see her brother, day in and day out?

I can stand you just fine. It's just hard to look at you and not want to bury my cock in you the second I see you.

I was already way too attracted to him.

I already knew he was bad for me, and that was an understatement.

Could I handle being around him if I knew he wanted me the same way I wanted him?

More, if he crooked his finger, would I go running?

A slight sound from the other end of the apartment had me lowering the cup of coffee. I craned my head around and looked down the hallway. That faint noise was all I heard for a few minutes, and I went back to slowly and steadily feeding my need for caffeine.

By the time he came out, I'd poured him a cup and myself a second. He took the mug gratefully, but in silence.

Neither of us said anything.

My phone rang after he'd taken a few sips, and I saw him start for the door.

I couldn't really say I was surprised.

Pissed off, sure.

But surprised?

No.

Unfortunately.

Chapter 4

Toni

The sound of the door closing didn't so much as *hurt* as it...echoed.

I could feel it, in a strange, surreal way. It echoed all the way down into my soul, and it was still echoing even when I told Victor I needed a few minutes, and could he please call back? I hung up before I heard his reply.

I took advantage of the brief respite and locked myself in the bathroom.

Ash had been in here.

I mean, I'd expected him to use the bathroom, but I hadn't expected to be able to walk in and sense his presence. He was neat, but I could see the telltale signs.

My shampoo wasn't in the same spot I usually put it. I always left my folded towels with the crease to the right. It was to the left now and slightly askew.

It wasn't anything major, and while I was something of a neat freak, I couldn't fault the condition he'd left my bathroom in. There were no seats left raised; no toothpaste left in the sink even though I knew he'd used mine. I only knew because I'd left it on the counter late last night when I'd brushed my teeth three times over, as if that would scrub the taste of him from my memory. It was back in the medicine cabinet.

The spare toothbrush I always left in the cabinet was

gone.

I made a mental note to buy another one even as I turned on the water and splashed icy wet over my face. It did nothing to cool the heat inside me.

I was still shaking, still unsteady, and still...wanting.

I still wanted him and I wanted to call him.

I didn't even know his number. I had it somewhere, of course, since part of being Isadora's assistant meant having the numbers of all of the people she might need to contact. Including her brother.

I was also half-sick with worry over Isadora, and if I'd thought the two of us would be able to wait it out together, I would've just asked him to stay. But I knew better.

He couldn't be around me without wanting to fight with me.

Well, fight me or fuck me.

One or both would put me in a very bad place and I knew it.

He wasn't good for me, no matter how badly I wanted him.

The phone ringing caught me off guard and I let out a startled sound. A quick look at my watch told me that I'd been in the bathroom for nearly twenty minutes.

"Time flies when you're freaking out," I muttered.

Grumbling the entire way, I hurried to the landline that sat above my kitchenette counter. I answered it, but didn't get to even finish a *hello* before my brother was talking.

"Geez, Toni," Vic said. "*I need to talk to you, Vic. It's urgent. Not now, Vic. I'm tied up.* Make up your mind already, why don't you?"

"Shut it, Vic." Tired already, I slumped against the counter and stared outside. The sky was so blue, dotted with puffy blue clouds. "So...ummm..."

Even though I couldn't see him, I already knew I'd just

made him suspicious.

"Just spit it out," he said, sounding annoyed.

Vaguely, I wondered if I'd caught him in his early morning sneak out – his typical way of finishing a hook-up.

Rolling my eyes, I shoved off the counter and tried to find the right way to approach the subject. At twenty-seven, Vic was the youngest of my four older brothers and the one who'd been in and out of trouble since he'd been a kid. Our parents and brothers had tried to keep him out of it, but he was even more stubborn than I was, and that was saying something. I sometimes wondered if it was partially my fault, if my having passed him up in school, always being the smartest kid in the room, if all of that had somehow made him feel like he needed something of his own, even if it meant breaking the law.

After being arrested at eighteen on felony drug charges, he'd served his time and then pulled back from the life. Sort of. He still kept in touch with some of the wrong people and, more importantly, kept his ear to the ground, always hoping he'd find that *one* thing that would let him make it rich, somehow.

Sadly, the one thing my big brother didn't want to do was hard work.

I loved him no matter what, but sometimes, he annoyed the hell out of me. Even though he was three years my senior, I sometimes – okay, most of the time – felt like the older sister.

Sighing, I rubbed the back of my neck. He was going to be pissed, but I reminded myself of what was at stake. "You been hanging out with any of your old crowd, Vic?" I asked softly.

He started to make a derisive noise, and I knew he was going to brush me off. I could practically hear the words. He tried to make us all believe he'd left that life behind him, and for the most part, he had. But we all knew better. Try as he might, there were shadows that would always follow him, mostly because he didn't want to let them go. He just wanted us to believe otherwise.

Too tired to argue it with him, I said, "Don't jerk me around, Vic."

"What?" His tone was borderline belligerent.

I'd been subconsciously pacing my apartment and found myself at the microscopic fire-escape I'd retrofitted into a mini-balcony. Ducking through the window, I stared out over the streets of the city. "Don't lie, Vic. I'm not looking to lecture you. If that's how you want to live your life, then...hell, it's your life. Right now, I just have a question. Yes or no. Have you had a chance to hook up with anybody from that old life?"

If he was at all suspicious, he didn't let it show. "Well, I guess I might see a few of my old pals down at the bar here and then. I don't hassle them, they don't hassle me. It's easy to just kind of glide on by like that, ya know?"

I reached up to pinch the bridge of my nose. Only my brother could make hanging out at a bar with drug dealers and pimps and members of organized crime sound like he just happened to run into them at the grocery store.

I loved him, but sometimes I wondered about him.

"I need to ask a favor." I focused on the reason I'd called. It would make it easier not to reach through the phone and slap him. I hoped.

"Yeah? Look, if you've got yourself some kind of bleeding heart at one of the places where you volunteer, Toni, I'm not turning on friends."

"Vic, shut *up*," I snapped. My nerves were frayed and I wasn't in the mood for his whole 'honor among thieves' bullshit. "This is important and it's not about you or me. So listen."

Something in my voice must've gotten through to him and Victor's voice gentled as he asked, "What's wrong?"

"There's a woman missing. My boss."

"Isadora Lang."

"Yeah."

He sighed. "Why you calling me? You know I'm out of that life, right? I might talk to some friends, but I promised Mom and Dad. I promised all of you that I was done."

"I know that." Swallowing the knot in my throat, I brought up a mental image of Isadora. Those stylish black curls and innocent olive green eyes. Her sweet, brilliant smile. "Look, I've just got this feeling she was kidnapped. You were in deep for a while with all sorts of people. I'm not accusing you of anything because I know you'd never hurt anyone, but sometimes…well, people talk."

"Toni…" Vic's voice was soft. "I've been out a long time."

Feeling defeated, I sagged back against the crumbled brick of my apartment building. I'd been grasping at straws, I knew. A part of me had just been hoping. "I know. I'm worried about her, Victor. She's like this…she's sweet and hopeful. She gets excited about pretty flowers in her office. She buys toys for kids in the hospital and group homes and takes them in herself because she loves seeing the the looks on their faces. She's one of the best people I know."

"Shit, kid." He was quiet for a moment, and then said, "I'll ask around."

My relief was so profound that my legs almost gave out.

"I gotta be careful, though. Once the cops start really digging into things, they're going to be looking at everyone close to her and that means you. They find out who you're related to and then it gets out that I've been asking around, they're going to think I had something to do with it."

"I'm sorry."

"Why?" Victor laughed humorlessly. "You weren't the dumbass who thought he could solve all of our money problems by making a drug run. If anybody should say they are sorry, it's me. You'll get hassled a lot more on this because of me than you would if some other chump was your brother."

I half-smiled. "I don't want some other chump."

Victor muttered something under his breath, but I heard him anyway and it made my heart hurt.

We ended the phone call a few seconds later, but not before I said, "You're wrong, you know. I've got exactly the brother I deserve. You might still have your flaws, but you turned your life around, Vic."

It was probably a waste of time, making the trip uptown. There were no police cars outside the monolith of a house, but that wasn't surprising. I was sure they'd set everything up in case a ransom call came in, but I knew the cops all thought that Isadora was just out doing what most rich twenty-somethings in New York City did and that she'd stagger home, drunk and /or high at some point.

Fifth Avenue was quieter than I could remember seeing it in quite some time and I had to wonder if maybe Ash had waved his magic wand made of green bills and somehow managed to clear the city street.

The idea amused me for some reason.

Maybe because I could actually picture Ashford Lang striding into some crowded and dim city official's office and shaking a fist of bills in his face. *See this? I'm Ashford Fucking Lang and I'm having a bad day. Make everybody go away.*

Not that it would work in the real world, but he was arrogant enough to think he could control everything and everybody. I wouldn't have put anything past him.

I control things.

His voice was a hot, raw echo in the back of my memory and I had to suppress a shudder.

I still felt his hands on me.

His cock inside me.

His mouth on me.

Oh, hell.

That mouth.

Even as much as I regretted last night, I regretted not having *more*. Like having him completely sober so that he couldn't blame what happened on lowered inhibitions. I regretted not having him completely naked and stretched out under me as I learned his body. Then me under him as he learned mine. I regretted not having had more time.

"Stop it," I told myself as I mounted the steps.

For once, nobody was there to open the door. I really hoped that didn't mean Ash had fired the entire staff. Isadora had told me that Doug had been with her family since she was a child and he'd been the one who'd stayed with her after her parents died while Ash had been on his way from college.

I told myself it wasn't a big deal to let myself in. I had a key. Isadora had given me one and told me that I could pretty much come and go as I pleased. I shook my head. Far too naïve and trusting.

There had been one thing she'd said though. *If you do let yourself in, make sure you either find me in my wing or stay in the main area up front, Toni, okay? Don't go in the west wing. That's pretty much all my brother's.*

She'd made a joke about *Beauty and the Beast*. I'd countered with one about Bluebeard and she'd laughed, a surprisingly loud and bawdy laugh that hadn't seemed to fit the elegant and sweet woman.

I could see now that her joke had been much more appropriate for her brother.

Slipping into the house, I locked the door behind me and quickly moved to disarm the system. The last thing I needed was for the alarm to go off and the cops to show up.

As the beeps hushed, my skin prickled. As a soon-to-be psychiatrist, I knew all about instinct and the sorts of primal things that our species had retained despite all of our civilizing.

It was that part of me that reacted when I heard the low, guttural moan. It was like nothing I'd ever heard before. I couldn't even tell if it was a sound of pain, but it was enough to tell me that something was happening.

Chapter 5

Ash

I was a coward.

I had a hell of a lot of character flaws, but I had to admit that one surprised me. I'd always considered my way of dealing with sex and women as being smart, the right thing to do since I wasn't interested in a relationship. Now, I saw it for what it really was.

I was a coward for sneaking away from Toni the way I did every other woman. I was worse, actually, because those other women had known what they were getting into.

I'd been wondering what in the hell I'd gotten myself into and how I could ever face Toni again when I'd been saved by the bell...more or less.

Toni had gotten a phone call, and judging by the grimace on her face, she'd seemed to think it was important, so rather than doing the polite thing and waiting to see if she wanted to talk, I used it as a chance to get the hell out of Brooklyn.

If I'd thought that thinking clearer would be any easier once I was away from her, away from the magic of her touch or the power of her eyes, then I was clearly an idiot.

I doubted she would've disagreed with that assessment.

All day, I tasted her kisses.

Instead of the pounding headache, I had a pounding cockache, brought on by residual memories of the way she'd stared at me, daring me to try to control her.

Damn, I wanted to control her.

And it pissed me off that I couldn't.

What was worse, the more I thought about her, the hotter I got, the more on edge I got.

And then my mood did a violent slide in the other direction as I recalled...*Iz*.

She was still missing.

Not that it mattered to the cops.

There was a set period of time she had to be missing, I'd been told. Forty-eight hours.

It had been less than twenty-four.

I was going to kill someone if I had to wait another day for them to get off their asses and do something.

"What do you mean *there's nothing you can do*?" I was talking to the Police Commissioner, but even his title wasn't enough to make me keep my voice down. "I'm telling you that my sister is missing. You're the NYPD. What, you don't investigate missing persons' cases anymore, Dyson?"

I stared hard at my computer screen.

The man who stared back at me over the monitor was a white-haired man with the distinguished sort of features that commanded authority. That wasn't why I'd backed him or why I still supported him though. He backed up his promises with real action.

Yet I wasn't seeing any sign of that here.

"You're not listening to me, Ashford. Now...*listen*..." He held up a hand when I opened my mouth. "I understand why you're so angry, but before you tear me a new one, try to remember what I had to go through about this time last year."

His jaw went tight, and I looked away. A year ago, his daughter had been gunned down in what was nothing more than a petty act of revenge. She'd only been fourteen. They still didn't have enough proof to arrest the guy who did it.

"But you need to understand, there are certain things that tie our hands for now. Isadora is an adult. She hasn't been missing for forty-eight hours. Trust me, we *are* keeping our eye out, but until we cross that deadline…"

"With kids, they say the first twenty-four hours or whatever…those are the golden hours. So why is it different with adults?"

"Because adults can, and *do*, just…leave."

I hammered at him for another few minutes and then hung up. I had other names on my list. Powerful names who I'd gotten to know through my business transactions…and some through my more…private life. I didn't make any other calls though.

It wasn't doing any good.

I had my own security out in force, combing the streets for her. I'd sent them out almost immediately after I'd talked to Doug. And actually, I'd gotten proof that the cops *were* looking for her. Just not officially. One of my men had run into a contact of his own the force and it turned out they were both doing the same thing. Looking for Isadora. My guy had texted me to let me know.

Tearing the city apart and threatening all the contacts I had – contacts I might need soon – wasn't going to serve any purpose.

I needed to focus.

Needed to think.

But I wouldn't be able to do that until I got rid of some of the energy, the anger inside me. There was only one way I knew to do that.

I picked up the phone and punched in a number.

A soft, throaty voice came on the line.

"Are you available?" I nearly barked out the words.

"Just say when, Sir."

Sibella Hall was a sub I only occasionally used.

She liked her play…dark.

I rarely went that dark, but today, I needed it.

The hour I'd spent tying her had done more to focus my brain than anything else could have. Yoga, meditation – that was what any number of people in my line of work did.

I had sex.

And I had it rough.

The more stress I needed to relieve, the rougher it got.

When I really needed to clear my head, I had sex with a Sub when she was bound and helpless, unable to move anything, sometimes not even her mouth.

I didn't gag Sibella this time, but I told her not to scream, not to moan. And I'd done that only because my mood was so dark, I didn't know if I was going to push her harder than I should. I doubted it. I'd taken plenty of subs to their limits, but Sibella didn't seem to have one. Still, I didn't gag her, just in case.

Once I had her bound securely, I moved to her head and wrapped her long ponytail around my hand.

She rolled her eyes to look up at me and I saw a familiar dazed look in them.

If I just jacked off and came right there, or had her take my cock in her mouth, fucking it until I emptied myself, she'd be more than satisfied. For Sibella, it was all about the submission. She was probably about ready to come and the only times I'd touched her had been to tie her up. And there hadn't been anything sexual about any of my touches.

I found myself thinking of Toni and frustrated need sank its teeth into me again. I needed more than just this.

"Open," I growled.

She parted her lips and I surged inside.

Closing my eyes, I tried to focus on the wet cave of her mouth, how she sucked and used her teeth and tongue. She was an artist, even when she couldn't use her hands–

I could still feel Toni's nails biting into my shoulders. See her hands as they slid down my torso.

She'd never wait for a man to *allow* her to climax. I'd had to fight to keep her from taking it.

With a snarl, I tore away from Sibella, my cock pulsing, nearly painful with need.

She was panting. "Sir?"

"Be quiet!" I snapped. I didn't want to hear her voice.

I moved up behind her. She was bound on a specially designed sawhorse I'd ordered last year. Each leg, wrapped in red rope from thigh to ankle, was secured to the horse's supports. She was wet, the lips of her bared sex open and vulnerable. Sibella always removed all of her body hair. Most of the subs I chose did the same.

Toni had a nice, neatly-trimmed thatch of hair, dark with just a hint of red and I...

Dammit! I shook my head, trying to clear it. I reached over to the side table and picked up the bottle of lubricant I always kept handy. I might like to get really rough with my Subs, but I wasn't cruel. I knew exactly how much preparation each Sub needed before each type of sex.

Fortunately for me, Sibella only needed a little and I knew just how to work it so that the lubricated finger slid in and out of her ass, drawing little suppressed whimpers from her as I twisted and curled it.

She was quivering by the time I mounted her. I pressed the head of my cock against her ass and paused.

"I want you to scream," I said. Maybe the noise would pull me out of my head.

I slammed into her and Sibella's high, needy scream echoed through the room. The muscles in her ass spasmed around my throbbing shaft. She loved taking it after very little prep and that was what I needed right now. I drove into her again, my balls slapping against her cunt.

Again, again, again...

In my head, Sibella had become somebody else. The furious sounds of her passion made it easier for that image to coalescence. Tired of fighting it, I let it happen. I spanked Sibella's ass while I let the memories play out, let the new fantasies take over.

"Beg me," I said out-loud.

"Please...please, Sir...Sir please..."

It wasn't enough. It wasn't *her*.

I brought my hand down on her naked ass, the round globes one of the few areas of her body I'd left untouched by the ropes. And exactly for this reason. "Keep it up. What do you want?"

Sibella's low, throaty voice was almost – *almost* – a match for Toni's. "I want you, Sir–"

I knew what was wrong. Why it sounded wrong. *She* hadn't done that.

"Don't call me, Sir. Just..." I squeezed my eyes closed. When I heard *her* call me...I wanted it to be real. Now, I just needed release. "Tell me what you want."

"You...fucking me. Just like this. Please, harder...harder...harder...I want to come, please, oh, please...let me..."

She lapsed into silence as her body stiffened, her ass tightening around me until it was almost painful.

She was close.

I knew the signs.

I should help. Get her to come so when I was ready...

A harsh gasp broke through my concentration, and I

opened my eyes.

Toni stood in the open doorway to the room.

My playroom, the one I'd designed solely for my kind of sexual play.

Her eyes tracked down over my naked chest to linger on Sibella and where my cock was half-way in the other woman's ass.

Her mouth trembled.

I rotated my hips and drove deep and hard into Sibella, her ass a hot, silken glove, even through the condom.

Without taking my eyes off the petite woman in the doorway, I spanked Sibella again. "Beg me," I rasped.

"Please, please, please, Sir!"

Toni's eyes narrowed and her face flushed a hot, angry red.

As I brought my hand down on Sibella's ass again, Toni spun on her heel and stormed away.

I buried myself balls-deep in Sibella's ass as she came...

Chapter 6

Toni

"That…that…that *asshole*!!" I said it through gritted teeth, and it wasn't even close to enough. There wasn't a word in the English language bad enough for the sort of person that bastard was.

Or for how fucking stupid I felt.

Shaking and hot with the anger inside me, I was almost all the way to the door when the phone rang.

I almost kept going.

I couldn't even explain why I stopped.

Maybe some part of me knew.

I hesitated and looked down the long hallway. Ash hadn't even stopped, hadn't even slowed. The fucker had his cock half in her ass and hadn't even blinked. In fact, he'd all but *taunted* me.

"Beg me…"

Like he wanted me to know what he wanted. Like he wanted me to know I'd come up short.

As if his exit this morning hadn't been enough to tell me that I hadn't measured up.

All those thoughts rushed through my head in a span of a second as I was turning to look at the phone. The name on the caller ID made my heart stop, then nearly burst out of my chest as I dove for the phone. I snatched it up, barely able to think.

"Hello?"

"I assume Mr. Lang has noticed that he's...missing something."

I sucked in a breath. "Who is this?"

A voice, disembodied and distorted, chuckled. "Now, now, Miss Gallagher. I'll do the talking in this conversation. Is Mr. Lang available?"

Shaking, I lowered the phone and looked down the hallway, back to where...back to Ash. I shouted his name. He didn't answer.

The screaming I'd heard earlier had gone silent. He must have told her to be quiet. She would've listened, of course. Because that was the kind of woman he wanted...I pushed the thought from my head. Not important.

A distant voice caught my attention and I stopped, lifting the phone to my ear as I started down the hallway. "I'm getting him."

"No time for that, Miss Gallagher. I'm afraid you'll have to work as the go-between for now."

I shot another look down the hall and tried to walk faster. If I ran, I wouldn't be able to hear. *Damn it, Ash...*

My knees went weak as the man laid out his demands.

The line went dead.

Too late.

I sank to the floor and stared at the plush carpet beneath me. I tried to breathe, tried to steady myself.

But I couldn't.

I ended up vomiting the entire contents of my stomach up on the floor.

Chapter 7

Toni

Thursday morning.

I mentally counted the days since Isadora had been kidnapped.

I wanted to puke.

Again.

As far as I knew, there hadn't been any more calls, no more contact from the kidnapper. Not since Tuesday afternoon. Instead of a comforting blur, it was stark and clear. Every memory from the moment I'd seen Ash – Mr. Lang – through the rest of the day and into the night had been seared into my brain.

I hadn't quite made it to my feet when Mr. Lang had appeared in the door, his jeans unzipped, a cruel smirk on his lips. "What are you…?"

That had been the last *semi*-civilized statement he'd said to me.

Everything else since then had either been shouted or snarled.

He'd been furious.

I hadn't deserved any of it. It hadn't been like I'd planned to walk in on his little kink-fest, and I'd sure as hell tried to get him on the phone. He had just been too busy, all balls-deep in the ass of his tied-up girlfriend.

Were they serious?

I didn't know.

I didn't care, I reminded myself.

But even if I didn't care, I didn't understand why he was so pissed at me. I had tried to get to him in time. I'd told the cops everything the kidnapper had said. I'd remembered everything.

But still, it hadn't been good enough.

Not surprising. A guy like him expected perfection, something I was sorely lacking in. I was also lacking in answers and he seemed to think I could pull those out of my ass.

The rest of the night's memories followed.

"Miss Gallagher?"

I tensed at the sound of my name. I hadn't been able to help it. I didn't hate cops, didn't distrust them, per se. But they'd made my life hell, had made my family's life hell back when Vic had gotten in trouble. They'd assumed some of us – if not all of us – had been involved in the crap he'd been doing.

The FBI agent had noticed my flinch and had lifted a trim black eyebrow. Her skin had been a lovely shade of warm brown, and she smiled as she'd come into the room and sat down. "Don't like cops, huh?"

"You're with the FBI," I'd said without thinking. "That's actually scarier than the cops."

She'd just chuckled. "You're very blunt, Miss Gallagher…or is it Dr. Gallagher?"

"Not yet." I'd grimaced at the thought of the final I'd had coming up the next morning and the notes I needed to study.

It hadn't ended up mattering. I hadn't gone in to take it. I'd still have a C even if I didn't retake the test. After a lifetime of perfection, one fucking C had barely even registered.

"Must be hard, working a job like this and still going to

school."

I'd shrugged. "I've always had to work. It's nothing new." I hadn't understood why she'd been asking about work rather than the phone call.

"I hear ya on that. I've been there." She'd smiled. "Special Agent Dionne Marcum, by the way. Man, I tell you...I look around this place, see all this money. I had to do what you did, bust my ass all the way through, working a job, sometimes two, and there would be some of these kids with their silver spoon choking them as they complained about how hard it was getting up for a nine a.m. class."

I'd leaned back, studying her. "I know the type."

"You're working for the type," she'd countered.

"Isadora's a doll. She's not a complainer." I'd blown out a sigh. "Please tell me you all have something."

"I wish I could."

Off in the distance, I'd heard Ash – Mr. Lang – his voice big and harsh. Dionne had grimaced. "That one isn't a doll. Why'd you come in today?"

"Because she wanted me to do a job for her, and..." I'd stopped. It hadn't been easy to say. "I'm scared. I'm worried about her. Being here...well, I was hoping I'll hear good news here, rather than something bad on the news."

She'd continued to study me. She'd had a good game face, but hey, I'd grown up with Victor. I'd known when I was being played and I'd seen the wheels churning, see them spinning in her head. Tired of the game, I'd leaned forward, elbows braced on the edge of the desk. It was neatly organized, everything I needed within reach, including a computer that was so top of the line, I didn't think it was even on the market yet.

"Can I make this easy on both of us?" I'd said softly.

There had been just the tiniest break in her *it's just us girls* mask. Then she'd cocked her eyebrow. "Excuse me?"

"Look..." I'd hitched up a shoulder. "I'll give you credit.

You're good at this – really good. But you can stop with the trying to bond with me thing. Just ask your questions."

The friendly look had drained out of her eyes and she'd cocked her head, indicated that I should continue.

"Let's just say I had a good crash course when it comes to cops. I know a routine when I see one." I'd given her a wry smile and shrugged. "You already pointed out that I'm blunt. I am. And I prefer it when people are the same with me. I gave your buddy over there everything the kidnapper said to me on the phone. What else do you want to know?"

"Fair enough," Dionne had said, giving me an appraising smile. "So let's look at it like this. You're busting your ass through school. Had a job that made it...well, *easier*. Not easy, though. But you could study, and it let you take the time you needed. Then life kicks you in the face, and you lose that job, had to find another. Here you are, working with people in the lap of luxury. Isadora Lang? If she wanted to, she'd never need to do anything but spend money and she wouldn't run out. Isn't that rough?"

"No. Why would it be?" I'd answered honestly and kept my eyes steady on her.

Dionne had leaned forward. "Toni, you have the smarts, drive and determination to do anything. But you had to work. You had a full ride offered to you, only to have it taken away because of things your brother did. That's hardly fair."

"Can I share a secret?" I'd dropped my voice. "Life's not fair. You learn to deal with it."

She'd started to say something else and I'd lifted a hand. I was tired of it by then. They needed to be out trying to track down the caller, not questioning me about my life.

"Nothing else." I'd said. "I get what you're poking at. Somebody decided that it was plausible that I might have gotten drawn into this because I'm hard up for money. Somebody offered me easy money...nobody would be hurt. I just had to do what they asked…how close am I?"

Dionne had shrugged, her gaze shrewd. "C
that I imagine you watch a lot of *Law & Order* or
of people get the rough idea of what they think happens,
Gallagher."

"Yeah, well. I lived it." Thinking about what happened with Victor had been enough to turn my stomach. If I'd had anything left in it, I might've thrown up again. "I lived it. It almost destroyed my family. If you think I would do something like that…"

She'd nodded and rose from her chair, heading toward the door. Halfway there, she'd paused and looked back. "If it helps? Personally, I don't think you would. But personally can't come into play here. It's about the job and what can be proved."

We'd stared at each other for a moment and then she'd nodded, turned around and left.

Things hadn't gotten any better from there. Like right now. It was Thursday morning and I was back at the Lang house, trying to find out what was going on. No one had told me anything.

I hovered outside the office, hardly daring to breathe. I had my eyes closed, and I kept having to unclench my hands from the fists I'd unconsciously knotted them into.

I wanted to barge inside and demand to know what was going on.

Not that it would do much good. Mr. Lang wasn't talking to me. He hadn't since he'd screamed at me two days ago.

So I was reduced to this. Sneaking outside the door to Mr. Lang's office. Just beyond the door, I could hear people talking.

"…sorry. There was just no reason to hold him." It was one of the FBI agents. I couldn't remember the name.

"What do you mean you had no reason to hold him?" Ash

napped. His voice I knew. Even if I wished I didn't.

"Holding him any longer than we did would have been a violation of Mr. Stevens' rights. There is simply no indication he's involved. His alibi is ironclad and—"

"I don't want to hear about anybody's rights when my sister is still missing!" Ash shouted.

My heart ached for him and I couldn't quite hate myself for it. No matter how I felt about him right now, his sister *was* missing.

"What about *her* rights?"

"We're looking, Mr. Lang." That firm no, nonsense voice...I recognized that one. Marcum. "But your sister's boyfriend had an alibi, and there's no sign he's involved in this."

"What do you expect him to do? Hang a sign in his window? *Kidnapped woman – ask me for details?*"

I closed my eyes at the angry desperation in his voice even as I eased away from the door. If I kept standing here, I'd get noticed by one of the household staff. They wouldn't yell at me, but it'd be awkward.

"I'm sorry, Mr. Lang. We've been monitoring his calls, his whereabouts, everything. He's not involved...oh, hello."

Marcum had opened the door. With her was a tall man, his blond hair already thinning. Marcum didn't look surprised. The guy looked a bit thrown to see me there, but he covered quickly. The two lawyers busied themselves with lawyerly things while the thickly muscled man at Ash's shoulder just stared at me. He was a member of Ash's security detail. He'd stared at me quite a bit since I was hired.

Mr. Lang did a lot of ignoring – at least when it came to me lately.

Fine. Let him.

I looked at Special Agent Marcum. "I guess there hasn't been any news."

She didn't respond, but her expression said it all.

Mr. Lang finally spoke to me. "Miss Gallagher, if you don't have anything specific to do, you can go."

"I don't work for you." I narrowed my eyes at him.

He flicked a look at me. "No. You work for Isadora. Since she's not...available, why'd you come in this morning?"

The disparaging tone got to me, and he gave me one of those looks, like I wasn't even worth his time. I had another sudden flash of memory – him burying himself inside that woman. My stomach twisted and I resorted to anger. He wasn't the only one who could be an ass. He was about the meet the bitch queen. Yeah, Isadora was his sister, but I was worried about her too, and he had no reason to be acting this way.

Stepping past the agents into the office, I stopped a few feet away from the desk and folded my arms over my chest.

"I don't recall inviting you to participate in this conversation," he snapped at me.

"Screw you." I didn't even glance at the lawyers, agents or the security guy looming in the background. This was between me and the ass. "You want to tell why you've got some bug up your ass about me, *Mr. Lang*?"

"I don't have a bug up my ass as you so elegantly put it." His jaw went tight and his eyes burned hot. "But as you are aware, my sister has gone missing. After you botched the call, the kidnapper hasn't–"

He said something else.

I knew he did.

But after those words "you botched the call" my head sort of exploded.

Or maybe I did.

Jerking back, my spine ramrod straight, I glared at him.

"Did you just say *I* botched the call?" I demanded, pointing a finger at him. "I screamed my lungs out for you, asshole. But you were too busy fucking some woman's brains out to be bothered."

There was a faint snap.

From the corner of my eye, I saw one of the lawyers – a portly, middle-aged man with salt and pepper hair – had a pencil. Or pencils, rather. He'd snapped the one he was holding in two and didn't even seem to notice.

The other one was staring stonily ahead as if he'd gone mute, blind and deaf.

Actually, save for my ragged breathing, there wasn't a sound in the room.

Ash rose from his desk, harsh flags of color riding high on his cheeks. But he wasn't blushing. He was furious.

Good.

Curling my lip at him, I said, "I was basically screaming for you, but that wasn't the screaming you were listening to, was it? I was practically running down the hall while trying to listen and remember everything that man was saying. He wasn't going to wait for you to get your dick out of her ass, much less walk to the phone."

The others in the room were trying so hard not to look at us, abruptly, I started to laugh at the sheer stupidity of it.

Spinning away, I tried to get myself under control. There was nothing humorous about this. Nothing. It was all just crazy…and sad. Scary. Once I had that final, bitter laugh out, I looked over at him one last time. "I was walking by the phone when it rang. I saw her number and started to call for you. It's not my fault that you were too busy to pay attention."

His eyes had turned to shards of ice, but I met them dead on and gave him a derisive sneer before I turned away.

"It's curious…" Ash's voice was even colder than his stare had been and I wouldn't have thought that was possible. But even more cutting than his tone, his gaze? The words. "You came in when you clearly weren't needed."

Or wanted. The words hung there, unsaid, but heard all

the same.

"And then the *one* fucking phone call that's received? Who's here to answer it, at the exact right time? You. One might call it a coincidence."

I turned and stared at him. A different kind of quiet covered the room.

"I don't believe in coincidences," he said softly.

The implication almost sent me staggering. But one lesson I'd learned early on. Never let them know they hurt you. I'd cry, later. Much later.

"Ash?" I gave him my most brazen smile. "Fuck you."

Victor looked decidedly aggravated as we sat down at the pub, finding a table in the far back, away from the noise, away from the band, away from the front door...and the cops.

"You've got cops following you again?" I asked as I slid into the seat across from him. After my little run-in with Ash – no matter how many times I tried to get myself to think of him as Mr. Lang, I kept reverting to Ash – I wasn't in the best of moods either.

"Happens from time to time. What am I going to do?" He jerked a shoulder like it didn't matter, but I knew him better than that. While he didn't seem to be able to completely stay away from the life, he hated the general assumption that he was up to no good. It was one of the reasons he rarely got to see his son. The judge hadn't even blinked when she'd given Rachelle full custody.

We sat in silence a moment, sipping from our respective drinks. Vic always went for the cheapest shit beer, which I'd always thought strange, since when it came to everything else, he went for the things that were out of his reach.

I was on my second rum and coke, and lamenting over my lack of foresight. I should have requested a double. I didn't care that it was barely mid-afternoon. I was going to need it, the way things were going. I was scared for Isadora. I'd missed an important final and even if I could pass my class without it, I didn't like not doing things. And, of course, there was always the looming question of my employment.

If I lost my job, what would I do?

I only had a couple more months until I finished my degree and I'd already started scouting out places to send my resumé. Hopefully, by the time I got my diploma, I'd have a job lined up. But that wouldn't do me any good if I lost this one now.

After the server put down a basket of fries, I swiped one before Victor could drown them in salt, then asked, "I guess you haven't heard of anything."

He shook his head. "No." He glanced around and then asked in a low voice, "How come none of this is on the news, Toni? She's a fucking heiress. It should be a headline story. I mean, people are talking, but not as much as they should be."

"Her brother shut them down, I guess." I tipped my glass in Vic's direction. "What can I say? Money talks."

"No, it doesn't." Victor sighed, his face grim. "It sings, Toni. Like a fucking siren."

"That's almost poetic."

He surprised me with a quick, rakish grin, the kind that had come much easier when he'd been younger.

"I'm a regular renaissance man." He reached out and put his hand over mine. "I'm sorry, Toni. I know you want to help and I want to help you. It feels like...I dunno, redemption, in a way. But nothing's turning up."

I wrapped both of my hands around his bigger one. "Keep

your ears open?"

"Bet your ass."

Chapter 8

Ash

"Yes, yes. I've got it." I closed my eyes as Melody Strum, my assistant, rattled off a few more details about the upcoming takeover.

I hadn't been to work since Isadora had been kidnapped, but it had been nearly a week and things had to be done. I had a board, but I was the CEO and I was usually the one who made all of the important decisions. Except, how was I expected to work at a time like this? My brain was feeding me every horror story I'd ever heard or read about kidnappings.

This was my worst nightmare. Only it was real.

And whenever I tried to stop thinking about Isadora and find something else to distract me, that something else was always Toni. I had a tangle inside me because of her – anger, need, frustration…amusement.

I wanted to bend her over my knee and spank her until she couldn't sit for some of the things she said, but at the same time, there was a part of me that still found her anger almost cute. She was just so tiny that seeing so much rage coming from her was shocking.

Even when she was yelling at me, I'd been torn between yelling back and kicking everybody else so I could take out my frustration in another way. Between her thighs while her nails sank into my shoulders, and I felt the hot, sweet grab of her pussy again.

"Mr. Lang?"

The sound of Melody's voice jerked me back to attention. "I'm sorry." Rubbing at my eyes, I said, "My mind was somewhere else."

"That's totally understandable." Her voice was apologetic, full of concern.

She'd been with me for nearly twelve years and knew me better than most. And the one thing I knew she understood was how much I loved my sister.

"If we could've waited on this, you know I wouldn't bother you."

I nodded, and then remembered we were on the telephone and she couldn't see me. "I know that. That's why you're paid big bucks, right?" I tried to lighten my tone for the last part.

She came back with a typical Melody response. "Well, that being the case, Mr. Lang, you do know I'm up for my annual review and raise next month?"

She managed to get a laugh out of me, and we were able to finish the rest of our business. As soon as I hung up, however, I was left to my own thoughts.

And those thoughts weren't good.

Mentally, I counted off each day since she'd disappeared. Monday evening to Friday morning. I broke those days down into hours, then minutes. So many things could be done to a helpless woman in that many minutes, hours, days. Had I even tried to make sure she knew how to take care of herself if she needed to? Or had I arrogantly assumed that my money could provide enough protection? Maybe instead of trying to protect her from the world, I should have been preparing her for it.

The kidnapper still hadn't called back.

It *was* my fault.

Knowing it didn't lessen my anger at Toni any, though. I'd been losing myself in a Sub because Toni had been on my mind too much, and I'd hoped I could clear her out so I could think about my sister. Toni was a distraction, and one I couldn't afford. Especially not now.

Pounding my fist on the arm of my chair, I stared into the gloomy corners of my shadowed office. I hadn't turned on the lights when I'd come in during the early hours of the morning. I hadn't been able to sleep. I hadn't showered. Or eaten breakfast. I wasn't even sure I'd eaten dinner last night either. I didn't care though. I wasn't hungry.

I sat in my office and brooded about Toni, worried about Isadora. I tried to think about work, but my thoughts kept going back to the two women, alternating between them and how I could've, should've, done things differently.

Lost in my thoughts, I didn't know how long I sat in the dark. The knock at the door and the subsequent opening allowed light to spin inside, forcing me to fling up a hand to block out the glare.

Doug stood in the door, his posture rigid. He turned on the lights and I grimaced. Light and I weren't getting along very well these days. I was pretty sure the alcohol wasn't helping in that respect.

"I'm quite certain you're not helping Isadora by sitting here in the dark, sir." Doug folded his hands in front of him. His face was polite, but I could hear the disapproval in his voice. It bothered me more than I liked.

Since when had Doug started to hate me? He'd taken me Christmas shopping as a child.

A lifetime ago.

"What do you want?" I demanded, wanting him to just leave me alone.

"You have a guest. A Stanley Kowalski. Are you home?"

"No." I glared at him with one eye while I rubbed at the other. "I'm on the damn moon. What's it look like?"

Doug's disapproving eyebrows drew lower and tighter

over his eyes. "Are you receiving visitors on the moon, sir?" He didn't even try to hide the sarcasm this time.

"Kowalski's not a visitor." I shoved a hand through my hair and tried to pull myself together. "He's the investigator I hired to look for Isadora. And Doug, yank that stick out of your ass before I beat you with it."

"You would have a hard time doing that, sitting in this room and letting guilt eat you alive. Sir." The older man's face softened slightly. "I'll allow you a few minutes to compose yourself before I bring Mr. Kowalski back."

"*Allow* me." Muttering under my breath, I shoved back from my desk instead up. Various kinks and stiff muscles protested movement. I hadn't been doing much of anything but sitting in this room when I didn't have the cops and FBI here. My clothes were wrinkled and I was pretty sure I didn't smell that good. No wonder Doug looked so disgusted.

I needed to get off my ass.

Ten minutes later, Doug showed Stanley Kowalski into my office.

The investigator was a skinny man with graying hair and sharp, intelligent eyes hidden behind narrow-rimmed spectacles. When I hired him, he'd told me he had gone into private work after he'd retired from the force. He didn't look like a cop. I figured that must be a bonus as an investigator. Somebody like him showed up at the door, a person would expect some sort of sales pitch or a request for donations to a local ministry.

Definitely not law enforcement.

"Please tell me you have something," I said as I stood.

"Afraid not." He shook my hand and then lowered himself into the chair across from my desk. "As soon as I have anything, I'll call you immediately."

"Yeah." I moved to the window and stared outside. It faced out over a small, private garden. Isadora loved our garden. We had a larger one at our house in the Hamptons, but she spent a lot of time here in this one. I sometimes thought she'd live out there if she could. What if she—

"Don't give up hope, Mr. Lang."

I looked over at Kowalski. He had a worn, lived-in sort of face. The kind of face that made you think he'd done it all and seen it all, the kind that made you want to believe him. I wanted to. But Isadora was the optimist. Not me. Not after everything I'd been through. Everything I'd lost.

"What brings you over here then?" I asked.

He didn't beleaguer his point.

Gesturing to my desk, he said, "May I?"

I nodded and pushed aside the clutter that had gathered there over the past few days. I watched as he pulled out a folder and began to lay out several black and whites, glossy, close-angle images of a man I didn't know. Suddenly, I clenched my jaw, reaching out to snag one of the pictures. It was of Toni. With the guy.

They were sitting in a bar or something.

The look on their faces…it was one of familiarity. My stomach clenched at the expression on her face. She was smiling, the sort of smile someone only gave to a person to whom they were close.

I continued to go through the pictures. In a few of them, I could tell they were trying hard to keep from being overheard, their heads and bodies bent towards each other. When I came to the end, I looked up at Kowalski.

"What is this?" I asked, my gut a tight, ugly snarl.

"I assume you recognize the woman."

"Get to the point." Flinging the images down on the desk, I crossed my arms over my chest and waited. My heart was pounding so hard, I almost felt sick. Kowalski had better have a good explanation or I was going to be even more pissed than I already was.

"The man with her is her brother, Victor Gallagher. Are you aware of his...?" Kowalski paused and then forged ahead. "His somewhat checkered past?"

I snorted. "Yes. He's a thug."

"He's a bit more than your typical thug." Kowalski rubbed his hands together and looked away, obviously taking care with his words. "Now, please understand. I'm not making accusations, but I think it's just worth...well, knowing. When Victor Gallagher was eighteen, he was arrested on felony drug charges, but testified against the guy he was running for. Word on the street was that the guy was trying to edge into some other family's business, and the kid was setting him up, but things went south. Kid got pinched. His lawyer made a deal, and because the guy wasn't from the neighborhood, the kid testified. He got six months and has been clean ever since. Or, at least, hasn't gotten caught. There have been rumors though."

"I know about the drug conviction." I trailed off when the investigator looked back at me. "What is it?"

"One of the things he's been rumored about being into since he got out? It was a kidnapping."

Chapter 9

Toni

I tried to ignore the ringing of the telephone. It had been ringing off and on for the past twenty minutes.

Maybe longer.

My body had shut down on me, and all it knew or understood was sleep.

If it wasn't for the fact that I had to pee, I probably would have blissfully ignored the phone indefinitely. I had the kind of brain that let me tune out the things I didn't need to worry about. A benefit of having grown up in a noisy home. But once my bladder made it known I'd have to get up soon, I slowly and subtly started to drift to wakefulness, even though I ignored even my body's urgent needs as long as I could.

A few more minutes.

I had my face under a pillow and if I could just have a few more minutes…

Another ring and I yanked the pillow off and lay there, staring up at the ceiling overhead. I wasn't going to get a few more minutes.

Then the phone stopped and I sighed at the sudden and welcomed silence.

After a quick run to the bathroom, I all but dived into bed and hauled my blankets up. I'd been trying to do too much on too little sleep since Isadora had gone missing. I needed the rest.

Technically, I should have been over at the Lang's house. But Isadora wasn't there. Ash had made it clear that my presence wasn't welcome. I had work that I could do, yes, but I could technically do most of it from here. I didn't think I needed to stress him out more than he already was. I certainly didn't need the added stress of being around him.

My eyes drifted closed and a dreamy lassitude fell over me. I was hovering in that space between sleep and waking when the damn phone started to ring again, the shrill sound of my landline jarring me back into wakefulness.

Slowly, I pushed up onto my elbows and stared across the room at the stupid thing.

Whoever it was, they'd just keep calling and calling...

The idea didn't help my voice sound any more pleasant when I finally grabbed it.

"This had better be important," I snapped without bothering with a greeting.

"If it wasn't, do you really think I would've spent forty-five minutes trying to get hold of you?" Ash said his voice cool. There was no doubt it was him. "You sleep like the dead."

"I spent two hours making up a final I missed, three hours trying to get my schedule set up for summer session, and then another two hours tutoring some punk who reminded me of you. Except he was ten years younger and a whole hell of lot stupider and he thinks he can be a doctor. At least you didn't try to do that." Irritation and lack of sleep tended to have a bad effect on my filter – as in, said filter didn't work. "And it isn't like I've been sleeping well over the past week. What do you want?"

There was a pause. "When are you coming over to work?"

Closing my eyes, I sighed. Was he fucking kidding me? "I'm not. You made it more than clear I'm not wanted there."

"You have a job to do. If you want to keep working here once Isadora comes home, I suggest you get your cute ass over here."

The threat in his voice made me roll my eyes. "Your sister adores me and she'd have to fire me before my job disappeared and you know it."

Wait a minute...had he just called my ass cute?

"I have news about Isadora. Just get here." A moment later, the phone slammed so loud, I flinched in reaction.

Glaring at the handset I still held, I mumbled, "You could have just said that."

I had gotten ready in record time, only bothering with the bare essentials. My hair was still wet when I left the house, and I twined it into a braid once I was on the subway. I didn't have time to dry it, but if I let it just dry, I'd regret it. The braid was my best bet. If it made me look about sixteen, oh, well. It was better than the pigtails. Those made me look twelve.

I got to the house on Fifth Avenue in record time and burst inside without knocking. It wasn't until I'd stepped inside that I realized the door had been unlocked.

And the house was oddly silent.

None of the staff were around. I paused to look for Doug. The front door seemed kind of naked without him. I called out his name. Only silence echoed back.

"I gave them the day off," Ash said from behind me.

I jumped, spinning around to find him standing right behind me. I'd moved farther into the silent house than I realized.

"You scared me to death."

He lifted one shoulder in a half-shrug.

I frowned. The normal response to that was an apology.

He turned and strode into the large salon to the far right of the elegant foyer. I'd been in the room once or twice, but never for more than a minute. To be honest, I didn't like it. It was informal and uncomfortable and…stiff. Cold, somehow.

Rather like Ash, I thought.

"Drink?" He looked up at me from the drink service where he was pouring something for himself.

"It's not even two o'clock," I pointed out.

"There's that annoying song…*it's five o'clock somewhere…*"

"You're in an odd mood."

"I am." He tossed back something that glittered amber in the light, and when he turned to me, I caught sight of his eyes. They were the coldest I'd ever seen them. No heat in them at all. Not even anger.

Slowly, I reached up to rub at my chest. "Please tell me that she hasn't been…"

"Still nothing." He gestured toward a seat. "Please."

I didn't want to. For some reason, all I wanted to do was get out of there. Fast. But I didn't think that was an option. Slowly, I moved over to one of the stiff-backed chairs and sat down. It was as miserable as it looked.

Ash poured himself another drink and came over to sit down in front of me. He looked like he belonged in that chair.

I held myself tense, uncertain as to what was going on. He gave me a smile that made my stomach turn. It was cold and brittle.

"Ash, what's going–?"

"Kidnapping, huh? That's your idea of living clean?" He looked at his glass, studying the contents and then tossed it all back before slamming the empty glass down on the table. In a blink, he was in front of me. "Your brother is a fucking *kidnapper.*"

"No!" What the hell...who had...no. It didn't matter, because he was wrong, the story was wrong. Victor had *stopped* a kidnapping. But nobody wanted to listen to him. He was a thug, a convicted dealer just a couple years out of prison, a few steps up from human trash as far as most people were concerned. He hadn't been charged with anything because there hadn't been any evidence, but the rumors had never gone away, even years later.

Ash put his hands on the arms of my chair and leaned down so that his face was only inches from mine. "What have you two been planning behind my back, Toni? How did you make it happen? Did you bribe somebody at Winter to help you get close to my sister?"

"What?" I gaped at him, my head spinning. My heart hammered in my chest; fear an acrid, ugly taste crawling up my throat. "I don't–"

"I've seen the fucking pictures, Toni!"

Ears ringing from the sheer ferocity of his bellow, I shoved him. He didn't move. Narrowing my eyes, I leaned back into the seat and brought my feet up. The movement caught him off guard and he didn't react in time. The double kick sent him stumbling back and I shoved upright. He may have towered over me by more than a foot, but at least I was on my feet now.

I pointed a finger at him and warned, "Don't ever try to corner me, Lang."

He rubbed at his gut. "How did you do it?" He glared at me.

"Do what?" I shouted. "I don't know what the fuck you're talking about?!"

He turned around and grabbed something. A moment later, pictures flew across the room. "Stop the innocent routine. I saw you with him. You've met with him more than once."

Confused, I looked down…at pictures of Vic and me. We were in the bar in some of them. A few…son of a bitch. He'd had me followed all the way to my parents' house. And it wasn't like before. Not like the time the investigator hadn't been hiding and had just stood around outside; like he'd been confirming that I didn't have some sort of hidden routine. These were close-ups. These were private. Somebody had been looking into the windows of my family's home. I could even place where they must've been standing when the shots had been taken, and it sure as hell hadn't been on public property.

He'd had me followed. Again. And this time he'd crossed the line.

Shit. A thought hit me. Vic said he'd had cops following me, but were they cops?

Or where they Ash's men? How many did he have?

I blew out a slow breath, tried to calm myself. He was going through something awful, something I couldn't imagine. We'd deal with the violation of my privacy later. It didn't mean I still didn't need a moment to reign in my temper.

"Explain," he demanded again.

My hands were shaking with anger and the quaver came through in my voice. I looked up at him. "Explain…you want me to explain?"

Selecting a photo at random, I turned it and met Ash's icy gaze. My grasp on my control was tenuous at best.

"This is Vic and me, having a drink at his favorite bar. We do it two or three times a month." I scowled at Ash. "I'll tell you what, your crack-shot investigator isn't worth shit, because if he'd asked around, anyone could tell you that. And sometimes it's all of us. Me, three of my brothers since Kory can't commute from Michigan. Deacon and Franky sometimes bring their wives. Sometimes I bring whatever guy I'm seeing. Not that any of that is your fucking business!"

My voice rose with every word, my control slipping, then

snapping. I tore the picture in half and grabbed another. My heart felt bruised, shredded, as I saw the image of a Friday night dinner. He'd invaded the sanctity of my parents' home. Not just my life, but their lives. Reaching up, I traced the edge of my mother's face. She wasn't completely in the frame since I was the center of the shot, me and Vic, but she was still there.

"You want a fucking explanation for this? It's called a family dinner. I'll be going to one tonight. We do it every Friday evening. Rain or shine. Snow, sleet or hail. It's my family." The picture fell from numb fingers and I looked at him, suddenly empty. "What else do you want from me?"

"Tell me where she is. I'll pay whatever you want. Just tell me where she is." His voice was so cold.

I stared at him as it hit me. He wasn't just lashing out or grasping at straws. He was serious. He thought I had something to do with this. That my family and I…

For a second, I couldn't feel anything, couldn't even think.

A disgust so thick and all-consuming settled inside me, I thought it might choke me. But I didn't know who it was directed at. Him…or me.

I'd had him *inside* me. Maybe I hadn't exactly been thinking clearly. But I'd liked him. Some parts of him, at least. I'd told myself that after all he'd been through, it was understandable that he'd put up some walls. I'd told myself that, deep down, he was a good guy. I'd counted on my usually accurate insight into people and it had let me down. How could I have taken a man so callow, so selfish inside me? How could I have not seen the sort of man he truly was?

"You son of a bitch," I whispered, my voice thick. I started to shake as I stared at him. I'd let him put his hands on me. His mouth. I'd comforted him. "You monstrous, evil son of a bitch."

"Cut the shit, Toni!" His green eyes glinted as he

glowered at me. Fury practically radiated off him and that only made me angrier. He wasn't the wronged party here.

We'd hadn't exchanged deep, heartfelt words of longing, but I'd…hell. I liked sex. A lot. But I'd never been flippant about it. I'd always prided myself on my discernment when it came to choosing who would share my bed. How could I have been so wrong?

He stalked toward me and shot out a hand, grabbing my arm and jerking me close to him. I didn't even fight. I didn't have it in me. I was still reeling from the betrayal.

His fingers dug into my arm, leaving bruises as he bit each word off, "Where. Is. She."

"I don't know." I stared into his eyes and it was like looking at a stranger. Sick inside, I said, "I like your sister. I would never hurt her."

His fingers tightened, just a little and he tugged me closer until there was less than an inch between our bodies. "That's your final answer?"

I just stared up at him. How could he think that of me? Had all of this only been an act?

"Lieutenant." His voice, so cool and calm now, sounded out of place.

I jerked away and surprisingly, he let me go.

He let me go.

Spinning around, I half-stumbled at the sight of the cop standing there. Her name escaped me. She slid a look from me to the man at my back. There was a curious look on her face. Later, I'd remember it. Later. Much later.

"Go on."

At first, I thought he was talking to me.

But then the cop looked at me. "Miss Gallagher, we'd like you to come into the station and answer some questions."

"About what?" I demanded as several uniformed officers swarmed me. One of them took my elbow. I jerked away, even though I knew better. Common sense and logic were taking a backseat to all of the shit going through my head.

"Miss Gallagher," the lieutenant said, her voice calm. "We just have some routine questions."

"Then ask them here," I said. "I answered questions here before."

"Get her out of here!" Ash bellowed.

I shot him an ugly look.

When I shifted my attention back to the lieutenant, I caught sight of something in her eyes. Regret.

She looked from me to Ash and then back at me.

I knew then that I was in trouble.

Vic's words came back to me. *Money doesn't talk…it sings….*

I looked around at the cops circling me, surrounding me. My chest tightened and I could barely breathe. Why was this happening? The question had a tinge of hysteria in it. Was I paying for Vic's mistakes? Again. God forgive me…I loved my brother, but I'd paid for his mistakes enough. Too many judged me by the things *he* had done. And what Ash had thought he knew about Vic…that wasn't even the truth. My brother had been innocent. Was innocent. And so was I.

But it looked like that didn't matter to anyone. Who cared if I was some scapegoat because I had a brother who'd done some dumb shit years ago? Nobody, that's who. I didn't have money. My family wasn't important. These cops didn't care if they hurt the people I loved, so long as the ones with money and power got what they wanted. Ash didn't care who got hurt, as long as people did what he told them to do.

Something inside me snapped, and when the cop to my left touched my elbow, I jerked back.

His jaw tightened and he gave me a look I knew too well.

I lifted my chin.

I was done.

The entire room went quiet.

"Miss, you need to get control of yourself and come with me," he said, his voice flat. He reached out again and I took a step back.

"Yeah? You've yet to give me a reason." I curled my lip and said, "I know my damn rights. You want to take me somewhere? Tell me what the problem is. What's the damn evidence against me?"

He went to catch my arm again and I smacked at his hand.

"Don't touch me," I warned. "Unless you have an arrest warrant, don't fucking touch me again."

"Toni, for fuck's sake." Ash's snarl barely even registered.

"That's it." It came from the tired-looking brunette at my side.

When she caught my arm, I acted without thinking. I pivoted and swung, driving my fist into her nose. I heard it crunch, saw the blood spurt out…and then I was thrown to the ground.

I wished it would've been Ash. And I wished I would've done a lot worse to him than just messing up his nose.

Chapter 10

Ash

I felt sick.

As Toni was half-dragged out of the salon, I leaned against the bar service and stared at the blood on the carpet. That was going to be hell to get out.

"Are you okay?"

Automatically, I started to answer, but when I looked up, I saw that Special Agent Marcum was talking to the cop with the bloody nose.

"Crazy bitch," the officer said, her words thick and distorted.

An instinctive response leaped to my lips and I had to clench my jaw to keep from saying that Toni had warned them not to touch her. It didn't matter what she'd said. They only cared about what she'd done.

A few moments later, the rest of the NYPD gang had been cleared out by Marcum's two agents. One of her people followed the cops outside, eying the bleeding brunette, but Marcum hadn't budged from her spot by the door.

"Why are you here?" I snapped at Marcum. "Don't you want to horn in on the action?"

"Sure. When there's action. But I know guilty and the girl? She isn't guilty." She hesitated a moment, and then tipped her head at me. "Are you proud of yourself for that set-up, Mr.

Lang?" She actually sounded curious.

"I didn't do shit," I bit off. "She's the one who helped somebody – probably her brother – kidnap my sister."

"Like hell she did." Marcum rolled her eyes and planted her hands on her hips. "If that girl is any kind of criminal, then I'm Lady Gaga. You tried to throw your weight around with me to get to her, and it didn't work, so you sicced your boys in blue on her."

She paused and I just stared at her, refusing to even blink.

"What did you do, call the mayor?"

Something in my face must've given me away, though I didn't know what, because Marcum made a disgusted sound.

"Wow. That's impressive. I wouldn't do what you wanted, so you shook your money around and intimidated people into violating that girl's rights."

"That's not–" I snapped my jaw shut as a red flush climbed up my cheeks. This was bullshit. It didn't matter *what* my methods had been if I found my sister. Period.

But the burn of humiliation did nothing to help the anger in my gut at all. I didn't want to feel like I was in the wrong here. But I kept seeing Toni's eyes. I couldn't wipe away the memory of the betrayed look on her face.

"Just shut up," I said, shaking my head.

Kowalski was on to something. He had to be. He'd just been cautious when he'd told me there wasn't any actual evidence. But if he hadn't been right, I had nothing. Absolutely nothing. And that was something I didn't even want to consider. I had to fix this. I had to find Isadora. No matter what.

"Don't say I didn't warn you."

From the corner of my eye, I could see the agent moving to the door.

Finally.

Marcum paused. "I hope she's as tough as she looks, Mr.

Lang."

"Isadora is tough," I answered automatically.

"Not your sister," Marcum said. "Toni Gallagher. She better be way tougher than she looks."

I shifted my weight from one foot to the other. "What are you talking about?"

"In case it's escaped your notice, it's Friday afternoon." She made a show of checking her watch. "By the time they get done processing her, it'll be pretty late. And she punched a cop. Nobody's going to be rushed to get her arraigned. She'll be spending some time behind bars. All weekend, to be blunt."

"What the hell ever. They can set bail on weekends." I tried not to think about how much that idea bothered me.

Marcum gave me an incredulous look. "I'd forgotten what world you lived in. Judges don't work weekends. Lawyers might. If a case fits certain, shall we say, *criteria*, she might be let out on bond. But I can tell you now, hitting a cop? Any kind of assault? That ain't gonna fly. No matter the circumstances. She's going to have to see a judge before they even come close to letting her out."

My gut started to get a little queasy as Marcum studied her slim gold watch, her lips pursed.

"She'll get through processing in a few hours if she's lucky. Then she's got all weekend in holding. She might see a judge on Monday. Tuesday is more likely. Her paperwork will probably get lost. And when she does see a judge, they're not going to do her any favors for bail. Now, I don't know the details of her family's financials, but I think it's safe to say that they probably can't afford whatever bail the judge sets." Her dark brown eyes narrowed as she looked at me. "See, she doesn't know all the big-time important people like you. She's just a regular person. She's fucked, in short."

"Am I supposed to care about that?" The thing was...I did. Even as I said the words, I knew I cared. What the fuck?

Why did I care? I'd been thinking about Isadora when I'd called in my favors, but now…

Now, I was just…

Shit.

"Pretty, mouthy girl like that, tucked away behind bars. She's never had to sit in the holding tank before, I bet. Neither have you, I'm sure." Her eyes gleamed. "It can get pretty ugly, especially since the cops will probably put her in with some unsavory people."

"She kidnapped my sister!"

"No, she didn't." Marcum's voice was cold and clear…and so certain.

I was torn between wanting to believe her and not wanting to. If the agent was right, then Toni was exactly who she'd always seemed to be…but that also meant I'd royally fucked things up.

"And here's the thing, Mr. Lang. It doesn't really even matter how the next couple days play out, because she's probably going to jail anyway."

"But here you stand insisting she didn't do anything." I snorted. "Some faith in the justice system you have."

Marcum started to laugh. It was caustic, bitter. It ended quickly though and she shook her head. "Educate yourself on the law, Mr. Lang. She struck a police officer while said officer was carrying out her civic duty. That's second-degree assault. Granted, there was no arrest warrant, no legal way for the cops to force her to come in. And never mind that, in all fairness, she'd told them not to touch her and they really didn't have a legal right to. Or the fact that she'd probably felt trapped, with no way out."

Trapped…

Toni had a reason to feel trapped. I'd lured her here. I'd told the cops to wait, then used them to ambush her. I'd set this all up and I had no doubt the cops had received the order to make sure Toni was brought in for questioning.

"Never mind that there was no reason for her to even be here in the first place," Marcum added softly. "No attorney will ask about that, I'm thinking. Why bother trying to set up a clear defense? There were witnesses. You were one of them. I was one of them." Her smile went even colder. "I guess she won't be finishing that degree...ever. She hit a cop. That's a felony."

Now, in slow motion, I saw it happen again.

The way Toni had stared at me, the anger and betrayal in her eyes. The pain. Then had come the panic as the cops had closed around her. The hurt under the fury when she'd told them not to touch her.

"Have fun," Marcum said, interrupting my mental reverie. "Explaining, I mean. Once I find Isadora – and I will – have fun explaining to her why her intelligent, caring, assistant is in jail. Why Toni Gallagher will never be a psychiatrist. Congratulations. You helped ruined that girl's life. Have a good day, Mr. Lang."

I stumbled backward and barely managed to catch myself on the couch. "That's...shit. She's..."

But Marcum was already gone.

I shook my head and focused on what I knew. Marcum was speculating. I had a good investigator.

He had pictures.

I looked down. My gaze landed on one of them. It was Toni. Toni and that brother of hers. An older woman, it had to be her mother, bent over both of them from behind while the two siblings were sitting down. The picture caught them laughing.

"Fuck, what were you doing, Kowalski, family portraits?"
It's family dinner.
Toni's voice echoed in my ear.
The way her voice had caught. The pain in the words.

Once again, I saw her driving her fist into the cop's nose.

Slowly, I stood up. I made my way over to the cabinet and helped myself to a bottle. It wasn't my favorite bourbon, but it didn't matter. I carried it over to the couch and sat down.

The burn of that first drink didn't undo anything.

So I had another.

Then a third.

Somewhere along the way, I passed out.

Then I woke up and it was dark, so I had another drink because I could still think, still remember.

I could even still hear Toni's voice. *It's family...*

At some point, I finally passed out and this time, I stayed that way.

I lurched awake, unsure what had pulled me from the blissful ignorance of unconsciousness.

A knock on the door?

I practically bolted to my feet, and the second I did, I regretted it.

My stomach rebelled and I swayed, slamming both hands against the wall as I struggled to stay upright, as I tried to make my stomach stay in control.

What was...?

My head abruptly cleared. Oh, the pain was still there. Plenty of that. And the headache, the nausea, the misery...

But I could think.

I'd heard something.

A knock.

Shuffling on stiff legs, I moved into the hallway and

stared at the front door. Doug wasn't here. None of the staff were. I'd given them the weekend off. Normally, Doug wouldn't have left no matter what, but he'd overheard me going over what I planned with the cops and he'd given me a look that said he wanted no part in it.

Toni. I saw her driving her fist into the officer's face.

I heard her voice as she said, *It's family dinner*. And the look of complete and utter betrayal that had slid into the deepest loathing.

"Son of a bitch!" I shouted, my voice echoing through the empty house. My headache pounded harder and harder and I bent over, thinking I might get sick. I deserved it.

Swallowing the bile in my throat, I straightened. I had to brace a hand on the wall to do it, but I was upright. I took one shambling step, then another. Out into the foyer. I squinted at the door.

Somebody had knocked.

That was what woke me up.

Somebody had knocked.

Swearing, I opened the door.

Nobody.

Absently, I glanced down. If I hadn't, I wouldn't have seen it.

But there it was.

A large padded manilla envelope, crumpled and battered, like it had been mailed to hell and back.

Mouth dry, I bent down and picked it up.

Blood started to roar in my ears and it wasn't from the alcohol. I knew what it was without needing to see my name scrawled in black marker on the front of it.

I half fell against the door to shut it as I opened the envelope with shaking hands.

"Sir—"

I vaguely recognized Doug's voice. I'd been wrong. He

hadn't left.

Several things fell out.

"Sir, you shouldn't touch—"

"Shut up," I said dully as I sank to my knees.

The thick, gleaming locks were tied together messily with a piece of what looked like twine. I had no trouble recognizing the heavy curls.

"Iz," I whispered, broken.

"I'll call the police." Doug's voice was quiet, oddly gentle.

My hand shook as I picked up the folded paper that had also fallen out and read it.

Printed on plain paper, block letters, it listed demands, simple and stark. Money in exchange for Isadora.

I read it through once, twice, three times.

I'd be contacted.

I'd better be ready.

The letter fell from my numb hands as I sat down. It was only then that I noticed the other envelope that had also dropped to the floor. It was smaller, bound closed with rubber bands. I picked it up.

Doug's voice came from above me. "If I tell you again, you shouldn't touch, will you listen?"

"No." I was careful though, only touching the rubber bands as much as I had to, handling only the edges of the envelope. Once I had it opened, though, the weight of its contents did the rest.

Photographs spilled out. Dozens of them. My eyes tracked over them, trying to make sense of what I was looking at.

It was Doug who started to reach out this time. I caught his wrist just before he would have touched the one lying nearest to us. The very sight of it chilled me right to the bone. It was Isadora and me, her hand tucked inside mine. I couldn't see either of our faces, but it was no puzzle as to who it was. It was us.

So was the next one, and the next one…

More than a dozen.

"Some of these are old," Doug said softly.

I nodded, staring at the photo of the younger images of my sister and me. Standing together, dressed in our finest, as we went to visit our parents' graves. It had been raining that year. I didn't remember anybody photographing us. But then again, I wouldn't have. Not on the anniversary of their death.

Whoever had taken this had wanted to make sure they weren't seen. There was something stealthy, secretive, about the pictures.

That feel was echoed in every last one of them, reading right up to the most recent one. It, like the others, had been taken on the anniversary of our parents' death, which had been three months ago.

It didn't matter if that one had been taken before or after Isadora and I met Toni. Even if she'd been some mastermind criminal and had been stalking us for months, there was no way she could've taken those old photographs. She would've only been twelve or thirteen when the first one had been taken. Her brother wouldn't have been much older. Their involvement didn't make any sense.

I closed my eyes, but I could still see the hurt on Toni's face. "What in the hell have I done?"

Marcum's voice answered my rhetorical question. *Congratulations. You helped ruin that girl's life.*

Blindfold Vol. III

Chapter 1

Toni

The burn from my injured knuckles was keeping me from falling asleep at the moment. Admittedly, I didn't think it would work for long because I was exhausted. Adrenaline had long since drained out of me, taking with it all of the numbness that'd been protecting me. All I could feel now was defeat, disgust, and more than a little despair.

To be honest, I kept hoping I'd wake up and discover this had all been a bad dream. But I couldn't wake up without falling asleep, right?

But a holding cell at the one-nine New York City Police Department wasn't exactly the kind of place I'd ever want to close my eyes.

My temper had always been a nasty one, but I'd usually been able to keep it under control. I'd always been the cool-headed one in the family – on the surface at least. This was the sort of thing I'd expect from one of my brothers. Vic, maybe. Or Franky. Even though Vic was the ex-con, Franky had always been the one our older brothers had to pull out of fights. My temper paled in comparison to his...but I was the one who'd hit a cop.

It wasn't entirely my fault, though. It wasn't like I'd expected to ever face a situation quite like the one I'd found myself in a couple hours ago.

The one I knew I should regret.

Part of me did.

I regretted hitting the cop. It hadn't been her fault Ashford Lang was an asshole. I regretted going over there and making it easy for him to set me up.

And it had been a set up.

I regretted humiliating myself like that.

Most of all, I regretted having taken that job in the first place. I wished I'd never heard of the Winter Corporation, or Isadora Lang...or her older asshole brother Ashford. Even as the guilt flooded me, I didn't stop wishing it.

My eyes started to burn, but I held the tears back through sheer stubbornness alone. Crying in here was the last thing I wanted to do. I'd grown up with four older brothers, and I knew how dumb it was to show weakness.

I rubbed at my gritty eyes and tried analyzing the situation even though I'd already gone through it a couple times already. I was still in holding. I hadn't gone through booking and processing yet. Thanks to Vic, I had a good idea of what happened once the cuffs went on. I sighed. I would've been more than happy to keep my knowledge all second-hand.

Why in the hell had I hit her?

I should have hit Ash.

He'd been the one who deserved it.

The woman sitting next to me shifted, her short skirt hiking up high enough that if she turned towards me, I'd have a good idea of her grooming habits. She'd been escorted in not long after I'd been unceremoniously shoved inside and I didn't have to ask to know what she was in for. After all, I could see her nipples through her barely-there halter-top.

I jerked my gaze away, but not quick enough because she saw me looking at her.

She shot me a look and smirked. "I do girls if you got the money. Could be a good way to pass the time."

My face went red and I cursed my fair skin. I wasn't usually so easily embarrassed, but I also wasn't used to being propositioned by women. In jail.

The other women in the cell laughed and I just sat there, not knowing what to say or do. Fortunately, once they'd finished, they went back to whatever it was they'd been doing before I came in.

I wasn't sure how much time had passed, only that I'd gotten lost in my thoughts when I felt a pair of eyes on me. I jerked my head up and saw the cop I hit looking at me.

"Have you been making friends?" Her voice sounded funny and I wondered if I'd broken her nose.

"I'm sorry for hitting you," I said, sincerely. "My temper got the better of me, and I shouldn't have taken it out on you."

"You think that's going to help?" She crossed her arms over her chest.

"No." I lifted a shoulder in a half-shrug and looked away. "I did something stupid, and now I'll have to deal with the consequences." After a pause, I muttered, "If you were Lang, I sure as hell wouldn't be apologizing."

She lifted a brow. "Maybe you shouldn't have kidnapped his sister."

I gave her a withering look. Now I was regretting the apology.

The prostitute next to me started to laugh. "You, a kidnapper? Bitch, you ain't never broke a law in your life. You can't even look at me without blushing."

I glared at her this time, but she held my gaze without wavering. It was the officer who walked away without a word.

"Who did you kidnap?"

The question came from a belligerent, heavy-set woman sitting on the bench across from me.

"Nobody." I sighed and dropped my face in my hands.

"Not what the cop thinks. Who does she think you kidnapped?"

"Does it matter?" I didn't want to talk about the Langs.

She asked again and I pretended not to hear.

Probably not the best action.

She came up off that bench. She was massive, easily six and a half feet tall. She'd break me in two. I was just about to tell her the answer – hell, I'd tell her anything she wanted – when the girl at my side stood up and got in front of me. "Leave her alone, Rita. She ain't causin' you no problem just sittin' there anyway."

The woman about to kick my butt – Rita, apparently – took a menacing step toward the prostitute. I hadn't realized how tall the woman next to me was and I suddenly felt smaller than I ever had before. If these two started a fight, there was no way I'd walk away without a scratch.

"What's it matter to you?" Rita took a step toward my unexpected savior, her eyes narrowing. "Maybe you should just sit down and shut up, Passion."

The prostitute responded by folding her arms and jutting out her chin.

I didn't want to know what might have happened if an officer hadn't appeared at the cell at that moment. "Gallagher, Toni."

I practically jumped up, thinking something was finally going right. Except it wasn't an answer to my prayers. I was simply going to booking. It was...humiliating.

I got my phone call first, though. Fun fact: it's not true that you're entitled to one phone call when you get arrested. The cops don't have to let you call anybody. But if you're polite, you can make a call, or even two or three. I went out of my way to be as polite as possible, and I made two phone calls. Neither call was to Ash because I planned on never speaking to him again.

Instead, I called my oldest brother, Deacon, who spent nearly five full minutes saying how he couldn't believe that I'd do something so stupid before he promised to explain to our parents what had happened and that I was okay. Then I called Vic. He was a thorn in my side at times, but he'd always understood me better than my older brothers. He didn't sound surprised when I told him, but his voice sounded a bit odd. After a moment, he told me to make sure I kept my mouth shut, and not to do anything or say anything.

"Anything," he practically snarled the word. "You understand, Toni?"

I wondered if the apology counted. Probably, but it was too late now. I agreed without telling him what I'd done, and we disconnected.

As I sat down next to a desk, Passion walked by with a hip-swinging gait. She winked when she saw me and flopped down in a chair as though she was ready to get her toes painted. She had an expression on her face that said she'd done all this before and she wasn't impressed.

Me, neither. I was fucking terrified.

"Allergies?"

I jerked my head around and stared at the officer. "Excuse me?"

He gave me a bored look. "Do you have any food allergies? Environmental? Things like latex–"

"I know what allergies are," I said, interrupting him. "I'm not an idiot."

He paused briefly, then jerked his shoulder and went back to typing. "Yeah, well, hitting a cop seems like a pretty idiotic thing to do."

He was right. I'd hit a cop. Best case scenario, I'd escape prison. Worst case, my entire life was ruined. I'd never be allowed to become a psychologist. Everything my parents had sacrificed, all of the work I'd done. All of it would be for nothing.

My head started to spin and black dots danced in front of my eyes.

Abruptly, a hand caught the back of my head and pressed down, reminding me of what I'd already known I should be doing.

"Breathe, Ms. Gallagher. The room looks a lot more normal if you breathe."

I sucked in one breath, then another.

"That's it..." It was a familiar voice, but not one I could place immediately. "Hey, why don't you go get her a soda...yeah, yeah, I know. Look, I know the kid. I'll watch her."

The pressure on the back of my neck eased and, a moment later, I found myself looking at a graying, grizzled cop. He wore a rumpled suit and his face was equally rumpled. Lived-in, I supposed. But I knew him anyway.

Scowling, I crossed my arms over my chest and looked away. "Thanks for the help, Detective Bowers. I'm fine now."

"It's Captain actually, Ms. Gallagher." He arched a brow at the frosty look I shot him. "It seems you've found yourself in trouble."

"It's a family trait."

"Hmmm..." He bent forward, his eyes focused on the screen in front of him. He winced as he shot me a look over the computer. "You went big for your one and only trouble ever. Assault of a cop, Ms. Gallagher?"

Stonily, I ignored him. Hearing the heavy tread of police-issue uniform shoes, I looked over. It was the officer who'd started booking me.

Bowers got up, groaning a bit as his knees popped. "You hang tight there, Ms. Gallagher."

Like I had a lot of choice.

As the older man walked away, I watched him go.

He was the one who'd arrested Vic all those years ago. It had been Bowers' face on media reports when everything had gone to hell. He'd been furious that Vic had only gotten six months and had made sure everyone knew what a scumbag my brother was.

I was led into a small concrete room before I could dwell on Captain Bowers much longer. I knew what was coming next.

The door opened and I turned around.

Shit. It was the officer I'd hit.

The harsh light shining down on her face did nothing to soften the bruising on her nose, spreading up to her left eye. Man, I'd really gotten her good. I silently cursed my brothers for having taught me how to fight.

"Apparently you've got friends in high places." Her voice was tight, angry.

I blinked.

That wasn't what I'd been expecting to hear.

She nodded at the table and said, "Sit."

I sat.

At this point, if she wanted me to twirl around and bark like a dog then hop like a bunny, I would.

"Captain Bowers talked to me. Asked that I consider...letting this go."

I blinked at her. No fucking way. "Ah..." I cleared my throat, then tried again. "Um..."

Nothing intelligent was coming out.

"You do know him," she prompted.

Numb, I nodded. I didn't understand. Why would Bowers do that for me? He'd never liked my family.

"Any idea why he'd like me to reconsider?" she asked. She touched the glorious bruise, already a deep, ugly purple. "I mean, I personally think there's a good reason to not reconsider."

I didn't say anything. What could I say? I had no reason to offer her.

"You must have something to say."

"I already did. I told you I was sorry and I meant it. What more do you want?"

She stared at me for a long moment, and then she got up and left.

I was alone in the room, and I stayed that way for a very long time.

The squeak of the opening door woke me.

I jerked my head up, groaning as pain lashed through me, my stiffened neck protesting the sudden movement. Bleary-eyed, I stared at the doorway. It took a moment for my brain to register what I was seeing. When it did, my jaw fell open.

"Deacon."

I launched myself at him and his arms caught me. My feet left the ground and over his shoulder, I saw Franky and Vic too. A rush of emotion swept over me.

"Let's get you home." Deacon kissed my temple and squeezed me even tighter before setting me on my feet. "You can give us all the details later. For now, let's get out of here."

"I can't." Confused, I looked around.

"Get out of here." It came from the officer I'd hit. She gave me a disgusted look from where she stood behind Franky. "Go on."

I remembered her comment. Friends in high places. Shit. "Ah...did Ashford Lang call? Did he have something to do with this?"

She snorted and muttered, "As if."

"Come on, little sister," Vic muttered as he took my arm. "Trust me. You don't want to stay here any longer than you have to."

I let him lead me out while Franky and Deacon followed behind like some weird little entourage. I didn't understand what had happened.

If it hadn't been Ash who'd gotten me out, then who was it?

Chapter 2

Ash

"What do you mean, you can't help me?"

I glared at the man on the other side of the glass. He smiled back at me, but there was nothing friendly, or even helpful about the smile. It was the smile of a tired man who didn't want to talk to me, but his job dictated that he do just that.

His gaze had skimmed along my clothes as I'd come rushing inside. I'd put up with enough of it in my life that I knew when somebody was taking my measure. The cop in front of me had already taken my measure, made a few rough estimates, and I felt sure he was probably fairly well on base.

The man knew I had money and so I got the smile when he told me politely that there was nothing he could do.

Leaning down, I braced my hands on the counter and glared at him through the glass. I'd already put the letter – sealed in a plastic Ziploc bag thanks to Doug's quick thinking – on the flat surface. He hadn't even looked at it.

"I need to speak with Lieutenant Green. She has a woman in custody for my sister's kidnapping and it isn't her."

"Yes, Mr. Lang." The cop nodded soberly. "So you've explained. I've already checked on this woman, and she's not under arrest for any kind of kidnapping. She's being processed for assault."

"I..." I snapped my jaw shot and looked away, staring off to the side as Agent Marcum's voice came back to haunt me. Only a couple hours had passed and already, she was proving to be right. "What do you mean she's being processed?"

I had to do something to stop this. I had to talk to the lieutenant about the fucking letter. But this idiot...

Forcing my teeth to unclench and my facial muscles to relax, I met the cop's eyes. Toni being here was my fault. Me being an ass wasn't going to speed things along. If anything, it would make things worse for her.

"She's being processed," the cop said again, talking slowly, like I hadn't understood him the first time.

I glanced at his badge and managed a smile. "Look, play along with me here, Officer. Pretend I'm an idiot. Imagine I have no idea how any of this works. Now. She's been brought in. She was supposed to be questioned for my sister's kidnapping. Now, what's going on?"

Trebek looked like he wanted to tell me to take a hike, but after a moment, he slumped back in his chair and gave me a short nod. "After she's processed, she goes back into a cell. She's got to get arraigned and then post bail if it's offered."

"How long does that take?"

He snorted then. "It's one-thirty on a Saturday morning. Won't be a judge in here before Monday. If she's lucky, she'll see one by Monday afternoon."

"That's not—"

A flurry of voices behind me drowned out my words – probably for the best – and I jerked my head around, ready to bellow for everybody to shut the hell up.

But then I saw the men in the doorway and recognition slammed into me. I curled a hand into a fist. My gaze landed on one in particular.

The man in the back. Dark red hair. Dark eyes. I'd seen his face before. In the pictures my PI had taken.

None of the brothers looked at me. I tried hard to do the same, although I couldn't keep my gaze from lingering on the tallest of the three men.

Victor Gallagher, Toni's brother. The other two men with him had to be Deacon and Franky. She had a third brother, but he didn't live here. I had a feeling he wouldn't mind making a trip back here for this, though. All of them looked pissed and it wouldn't take long for their anger to find a target.

Rightfully, it should be me. I'd been the one to get her into this mess.

Vic's gaze slid to mine. There was no recognition, but his gaze narrowed nonetheless, lingered for just a moment.

He shouldn't know me. Just as I shouldn't know him. Yet we both recognized the other. If it hadn't been for the letter I'd found at my door, I might've felt more justification at having set Toni up. Now I was just frustrated. They'd get back there to see Toni, find out what I'd done, and this ass at the desk wouldn't even give me a simple answer about what was happening.

As the Gallagher brothers disappeared through the door, my gut twisted into newer, tighter knots. I turned back to the officer. "I've got new evidence. Please let Lieutenant Green know that."

I walked away from the counter, unsure what to do next. After a moment, I sat down and pulled out my wallet.

Green had given me a card.

Why hadn't I thought of that before now?

People were always giving me cards. More often than not, I threw them away. Sometimes, I passed them on to my administrative assistant. I rarely kept them. But I'd kept the lieutenant's, shoved it into my wallet along with the cards from the FBI agents.

Now, I punched Green's number into my cell phone and waited. When it went to voicemail, I left a message, reading the letter from memory.

Then I called the numbers on the other cards I'd gotten. Nobody answered, so I left the same message on their voicemails too.

That done, I didn't know what else to do, so I sat...and waited.

Sitting out in the waiting room of any police department, a man could make millions in a year, or he could make nothing, and there would be people in uniform who just didn't care.

It wasn't something I was used to. I was accustomed to getting what I wanted, to having all of the connections I needed to get things done. Maybe if I could get the attention of the people striding around or talking on the phone, I could do something. But what was I supposed to do? Throw my weight around? Make calls?

I'd done that bit before and it hadn't really worked out well.

I stroked my thumb down the plastic that held the letter and looked up.

I still didn't have a single response to any of my calls. I had to try again. It had been after one when I'd gotten here and it was coming up on four in the morning.

Getting to my feet, I made my way back over to the man at the desk. I saw him take a slow breath and plaster another fake smile on his face.

"Have you had any luck contacting the lieutenant?" I asked.

"She's here." He nodded. "She's tied up with a suspect. As soon as she's available—"

"Toni Gallagher isn't a fucking suspect," I said. I didn't raise my voice. Instead, it came out cold as ice.

The officer's eyes widened, then narrowed.

The letter was still sitting next to him. I reached over and tapped it, fighting to keep my voice even and polite. "Would you please take thirty seconds and read this?"

Maybe it was the please that did it.

This time, he did more than just take a cursory glance. And his eyes widened halfway through.

He shoved up to his feet, calling out to somebody whose name I didn't catch.

"I'm taking this," he said to me, voice clipped.

"What are you—?"

But he was already striding off.

A couple more hours passed. It was a little after seven now. Another cop, dressed in a rumpled suit, had come out, asked me several questions, made notes, and then nodded. A woman, her shirt crisp and fresh, had come out and asked the same questions, in a different order.

When a third person, another man, came out, I finally held up a hand. "I want to see Lieutenant Green."

"Mr. Lang—"

"Lieutenant Green." I was fucking tired of playing nice, and I let it show in my voice. It was too early – or late, depending on how you looked at it – and I hadn't gotten shit accomplished. I'd been here for six hours and the hangover wasn't helping.

Toni had been here for over fourteen, a snide voice in the back of my head said.

And I was trying to fix that.

The man – his badge said Reardon – peered at me for a moment and then he nodded. This time, when he walked off, I didn't sit back down. I moved over to the window and stared outside, watching as a misty, gloomy morning dawned.

The door to the back had opened and closed so many times, I'd finally stopped looking.

This time, though, I did look, more out of reflex than anything else, my head already half turning back to the window when my brain kicked in.

Swinging my gaze back around, I stared intently at the petite woman who'd just come striding through the door, her head high and shoulders straight. Her chin was lifted and her hair, all that rich, dark red, hung in a tangle down her back. There were shadows like bruises under her lovely eyes, but other than that, she looked fine.

Nobody had hurt her.

I breathed a bit easier.

It lasted for all of two seconds, because then Toni was shifting her gaze around and she saw me.

She stumbled and the shortest of her brothers caught her, concern clear in his dark blue eyes. She gave him a quick smile and went back to glaring at me.

After a moment, she curled her lip and looked away, saying something in a low voice to the brother who'd caught her. He looked a little older than the others, which meant he was probably the oldest of the lot, Deacon.

I couldn't stop myself. I should have, but I couldn't.

"Toni."

I took a step toward her and watched as those smoky blue eyes swung back to mine. She inclined her head and a cool smile settled on her lips. But she didn't say anything. She just continued walking with her brothers.

One of them peeled himself away from her and placed himself between us when I took another step toward her.

It was Victor.

He was a few inches shorter than my own six foot three inches, and lanky, but he held himself in such a way that told me he wasn't someone to be trifled with. He raked his gaze up and down. My spine stiffened at the obvious derision in that look, but I didn't react.

What would I be doing if someone had done to Isadora what I'd done to Toni? And that was assuming they didn't know that Toni and I had slept together.

I'd beat the shit out of anyone who hurt my baby sister. Something I fully intended to do as soon as I found out who'd taken her. I couldn't fault these guys for standing up for Toni. But she was walking away. Cutting around Vic, I said her name again.

"She doesn't want to talk to you."

"I understand that, but I have things I need to say." I held his gaze for a moment, and then looked back to see Toni almost to the door.

She wasn't even looking back this way.

"Toni, just listen to me, dammit!"

"This him, Vic?" The stockier of the brothers had left his place at Toni's side to join Vic. If the other one was Deacon, I assumed this one would be Franky. He had a broad face, reddish-brown hair, and pissed off light brown eyes.

"It is, Franky." Vic reached up, scraped his nails down his cheek. He had his sister's hair color. Her stubborn jaw too, and he lifted it pugnaciously, like he was daring me to do something.

"I just need to talk to her," I said. "I want to apologize."

"Is that a fact?" Franky nudged Vic to the side and I looked down, hoping he might be more reasonable.

Almost instantly, I knew I'd wasted that hope.

From the corner of my eye, I saw that Toni had slowed down, but she wasn't looking at me. She was gesturing toward her brothers, and I had a feeling she was more worried about them than anything I had to say.

It's a family dinner.

Knowing my chance was sliding away, I knew I had to make a choice. Let her go, or say it in front of everyone. I raised my voice. "Toni, I'm sorry. I was..."

She didn't look at me, but everybody else was.

"Toni, for fuck's sake!"

She glanced down at her hands, nails folded in so she could study them. She pursed her lips as she gazed down at her manicure as if her fingers were of utmost importance.

That was it. My temper flared and I shoved between her brothers.

That was yet another big mistake, I realized.

They caught my arms before I made it a full step. I tried to jerk away and they just put more muscle into it. They were shorter than me, but they were far from weak. Getting away might involve some serious physical force here.

"Toni."

Finally, she looked at me. After a moment, she turned towards her brothers. "Vic, Franky...don't. He's not worth it."

Their hands fell away and Vic shoulder-checked me hard as he headed back to his sister's side. She folded her arms over her chest as she met my eyes. There were shadows in her eyes.

"Go away," she said quietly. "You've got other things to focus on besides me, so maybe you should do that."

While I tried to adjust to the dull tone of her normally vibrant voice, she looked up at the brother who'd stayed by her side. "Deacon, I'm exhausted. Take me home, please?"

I tried one more time. "Toni–"

"No!" She spun back to me, her hands clenched into fists at her side and for the first time since I first met her, I saw the glitter of tears in her eyes. "I'm exhausted. The only sleep I got was a nap in the interrogation room. The last time I peed, I had to do it on a toilet in front of ten other women. I want to take a shower. I want some food. I want to sleep for about twenty hours straight. What I don't want is to see you. Ever again."

Numb, I stared at her. She couldn't mean it. She was understandably upset, but she couldn't mean she never wanted to see me again. Into the raw silence, I finally managed to speak.

"I...Toni, I'm sorry. Let me...I'll fix this. Let me make it up to you."

"How?" Her voice cracked as she shouted at me. "Your fucking money? Guess what? It doesn't solve everything. Grow up, *Ashford*."

She spun on her heel and stormed towards the doors, her brothers following right behind her.

"Well. I do hate to say I told you so..."

Marcum's caustic voice came from behind me.

I didn't know where she'd come from. I didn't really care. Looking back, I saw that Marcum had joined Lieutenant Green and the other cops at some point in the past few minutes. Great. They'd all just witnessed everything Toni had yelled at me. Dropping onto a bench, I propped my elbows on my knees and stared at nothing.

Shit.

"That went well."

It was Green who spoke first. She cleared her throat and when I glanced up, she was running her thumb up and down the crease of the envelope containing the ransom letter.

"Perhaps we could move on to the real concern, Mr. Lang. Your sister. And this new...letter?"

Chapter 3

Toni

I was going to regret this.

Shaking with exhaustion, my head pounding, I still found myself turning around. The doors were within my reach, but I couldn't bring myself to open them. Not yet.

"What letter?"

Ash's shoulders had been slumped, but as soon as I spoke, his entire body tensed.

"Come on, Toni," Deacon said, resting his hand on my arm. "Let's go. You're exhausted and if I don't get you home so you can rest, Mom's going to have all of our hides."

I gave Deacon a strained smile. "Isadora's my friend."

They knew about her, of course. I'd told my family all about her, all about my job and how much I enjoyed working with the sweetest twenty year-old I'd ever met. Deacon's eyes bore into mine, almost grim in their intensity, but he nodded and his hand fell away. I knew he'd understand. True friends came second only to family.

Lieutenant Green gave me a tight smile. "I'm sorry, Ms. Gallagher, but we can't discuss an ongoing investigation."

"No." Ash's voice was low as he slowly raised his head.

I let my gaze shift back to him, but he didn't meet my eyes. Fine. If that was how he wanted to play it.

"You can tell her. She cares about my sister."

Green bristled. "Mr. Lang, that's not how we do things."

Angling my head, I studied the two of them, watching the power struggle as it played out between cop and...whatever in the hell Ashford Lang was. Mega-millionaire, sure. But this was New York. They were practically a dime a dozen. He needed to have friends in powerful places as well as money.

"Did he ask you to arrest me?" I asked abruptly.

Next to me, my brothers stiffened. In front of me, Ash went pale, his jaw going tight.

Lieutenant Green, though, could have done a soldier proud. Her shoulders went back and her chin angled high. "What a citizen of this city requests of me doesn't dictate my duty, Ms. Gallagher. I do what I swore to do when I picked up my badge."

"Nicely said," I told her dryly. "You neither denied nor confirmed. You should go into politics." I looked at Ash. "You're an asshole."

In addition to his clenched jaw, a vein started to pulse in his temple. "My sister's life could be at stake."

"Yeah. And how much time did you waste having the cops hassle me? How much was wasted having people trail Vic?" I shook my head and shifted my gaze elsewhere, hoping that sense of betrayal would fade.

It didn't.

"Ms. Gallagher."

I looked over to find Agent Marcum standing a few feet away. Her gaze was compassionate. She flicked a look at Ash, a bit of curl to her lip, a sneer. I found myself liking her, despite the side of the badge she stood on. I wasn't feeling very friendly toward badges right now. But I liked her.

"Regardless of how he pushed, we would have ended up looking." She shrugged and shot Vic a glance and then shifted her focus back to me. "Maybe not as hard and definitely not as...intrusively. But we would have looked. Now it's done and we can focus on Isadora again. She's what matters, right?"

Marcum was right. Isadora was what mattered.

When Ash asked if I wanted to come with them after Green said she wouldn't discuss aspects of the case in the middle of the station, I agreed. I didn't want to be anywhere near Ash, but I needed to know what was happening with Isadora.

I left my brothers to cool their heels in the main lobby while Green, Marcum, Ash and I squeezed into a conference room, along with a handful of agents and detectives. I tucked myself into a corner and pretended Ash wasn't there as the cops went about setting up a board and passing out sheets of paper.

"Who's this?" I asked softly after Marcum finished placing one large picture square in the middle of the board.

"That is our one connection." She slid me a look. "We'll get you up to speed here shortly."

Up to speed? A few minutes later, after Green and Marcum had each taken turns talking, I had to fight the urge to ask them to go over it just one more time.

Up to speed. Not so much. My brain was taking in what I was being told, but I didn't know if I was really processing it. The one thing I did know was that I needed to be able to examine that picture when I was more coherent.

As they started to pass around files, I edged around the table to look at the picture. While everybody behind me was talking, I casually lifted the phone I'd slid out of my pocket and snapped an image for myself. I didn't know if I'd managed to pull it off or not, but when I turned back, everybody was still busy flipping through the files. No one had seen me.

"If you're curious..."

I blinked. Marcum was standing in front of me, holding out a file.

"It can't leave this room, but you're welcome to look at

the photos. As far as him." She looked over at the board. "We'll have to put out an alert on him soon, so we're not sharing anything you won't see soon enough."

Ash's gaze shot our way. "An alert." A muscle pulsed in his cheek as he shook his head. "I want this kept quiet."

"I'm aware of your desires, Mr. Lang." Marcum gestured toward the board, and the picture of the unknown man. "But I'm going to be frank here. Our mystery man doesn't have a record and your sister has been missing for quite some time. At some point, we may need help from the public. Assuming you want your sister found."

Ash snapped his jaw shut, but the desperation in his eyes spoke volumes. He was angry, but he was also hurting and frightened for his sister.

"Please let us do our job," Lieutenant Green said.

She flicked a glance at me and I wondered how long it would take her to figure out a way to get me kicked out.

Clearing my throat, I looked back down at the photographs. Pointedly, I asked, "What's with the pictures?"

That was what the file held. Pictures. Or, rather, copies of them. One of the officers had put original photos in sealed bags down the middle of the table in a straight line. When had these come into play? As soon as I asked myself the question, I knew the answer. Someone had gotten these while I'd been under arrest. I wondered if they'd been delivered to the station or to Ash.

Marcum pulled out a chair across from me and sat down. "If you read the copy of the letter delivered to Mr. Lang late last night, it'll give you a decent idea of what is going on."

Frowning, I found the letter in the file and read it. Then I read it again. There wasn't much to it so I had it memorized by the time I finished. I couldn't see how the cops might read into anything it and I was trying hard. It was short, simple and to the point.

As the cops and agents fired questions at Ash, I shifted my attention to the pictures. Okay...these were a little different. I went through them slowly, seeing younger and younger versions of both Isadora and Ash.

Feeling a pair of eyes on me in that moment, I looked up. Ash was staring directly at me. I set my jaw and lifted my chin, pretending to focus on what was being said.

He felt bad. I knew he did. Part of me could even understand. My brothers...

No.

Even as my brain tried to feed me that bit of bullshit, my conscious mind rejected it. My brothers wouldn't have pulled strings to get someone arrested, not even if it had been me missing. Unless their gut absolutely screamed yes, she's guilty, yes, she did it, they wouldn't have gone after somebody the way Ash had gone after me. And if that had been the case?

They wouldn't have slept with the woman.

So either Ashford Lang was a bigger dick than I'd realized...or I was a bigger fool.

"We're looking at somebody with an obsession," Green continued with whatever she was saying.

"A grudge." The words popped out of me without any conscious decision to say anything.

Everybody in the room shifted their attention to me.

"Excuse me?" The lieutenant's voice was coolly polite.

Marcum's gaze slid to me. "Excuse me?"

"Ah...I'm sorry. I just..." I forced a smile. "Never mind. I'm speculating."

Green gave a short nod and looked back at the board, but before she could speak, Marcum held up a hand to stop her.

"Speculating about what, exactly, Ms. Gallagher?"

Nervous, I reached up and twisted a snarled lock of hair. "Nothing important, Agent Marcum. You guys are the professionals here."

"And you're just shy of your psychology degree. What do you think you see?" Marcum's eyes narrowed.

Ash wasn't the only one staring at me now. I was more nervous than I could remember being in a long, long time. "Ahhhh..." I glanced down at the photographs again. "It's the pictures. She was...um, well...prepubescent when the first few were taken? Most obsessions don't start when a girl is still at that stage, do they? Or if they start with a child, they usually stop once the child hits puberty. Most obsessions don't cover both. And Ash – Mr. Lang – is in these photos as well. Besides, how often do kidnappers grab a woman they want to assault, and then make a demand?"

"We've already come to that conclusion, Ms. Gallagher." Lieutenant Green looked annoyed. "But there are different kinds of obsession, and these pictures do indicate a certain focus on the Lang family. Since Ms. Lang is the one they grabbed, it makes sense she's the focus of the obsession."

"Does it?" I stared at the headstones and how precisely they appeared in the majority of the images. Focal points, even. There wasn't a single shot that included the stones where the stones were obscured. "I'm not sure she is the focus. Look at most of the pictures. There are a couple of other Langs in them."

Confusion flickered in several faces. Except the FBI agents.

Looking at Agent Marcum, I said softly, "You're already considering that angle."

"The parents?" She picked up one of the copies they'd copied of each photo. "Yes. We're considering it."

"My parents?" Ash nudged one of the images toward Agent Marcum. "In case you didn't notice, they're dead."

"Dead doesn't mean forgotten, does it, Mr. Lang?" the agent countered.

He flicked me another look, one I couldn't read.

Instead of trying to, I just sat down and closed my eyes, letting the voices wash over me.

The meeting dragged on so long, I thought I'd fall asleep, but I powered through. When I finally escaped into the slightly fresher air of the main hallway, my brothers were waiting. None of them spoke. Franky pushed a diet soda into my hand while Deacon turned over a bagel. Vic hooked an arm around my neck and hugged me, ignoring the fact that I had already shoved nearly half the bagel into my mouth.

He held on so tight, I had to nudge him back to take the next bite. "What gives?" I said around the yummy, yeasty goodness.

Vic just shook his head. "Come on, kid. Let's get you..." His voice trailed off, his eyes sliding past my shoulder.

Sighing, I turned and saw Ash standing there.

He looked as rumpled and worn as I'd ever seen him. He'd shoved up the sleeves of his dress shirt at some point during the discussion, and his hair looked like he'd combed it with a chainsaw, sans blade. There were shadows under his bloodshot eyes. And damn him to hell, he was still gorgeous.

All three of my brothers gathered at my side, and I could practically see the testosterone oozing in the air. In the middle of a police station, this was the last thing we needed.

"Guys, let's go outside," I said softly.

I knew they weren't in the mood to listen, so I hooked one arm through Franky's to keep him at my side. He was easily the most volatile one of the group. Vic would do almost anything to avoid getting in trouble again, and Deacon had always been the level-headed one.

As I started to walk, I pulled my brother with me. He didn't resist, but he did grumble under his breath, "You never let me have any fun, Toni."

"Yeah, picking a fight in a police station. That's fun, all right. Or are you looking to top my experience of having a hooker proposition you while you're in holding?"

As I'd hoped, that caught their attention. All three of my brothers were suddenly demanding to know what in the hell I was talking about. Needing distance between me and the station, I didn't stop to explain, but rather kept walking towards the nearest subway entrance. As I walked, I told them about the oh-so-subtle offer from the prostitute in the holding cell. I forced a smile and a laugh. "But I turned her down. I'm not into girls and I didn't have any cash on me."

"If you tell Mom, she'll have a heart attack," Franky said, shaking his head.

"That's why we're not telling her." Deacon cuffed him on the back of the head, rolling his eyes.

"Guys." I couldn't help but laugh for real this time. "Mom's the one who gave all of us the sex talk. I don't think she'd be surprised to hear there was a hooker in a holding cell."

I glanced around for Vic to see what his take was, but he wasn't behind me.

"Shit."

Deacon grunted a similar sentiment under his breath as the three of us turned to see our brother a couple yards back, standing not more than an arm's length from Ash.

This could end badly.

I started back towards the pair. "Vic."

I shoved hair back from my face. Annoyed, I gathered it all together with a half-thought of shoving it into a knot when I realized I didn't have my purse. "Shit. Shit. Shit. My purse."

My brothers knew me well enough to know I wasn't upset because I had some sort of expensive little bag. Unless I was going to something special, like a wedding or a club, my purse wasn't an accessory. I had everything in it. Wallet, phone, pictures, notes for work and school...

At least my voice caught my brother's attention, pulling

him away from Ash.

"Did you have it with you when you were arrested?"

"Yes – no. I don't know!" I could feel the panic I'd managed to keep at bay all night threatening to come back.

"It's at my house."

I whipped my head around. Ash had moved closer without any of us knowing and now he was only a few feet away.

"Your house," Deacon said, his voice flat.

Closing my eyes, I flipped back through my memories of what had happened before I'd gotten arrested – skipping quickly over certain parts I didn't want to remember – and then blew out a breath. "Yeah. I put it in the room where I usually work with Isadora. Habit. Then I just...forgot." I didn't need to remind anyone why I'd forgotten.

"Fine." Franky gave Ash a toothy smile. "I can run on over there with Lang here and pick it right up."

Ash didn't even look at my brother. "Are you going to talk to me?"

I couldn't avoid him forever. I wanted to. But I knew I couldn't. It just wasn't me. Plus, I wasn't about to ruin what I had with Isadora because her brother was an ass.

Taking a slow breath, I walked over to him. "You know, the entire time I was in there, I kept thinking…wondering if I could have done anything differently yesterday. Done anything that would've changed how things ended up. And I realized I could have…"

"I could have done a thousand things differently too," Ash said, his voice hoarse. "Toni, I'm sorry. I–"

"This isn't about you." I held up a hand. "It's about me. You want to make things square with us?"

He nodded.

Surprise widened his eyes a fraction of a second before my fist slammed into his nose. I pulled the punch at the last second when I remembered that my knuckles were already bruised, but I still hit him with considerable force.

Pain burst up my arm as he stumbled back. He didn't fall and I didn't see any blood, but I still felt better.

As he shook his head to clear it, I gave him a hard look. "You're the one I should've hit yesterday. Consider your apology accepted."

Chapter 4

Toni

    I opened my eyes.
    Confused, I looked around only to wince as a crick in my neck decided to send a shooting pain straight up into my head. The headache that had been lying in wait sprang to life as I peered through tinted glass and tried to remember just where the hell I was.
    "You fell asleep."
    Groaning, I rubbed at my stiff neck as I looked over at Ash.
    He was sitting on the leather seat across from me.
    My memory turned on and, just like that, the events of the past day came rushing back at me.
    He'd called and said he had some news about Isadora. I'd gone over to his house and he'd had me arrested after accusing me of having something to do with Isadora's kidnapping. I'd spent the night in jail. My brothers had shown up at the station. The officer had declined to press charges. Ash had been there too. I realized I'd left my purse at his house. I vaguely remembered him offering me a ride to his house to get my purse and me accepting just to prove that I could be an adult about this. After that, things started getting hazy.
    I rubbed at my eyes, and out of habit, checked my watch. Then, blinking, I checked it a second time. It was three hours

later than it had been when I'd left the police station. I frowned at Ash as I straightened.

"Where are we?"

"My house. You needed to get your purse, right?"

My eyes narrowed. "It doesn't take three hours to get from the police station to your house."

The corner of Ash's mouth twitched as if he was amused. "You fell asleep and I didn't want to wake you."

"So you've been sitting in your driveway, in the back of a limo, watching me while I slept?" I pinched the bridge of my nose and closed my eyes for a moment. Under my breath, I muttered, "Yeah, that's not creepy at all."

"You did say we needed to talk."

I opened my eyes to find that smug smile back on his face. The fact that his nose was slightly puffy made it a bit less irritating. But only a little bit less.

The door next to me opened and I stared at the hand extended by the driver. I wasn't opposed to men opening doors for me. I actually rather enjoyed it. But I wasn't entirely sure just what I was willing to accept from Ash right now, and that included things like a hand from the man he paid to chauffeur him around. Ignoring the proffered hand, I climbed out on my own and turned to give the car a pointed look as Ash got out on the other side.

"You know," I said. "Plenty of people just use a town car to get around New York."

Ash opened his mouth, then closed it. After a moment, a sheepish expression crossed his face. "Usually I do. Or I drive my Porsche. I thought..." He stopped and shook his head, his cheeks an amusing shade of red. "Never mind. Come on."

His Porsche? Was he kidding, letting that drop? I let some of my waspish temper out. "Let me guess...you decided to see if you could impress me by calling a limo to pick us up?"

His shoulders stiffened. To my surprise, he turned and

met my gaze. He didn't answer right away, but rather spoke to his driver, "Lewis, I'll let you know if I'll need you later. Thank you."

As the man climbed back into the car, Ash reached up to rub at his jaw. After the limo pulled away, Ash came towards me. With just a few seconds, he was closer than I liked. Close enough that I could smell the heady, masculine scent of him, and it brought back memories of his body rubbing against mine, his hands on my hips, in my hair, tugging, pulling, driving me on.

"I never make an effort to impress people, Toni. It just happens," he said, his voice low. "Did I use the limo to maybe throw you off balance?" He half-smirked. "Obviously, it didn't work."

"I just spent the night in jail being propositioned by a hooker." I gave him a brightly false smile. "You'll have to try harder."

I cut around him and headed up the steps. My legs felt like blocks of cement and my eyes seemed to be coated with sand. The little nap in the limo had helped a bit. If I could get some coffee and use a bathroom for about five minutes, I'd be good to go for a few hours.

I caught sight of Doug as I stepped inside the house. His face softened when he saw me. I knew he'd been hoping I was Isadora, but he didn't show any disappointment.

"Ms. Gallagher." He smiled. "Is there anything I can get you?"

I smiled back, grateful he wasn't mentioning anything about the arrest. Then again, it was possible he didn't know. "I'd love some coffee."

The butler nodded. "Just a moment then."

As he disappeared, I glanced over my shoulder at Ash as he walked into the house. "I'm using the restroom."

I didn't go to the closest one, however. That was the one

Ash and I had been in when we'd heard the news about Isadora...after we'd gotten a little too friendly with each other. The thought of being in there again...even thinking about it was enough to make my nipples draw tight.

Distance. I needed distance and probably a solid hit upside the head to knock these insane thoughts out.

Ducking into the larger bathroom just off the main hall, I locked the door and pressed my back against it. I closed my eyes, and took a slow deep breath. I did it again and again until my brain felt a little more awake and my mood felt level. Only then did I open my eyes and go over to the sink.

A few seconds of digging around unearthed a variety of expensive toiletries. Never let it be said that the Lang family didn't know how to provide for unexpected company. I scrubbed my face, then did a quick wash-up before freshening up with lotion and one of the small deodorants I found. The place was better than a hotel. By the time I was done, I felt marginally better. I used the toilet, washed my hands and brushed my teeth. I felt almost human again.

As I was rinsing, I heard a knock on the door.

"A moment."

When I opened the door, Beth was standing there, a small bundle in her hands. She looked older than she had when she'd told us about Isadora being gone. Older and almost fragile. "Doug thought you might like to change your clothes. These should fit."

"I...ah..." I hesitated, then looked down. It took only a glance at the clothes I'd been wearing for way too long and I nodded, taking the garments with a grateful smile.

I left the bathroom wearing a silk blouse and a loose pair of trousers. The entire outfit probably cost more than I made in a month, the silk sliding against my skin and making me very aware of the inexpensive panties and bra I put with the rest of my inexpensive clothes. My skin was flushed as I stepped out of the restroom, self-conscious of my lack of undergarments.

Ash was waiting in the room Isadora and I usually used. I almost turned around and walked back out, but this was where my purse was and I'd be damned if I gave Ash the satisfaction of knowing how much he disconcerted me.

Ash turned to look at me, but before he could say anything, Doug came in, pushing a wheeled cart. There was a silver pot of coffee, and my belly started to rumble as I caught the scent of food.

"I didn't know if you'd eaten, Miss Toni." The older gentleman gave me a smile.

The yowling of my belly at that precise moment seemed to be answer enough. Blushing, I pressed a hand to it. "I had a bagel earlier."

"Perhaps you'd like something more filling?"

"You're my hero, Doug. Thank you."

He gave me a nod, then left without looking at Ash. Neither one spoke, and the silence was filled with ice.

"He seems mad at you," I said as I poured myself a cup of coffee.

"They all are." Ash sounded weary.

I didn't have any sympathy for him. "Have you put them up for the chopping block yet?"

"I'm..." He blew out a breath. "I'm not going to fire them. Isadora..." The hesitation was almost imperceptible. "She's in charge of the household staff. She'd never forgive me if I did anything like that...rashly."

"Hmmm." I wondered why the staff was mad, but I didn't ask. It wasn't my business.

I sipped the coffee, desperate for the buzz of caffeine. On the cart was selection of light sandwiches, fruits and cheese. I took a plate and filled it with a bit of everything before heading over to a chair. It faced outside, which meant it was angled away from the couch so, if I wanted, I didn't even have to look at Ash.

"I'm sorry."

I glanced at him as I took another sip of my coffee. "So you've said." His nose looked more swollen and discolored in this light. "Does your nose hurt?"

His lips twitched. "Have you ever been hit in the nose?"

"Yep."

"Then what do you think?"

I grinned at him. "That it hurts like a bitch." I paused, and couldn't help but add, "I'm not sorry."

"I wouldn't expect you to be." He moved from the couch to the chair across from me, his expression serious. "I don't know where to go from here."

"I'd rather you not keep apologizing." I kept my voice nonchalant. Selecting a strawberry, I popped it into my mouth and waited until after I swallowed before I said anything else. "I get it, you're sorry. I'm sure you regret it. And I bet you'd do the same thing tomorrow if you thought it necessary."

"Not to you."

My hand stilled over the plate and I pulled it back to drop it onto my lap.

"You want me to believe that?" The question came out flat.

"I don't expect you to," he said softly. "But it's the truth."

He closed his hands into fists, then opened them, flexing as he stared off into the distance. "It won't help, but I'd like to explain, if I could."

"Feel free." I shrugged and settled more comfortably in my chair, prepared to be entertained if nothing else.

Entertained...

That wasn't the word I was thinking right now.

I was...disgusted. Disillusioned. Tired. Not even close to entertained.

After reading the PI's report a second time, I tossed it on the table and stood up, moving over to the window and staring outside.

Ash had explained everything in short, simple terms and then he'd given me the images that had been shot of me with my brother, and all of the ones taken of us at my parents' house. There had been a report too. A neat and concise one that started with all our meetings together and ended with an in-depth report on my brother's history.

Including his arrest on felony drug charges when he'd been eighteen. But Ash had already known about that. I knew for a fact that he did because I'd been the one who'd told him.

What I hadn't told him about were the rumors. Specifically, the ones about Vic being involved in a kidnapping attempt.

"Vic wasn't trying to kidnap that girl," I said softly, staring out the window. "He was the reason she was rescued."

"It doesn't matter. Toni, I–"

Slowly, I turned to him. The look in his eyes was carefully blank, but I knew what that meant. He didn't believe me.

"He wasn't involved," I said again, carefully and slowly saying each word. No one outside of our family and a couple of cops knew what I was about to say, but Ash needed to hear it. "Vic was supposed to be flirting with her, charming her...then when he asked her out, he was supposed to grab her. He went to the police instead. He wore a wire. For two whole days, he wore a wire. If he'd been found out, he could have been killed. My brother is the reason that girl didn't end up dead."

Ash started to say something and then he stopped, shaking his head.

I grabbed the report and wadded it up into a ball. "Ask your source if he had access to confidential reports or to the undercover officers in the gang unit. Because that's who my brother was working with. If your source hasn't talked to one of them, he doesn't know shit. Vic risked his life to save that girl and if anyone ever found out what he'd done, his life would be at risk again." Wrapping my arms around my middle, I turned back to the window. "Some things are worth more than money."

He was quiet for so long that when he did speak, I actually jumped a little.

"I know you don't want me to keep apologizing."

He was closer now. Nervously, I darted a look back at him. He was only a foot away. "No. I don't."

"Want to take another swing at me then?"

My gaze dropped to his nose. Then, to my surprise, I laughed. "No." Flexing my right hand, I winced at the bruises. "You've got a face like a rock. Next time you need to get hit, I'll let Franky do it."

"But you seemed to enjoy it so much." There was a hint of amusement in his voice.

I shrugged. "There's something to be said for a physical outlet when it comes to blowing off steam." I kept my voice light, but I made the mistake of looking at him when I said it.

Our gazes connected.

Heat arced, snapped.

I spun around. I should go. I really, really should go.

"If you're still in the need to blow off steam, I have an idea."

Blowing off steam didn't involve a bed.

Part of me – a very bad, bad part of me – was disappointed. Not that I would've given in anyway. Sex with Ash was one thing I didn't plan on letting happen again. Ever again.

But this, well, this wasn't bad.

Instead of suggesting we go to his bedroom, his playroom or even the couch, he'd escorted me down to a personal gym that was better outfitted than some of the ones I'd seen people pay for.

We weren't using any of the equipment, though.

I had a pair of gloves on, as well as padded protectors on my feet. Ash had told me they weren't necessary, but then I'd caught him with a roundhouse to the side of the head, and he'd decided that maybe they weren't a bad idea. Then he'd grinned and come at me.

We were now flat on the floor. Ash had dropped down first after we'd agreed to a time-out. Right after he'd gotten me in the ribs with a punch I hadn't been able to block, I'd plowed a sidekick directly into his gut and knocked the air right out of him.

Panting, more than a little exhilarated, I closed my eyes and tried to focus on letting my pulse slow.

"I haven't had a match like that in a long while."

I twitched and opened my eyes. Ash rolled over to his stomach and was staring at me, his eyes just a few inches away.

Sweat gleamed along his shoulders and as I stared at him, one bead started to roll down his jaw to his neck.

I had an overpowering urge to lean in and lick it away.

Bad, bad, bad thoughts. Pull it together.

His gaze slid to my mouth.

I rolled away from him and got to my feet. My legs were rubbery under me and I covered my nervousness with a laugh that sounded so fake. I grabbed some water and gulped down half a bottle before turning towards him.

Ash had risen and was staring at me, his gaze hot and intent. My heart was still racing away, but it wasn't all from exertion now. He came toward me and my fingers tightened around the water bottle. Anticipation clamored inside me while common sense tried to get a foothold.

But he veered to the left and I spent the next few seconds telling myself I wasn't disappointed while he chugged water. He'd stripped away his shirt and swapped out his trousers for a pair of loose gym shorts. For the past thirty minutes, that hot body had been moving with mine and I'd been almost immune.

Of course, we'd been otherwise engaged, and I'd managed to preoccupy myself with punches and kicks.

Now though...

I busied myself with screwing the top back on the water bottle, my head lowered as I studied his physique from under my lashes. He was seriously a walking work of art, everything about him wonderfully defined, strong shoulders, his pecs solid and tapering down to a flat, chiseled abdomen and narrow hips.

I could remember sinking my nails into those hips, gripping him as he'd ridden me, driving me to the heights of pleasure.

He looked up as that thought flickered through my mind as if he'd heard the echo of it. He sucked in a harsh breath and closed the distance between us. We stood barely a foot apart now. Close enough that he could he reach out and touch me. Close enough that he could reach out and grab me, kiss me, take me...

Please...

His body tensed.

I caught my breath, held it.

Then he turned away.

"There's a shower you can use down here," he said, his voice brusque. Gesturing off to the far side of the sleek gym, he added, "Feel free to use whatever you need. Iz...sometimes she has friends drop by and hang out for a while so there's always plenty of toiletries, extra clothes in different sizes. Take whatever you need."

An ache pulsed deep inside as he strode away and before I could even say anything more than thanks, he was gone.

He wasn't upstairs when I finished. Torn between leaving and looking for him, I wandered back to the small sitting room. I had some vague thought of trying to get some work done, but I'd reached the point where there really wasn't much I could do until either a few people got back to me or Isadora returned.

So I didn't have anything left to distract me from my memories.

Ash had been such an ass earlier and it was foolish of me to think a round of sparring had changed anything. I should just leave. I didn't need to be here. For that matter, I could just let him know to call me when there was news, and let my dad know I'd help out with the family business temporarily. My father would understand. It was the perfectly logical thing to do.

But I couldn't leave.

"I can call a car for you if you're ready to go."

Ash's voice caught me off-guard and I spun around,

staring at him. He'd showered and changed. And whoa...what a change.

He wore a silvery gray shirt, silk clearly, and it rippled against his muscular frame like it had been designed for him. Hell, I had no doubt it'd been designed for him. There probably wasn't a single piece of clothing in his wardrobe that wasn't tailor-made for that magnificent body. He'd paired the shirt with a pair of black trousers that fit like a dream and made me recall just how good those thighs had felt as he'd moved against me.

"You're going out." The words popped out of my mouth without me thinking about how they sounded.

He cocked his eyebrow at me. "Yes. I..." He blew out a breath and then shrugged, sending that silvery silk rippling again.

I wanted to drag my hands down his chest and mentally scolded myself. One night had been bad enough, but I could excuse one slip up, especially when taking into consideration the emotions that had been running high. Now, I needed to listen to common sense. Still, I had to ask, "You what?"

"I need to get out of here," he admitted. "Everywhere I look, I see my sister and I need to stop thinking."

"I understand," I said softly.

"Okay, then." He paused, clearly waiting for something.

"Yes?"

"Should I have a car brought for you or would you prefer a taxi?"

I managed a smile. He had the right idea. "You know what? I think I'll just walk to the subway. Going out doesn't sound like a bad idea."

I didn't let myself look at him as I moved past him to grab my purse. Next to it was a bag. I peeked inside and had to smile. Doug, on top of his game. He'd already had the clothes I'd been wearing yesterday laundered and folded. As I headed to the door, I gave Ash a vague smile.

"I'm going to a club."

His words made me pause.

"Okay." I glanced over at him, unsure of why he'd said it. After a moment, I added, "I'm thinking of doing the very same thing."

"Going to a club?" His gaze slid over me again and the air began to superheat, charged with the same kind of tension that had flooded the gym not long ago.

"Yes."

He put me on edge like nothing I'd ever known before. Put me on edge and pissed me off. Getting me worked up and then turning away like he did. I reached for the glib humor that had pulled me through whenever my brothers were riding me or when teachers were being asses.

"Shocking as this may sound, I actually go to clubs quite a bit."

"Not like mine." He took a step toward me.

The intensity of his voice might have had me backing up a bit. If I'd been the kind of person who ever backed down. I chuckled, but there wasn't really anything funny about what came out of my mouth.

"Wait, let me guess. You're one of those guys who go blow off steam at the kink palace, aren't you? What is it called? Olympus?"

The memory of seeing him with some woman popped into my head. Her bound, moaning and begging as he fucked her ass. The way he hadn't even flinched when I'd caught him.

I didn't need to hear him say it, but he did anyway.

"Yes."

Chapter 5

Ash

I should have kept my mouth shut.

I'd been almost rock hard ever since she'd come out of the changing room, wearing some of the extra workout gear Isadora insisted we keep on hand in case any of the staff or her friends wanted to use the gym. I didn't know of any of my sister's friends who were as tiny as Toni, but she'd managed to find a pair of yoga pants and a tank top that both fit her perfectly.

Too perfectly.

I'd been so distracted by her lithe body that she'd almost knocked me on my ass the first time out. She'd moved like a deadly dancer as we'd sparred, her eyes glowing, a grim sort of smile on her face. She'd gotten in more blows than I'd expected before I'd stopped thinking about what I wanted to do with her body and started paying attention. And it worked...until we stopped and all of those thoughts came rushing back.

I wanted to haul her to the floor and strip her naked, have an altogether different sort of battle with her, the kind she couldn't hope to win.

Now, as she stared at me, her eyes wide, I said something else I knew I'd regret. "Want to come with me?"

I watched her carefully, waiting for the freak out since

she'd obviously heard rumors about Olympus. Except it didn't come. She'd been surprised at first, but now she was...interested. Fuck. I wanted her to say yes. Wanted her to come to the club so I could show her a hundred, a thousand, things she'd probably never even dreamed of. I wanted to show her my world so I could make her a part of it. I'd never wanted anyone as much as I wanted her.

"It's..." She paused, touching her tongue to her lower lip.

I had visions of her on her knees, doing that very thing right before I guided her mouth to my cock.

Her voice was soft, as if she was trying to ask her question without sounding insulting. "It's really a sex club?"

"Technically, it's a private club for those with an interest in alternative lifestyles," I said blandly, quoting the public lines before I explained further. "It gets dicey if you use a phrase like 'sex club.' But basically, yes, it is. There're any number of things that happen there, and it all depends to what you want to do. Have a drink, look around, enjoy the atmosphere...or take in other...options. As long as it's consensual, pretty much anything's allowed."

I forced myself to quit talking, aware I was bordering on babbling. I just wanted her to say yes.

She blew out a slow breath, and then looked down at the clothes she'd changed into after our sparring session. "I'm not sure if I'm dressed right." There was a strange undercurrent of vulnerability to her words; as if she was afraid she wouldn't fit in.

The black silk shirt she wore paired with slim-fitting pants would be sedate compared to what most of the women at Olympus wore, but she'd still stand out. She was simply that kind of woman.

"The club doesn't have a dress code." I smiled slowly, hardly daring to hope that she'd agree. "You can wear as much, or as little, as you like."

Her eyes met mine.

Heads turned as Toni walked along with me.

While I realized new faces always caught attention here, I also knew the interest wasn't solely because she was new.

Several of the Subs I knew checked her out, male and female alike, their expressions puzzled. Some of the Dominants did the same thing, wearing similar expressions, although for different reasons. Everyone knew who I was, knew what I was, and they were all trying to figure out what the two of us were doing together.

Nothing about Toni Gallagher spoke of submissive. As a matter of fact, it was the opposite. The way she held herself, the look in her eyes, everything about her screamed that she wouldn't submit to anyone.

More than one of the Subs had speculative looks in their eyes and I knew what they were thinking. They wanted her, wanted her to dominate them, to take control. They wanted to be hers.

It shouldn't have bothered me. She wasn't mine in any way.

That shouldn't have bothered me either.

But it did.

I resisted the urge to snap at everyone who was staring, to lay claim to her right then and there. I didn't, however, resist the urge to touch her. Using direction as an excuse, I put my hand lightly on her lower back and steered her towards the VIP section.

Once there, I took her to the seats closest to the railing.

She settled on the plush love seat and I sat next to her. I told myself it was only because I didn't want someone else to sit there and make her feel uncomfortable. It had nothing to do with the fact that I simply wanted to be near her.

Before I could say or do something I'd regret, I gestured toward the stage in the middle of the lower area. The VIP section was on the highest level, which meant we had a prime view of any of the live shows going on below us. It was almost time for one of them to start, which was ideal. I needed a distraction. Coming here was supposed to be the distraction. It wasn't working as I'd planned.

Because I'd been dumb enough to ask Toni to come with me.

"What's going on?" Toni asked, leaning in close enough that her breasts brushed my arm.

"There's a show." The words came out more abruptly than I'd intended.

"What?"

Damn music. Turning my head, I pressed my mouth to her ear and tried not to think about how good she smelled.

The dance music abruptly cut off as I spoke, "There–" Toni jerked back with a laugh, rubbing at her ear as I finished in a normal voice. "A show."

Heat rose to my face and I silently cursed myself. That had been real smooth. I felt like an idiot and that wasn't something I was accustomed to. I didn't like it, especially not around her.

"What kind of show?" Her eyes widened as she braced her arms on the railing.

The fascination on her face pulled at me, helping me to push aside my embarrassment. I wanted to tell her to forget the show. Wanted to ask her to come with me to one of the rooms, tell her that I'd teach her anything she wanted to know.

Blurred memories of the night we'd had together haunted

me. I'd been drunk enough that things weren't as clear as I wished, but there were a few fragments that stood out with crystal clarity. Her moving against me. Her on her hands and knees, my fist in her hair. The tight, wet heat of her gripping my cock.

I forced myself to answer her question instead. "It's always different. You'll just have to wait and see," I said, tearing my gaze away from her. If I kept staring at her, I was going to put my hands on her.

And if I did that, I'd lose what little control I still had.

Chapter 6

Toni

The way he kept staring at me was driving me nuts. My body ached for him to put his hands on me. At the same time, I thought I might hit him if he did. Really hit him.

This hot and cold thing with him was going to send me over the edge, and not in a good way.

I might have said something, but before I could, the air was once more charged with music. It all but bled sexuality and promise, and I found my gaze shifting over to the stage, my curiosity overcoming my other thoughts.

"It's starting," Ash said.

"I can tell," I replied absently. Licking my lips, I lowered my head and rested my chin on my hands, my eyes on the woman who was walking onto the stage.

She wore a black dress that pooled around her thighs as she knelt in the center of the spot lit stage, facing towards us. She had pale blonde hair drawn up into a knot, revealing an elegant neck, and as the music slowed, her head lifted long enough for everyone to see the fine features of her face.

A man walked onto the stage and she immediately lowered her head again. He walked toward her and lifted her chin, one finger under it. She gazed up at him, dark eyes filled with something I couldn't quite recognize.

"This is something new," Ash said softly.

"Hush." Already, I was caught up in the artistry. I felt like I'd somehow ended up at some sort of Broadway show. Even Ash sitting right next to me couldn't tear my attention away.

As I watched, the man helped the woman to her feet. It was a slow, easy sort of dance, and the movements evoked the sense that he was guiding her every movement before pulling her up against him. After a minute or so, the rhythm of the music picked up and he spun her out and away. She went.

The black dress didn't.

She stood wearing what looked like a corset or a bustier and panties, staring down at herself. Her body language and expression communicated dismay and when the man started to approach her, she looked up, her hands moving to cover herself.

"Shibari."

I heard Ash say it next to me and filed it away for future reference. I saw the rope descending from the ceiling then. It wasn't like the kind of rope someone would buy at a hardware store and I wondered what the texture would be like, how it would feel against my skin. Despite how foreign everything around me was, I was mesmerized by the display of rope and rhythm unfolding in front of me. The pair never stopped moving, every pass of his hands over her, every time he twisted her away, there was a new twist of the rope. I couldn't even tell when it was happening, when the dance had changed into restraint.

By the time the music rose to a swelling crescendo, the rope had created a complicated cage of sorts and she was kneeling again in the very same position she'd been in when the dance had started. As she bowed her head once more, the man came up to kneel behind her, their height difference enough to allow the audience to see both of their faces. He slid his hands down her torso, along her still-covered breasts. When he cupped them, my nipples began to pulse.

One of his hands slid lower and I realized I was clenching my legs.

When he eased his weight back, shifting just slightly, I bit my lip.

Then he slid his hand down to the curve of her butt.

My chest started to ache, and I suddenly realized that I was holding my breath in anticipation. What was he going to do next?

The spotlight suddenly went out, bathing the entire place in darkness as the crowd erupted in applause.

I jolted at the unexpected ending and sat upright, swinging my head around to Ash, intending to ask about what I'd just seen.

He wasn't looking at the stage. He was staring at me. And I had a feeling he'd been watching me for a long, long while.

"Ash..."

His gaze slid to my mouth.

If he didn't kiss me soon...

Screw that. You kiss him, my libido screamed. Common sense argued back, and while those two were battling it out, we were interrupted.

"Ash, how are you?"

The strange voice caught my attention, and I took a few seconds to compose myself while Ash shook hands with the man who'd stopped by our seats. Ash told me his name, but my brain was barely functioning enough for me to smile and shake his hand. It didn't seem important that I remember his name since, less than two minutes after he'd come over, he excused himself, winking at Ash and saying that his sub was waiting.

"His sub?" I was fairly certain I knew what that meant, but I wanted to hear Ash's explanation rather than assuming anything.

He turned his gaze back to me. Eyes glittering with

something that looked a lot like desire, he gestured to the stage. "The woman who was being bound, she's a sub. The man who was tying her, he's a Dominant. Probably permanent partners. They move too well together and that required too much practice for this to have been a one-time thing."

Permanent partners. I'd never even considered that before. When I thought of a sex club, I immediately thought of people who were looking to have casual sex, probably with a bit of kink, and never any strings attached. It had been both naïve and judgmental of me, I realized. I made a mental promise to be more open-minded.

"For first-timers, it's sometimes difficult to know who's a Dominant and who's Submissive, but after a while, you know what to look for and it's almost automatic."

His eyes were intent on mine, as if he was trying to communicate something. I was pretty sure I knew what that something was. "I've already figured out that you're sexually dominant, Ash," I said, looking away to hide the rush of warmth adding to my already overheated cheeks. "You're too controlling to be anything but in charge."

His response was simple. "Yes."

Even though the couple was gone, I looked back to the stage. My entire body ached. I'd never felt like this before. It was the kind of empty ache that wouldn't be satisfied with good old-fashioned self-service or even the best vibrator money could buy. I wasn't even sure that regular sex would satisfy it.

A sound halfway between a sob and a moan caught my attention and I suddenly realized that the stage wasn't empty anymore. A woman was on the stage. A naked woman. And there was a man standing behind her, clad only in black leather pants. His torso was bulky, just a bit too soft to be considered muscular, and he exuded the sort of persona I associated with men in positions of power.

As I watched, he braced a hand on her neck, holding her face down on a strange, bench-like contraption. It was wide enough for her knees to be several inches apart, and with her ass up in the air, there wasn't much hidden. It was a vulnerable, open position and just looking at her made me want to squirm in embarrassment.

Then he brought his hand down on her exposed ass, the crack audible despite the music.

Desire exploded through me as she moaned, and I had to bite my lip to keep from doing the same. That shouldn't have been so hot.

"Would you care for a drink, Sir?"

The woman's voice was an intrusion and I had to grit my teeth to keep from scowling. From the corner of my eye, I saw a tall, slender woman speaking to Ash. I glanced over when he said my name, suddenly realizing my throat was terribly dry. "Vodka cranberry, please."

She gave us both a quick nod and I went back to watching the stage.

Down on the platform, another man had joined the original pair.

I didn't consider myself sheltered or naive, but watching the two men running their hands over her was pushing me far past my comfort zone. But I still couldn't look away. They were tying her up, the ropes forming a complicated twist between her spine, ankles and thighs. When they were done, it left her with her ankles pulled up until they were almost touching her ass while her wrists were bound at the small of her back.

It looked uncomfortable. And erotic as hell.

One of the men – the second one – bent over and kissed her. It was a rough and wild kiss, nothing gentle or kind about it. I bit my bottom lip. Some part of me wanted to be down there. But I wouldn't be a passive recipient, though.

I'd...

"Your drink, Lady."

I jumped a little as the server spoke from my side. I'd totally forgotten about her and the cocktail. Nodding, I took it and tossed back half of it before she'd even served Ash.

"Thirsty?" he asked, his tone amused.

I gave him a partial smile. "A bit."

"Bring her another," he said before the server left. "And a pitcher of water."

"Of course."

It was a bad idea, I thought, having another drink considering I was running on a short nap and the food Doug had given me a couple hours ago. But with all the adrenaline I had coursing through my body mingling with the need now clamoring inside, I thought the alcohol would be a good way to help calm my nerves.

Of course, if I didn't look away from the platform, all the alcohol in the world wouldn't be enough to calm me down.

The first man was behind her now, his hands on her hips as he pumped against her in a primal rhythm that had my core pulsing. He moved with rapid thrusts, and each time, I had to clench my knees together.

Finally, I tore my gaze away because if I didn't, I would...well, I didn't know what I would do. I couldn't come just watching, but if I didn't come soon, I thought I'd explode.

I closed my hand around my second glass of vodka cranberry. I sipped at it while trying to figure out how to deal with what I was feeling. Before I could though, Ash said my name and I looked over at him, unsure if I was grateful for the interruption.

"Are you ready to go?"

I wasn't, not while the show was still going on, but if we didn't leave now, I knew I'd probably end up doing something stupid.

Chapter 7

Ash

Her eyes were dark, but I couldn't read the expression in them. Her face was equally blank, making it impossible for me to truly know how she felt about what she'd seen.

Except...her nipples were tight and hard, and they'd been that way almost from the moment we'd stepped inside the club. And I knew that because it'd been nearly impossible for me to stop staring at her the entire time we were at Olympus.

It was almost as difficult now to keep my eyes to myself. She kept shifting around on the smooth leather of the seat next to me as if she couldn't get comfortable. After the first couple miles, I couldn't help but think it was a good thing I'd decided to drive or I might've lost control and put my hands on her.

I wanted to do it anyway.

"Was it a mistake taking you there?" I finally asked, keeping my voice soft.

"What?" She seemed startled that I'd said anything. "Oh, no. Not a mistake. It was...intense."

From the corner of my eye, I saw her pressing her knees together, and I had to squeeze the steering wheel to keep from reaching over and sliding my hand between them. She needed a man's cock inside her and I wanted it to be mine.

"I can't say I've ever been someone who's been curious

about that sort of thing," Toni continued. "I mean, you've probably figured out there's no way in hell I could ever be anybody's sub."

I had, and it bothered me more than it should have.

She kept going. "I also don't much see myself wanting to be...well. You know."

"Yes." My stomach clenched.

There was a few seconds of silence and then she spoke again, "But it..."

The light ahead turned yellow and instead of speeding through as I usually did, I brought the Porsche to a stop and looked over at her. "It what?"

For too long, she didn't answer, but when she did, her voice was husky, sending a bolt of desire right through me. "I'm the kind of person who's always known what I want. In life, in general. I'm strong-willed, stubborn and opinionated. I don't need a man to do anything for me. But..."

Her voice trailed off and I could almost feel what she was thinking.

"Needing a man to do something, and wanting it, are two very different things, Toni." I couldn't stop myself this time. I reached over and put my hand on her knee.

She froze.

Slowly, I dragged my hand up, the material of her pants thin enough I could feel the heat of her skin. Her breath was ragged and I knew she was just as affected as I was. "You were sitting in there, watching them, so aroused it almost hurt. Am I right?"

"Yes." The word came out in a low whisper.

I slid my hand higher so that my fingers brushed the inside of her thigh. "I wanted to put my hands on you then. Just like I'm doing now. More." I could hear the rough edge to my voice. "I know what you need, Toni. I can give it to you. If that's what you want." The light turned green, but I didn't hit the gas just yet. Instead, I looked at her. "Or I can take you home. What do you want?"

She was still for a moment, and then, without saying a word, she covered my hand with hers and rocked against them both. I could feel the crotch of her pants were damp.

It wasn't enough. I was going to make her wet.

Twenty minutes later, we were standing in my bedroom.

Part of me wished I'd done this back at the club. If we'd taken one of the private rooms, there were so many things I could have done. So many things I could have showed her.

And patience wasn't exactly the utmost of my virtues.

But maybe this was better. I had my playroom if I wanted more toys, but I didn't. I wanted to show her all of the ways I could bring her pleasure, but I knew this was going to be different from anything else I'd experienced. She wasn't a Sub by nature or through training. I couldn't just jump right into this with her.

I had to do it right.

"So..." Toni was looking at the bed. "How do we...?"

I tipped her chin up, using one finger to guide her face upwards until she was looking at me.

"The most important thing you need to know is that this needs trust." I smoothed a hand down her hair. "I need you to trust me. Can you do that?"

"After everything that's happened, you're really asking me to trust you?" She raised an eyebrow. "Maybe this wasn't such a good idea."

No. I couldn't lose her. Not when I was so close.

She blew out a breath, her tongue darting out to wet her lips. I pressed my thumb to the fuller lower one, tracing the damp path.

"You'll need to trust me at least a little or this won't work." It was asking a lot. Maybe too much. But I wanted it. Wanted her.

For a frightening moment, I thought she was going to call the whole thing off. Then she lifted her hands and placed them on my chest, making my heart thud painfully against my ribcage.

"I didn't come here to back away now."

A flare of hope went through me.

"I can trust you enough," she said. "For now."

I supposed that would have to do.

I opened the top drawer of my dresser and drew out a silk scarf. "Silk is a tricky thing. It makes one hell of a restraint, smooth, strong...sensual. But when you tug against the bonds, the knots tighten. It can be dangerous."

Toni's eyes dropped to the black scarf. "Are you warning me?"

"Just letting you know. I'll use something other than silk to restrain you. If that's a problem, you better let me know now." I raised the scarf with both hands.

"Wait." She held up a hand. "I said I trust you a little. I don't trust you enough for that."

I stilled. "For which one?"

She tugged on the silk and I let it go. Her eyes stayed on me as she reached around me and put the scarf on the dresser. Her expression was serious, but not upset.

"I don't trust you enough to blindfold me." Her voice was matter-of-fact. She reached up and ran her finger along my jaw. "And I need to know I can get out of however you restrain me. But I want this."

I nodded. It was strange, having a Sub telling me what I could do to her, but I'd known from the moment I'd first seen Toni that nothing about her would be usual.

"Good." I reached behind her head and pulled out the pins that had held her hair in place. "Now that we have that settled, are you going to trust me to take things from here?"

She nodded and my stomach clenched as I moved around

to stand behind her. It was time.

"I'm in charge now." I spoke softly in her ear. "And I'm going to give you everything you want." My fingers ghosted over her neck. "I might do some things you don't like, or you're not sure if you like. Before I go any further, we need a safe word. Do you know what that means?"

"Vaguely." She glanced over her shoulder at me, a puzzled expression on her face. "Why can't I just say stop?"

I smiled, letting everything I was thinking show on my face and in my eyes. "Because I'm going to do things to you that will make you say all sorts of things. I'm going to lick your pussy and make you come harder than you ever have and then I'll do it again. I'll fill you and drive you to your limit. In my world, stop sometimes means...more. So we need something that only means stop. Something that can't be confused with anything else, and it needs to be something you won't forget."

Her breath came out of her on a rough sigh. Her brow furrowed and I could see her trying to think of something. "I...hell. Ash, my mind is blank." Then she pursed her lips and I could tell she'd thought of something else. "For the record, are you one of those guys who wants his...ah, whatever calling him Master?"

I curled my hand around the side of her neck and drew her back against me. Her pulse beat wildly against my fingers. "You're not the kind of woman who'll ever let any man be her master. I'll settle for control." Dragging my hand from her neck downward, I cupped her breast and she arched against my hand. "What's your favorite color?"

"Pink." It came out immediately.

It surprised me a little. She was feminine, but not in the same way my sister was, and Isadora was the sort of woman with whom I associated pink and pastels. Toni, I would've thought crimson or something like that.

Not that it mattered. We just both had to remember it.

"That's your safe word, then. You'll remember it?"

"Yes."

I rubbed my thumb over her nipple, feeling it harden beneath my touch. One more thing to cover. "Is there anything else you don't want me to do?"

"Nobody else."

I didn't have to guess at what she meant. "Don't worry, Toni. I don't plan on letting another person near you." Just the thought of someone else touching her made my hands want to curl into fists. "Then let's begin."

Her breathing hitched as I settled my hands down on her shoulders, slid them down to free each of the small, round buttons that held her blouse closed.

"There's a mirror across the room. Do you see it?"

"Yes." Her body shuddered.

"Look at it. Look at yourself."

Smoothing her shirt off her shoulders, I studied her for a moment in the mirror. Her eyes met mine and I was again reminded of how this wasn't going to be like any other Dom-Sub experience I'd ever had.

I pressed my lips against the side of her neck, watching as her lips parted. Her breasts rose and fell as her breathing increased. Her bra was plain black cotton, nothing special, but she made it better than the most expensive lingerie.

"Do your panties match?" I asked quietly. It was a rhetorical question. I didn't want an answer. I wanted to find out for myself.

My hands went to the button of her pants and a few seconds later, I had my answer.

Yes. They did match.

Once she was wearing nothing more than her panties and bra, I led her to the bed. Her movements were stiff and I could feel a rush of anxiety going through her. Her nervousness was almost as erotic as the sight of her nearly naked body.

I eased her down on her knees and then slipped off her bra. I took a moment to admire her small, firm breasts, and then straightened to stand over her. As I started to unbutton my shirt, I was glad she'd stopped me from blindfolding her. Nothing could be as hot as seeing her desire-filled eyes running over me as I slowly exposed my chest, and then shrugged the shirt off. I tossed it aside and then smiled down at her.

"I'm going to tie you. For now, your hands will be in front of you."

Chapter 8

Toni

Trepidation had my heart hammering hard and fast against my ribs as Ash bound my hands together in front of me. I didn't know if I was ready for this, but one thing was damn certain, there was no way I would back out now, and I definitely wasn't going to cry pink, either.

It was both a challenge and an enticement, kneeling on the floor as he finished binding my hands together. He paused after he finished and I knew he was giving me the chance to test them and make sure I felt secure. I twisted my hands and felt a bit of give. I wasn't sure how easy it would be to get free, but I didn't feel trapped, so I nodded.

Even though I was still wearing my underwear, I'd never felt so exposed. As if he could sense my discomfort, he cupped my face and ran a thumb over my lower lip. Electricity and heat rushed through me. I was excruciatingly aware of everything. The way the air felt dancing over my skin. The sound of a clock ticking somewhere nearby. The scent of Ash, unmistakably male.

"Your mouth has driven me crazy almost from day one, you know that?" His tone was conversational as he stroked my lips.

Was I supposed to answer? It didn't matter. I wasn't going to ask permission to talk. "I get that a lot."

He chuckled. "I'm not just talking about that smart tongue of yours. I can't tell you how many times I've thought about seeing those pretty lips wrapped around my cock."

Damn. I clenched my thighs together. Lava had replaced all the blood in my body, and I felt like I was going to spontaneously combust if I didn't get relief soon. My mouth was practically watering at the thought of tasting him. When he unzipped his pants, my stomach flipped. As he removed his pants, I saw that my memory hadn't done him justice. He was thick and hard, jutting out from dark curls, a bead of pre-cum glistening at the tip of his cock.

He reached out, his fingers in my hair, hand cupping the back of my neck. "You're going to do what I tell you now, Toni. Say you understand." His voice had taken on that authoritative note that usually made me bristle.

Right now, it turned me on.

"I understand." Saying something smart didn't even come to mind just then. His hand on the back of my neck, the firm pressure, knowing that he was going to control things...it had me all but shaking with want.

"You're going to kiss my cock."

I opened my mouth as he pressed the broad head to my lips, eager to feel him slide across my tongue.

He tugged me back as soon as I tried to take him inside, his fingers twisting in my hair.

"I said kiss it."

Groaning, I held still. Not because I wanted to, but because he didn't release his grip on me. "Do you understand?"

"Yes, Ash," I said automatically.

"Good girl."

This time, I pressed my lips to his cock, but my mind was already set on one thing. When he decided he was going to quit the game, I was going to give him the blowjob of his life. He'd be the one groaning by the time I was done with him.

"Now you can open your mouth and take me inside. Use..."

His breath tripped. I hadn't wasted any time, taking the tip of him into my mouth and pressed my tongue to the pulsing vein on the underside as I slid down on him. I only went down an inch or so and when I came back up, I let him feel the edge of my teeth. He swore and it was all I could do not to grin. I repeated it again, taking him deeper on each successive stroke.

By the fourth one, he had both of his hands gripping my head, reminding me who was in charge, but letting me take control.

"You're good at this," Ash muttered, his voice raw.

He had no idea. One thing about being wicked smart and wicked curious, when you decided you want to learn about something, anything, you did just that.

After the first guy I'd ever slept with told me I was just as bad at giving head as I was being a girlfriend, I'd decided to become an expert. Books and movies of a certain kind could teach a girl all sorts of things. And having access to several of my brothers' girlfriends over a period of a few months hadn't hurt either. After a little over a month, I'd shown up at my ex's dorm room and I'd teased him into letting me in, teased him into playing a game that had resulted in me going down on him until he was right on the edge.

And then I'd left him, laughing as he cursed me for not finishing him off.

It had been one of the most thrilling and satisfying experiences of my life.

But it paled in comparison to this.

Ash's body was tensed and hard. I could feel the tension coming from him, felt his cock swell in my mouth. He was so close...

And then he stopped, pulling his cock out of my mouth

with an almost obscene pop.

I made a sound of protest, watching as he wrapped his hand around his cock and started to stroke. In a rapid rhythm, he dragged his hand down and back up again. The head was swallowed by his fist only to bob back out. Again and again...

Then he came and I gasped as semen jetted up and out across my breasts.

Fuck.

Need was a living, breathing ache inside me. "That was just mean."

"I'm in charge, remember?"

I gasped as he reached down and trailed his fingers across my breasts, his seed slick against my skin.

This was torture. Pure and simple torture. I moaned as he circled my nipple, the sensitive flesh hardening under his touch.

"Are you ready to be good?"

There was a challenge in his voice.

Never one to back down from a dare, I let my head fall back until I was meeting his eyes. With a taunting smile, I said, "Not on your life."

He pinched my nipple, bringing a startled cry to my lips.

Then, in a move so quick, it left me disoriented, I found myself swept up into his arms. "I was hoping you'd say that."

I vaguely recalled seeing a chair when we came into the room. It had been a simple, ladder-back affair, rather plain in the elegant masculinity that was Ash's bedroom. Before I could register much else about it, he was sitting and I was lying across his lap.

Oh shit.

I had only a few seconds to consider the absolute indignity, though, because he laid a hand on my ass and the heat of his palm was shocking and intimate.

"Are you ready?"

His voice held both promise and threat, making me shiver.

"Do your worst." The words came out without me thinking about them and I almost winced the second they left my mouth.

He chuckled. "Toni, you're either going to be really sorry you said that...or really, really glad."

He brought his hand down, hard and fast. It was a shock, the blow of his hand on my ass. I was still processing whether or not it hurt when he did it again.

Then, before anything else happened, he slid his hand between my thighs and pressed his fingers against the wet crotch of my panties. I was shockingly, achingly wet. He circled my clit hard and fast, the rhythm so spot on, I could feel myself getting close to climax already.

He stopped and I cried out in frustration. How could he keep doing that?

He spanked me again, three times in rapid succession. Then he went back to toying with my clit, sliding the thin material of my panties over me until I was hovering right on the edge. Again. And again.

The world narrowed down to just that. Him, the sharp bite of his hand on my skin, and then the sweet bliss of his fingers circling over my clit or occasionally dipping beneath my panties to thrust into my pussy.

After a while, I was no longer rising to the edge of orgasm. I was just there, hovering, but Ash knew exactly when to stop, exactly when to change what he was doing to keep me from going over.

It was torture. I was ready to beg, just so I could come.

And he knew it.

"Do you want to come?"

He stopped touching me when he said it.

That was probably the mistake.

Had he been manipulating my clit or spanking me, who

knew what I might have said. But he slid his hand up to stroke my hair and in those few seconds, my head cleared enough for me to think of how smug he'd be if I gave in so easily.

"Talk to me, baby," he murmured. "Do you want to come?"

"I don't know," I panted as I smirked up at him. "I think I kind of like this."

His voice dropped even lower than before. "Let's see if we can find something else you like."

I arched up in desperation as his teeth scraped over my clit, a wail coming out of me despite my attempt to contain it.

He chuckled and I swore at him. I wasn't so sure I liked this anymore.

But there was no way in hell I was going to use my safe word.

He'd tied me down on the bed, my arms overhead, my legs spread-eagle. Now, he lay between them, the lower half of his face glistening and wet. His eyes burned hot as he looked up at me, grinning wickedly. "That didn't sound like please."

"Damn you," I gasped.

He placed a hand on my belly, his palm hot and rough. The other hand slid between my thighs and I whimpered as he started to stroke the overly sensitive skin. He pushed two fingers in, then pulled them out. In then out. I moved as much as I could, which wasn't much considering the restraints. There was something blisteringly erotic about the entire thing. His hand on my belly while he stroked me. The ropes biting into my skin. The smile on his face. My total inability to control anything.

"Do you want to come?" he asked again.

Fuck it all.

"Yes!"

He surged up onto his knees, one hand rolling on the condom even as he went. And then he was inside me, hard and full and fast. No hesitation, no easing me into it. The orgasm took my breath away. I had been so ready, had hovered on the edge for too long, and him driving into me was too much.

"Fuck, Toni..."

Vaguely, I heard his voice, felt him pumping against me, moving deep and hard, but all that mattered to me in that moment was the climax. I shuddered under him, tightened around him when he withdrew, seeking to draw it out as long as I could.

"That's it, baby. Damn..."

His voice was raw.

He was thick and deep, pushing inside and stretching me, impossibly stretching. I cried out as he withdrew and surged forward again. Blinking up at him, I managed to focus on his face above me.

He had a savage look on his face, and when he saw me watching, his hand grasped my chin, holding my face in place.

"Again," he growled fiercely. "Come again."

I didn't think I'd be able to come like that again – ever.

Moaning, I shifted under him. His thrusts were so powerful, I could feel him all the way to the core of me. I wanted more. I wanted to curl my body around his, wanted to wrap my arms around him and lose myself in him. Then his mouth slammed down on mine, his lips hard and demanding. When his tongue slid into my mouth, I bit him and he growled. And he didn't stop. His tongue tangled and stroked against mine, a sinuous, teasing dance that I thought would drive me insane.

"Please," I whispered when he tore his mouth away. "Please."

There was no response, just the endless driving thrusts that still weren't enough. My body was too full of everything, nerves firing too fast and hard for my body and brain to be able to process.

When he pulled away, I swore. If my hands had been free, I would've grabbed him, held him to me. Since they weren't, I had to settle for glaring at him and calling him a few choice names.

But he was too busy tearing at the ropes that held me down to even respond.

They were made of nylon, he'd told me and they must have been specially designed for this. In a moment, I was free, but before I could sit up and grab him, he flipped me over. Now, on my hands and knees, I sucked in one breath and tried to brace myself because I knew what was coming.

He drove into me, harder and deeper than ever before. A moment later, his hand came down on my ass in a stinging blow and I cried out. He did it again and I could feel the orgasm building up inside me. It was too much. I needed to come.

Ash fisted a hand in my hair and yanked, pulling me upward so that my back arched at an impossible angle. "Tell me what you want," he snarled the words into my ear, a command I couldn't deny.

"I want to come. Damn you! Make me come."

"Bossy, bossy." He closed one hand around my wrist and guided my hand between my thighs. "You want to come, then do it."

I was shaking as I started to stroke my clit. And then my eyes caught the movement of our reflection in the mirror. Fuck. I'd never watched myself with someone before and it took my breath away. A stunning display of him taking me, his eyes on my hand as he waited for me to do what he'd said.

I let my head fall back against his chest as he rolled his hips and surged up inside me once more. My back arched, pushing my breasts forward. His gaze moved there and it was like he'd touched me, my nipples tightening, hardening.

Slowly, I slid my hand up, circled one nipple. His next thrust was harder, lifting me off the bed. I cried out again and shifted my hand to my other breast, cupping it in my palm and staring into his eyes as I pinched my nipple.

Ash snarled.

I felt the balance of power between us shifting.

I smiled at him as I dragged my hand down my torso and let my fingers brush against the curls between my thighs. In the mirror, I could see him, the thickness of his penis as it speared into me. I groaned and pushed back against him as best as I could. Because he was so much taller than me, I had no leverage. Instinctively, I lifted my arm and curled my hand around his neck, using the strength of his body to grind myself against him.

"Toni..."

The guttural sound of his voice drew my gaze back to his eyes.

He was still staring at the hand that hovered between my thighs.

I hadn't done much yet.

But now...

Slowly, I let my fingers brush against my clit. It was swollen, so engorged that one touch was almost torture. Whimpering, I did it again, the contact hesitant. I was so aroused, the line between pleasure and pain had all but disappeared and I didn't know how much more I could take.

Ash swore and caught my wrist with one hand, pinning it to my belly. His other hand replaced mine and I wailed as he flicked his forefinger against my clit. It was a blunt, hard contact, and the sensitive, nerve-filled flesh felt like it would explode. Then he did it again, and again, each one drawing a scream from me.

His cock swelled inside me and he growled my name.

In the next breath, we were both coming. My vision started to gray around the edges and we swayed forward. At the last moment, Ash shifted and took us down so that we hit the bed on our sides. He curled up against my back and murmured my name again. His lips pressed against the base of my neck.

I tried not to think much of it.

I really, really tried.

But that sexy, sated sound had my heart clenching up into a hard little knot.

This had probably been the best and worst mistake of my life.

That was my last clear thought before exhaustion swept up to claim me.

Chapter 9

Ash

Awareness came slowly, but I didn't open my eyes. Not yet.

I was laying on my bed and although it was quiet, I knew I wasn't alone.

That was strange, to say the least. I didn't bring women home with me often and when I did, they never stayed. It was always fuck and then good-bye.

Still, in those odd minutes between sleeping and waking, I couldn't find anything really wrong about the female body curled up against me. She was slim and small, my arms wrapped around her to hold her back to my chest. Certain parts of my anatomy already appreciated the feel of her. My cock was at attention, nearly painfully hard.

As I drifted closer and closer to wakefulness, she made a grumbling noise, then sighed and wedged her ass more firmly against me.

It was instinct to catch her thigh, raising it high enough for me to push inside. She was damp. Not wet, not yet, and her pussy clung to me, dragging against my cock as I rocked into her.

A low moan escaped, but I knew she wasn't awake.

Gripping her hip, I pushed up onto my elbow. Her hair was trapped under us, pinning her head down. It felt soft and satiny under my arm. I wanted to wrap it around my fists, my wrists, use it to hold her captive as I thrust my cock into her mouth...

"Toni."

The name slipped out without any conscious acknowledgement of who she was, her presence still vague in my half-asleep state. She whimpered and my stomach clenched. Her hand closed around mine, the one gripping her hip.

It was the prick of her nails into my flesh that finally jerked me into full awareness. My eyes finally flew open as she rotated her hips and sobbed out my name.

"Ash, please..."

Common sense screamed at me to stop now.

Lust screamed louder, and I rolled her flat onto her belly. Without missing a stroke, I pulled her to her knees and thrust deep, hard. The rhythmic sound of my hips slapping against her ass filled the room. It was underscored by the harsh, hungry noises that slid past her lips. She clamped down on me, tight, her muscles milking me as she started to come.

Pressing my hand against her back just between her shoulders, I rode her harder, making her cry out. Just as her climax began to ebb, my balls drew tight in warning and then the orgasm slammed into me. I ground down against her, drawing out the pleasure crashing through me. My eyes squeezed closed and I gritted my teeth to keep from saying her name again.

I wanted to sink down on top of her, cuddle her up against me.

Instead, as I began to come down from my high, I withdrew.

That was when I realized I'd made a mistake. Another mistake. Last night had been a series of them. Touching her this morning had set off another chain reaction of mistakes, culminating in this.

I hadn't worn a fucking rubber.

"I need to get dressed," I said shortly as I climbed off the bed.

From the corner of my eye, I saw Toni sitting up, but I didn't spare her a look as I strode to my bathroom. I mentally cursed myself for losing control. How could I have been so stupid?

I was a hundred different kinds of fool.

From the very first moment I'd asked her to come to Olympus with me, I'd been messing up.

Before that, really.

I should have just made my apologies at the police station and left. I could've had someone take her purse to her, and we could have continued on in whatever non-relationship we had.

Instead, I'd told her about the club, given her an inside look at just how perverse my sexual life was, and not only that, I'd given her a taste. Taken a taste for myself.

No, not a taste.

She was a fucking banquet.

"Idiot," I muttered, viciously scrubbing at my hair while the shower pounded down on me. I could smell her on me. The sweet female scent clung to my skin, and part of me hadn't even wanted to shower, because I didn't want that smell to disappear. I didn't want her to disappear.

Dammit.

I'd messed this up so bad, I didn't know how to begin to fix it, but I had to.

Toni worked for Isadora.

No matter what my doubts were telling me, my sister would be found. She would come home, and she'd need normalcy when it happened. Toni had been there when she disappeared, so Toni would be here when Isadora came back. They'd be able to pick up where they'd left off.

But I had to make sure I didn't do something stupid like touch her again. Sleep with her again. Kiss her.

Remember how her face had looked as she stared down at the shibari display playing itself out in front of us. The look of avid hunger as a young Submissive was hogtied and two Dominants worked her up to a fever pitch. They'd done the same to Toni, all without even touching her.

I'd have to forget that. Forget all of it.

I closed my eyes. Like hell.

Forgetting any of that would be just about impossible. So what I needed to do was just stay away from her. That would be easier said than done, but it wouldn't be impossible.

I just had to make sure she understood that this couldn't happen again.

There were perfectly logical reasons why any of it had happened to begin with. Toni was a smart woman. Chances are, she was out there brooding over the very things that had me on edge.

All I had to do was go out there, talk to her, lay it all out.

I could be a grown-up about this, and I knew she could be. She'd proven to be the more mature of the two of us time and again.

With that plan in mind, I headed out of the bathroom, a towel around my waist. Toni was still sitting in the bed, the sheets pulled over her chest. She caught sight of me and smiled.

I acted like I didn't see as I strode past her over to the dresser. It would be better to do this once I was dressed. Having rational discussions while naked just seemed to put a man on uneven ground. At least most of her was covered. I couldn't have done this if I saw those perfect breasts.

Since it was Sunday and I had no plans to go anywhere, I just pulled on a T-shirt and a pair of jeans, leaving my feet bare. It seemed best to get clothes on as quickly as possible...before I decided to climb back into bed and try for round three.

Once I was dressed, I turned and found that Toni had slid soundlessly off the bed and was gathering up her clothes.

Shit.

Her ass was amazing.

"Last night was a mistake."

I blurted the words out and nearly winced at how they sounded. I'd mentally rehearsed this several times over in the bathroom, but I sounded like this conclusion had just suddenly occurred to me.

She looked over at me, cocking her head as she straightened and turned. Holding her clothes casually, she studied me. "Which part was a mistake?"

"All of it."

"I see." She shrugged. "Okay. I'm going to use your bathroom if you don't mind."

That was it. No tears, no shouting. Not even a 'fuck you.' Nothing except 'I'm going to use your bathroom.'

That was...well. Perfect. My little speech that I'd rehearsed seemed kind of wasted now. Wasted and pointless. Big relief, really.

Toni strode past me and I caught her arm.

Immediately, I wanted to haul her against me and cover that smiling mouth with mine. Put her up against the wall and fuck her again. Fuck her hard and fast and then slow, soft. I wanted to make her moan, then make her beg. I wanted to be awake enough to feel those silken walls sliding against my bare cock.

"You understand, Toni." I managed an easy smile despite the lust that was turning my brain to mush. "You work for Isadora. When she comes home, I don't want things to be weird."

"Ash." She gave me a lazy smile. Then she reached up

and patted my cheek. "I understand completely. I'm going to shower now. Then I'll get out of your hair."

She patted me on the fucking cheek.

It was still burning me fifteen minutes later when she came strolling out of the bathroom. She had a towel wrapped around her and I almost swallowed my tongue as a bead of water slid down her neck and then the slope of her left breast before soaking into the towel.

Professional, I reminded myself. I was going to be professional about this.

"Oh." She stopped as she saw me, frowning a little. "I thought you'd already be doing...well, whatever you do. I just wanted to grab the bag of clothes Doug washed for me."

She said nothing else as she walked past me and out of the bedroom.

In a towel.

My towel.

My gaze zeroed in on her barely-covered ass and my fingers itched to grab her hips, pull off the towel. I wanted to turn her over my knee and watch her skin turn that same rosy pink it had last night.

Shit.

She had me twisted in knots, and all she'd done was walk out of the bathroom. In a fucking towel. For some reason, that pissed me off.

"You know, I have a robe in there," I pointed out, following her out into the hall.

She shot me a wide, innocent look. "I wouldn't want to be

presumptuous, Mr. Lang. Borrowing something so personal seems rather rude."

I scowled at her. "But you're fine walking around my house wearing my towel."

She looked down at the towel, and then up at me. "Good point."

I knew what she was going to do before she did it and I took a step forward. "Dammit, Toni!"

Too late. She tossed the towel at me and it hit me in the face. Instantly, my head flooded with the lush, warm scent of her, and the pulse of lust turned into a roaring inferno. I dragged the towel off my face and threw it in the vicinity of my bedroom.

She was already several feet ahead of me, naked as a jaybird, walking toward the stairs.

"Toni, you are not walking around my house naked!"

"Don't worry. I know where the bag is, Mr. Lang. I'm trying to be quick, though. I want to get out of your hair so you can forget all about that mistake." Her voice was cheerful.

The look she fired at me as she started down the stairs was anything but.

I caught up with her just as she entered the small sitting room and I froze in the doorway. My heart thudded to a stop, though, because she suddenly bent over. My cock went on red alert at the sight. Her firm ass flexing. Her naked cunt was open. Two steps and I could be inside her...

She straightened and glanced back at me. "Don't worry, Mr. Lang. Two minutes and I'll be gone."

"Sir, may I...oh, dear."

Doug stood in the doorway, his eyes wide. Wide and glazing over. I covered them with my hand as new flash of anger went through me. Anger that someone else was seeing her...

"Toni, get your ass dressed."

"I am, Mr. Lang. I'm sorry, Doug." She smiled again, still so cheerful. But the smile had an edge of violence to it. "Mr. Lang and I had an encounter last night, but he realizes now it was a mistake. I think he wanted to keep things professional after he had me arrested, but didn't quite manage it."

"Yes..." Doug's voice had a dazed tone to it.

I shot him a look. He leaned slightly to the side.

"Doug!" I snapped at him.

"Sir!" He turned his back, clearing his throat. Every inch of his visible skin was flushed. "Miss Toni, is there anything...shall I fetch anything else for you?"

"Nope!" She shimmied into her pants, sans underwear. The top went on over her braless breasts just as I recalled her bra and panties were up in my room.

"I can get your–"

"I promised minutes," she said, cutting me off as she turned towards me. "I'm down to one."

I sucked in a breath. Her nipples stabbed into the thin material of her sapphire blue top. Shit. There was no way I was going to let her go out like that.

"Doug. Please have a car brought around–"

"There." She shoved her feet into her shoes. "Okay. I'm done. Later!"

Later?

Dumbfounded, I watched as she sailed toward the front door. Surprised by the nonchalant farewell, I almost didn't move in time. Lurching after her, I caught her arm. "You're not leaving yet. We need to talk."

She lowered her gaze to my arm, studying it for a moment before looking up at me with those cool eyes. Her voice lost its cheerful quality and went straight to flat. "No. I don't think we do. You established we'd made a mistake. Now if I've made a false presumption and you don't want to pretend it never happened, that us having sex last night wasn't the mistake you were talking about...?"

Her words trailed off and she stared at me expectantly.

I opened my mouth. I could talk my way through this. It was what I did.

But nothing came out.

"Okay, then. We talked. It's settled." She patted my hand, then tugged it off. "I should go." She took a couple steps and then paused, throwing her final comments over her shoulder. "And, by the way, you should probably start calling me Ms. Gallagher. We want to keep things professional, right?"

She was gone before I had a chance to say another thing.

It took me nearly a full minute to get the taste of my size twelves out of my mouth. Just how had I managed to mess this up so badly? I hadn't just shoved my foot in my mouth. I'd shoved both feet in, past my ankles and all the way to my knees.

Shit.

Chapter 10

Toni

There were days when there was only one way to handle all of the craziness inside, and I knew that was where I was going very soon. At the moment, however, I sat on the subway with my arms wrapped around myself, staring out the window as if mesmerized by the sight of the tunnel speeding by my window.

When a guy took the seat next to mine and slouched down low, spreading his legs wide the way guys did when trying to direct attention to a certain part of their anatomy, I ignored him. He tried to talk to me and I deliberately put my earbuds in, even though I didn't turn them on. He called me a bitch, got up and wandered off to try his tactics somewhere else. Mentally counting down the stops, I prayed nobody else would settle in the now vacant seat. I'd never been in less of a mood to socialize.

Ashford Lang was a bastard. A stupid, self-centered bastard.

I should have just punched him again. Maybe a knee in the crotch.

Why in the hell had I gone to Olympus with him?

And why had I…immediately…

I closed my eyes and tried to pretend I wasn't remembering every detail of the past night. No, the past day.

Even him showing up at the station house. The stilted apology, us sparring down in the gym. Those hot, torrid moments at Olympus...and then even hotter moments that had followed at his house last night. And again this morning.

I hadn't been expecting any diehard declaration of love, but for him to go and turn all asshole on me again just seconds after he'd woken me up by sliding inside me...

The car lurched to a stop. At the last moment, I realized it was my stop and I darted through the doors just in time. Moving through the ever-jostling crowd, I emerged out into the brilliance of another hot New York day. It was Sunday, I realized. Since my usual Friday evening family dinner had been interrupted by my stint in jail, I was supposed to go today. But if I wanted to deal with the family's response to what had happened, I'd need to work out some of my issues first.

I hurried home and immediately changed into my own workout gear.

It took me less than ten minutes from the time I hit my lobby to be back outside again, earbuds in place. The music was loud, blasting the hardest, fastest rock I could find. I settled into a quick pace and tried to outrun the anger. I couldn't, but between the lingering exhaustion from yesterday, and my worry about Isadora, I knew I could at least run myself to empty.

After five miles on the city streets, I was back at my house and in the shower. As the hot water beat down on me, I willed my brain to empty. When I was done showering, I planned to lay down and grab a nap. Then I'd go to my parents' house, hang out with my family and recharge. Maybe tonight, I'd go somewhere and get a drink. Or just come home and read, have a glass of wine. Anything to unwind and try to forget about the past few days.

About Ash.

That was the plan.

After I talked to my brother about a slightly uncomfortable subject.

Vic leaned against the railing of the small deck my parents had built onto the back of their house this past spring, studying my phone. After a minute, he frowned at it. "That's the best picture you got? You couldn't have had them email you a decent one?"

"I'm not even supposed to have this copy, Vic. I need to keep it quiet that I have it, but..."

Vic cocked a brow, studying me with his dark eyes.

I forced myself to ask the question I knew he didn't want to answer. "Can you show it around?"

Vic looked away, the set of his jaw grim. "Show it where, Sis? It's not like I..."

"Vic, you still have connections. I know you do." My voice was soft but I wasn't going to let it go.

He pushed my phone back into my hand and shoved away from the fence. He paced across the planks, putting as much distance between us as the small deck allowed. Long moments passed before he said anything else. "I'll do what I can. But you stay out of it, Toni, okay? Kidnapping...hell, this isn't some prank. This is serious. Let me talk to some people, but you keep out of it. That's the deal."

I folded my arms and scowled. "I'm not an idiot, Vic."

"Nah. That's my job," he said wryly.

Joining him at the railing, I shoulder-bumped him. "You're not an idiot."

"Eh, I suppose I've wised up some." He hooked an arm around my neck. "How are you doing?"

"I'm...okay." Resting my head against his shoulder, I sighed. It was the truth. Sort of. I was mostly okay. I was tired and sore, and not just from the sparring or the running. Of course, I wasn't going to tell Vic that.

I loved my brother, but that would be a total overshare.

Chapter 11

Toni

If I was smart, I would've stayed home.

Or I'd have called my dad and talked to him about coming to work at the company for a while. I wasn't any good with electricity like my dad or Deacon or Franky, but I could file invoices, take and make calls, and it wasn't like I couldn't learn fast.

That had been one of Deacon's points when suggesting the personal assistant gig to begin with. My intelligence should've been an asset with pretty much anything I wanted to do, but I was beginning to suspect I was lacking in the common sense area.

Case in point, was I taking my own advice about work?
Nope.

I was on my way over to the Lang house, and I had no doubt I'd see Ash. He hadn't gone into work since Isadora disappeared. I couldn't say I blamed him. If something happened to one of my brothers, I wouldn't want to go to work either. No, actually, I would work, because I'd never be able to just sit and do nothing.

Then again, I didn't think Ash was doing nothing. I was pretty sure he was spending quite a bit of his free time drinking. The man was a mess, and not just because of the way he was acting around me. In his shoes, controlling an empire worth millions or billions, it probably didn't sit well not being able to control things.

She wasn't my family and I hated not being in control.

I tugged at the trim black pants I'd pulled on, paired with a simple white tunic shirt. The clothes were plainer than what I normally wore, and they hid my body well. So well that I'd almost turned around twice so I could change, prove to myself that I didn't need the armor.

Then again, Ash was being an ass, and if I needed some sort of armor to protect myself around him, then fine. He was the one freaking out about the other night, not me. I'd...loved what we'd done. I could come to crave it.

With somebody else, of course. No way, no how, was I going to subject myself to that kind of shit with him again. I was done with making stupid decisions. I was so...done.

Tired already, I started up the subway steps. Even though I still had a good block or so to walk before I reached the house, it was already so much quieter here. This part of New York was like a world away from what I knew. The only thing that seemed the same were the taxis and even at this time of morning, at the tail end of rush hour, the yellow cars that swarmed around the streets of the city like hornets seemed to be a little less...swarmy here. Except I knew that just because the place was wealthy didn't mean it was any better than the place I'd grown up.

Isadora had been targeted, in part, because of her money. These walls and that money didn't promise any more peace or security because of it. Or despite it.

The steps up to the Lang house seemed more daunting than normal, and when I went to knock, my palms were damp. I resisted the urge to swipe them down my pants. Relief flooded me as Doug was the one to open the door instead of Ash. Not really a surprise, but still a relief.

I eased inside as he nodded at me.

The quiet of the house wrapped around me like a tomb. "Has there been anything new?" I asked, my voice a bare whisper.

"No." He gave a somber shake of his head. "If there is, rest assured I'll call you. You have my word."

Impulsively, I kissed his cheek.

He blushed red. "Thank you."

And then I realized he was staring at me. And probably what he was remembering. Now I was the one blushing as I realized one very unintentional consequence of my previous impulsiveness.

This could quickly become very embarrassing.

But all he did was give me a soft smile. "You know you don't need to keep coming out here," he said quietly. "It's kind of you. You're a good friend to Isadora. But this isn't your responsibility."

"This isn't about responsibility." I shrugged. "I'm not sleeping very well at night. I'm worried for her."

I might have said something else, but the hair on the back of my neck stood on end and I realize Doug and I were no longer alone. *He* was here. I had no desire to give Ash any more of my attention. He had already taken too much of it. I reached out and caught Doug's hand, giving it a quick squeeze.

"I heard back from some of the contacts Isadora wanted me to reach out to, so I'm going to try to see if I can get a little bit more work done on that project she put me on."

"Of course." He nodded at me. "Let me know if you need anything else."

The look he gave me as he turned to walk away looked strangely sympathetic. As if he knew Ash wouldn't let me simply ignore him.

"Why are you here?" Ash asked as Doug left the room. The question was surly.

"What do you think?" I shot him a sour look as I pulled

the strap of my purse over my head and put it down on the nearest table. Without bothering to look at him, I moved over to the desk where Isadora kept the laptop we worked on.

As I moved, I was acutely aware of Ash's gaze locked on my back. I almost called out for Doug, thinking that having him around would be useful. I could lie, say I was hungry and ask him to fix me something to eat. But I wasn't a coward. I never had been. I wasn't going to let Ashford Lang turn me into one.

Dropping down into the chair behind the desk, I glanced over at Ash. He stood in the doorway, wearing casual clothes that looked entirely not casual on him. That long, sexy frame could wear just about anything. It didn't seem fair. His hair was rumpled, reminding me of how it felt to fist my hands in it the first night we were together.

"Yes?" I forced myself to look directly at him. I just hoped I could keep my voice cool enough to get through this conversation.

"Why are you here?" he asked again. "You spent most of last week fussing around and not doing much of anything."

"I spent most of last week finishing up what I could do with the information I had," I replied in as bland a voice as I could manage. "Since then, however, I received information back on the queries I'd sent out for Isadora, so now I can get a little more work done. She did hire me to do a job. The job is still there and I'd like to have some progress to report when she gets back."

Ash reached up and rubbed at his jaw. It was rough with stubble. His eyes were heavy-lidded, and the overall look was of a man who had just rolled out of bed. I doubted that was the case. I didn't think he had been sleeping all that much since Isadora disappeared. Although he had slept the other night...

Don't think about that, I told myself.

Thinking about our time together was the absolute worst

thing I could do. Under his gaze, I could feel the tension growing inside me and I had to resist the urge to squirm on the chair. Heat gathered inside my belly, a burgeoning inferno, and I knew I needed to get it under control. The man was too observant about certain things. I didn't want him knowing anything about what I was thinking.

Of course, he knew anyway. An answering flare of heat lit his eyes and he came closer. He stopped in front of the desk and leaned forward, bracing his hands on the edge. He gave me a wicked smirk. "You rushed out of here so fast yesterday morning. Now here you are, already back. You looking for more, Toni?"

It wasn't easy for me to be stunned into silence, but he'd managed it.

I wasn't shy, and I wasn't particularly naïve. Plus I had four brothers who'd made it their business to try to embarrass me, especially around cute guys. I'd learned early on how to brush things off. But Ashford Lang had just managed a near impossible feat. For a span of maybe fifteen seconds, I couldn't utter a single word.

Then anger burned away the shock. Shoving up right, I glared at him across the desk. "You are a monumental asshole. You know that, Ashford? An asshole. You're also an arrogant son of a bitch!" He opened his mouth to say something, and I held up a hand. "No! You don't get to talk to me that way!"

The look on his face was almost laughable. I doubted he'd had a lot of people in his life who'd raised their voices to him.

But I was too mad to be amused just then.

I kept going. "You don't get to talk right now. You had a chance when I walked in the door and you decided to be a dick about it. It's my turn to talk. I'm not your employee or subordinate. And I'm sure as hell not here for a booty call. You want to be freaked out about what happened? That's your problem. But you're not gonna talk to me like I'm one your little subs from the club. I'm not gonna put up with it, do you hear me?"

He stared at me, eyes glittering. Then, as I was bracing myself for what was bound to be one ugly argument, he turned on his heel and walked out. I sat in my chair and blew out a breath.

Yeah. No doubt about it. I might've had an IQ that was up there in the stratosphere, but sometimes I really wasn't all that smart.

Chapter 12

Ash

I took a shower. I lingered a little longer than normal because seeing Toni did what it always did and I wasn't about to walk down there with a hard-on. And I couldn't leave because I'd planned to stay home in case there was another phone call. Not that it was necessary since I had already arranged for any calls to be directed to my cell phone. But I felt more in control if I was actually here.

However, if Toni was here, I couldn't be. I couldn't even be in the same fucking house, no matter how far away she was from me. I could feel her.

Yet I didn't want to tell her to leave. She was here for Isadora and it felt...right. It felt right that somebody else was here for my sister. I couldn't tell her to leave. Besides, some crazy part of me liked knowing she was here. It was that same stupid part of me that had enjoyed waking up with her in my bed.

It had nothing to do with common sense, and everything to do with some base instinct that I didn't even know I possessed. The same base instinct that had me locked in my shower while I fantasized about the woman downstairs.

I dragged my hand up and down my cock, imagining that I had Toni in front of me. On her knees. Her hands tied behind her back, those wide blue eyes staring up at me as I slowly fed my cock into her mouth. She was so good at it...and she enjoyed it. My penis jerked in my hand and I gritted my teeth.

Thinking about her had me coming quick, maybe too quick, because I wanted to draw it out. But it was over and done in minutes, and then the shower was washing away the evidence. I hadn't come that fast since I'd been a teenager. Frankly, it was annoying.

Yet another reason to get the hell out of the house and stay out while Toni was here.

Less than thirty minutes after she'd arrived, I was jogging back down the stairs, dressed in a suit and ready to go to work. Well, not particularly ready, but I was going anyway. I doubted I would get much done at the office, but if I stayed here, I knew I'd say more things to Toni that I didn't necessarily mean.

Or I'd do things that I'd end up regretting.

I'd definitely enjoy them at the moment, and I was already itching to do them again, but all of this had to stop.

A relationship with her just wasn't possible. I didn't have sex with employees, and while she wasn't my employee, she was close enough that it just wasn't going to happen again.

And I didn't do relationships at all. Not in years. Not since...

I paused at the door, and no sooner had I stopped she looked up. An eyebrow rose. The look in them was so icy, it was a wonder frost didn't fill the room.

"Yes?" she asked coolly.

If I'd thought her eyes were cold, then her voice was doubly so. An apology came to my lips, but I grabbed it back. It was better this way. I'd been a jerk, and I knew it, but keeping distance between us was for the best.

"Are you planning on being here for most of the day?" I asked.

"Why?"

There was no softness left in her now, no humor, no gentleness, no understanding. She managed to pull off the business-like exterior that I'd been struggling, and failing, to find.

There was absolutely no emotion to her right now and I hated it.

She picked up her phone and studied it. Hardly anybody wore a watch anymore, except those smartwatches. It was always the phone. Toni pursed her lips as she continued to gaze at the screen although what took so long to judge the time, I had no idea. Then she shrugged.

"I'll be here until mid-afternoon at least. Unless..." she paused and arched her eyebrow. "You would rather I leave, Mr. Lang."

She said my name mockingly, somehow managing to turn it into an insult. I had no idea how she did that. She could probably tell me I was the best fuck she'd ever had and she'd still manage to pull off that snide, insulting tone.

"You don't need to leave." I slid my hands into my pockets. If I didn't keep them occupied, I was likely to wrap it around her neck and throttle her. Or something worse. "Actually, I need you here, if you don't mind. Since you're already occupied with...well, occupied, I have to go into the office. I need somebody by the phone."

I didn't really need somebody by the phone, but I'd feel better if somebody was here. Somebody besides the staff. They all cared about Isadora too, but it wasn't the same thing. And since she'd already talked to the kidnapper...

"Are you expecting a call?"

I opened my mouth, then snapped it shut. In the few seconds between her comment and the time I forced myself to calm down, I saw the glint in her eyes. She was going to twist that knife as much as she could. I'd bet my left nut that she knew exactly what the problem was, exactly why I was being such an ass.

"Are you able to stay or not?" I kept my voice calm this time, casual. If she could pull of that ice princess routine, I could manage some control myself.

"As I already said, I'm available until mid-afternoon."

With a terse nod, I turned and left.

As I walked to my car, I couldn't stop from thinking just why in the hell she had to leave by mid-afternoon. She never had to leave at a specific time when she'd been here with Isadora.

Was she meeting someone? A male someone? Who wasn't her brother? A man who wouldn't treat her like...

I shut the thought down before it could finish. It didn't matter. The vicious tug of denial and envy was already there.

I didn't want there to be another man in her life.

"What do you think, Ashford?"

It took me a good thirty seconds to realize he'd been speaking to me.

He being one Anton Phillips. He was the son of the man who owned the law firm that represented Phenecie-Lang on all fronts and they'd come by to talk to me about...something.

I hadn't been able to hold a thought in my head all day.

Every time I closed my eyes, it was like I saw a giant calendar and the days that had passed since Isadora had disappeared were slowly being X'd off with a blood red marker.

Over and over.

The marker would hit today and then it would start all over again.

How was this happening?

And why was I here?

As Anton opened his mouth again, I held up a hand. "Look, I don't think now is the ideal time for this meeting." We'd kept Isadora's kidnapping from the media, and I planned on continuing down that road as long as I could, but I needed something. "My head isn't on the job today, Anton. I've had family issues going on recently and, to be honest, I shouldn't have even come in."

This time, it was Anton's father who stopped him from speaking.

Brooks Phillips was the reason I continued to use the firm. Once he was gone, I'd find someplace else, because I just didn't like Anton. I had to wonder how a man like Brooks had managed to raise a kid as spineless and useless as Anton. But then again, my parents had raised a total bastard – me – and a total sweetheart – Isadora.

And, of course, it was her who'd been taken.

"Are you feeling well, Son?" Brooks asked, his voice gentle.

Usually, I didn't let people call me 'son,' but with Brooks, I didn't mind. He didn't say it in a condescending way.

"I've been better, Sir." I managed a tired smile as I stood up from behind the desk. I went around to shake his hand before looking at Anton. "I know you've got your heart set on me endorsing this charity event, but I need to look at it harder and I just can't right now."

It took a few more minutes to get them out of there. It took even less for me to wrap up what little I had going on. I couldn't pretend to work anymore.

I wanted to go home. I wanted to see Toni, assuming she was even still there. But I couldn't do that. I'd wedged some distance between us and it needed to stay there.

I'd go to the club. If nothing else, I could find a Sub and

burn off some of this restless energy.

Chapter 13

Toni

"The clock strikes four, he'll walk through the door and then he'll call me a whore..."

I made up a nonsensical tune to the beat of Hickory Dickory Dock as I checked one more thing off my list.

It was edging up on three-thirty and Ash was usually home by four. I wanted to finish up before then so I could be ready to go as soon as he stepped inside. I didn't want to have another confrontation.

Well, part of me did. Part of me wanted to go head to head with him, challenge him, make him back down. But I was afraid if I kept pushing things, I'd be the one backing down. Not just about how rude he was, but about everything.

He'd pushed me away, then he'd reached for me. I knew that's how things would go if I faced off with him. He'd do it again and again. And I'd take him back again and again.

And I'd grow to hate myself because of it.

I had too much self-respect for that.

I had to get out of here.

Gathering up my files and notes, I took a few minutes to document everything that had been done. When Isadora came back, she'd want to know, and I was going to make sure she didn't miss out on anything.

Soon, I thought.

She'd come soon.

She had to...right?

On my way out, I lingered at the door a few moments longer than normal. But I wasn't really waiting for him.

That was what I told myself. I didn't believe it, though.

Deacon and Franky were settled down, doing the responsible daddy thing. Part of me was wistful with envy at the lives they had. The one between those two was Kory. He didn't even live in New York anymore. In high school, he'd decided that he didn't want to live in the city, and he'd gone to a small arts school in Ohio before settling in Michigan.

Then there was Vic. I knew it sometimes confounded people, but out of all of my brothers, the one I was closest to was Vic. We were only three years apart in age, and we'd fought like crazy growing up. For a while, I'd hated him a little. I would have gone to one of the best Ivy League colleges with a full ride if it hadn't been for him.

But Vic wasn't the man now that he'd been then. He was a different man now, a better one.

It wasn't much surprise that I knew exactly where to find him that evening. He'd finished work – I still wasn't entirely sure what he did, and sometimes, I thought it was better that I didn't. I had my brother's schedule memorized. Twice a month, he got to see his son. Fridays, he and I hit the same place: our parents' house for dinner. Once or twice a week, he'd hit a pub.

But Mondays and Thursdays, Vic had one place he'd go and that was the basketball court in the park near where we'd grown up.

Moving up to the fence, I curled my fingers around the chain link and watched the game in progress. A few people called my name or shouted greetings. I waved but kept my focus on the game.

It was pretty obvious I couldn't get Ash or Isadora out of my head on my own, so I needed help.

Nothing did it quite like family.

I hadn't been there more than ten minutes before Deacon showed up.

"You in the mood to kick his ass?" My oldest brother slid me a sidelong look, a smile crooking at his lips.

"Eh, well. It was this or go pick a fight." I shrugged. "I figured I should avoid getting arrested again since I'd lucked out Friday."

"Try to avoid punching cops in the future, sweetheart." He hooked an arm around my neck and hugged me.

I snorted.

The game ended and Deacon and I moved onto the court. Deacon met Vic's questioning look with a cocky grin before he looked at me.

"What are you up to, Toni? Hanging out with that loser?" He jutted his chin toward Deacon and fired the ball at me.

I caught it and shot it back almost as hard. "Was in the mood for a game. You up?"

"Any time."

I didn't know when Franky hit the court, but I heard his wife, Yvette, hollering out my name in the distance. "Kick his ass!"

"Which one!" I shouted back. Then I was scrambling to grab the ball before Deacon had it, and all I had in my head was the game.

Two long, sweaty hours later, I collapsed back against the door of my apartment and closed my eyes. My legs felt like noodles and my arms had turned into cement weights.

If nothing else, a couple of hours with my brothers were able to accomplish something nothing else could. My brain felt empty now and I was so tired, it was an effort just to walk across the room and lock myself into the bathroom to shower.

Not even twenty minutes later, I collapsed face down on the bed.

I slid into dreams.

And in my dreams, I slid into Ash's arms.

Although, really, it wasn't his arms that held me so enraptured.

It was...everything.

Chapter 14

Toni

I couldn't move my arms.
I couldn't move my legs.
I could move my head, though.
My head and my mouth were under my control, as were my eyes.
When Ash had told me that he'd spank me if I didn't watch my mouth, I'd laughed.
Then I'd moaned.
Moaned, shook, shuddered...
His hand came down on my ass and the hot lick of pleasure was so intense, I almost couldn't stand it. His voice slid over me like liquid sex.
"You're going to come. Don't try to fight it. You're going to come and I'm going to feel it. I'm going to draw it out and you're going to be wet and hot..."
"Just do it already!" I snarled.
He laughed and the sound of his laugh wrapped around me, sending tendrils of heat racing through me and I wanted to reach up, grab him by the back of his head and pull him down so I could kiss him.
His mouth on mine. His tongue rubbing against mine.
His hands...then his hands were on me. Fingers plucking at my nipples until I was arched up and whimpering. His knee came between my thighs.
I'd been on my belly. Bound. Tied.
Now, I was free and I intended to take advantage of it.
"Kiss me." I shoved my hands into his hair.
His cock was inside me. Stroking deep and hard, stretching me and burning me. He was hotter than he'd ever been, his hands firmer. He gripped my hips as he lifted me up,

then dragged me down. "You're going to come," he said again. "Come for me."

An electronic peel cut through my head, out of place and discordant.

I twitched.

It sounded again.

My phone. Shit.

The dream shattered and I jerked upright in bed as the phone rang again.

Grabbing at it, I brought it to my ear. "What?" I demanded.

The need to come was riding me hard and I was breathless, aching and empty.

"Toni."

The sound of Vic's voice was like the coldest of cold showers. Nothing like a brother to cool the libido.

Groaning, I flopped back on the bed. "Is this urgent?"

"No. I just…"

"Fine. Call back in twenty." I slammed the phone down and flopped back on the bed, desperate to take care of the need twisting inside me.

Memories flooded me as I slid my hand down the middle of my body. There were dreams and there were dreams. Sometimes, you just had to let your body have what it needed.

"You are so not a morning person."

I looked at the clock before answering. "The clock might read two a.m. but that doesn't make it morning. You're calling in the no-man's land hours, pal. What's the deal?"

"Well..."

Blowing out a breath, I reached for patience. When it came to my brothers, especially Vic, patience was crucial. Fortunately, I'd had a lifetime of practice.

"If you're mad I kicked your ass on the court..."

"You wish," Vic shot back at me, his voice amused. "No, it's just that picture you gave me. It's weird, Toni. I've been asking, and I've been asking a lot of people, the right people. Nobody knows him. Nobody's seen him. That's not normal."

"What do you mean, it's not normal?" Knuckling at my eyes, I tried to coax my brain into waking up. I had to get better about this. There would be times I'd be dragged out of sound sleep in the coming years and I'd have to make some seriously crucial decisions. Psychological emergencies weren't for wusses. "Plenty of people don't exactly make a career out of the criminal life."

"Yeah, but almost everybody has an electronic fingerprint anymore, Toni." He hesitated, then added, "I called in a couple favors to some people who specialize in tracing those fingerprints. Just about everybody in the modern world has them. Their face is somewhere. Driver's licenses, passports, you name it. Not this guy. He's like a ghost."

An icy hand gripped my heart. If the only suspect was a ghost, I was afraid Isadora was already as good as dead.

D as dead.

Blindfold Vol. IV

Chapter 1

Ash

The sidewalk slapped against the soles of my shoes with a rhythmic familiarity.

It was predawn. Way too early to be up and way too early to be running, much less thinking, but I was doing all of those things. And why not? It wasn't like I could sleep.

I hadn't heard from the kidnapper again since that one phone call and the ransom letter. No contact about a drop off point or how the money should be delivered.

No proof of life.

I was starting to lose hope.

And I was pretty sure I was losing my mind.

The rare times when my mind wasn't occupied with my sister and what might have happened to her, what could be happening to her, I was mentally kicking my ass over the way things had gone with Toni.

It was a never-ending fucking loop.

That was what had driven me out of the house and onto the streets rather than down into my personal gym for my morning run. Being down there made me think about how it had been sparring with her. Then it made me think of how badly I'd screwed things up. I'd been an idiot virtually every step of the way, and then, when I'd almost gotten things on an even keel, I'd let my dick take control and made things even worse. I hadn't even realized that was possible until I'd done it.

Dodging a busty blonde in running tights and micro-sized bra, I pounded the pavement harder. My head pounded in time with my feet striking the ground, and I ground my teeth together. Of course, that just made my headache worse, but I kept doing it. I was miserable and part of me wanted to stay that way. I deserved it.

For the first time in my life, I'd had somebody who was trying to actually help me, or at least *be* there with me when everything was going to shit. And what had I done? I hadn't even been satisfied to just push her away. I'd had to annihilate any chance of her ever forgiving me.

I had to stop before I drove away everyone.

If I didn't find a way, Toni was going to quit. I could already see it in her eyes. The only reason she hadn't told me to go fuck myself was because of her connection to Isadora. It didn't surprise me that Toni felt so strongly about Isadora. Everyone who met my little sister loved her. She was just that kind of person.

The complete opposite of me.

I'd never connected to anybody but Isadora like that in my life. She was all I had.

It wasn't a mystery why. I went out of my way to hold people at arm's length. I'd learned too young that if I let people get close, they could hurt me. They *would* hurt me. The only reason I'd kept my sister close was because I'd known she needed it. And yet, even with her, there were parts of myself I didn't share.

As I rounded the corner, I caught sight of a couple lingering on the curb. I slowed to a walk, unable to look away.

They looked like they were maybe in their early fifties. My parents' age before they died. He was standing in front of a car, a briefcase in hand, and she was looking at him. Only at him. It was like the two of them were all that mattered in the world.

Something hit me then. I stumbled and had to catch myself on the nearby light post. Bending over, I pretended to struggle to catch my breath. I was three miles into my run, an easy one over all, but I was feeling as if I couldn't get enough air. It just wasn't related to the run.

It was because of them.

My parents had enjoyed that kind of connection. They'd had each other, and they had me. Then, after years of thinking I was it, they had their miracle baby. And no matter how much they loved Isadora, they never made me feel like I wasn't enough. We'd been a family and I was old enough when they passed to understand what that really meant.

Envy had a bitter aftertaste.

I straightened, unable to stop myself from watching the couple again.

The woman pressed one last kiss to the man's cheek, and then turned, going toward the apartment building behind her. She never even noticed me. The man did, though. His gaze lingered for a moment, not a trace of embarrassment or chagrin to be seen. After a few seconds, he gave me a polite nod.

It was the smile on his face that made my heart twist though.

It was one that said he knew exactly how lucky he was to have what he had.

And that he pitied the rest of us who didn't.

I lingered at the house for the rest of the morning until well after the time Toni usually arrived.

Except this time, she didn't.

Although I planned to go into the office, I called and let my administrative assistant know I'd be late, if I came in at all. She was one of the few people outside of the small circle who knew what was going on. She immediately told me she had everything under control, and I knew she did. I needed to give her a raise. And a promotion. And some serious vacation time when this was all over.

By early afternoon, Toni still wasn't there, but instead of continuing to wait, I had my car brought around. Not the Porsche though. That was what I drove when I was trying to show off at a club with something other than a chauffeured limo.

That sort of thing wouldn't help with Toni, I knew. If anything, it might make things worse.

I picked one of the sedans I usually drove to work or when I wanted to be inconspicuous. After stowing my briefcase in the trunk, I headed for Brooklyn. If she wasn't at her apartment, I'd go into work and try again later, but I was going to find her, no matter how long it took.

This shit had to stop.

As it turned out, something finally went my way.

She opened the door less than a minute after I knocked and my gut knotted into hot little snarls at the sight of her.

"Yes?" She gave me a cool look from where she stood in the doorway, blocking it.

I had the feeling if I tried to push the issue and get inside, things wouldn't end well for me. My nose throbbed with the memory of how hard she'd hit me and I had a feeling she'd even pulled the punch at the last second. I wasn't dumb enough to risk that again. As for means other than force, well, she definitely wasn't somebody I could intimidate, and I knew she wouldn't back down. I didn't think she knew how.

Something inside me gave a sharp tug. No. It was something inside *her* that was tugging me...toward her.

There wasn't a question of swallowing my pride this time. Pride didn't even get a say in this.

"May I come in?"

"Why?" The word was sharp, cold.

"Toni. Please. I want to talk to you."

She blew out a sharp breath, her nostrils flaring. Then she jerked a shoulder in a shrug.

"Fine."

She shifted to the side, allowing me enough room to come inside without any risk of us touching. Still, the scent of her hit me hard and my blood rushed south, making me half-hard in a matter of seconds.

I put the entire span of the living room between us, but it still wasn't enough room. Maybe if the room had been the size of Grand Central Station, I would've stood a chance. Somehow, I doubted it though. I turned to look at her and saw she hadn't moved from her spot by the door.

She glanced at her watch and then back up at me. "I have a lot of work to get done," she said. "Temporary jobs to look for."

I didn't let myself show a reaction to her words, but inside, I was roiling. I'd be damned if I let her go anywhere, even if it was only temporary.

"I'll be brief then." I studied her face. She didn't look like she'd been sleeping very well and I knew at least some of that was my fault. Guilt overcame desire. "I'm sorry."

"This again?" She snorted. She flicked another look at her watch and then moved over to the couch. I watched as she drew her legs up underneath her before reaching for her laptop. "Didn't we have this conversation already? And if this is about the whole 'no condom' thing, unless you plan on telling me that you gave me something, you don't have to apologize for that either."

I could tell she was trying to make light of it.

"Toni, please."

She waved a dismissive hand. "I've been on the pill since I was seventeen and I'm clean, so you're safe. It was as much my fault as yours..."

"Could you stop, please?" Dragging a hand down my face, I reached for the words to tell her what I needed, but they didn't want to come. "I'm serious. It's just...everything is so fucked up right now. Isadora is missing, and I can't think straight, and you're there..."

"I'm there." The words had no inflection.

I sighed and gave in, blurting out exactly what I was thinking. "Shit. Yes. You're there. If you haven't figured out that you short-circuit my brain and make all the blood flow to my dick instead, then I have to question if you're as smart as you're supposed to be."

She surprised me with a quick, easy laugh. "Oh, trust me. I'm well aware of the fact that you want to fuck me. You've made it pretty clear what I am to you."

Guilt sliced through me as I moved across the room to her. "If it was just sex, then it would be easy. Sex is easy, and it doesn't matter. Not to me."

Her jaw went tight and I instantly realized how that sounded. Shit. I was fucking it all up again.

My voice softened and I willed her to believe my words, "But you matter."

She didn't look at me, her expression tired. "Look, Ash. I'm not up for your bullshit right now. You're forgiven, okay? Just go."

"I'm not feeding you bullshit." I took a few hesitant steps toward her. When she didn't immediately stiffen up, I took a few more until I was standing directly in front of her. "The morning after we..." I searched for words.

"Fucked. We fucked, Ash." Her voice was sickly sweet. "More than once, so I'll need to you to be specific as to which time."

"The second." My face went red. "When I woke up holding you. It felt..."

She stepped around me. "Look, enough. You're sorry. I get it. Fine." She gave me a wide smile as she all but tore the door open. "We're all good, okay?"

It hit me then and I knew it with a certainty I rarely felt outside of business.

Shit.

She was scared.

I forced myself to finish my sentence. "It felt right."

Her gaze fell away.

Slowly, I closed the distance between us. Her gaze swung back to mine and she jutted her chin up, her gaze defiant. I didn't let myself give in to what I wanted. Cup her face in my hands and taste that hot, silky mouth. Bite her lower lip. Pick her up, carry her to her bed and make love to her.

Make love.

Shit.

My heart squeezed as I fought back the desire as well as the edge of panic that welled up inside me. If I gave in, I knew I'd fall back into the same pattern as before and end up losing her for good.

Instead, I repeated what I said before. "It felt right, Toni." I swallowed hard and then added, "And that scared the hell out of me."

"Ash..." She sighed and some of the tension left her body, but the expression on her face was still guarded. She looked around for a moment and then crossed over to the small love seat on the other side of the apartment. She didn't say another word as she sat down, head bowed, eyes focused on her hands.

I looked around the room. Her apartment was small, an efficiency, typical of New York, although it had more room than some of the ones in Manhattan. I knew more about apartments than people would think. Half of the Phenecie-Lang empire was based on real estate and we owned a fair amount of property in New York. Still, small as the space was, Toni had put her stamp on it and made it hers. The love seat was the largest piece of furniture in the room, but there was another chair, sitting at an angle. I took that one, despite the fact that I wanted to be closer to her.

Her gaze flicked toward me as I sat down, but she still didn't say anything.

After a moment, I broke the silence. "Are you going to laugh at me if I ask if we can start over?"

Toni snorted. An inelegant, unladylike sound that should have made me want to dismiss her. Except it made me want to smile because it was so genuine, so unpretentious. And I liked it. From her, it wasn't rude. It was honest.

I opened my mouth to try to explain exactly what I'd meant by my question when her eyes met mine and my jaw snapped shut.

"I don't want to start over. I don't want to keep doing this. I'm tired, Ash. I never know which version of you I'm going to get. If it's going to be the man I trusted enough to..." Her voice trailed off for a moment and then she continued, "Or if you're going to dismiss me like some..."

She didn't finish the sentence, but whatever words she was going to use wouldn't have been complimentary, I knew that much. I locked my jaw to keep from saying something. What, I wasn't sure, but I had a feeling that no matter what it was, it wouldn't make things better.

"Why?" she asked finally, her voice soft. "Why are you even here? Why do you care?"

"Because it's you." I had very little time, I suddenly realized. Very little time to make her understand that I was done. Done fighting what we had between us and done pushing her away. I was chewed up inside with worry over Isadora. Fighting with Toni wasn't making it better. It was making things worse. She'd been a solid wall of support from the beginning and I'd done my best to tear her down.

No more.

I just didn't know how to put any of that into words that she'd believe. "Part of me is glad you're here for Isadora, that you care about her. But another part of me sees you and just...wants."

"I'm not having sex with you again." She delivered the words in a cool, flat tone that told me she wasn't buying anything I was saying.

"I'm not asking you to." I might want it, but I wasn't asking. Although, *want* was a pretty mild word for how I felt. "I need to get my head on straight when it comes to you and I know it. I don't..." I ran my hand through my hair. "Fuck, that's bullshit. I can't say I don't want sex with you. I can't look at you without wanting to take you, to make you mine."

Fuck. My heart hammered in my chest. Had I really said that?

I swallowed hard and tried to pull things back. "I want to have sex with you, Toni. But there are other things I want more."

"Yeah?" She lifted a dark red eyebrow, an amused smirk on her lips that didn't reach those smoky blue eyes. "What things are those, Ash?"

"A chance to make things right. To prove to you that I'm done fighting." I met her eyes and prayed she'd believe me. "To prove that I can be a better man."

Chapter 2

Toni

The part of me that knew better insisted I tell Ash to get the hell out. That he'd blown whatever little bit of trust I'd had in him. I didn't want to go through this anymore. I couldn't keep going through this. I knew all too well the sort of psychological bullshit he was putting me through and I'd promised myself years ago that I'd never let a man mess with me like that.

I'd decided sometime during the late hours of the night that I'd do better working from home for a while. The research material Isadora wanted for her next charity dinner was something that I could do from here, and now that I'd heard back from the two speakers she'd wanted to attend, I could move forward and keep myself occupied for a few weeks. Once that was done, though, it would all depend on whether or not Isadora had been found...

I pushed the thought out of my head because I couldn't bear to think about it.

I slid Ash a look. It was almost as hard to handle him as it was to think about Isadora. The fact that I wanted him, that my body craved his touch, wasn't helping matters much.

Was he serious?

He'd seemed serious the last time he'd apologized. Right after I'd gotten out of jail. I'd forgiven him, and then we'd ended up having sex...again. And he'd behaved like a total asshole...again.

I didn't know if I could trust him this time.

Fuck that, I knew I couldn't trust him.

But still...I wanted to.

Getting up, I walked over to him. His gaze slid up to meet mine and I studied him before speaking. "Let's say, for argument's sake, that I'm willing to believe you're serious. What exactly do you want from me? It's not like I'm going to quit. I wouldn't do that to Isadora."

To my surprise, he reached out and took my hand. He tugged gently and I resisted for a moment before letting him pull me down until I was sitting on the arm of the chair, my legs against his. That was all the contact between us, save for the casual intimacy of my hand in his, but it was too much. My body reacted the same as if he had slid a hand up my skirt and touched me. I compromised, pulling my hand away but not moving from the chair.

"I just want to start over. I want to show you I'm not the asshole I've been in the past..." His words trailed off and he looked away.

"Since the first moment we met," I supplied. Yes, things had gotten worse after Isadora's disappearance, but Ash hadn't exactly been the nicest guy in the world to me from moment one.

"Yeah."

He surprised me with the admission, but I didn't comment on it.

Silence grew between us. He looked exhausted. Something inside my heart loosened. I couldn't imagine the stress he was dealing with, the fear. I liked Isadora, but I'd only known her a little while. She was his little sister. If anyone could understand overprotective brothers, it was me.

I mean, mine had been ready to kick Ash's ass when he'd

had me arrested. Kory had been ready to fly back to New York from where he lived in Michigan to get a piece of Ash once he'd heard about it.

And it had to be worse for Ash. My brothers all sometimes acted like they were my parents instead of siblings, especially the oldest one, Deacon, but Ash had a right to feel that way about Isadora. He'd raised her since their parents died when she was seven. For thirteen years, everything he'd done had been to protect her, to keep her safe, and now, she was gone and there was nothing he could do.

"Okay."

Ash lifted his head and his eyes met mine. I held his gaze for a moment, and then slid off the arm of the chair and went back to the couch. I had my laptop open, a practice test pulled up on the screen. I read the question and selected an answer, unsure if I'd managed to pick the right one.

I glanced up at him. "We can try again. Clean slate. But Ash, I'm not kidding. Jerk me around again and I won't stop my brothers from coming after you. You haven't seen anything until you've seen them pissed off."

"Got it." His ghost of a smile only added to the strain on his face.

He stood up and started toward the door. Every step, every movement seemed weighted down.

"How long has it been since you've had a decent night's sleep?" The words popped out of me without me realizing I planned to ask them.

Ash paused, thinking. "Only once since Isadora was taken."

He glanced at me over his shoulder and I knew which night that had been because it had been my only good night's sleep since then too.

"How long since you've had a decent meal?"

He laughed and shook his head. "I'm not sure."

I was going to regret this, I knew, but my heart was aching for him. "Why don't you hang around a while? I haven't had lunch yet." Hesitating just a bit, I added, "I have something I need to tell you anyway."

"A ghost."

Lifting my shoulders in a shrug, I said, "That's what Vic tells me. He doesn't exactly run with the same crowd he used to, but he knows people. He knows a *lot* of people. He's asked around, shown the picture. The guy doesn't have any kind of online footprint, no known visual presence. Nothing."

"The cops would have run his face through facial recognition software, too," he said after a few minutes of silence. "It can take a while, but by now, we should have had something."

"How can a guy not have any sort of presence? Driver's license, tickets, passport...something?"

"I don't know." The look he gave me was grim and intense. "But I don't think it means anything good."

Before I could say anything else, my phone rang. Excusing myself to answer it, I slid out of the room and ducked into the only place that afforded any privacy in my simple studio apartment – the bathroom. Leaning back against the counter of the sink, I listened as my mother invited me for dinner. Again.

"No, Mom." I smiled despite how tired I was of her matchmaking attempts. For most people, a twenty-four-year-old single woman focusing on her career was normal. For Mom, it meant she'd never get to help me plan my wedding. "I'm sure Hank is a perfectly nice guy, but I don't need help meeting men, I promise."

There was an odd pause.

Moms might have a weird sense when it comes to their kids, but I think kids – even us grown-up ones – have a similar sense. It's the *oh, shit* sense. The one that starts to tingle like a Spidey sense when they let something slip or did something that somehow their mothers picked up on.

Mine was screaming now. The problem was that I didn't know exactly what it was I'd done that had made her 'mom alert' flare up.

"You've met somebody." Her voice was sly and soft.

"What?" I lowered the phone and stared at it, confused. That was my mom's number. She'd called me. Her single daughter who hadn't had a serious boyfriend since Greg McKinney dumped me my freshman year of college. "No, I haven't."

"Yes, you have." She was insistent. "This is the first time in years that I've tried to set you up and your response hasn't been some form of *Mom, I don't have time for a relationship right now*. You just told me that you found a guy on your own."

"No, I didn't." I shook my head despite the fact that she couldn't see me. What was she talking about?

"You did. You said you don't need help to find a guy, which means you've already found one."

"I did not." I still protested, but Ash's face was looming in my mind. His mouth. His hands. The way his eyes softened when he looked at me. The way *everything* in me softened when I looked at him. Shoving him out of my head, I reached for the humor that was one of my first defenses when it came to deflection. "Come on, Mom. Don't you think I would've introduced you by now if I'd met somebody? Especially after my little stint as a jailbird."

"Don't joke about that," she said automatically. But her

tone had changed. She sounded a little less sure of herself.

Good.

"I'm not joking. If I were with somebody, one of the first people I would have called that night would've been him. He would have been there waiting when I got out of jail and he would have met the boys."

Except Ash had been there. He had met my brothers...

That's not the same thing, I quickly told myself.

I didn't want to have this conversation. "Mom, I appreciate the offer, really, but even if you weren't trying to set me up, I wouldn't be able to come. I'm behind on work and I need to start looking into my summer semester classes."

The rest of the call wrapped up quickly, though not quickly enough for me.

A look at my phone said nearly twenty minutes had passed and I grimaced as I slid out of the bathroom. The apartment was almost eerily quiet. Ash must have left. I couldn't say I blamed him. If it had been anybody but my mother, I would have ended the conversation a lot sooner, but she was my mother. I'd never do that.

I came to a halt just a few steps into the room.

Ash was sprawled out on my couch. His face and body were relaxed, his breathing slow and regular.

He'd fallen asleep.

"Ash?" I said his name softly.

He didn't even stir.

Blowing out a breath, I glanced over at my work and shrugged. I could work with a guy sleeping a few feet away. It'd be a lot like being back home with my brothers again.

Except what I felt for Ash wasn't even close to how I felt for my brothers. There was definitely nothing familial about it.

Twilight was spreading across the city when he finally started to stir.

I didn't know if the ten hours he'd slept on my couch had finally been enough, or if the smell of food drifting through the studio was what finally penetrated his exhausted daze.

I jabbed at the tofu I had browning in the wok. I wasn't vegetarian, but tofu was good for the budget. When I was in the mood for Chinese or Indian, it worked in a pinch. Tonight, I was craving curry and the scent of it had my mouth watering and my belly grumbling in demand.

The couch creaked as he stretched and I glanced at him. The confusion on his features shifted into stark surprise when his gaze landed on me.

"Good morning, or rather, good evening." I gestured at the clock. "You've been asleep going on ten hours now."

Ash blinked at me. Then, in a surge of energy, he shot upright. "Did you say *ten hours*?"

"Yep." I nodded at his phone. It had been on the table where he'd put it when he came in. He must have silenced it before he came inside. "You've had both phone calls and texts. The texts were all from your administrative assistant. The basic summary is that she has things under control, and she hopes you changed your mind and decided to take the day off to rest. I didn't respond to those. Doug contacted you several times and I finally did answer one from him to let him know you'd swung by here and then pretty much passed out on my couch." I softened my voice to add, "Nothing about Isadora."

He stared at the phone and then looked at me. "How'd you get into my phone? It's password protected."

"Yeah. With your sister's date of birth." I gave him a stern look. "There's a warning about that kind of thing for a reason, Ash."

"I..." He frowned as if he had no idea what he wanted to say. He looked still muddled by sleep, almost hung over.

"Thanks for letting me crash here."

"You needed the sleep." I shrugged.

His voice was quiet as he spoke, "I can't sleep. I see a million things that could be happening to her. A thousand thugs and a hundred bad outcomes. I can't shut it off."

I gave the food cooking in the pot one final stir.

"I better go." He stood.

I made my decision.

"Why don't you sit down?" I gestured to my small table. "There's enough for both of us. You can have a meal and relax for a little while."

Chapter 3

Toni

We had a nice night, a decent meal, and good conversation. He stayed until late that night. Still, the next morning as I headed over to the Lang house, I couldn't help the nervous feeling in my gut.

I was giving Ash the benefit of the doubt. I had to if we were going to make this work. This 'professional' relationship we were going to have.

I had hours' worth of work ahead of me that could keep me occupied, and a small scheduling window to keep me busy over my lunch hour, so even if Ash did stay home, I wasn't going to spend an untold amount of time caught up in his spell again.

I had work.

I had a life.

I had school to finish and then a career to begin.

I *didn't* have time for an obsession with a man who swung hot and cold. A man who, despite what he told me, I couldn't trust.

He was already gone when I arrived and I was grateful for that. Doug was there along with several more staff members than I was used to seeing. I could tell by their grim faces there'd been no news overnight. It took me a moment to realize that I wasn't disappointed because I hadn't even hoped for anything different.

"Mr. Lang has us watching the phones and the house," Doug said, his voice somber.

I put my hand on his arm and gave it a squeeze. "She'll be back soon." I gave him a comforting smile before heading for the living room.

I hated this. Hated the situation, my complete lack of control. I hated that I hadn't been able to do anything to protect Isadora. No, it hadn't been my job, but I still felt responsible. I hadn't been able to do anything to help her or to help Ash.

And it pissed me off.

I liked being the one with answers, the one who helped people. Hell, that was why I wanted to go into psychology, to help people.

And I couldn't. I couldn't help Ash. I couldn't help Isadora. The kidnapper hadn't called, hadn't reached out to us, hadn't...

"Us," I whispered as I chuckled bitterly.

There was no *us*.

There was just Ash, and to some extent the staff here at the Lang household. And Isadora's boyfriend who I hadn't met yet.

I wasn't part of this.

Not really.

Twenty minutes into my lunch break and I was already going blind.

I'd just finished scheduling the last couple classes I needed and figured I'd try to get ahead on the required readings. I'd always been a good student, with an excellent memory and great comprehension skills. So studying usually wasn't an issue.

But usually, I wasn't stressed out like I this.

I'd been going over the same material for the past twenty minutes and I had yet to make any progress. Frustrated, I hurled my pen down just as a knock came to the door. Caught off guard, I jumped and my elbow hit the glass of water I'd poured. I caught it, barely, but some of it splashed out and I swore.

"Miss Toni? Is everything alright in there?" Doug called through the door.

"It's fine," I said, irritation clear in my voice. "Come on in, Doug."

The door opened to reveal him standing there in his severe suit of black and white. His eyes scanned the room before coming to rest on me as I mopped up the splashes of water with a couple of tissues. "Is everything well?"

"Oh, sure. I'm just a klutz."

A faint smiled appeared on his face. "Of course you're not." He held up a phone. "Mr. Lang is on the phone. Are you available?"

"Ah..." I looked down at myself. "I guess I am."

Doug passed the phone off to me and I lifted it to my ear, my belly fluttering. I hated the way I reacted to the simple sound of his name. If life had been fair, I wouldn't have reacted with anything but boredom or irritation to it at this point. But my heart raced and my body went tight. And everything in me just...wanted.

You've met somebody, my mother had said.

No. I really hadn't.

But I wanted somebody.

I closed my eyes. "Hello?"

"Toni. How are you?"

The sound of his voice shouldn't have set my heart to

racing the way it did. It shouldn't have made me ache and want and wish. But it did. Still, I managed to keep my voice neutral and calm as I answered, "I'm fine. How are you?"

"I'm...getting by."

I could appreciate the honesty of the answer. He hadn't offered a polite lie, nor had he unloaded everything. "I guess that's all you can do in a situation like this, isn't it?"

"At his point, yes." He blew out a sigh. "Listen, I was wondering if maybe you'd join me for dinner tonight."

My heart tripped inside my chest. I could practically feel the stuttering beats before it slowed to a complete and total halt for a period of maybe three counts. "Ah, dinner?"

"Yes. You were kind enough to feed me last night. I wanted to repay the favor."

"It was just tofu and curry." Keeping my voice light, I tried to shrug off my desire to say yes. To anything. To everything. "It's not like I wasn't eating anyway."

"It was more than tofu and curry, Toni." His voice was short. "But if you don't want to eat dinner with me, I understand."

If I didn't *want* to.

Yeah, right.

But I shouldn't. There was no question about that. But that didn't keep me from answering the way I wanted to.

"Yeah, Ash. I think I can do dinner." I hesitated only a second before I added, "I can't stay late, though. I'm falling behind on stuff and I can't do that."

"Understood."

I finished everything I'd planned to get done for the day

by two so I jotted down the hours. I'd been tracking my time on a pad of paper since I wasn't sure what to do with my hours since Isadora had been kidnapped.

I hadn't been paid at all since I'd started working and I wasn't sure how to address that. It felt odd talking to Ash about it, but I couldn't go much longer without a check. The Winter Corporation had placed me with Isadora, but she was my employer, not them. And she wasn't here.

Brooding as I counted up the hours, I tried to figure out the best way to approach things, but I hadn't found a resolution by the time the door opened in the foyer. I heard Doug's low, polite voice, and knew that Ash was home.

I kept my attention focused on the pages and notes neatly arranged in front of me, even when his footsteps stopped in the doorway. I didn't look up right away. Mentally, I counted to ten, then fifteen, before I glanced up, keeping it casual, then blinking in surprised when I saw him. "Oh. Hey."

Ash stepped inside the room. "Hey."

I offered him a faint smile before looking back down at the desk.

There was nothing here that I could even pretend was important. Not for long anyway. But I had to pretend like I hadn't been thinking about seeing him all day.

After a few more seconds of faked activity, I made a show of shuffling papers and then smiled up at him. "I'm pretty much done."

"Good." He tapped his briefcase against his thigh and came deeper into the room. "You know, it's...nice having you be here...for Isadora."

"I..." Pursing my lips, I tried to figure out the right way to respond. "I'm just doing my job."

"Your job isn't taking care of my sister, or trying to. Part of why you're here is because you're worried about her. You don't have to be here. You don't even have to keep working for her. But you're doing it." His green eyes were intense. "You don't have to care or try to help. But you're doing it. Thank you."

The sincerity of the words knocked me off balance. I didn't know how to handle Ash when he wasn't being a jerk or trying to get into my pants. So I shrugged it off. "I'm just doing what anybody would do."

"You're wrong." He smiled at me, his gaze staring straight through me. Then he skimmed the surface of the desk with his fingertips. "You said you were wrapping up. You're done, then?"

"Yes."

He held out a hand.

Uncertain, I stared.

"Aren't you hungry? Doug said you didn't eat lunch."

As if on cue, my belly rumbled. "I forgot," I answered honestly.

"Good thing I made sure we'll have plenty to eat then." He smiled at me but didn't retract his hand.

After a moment, I accepted it. I tried to ignore the hot pricks of electricity that ran along my nerves as I followed him out of the living room and down the hallway.

Off the back of the house, there was a small, intimate terrace. Grapevines and other flowering plants climbed up the trellis. There was a sweet perfume in the air, something sweet and intoxicating. I hadn't been out here before, but I was officially making it my favorite place now.

The small table was intimate, set for just two, and Ash sipped his wine as Doug gestured for a man clad in a white shirt and apron to come forward. The scent of the food made my stomach stopped growling, taking it up a notch. It started yowling.

After we'd been served, we were left alone and I busied myself with trying every dish that was offered. Part of it was because I was hungrier than I'd realized, but I couldn't deny that eating was easier than facing being alone with Ash.

I didn't stop until my belly was ready to pop and when I finally looked up, Ash was still watching me over the rim of his glass. He'd eaten some of his food, but not a lot.

"You don't seem very hungry." I smiled as I reached for my napkin and dabbed at my mouth. I wasn't embarrassed by how much I'd eaten, but I did hope I didn't have anything on my face.

"I ate lunch." He crooked a smile at me. "You didn't."

"Yeah, well. I've always had a healthy appetite. Me and skipping meals, we don't go together well." I reached for my water and took a sip, sighing as my belly, now beyond full, gurgled a little in protest. I leaned back in my seat. "My parents always joked that they'd thought they'd lucked out when I was born because they had their hands full trying to feed four boys, but I'd always managed to hold my own with the best of them."

"You're close to your family." There was something sad in his voice.

"Yeah. They're amazing."

"You're lucky." Focused on the glass he held, Ash spoke in a distant sort of voice. "You never know the kind of things you have, and how much you take them for granted, until you just don't have them anymore."

"I know I'm lucky." I hesitated only a few seconds before I asked, "What happened to them?" When he glanced at me, I clarified. "Your parents, I mean. Isadora said it was a car accident when she was seven, but..."

"Yeah, I was nineteen." He tossed back the rest of his wine like it was a two-dollar shot. "It was a country highway, up-state New York. No other cars, no one to say what really happened. The theory is that my dad lost control of the car. Maybe fell asleep." His mouth twisted in a snarl, but I knew he wasn't angry at me. "The officers who investigated it had a theory that they'd been arguing and he was distracted. It's shit. My parents hardly ever argued and he never would have gotten into an argument with her in the car. He was..."

"Like you?" I propped my elbow on my chin as I studied him, intrigued by this side of him. "If he was anything like you and Isadora is anything like your mom, then he would've been too protective of her to..." I stopped suddenly, realizing how it sounded.

Ash's lips twisted sardonically. "Let me guess. You think he would have coddled my mom, the way I coddle my sister." With a shrug, he said, "You'd be right. Dad doted on Mom and on Iz. He was the head of the household, the man. Responsible for taking care of everybody, for running the family business and making sure none of us wanted for anything. And I was being groomed to be the same way. Mom, Isadora...they were there to be loved, protected."

My heart twisted at his words, at the wistful tone. "Were they happy?"

"Yeah." Staring into his now-empty wineglass, he nodded. "They were so happy, it was almost embarrassing. Your mom ever kiss you in front of your friends? Or did your friends ever see your parents kissing? It was such a regular thing with my folks that my friends didn't even notice. Then it was just...gone. And it was me, this stupid nineteen year-old kid trying to figure out how to be a dad to a heart-broken little girl."

Tears burned my eyelids. "You don't have any other family, do you?"

"Not really. Some very distant relatives that we don't really see. They were going to take Iz so I could stay away at school, but I wouldn't let them."

His voice hitched at the end and I knew he was struggling to keep his emotions in check.

Unable to take sitting anymore, I got up and went around the table. He'd already pushed back, and it made it easy to kneel down next to him. Almost too easy to slide my hands up and grip his hips as I leaned in to press a kiss to his jawline.

"I'm sorry," I whispered against his skin. His dark stubble was rough against my lips and a thrill went through me before I could stop it.

His hand came up to cup the side of my head for a moment, and then he dropped his hand. He turned his face away. "I appreciate that, Toni."

And then he stood and walked away without even a glance in my direction. I closed my eyes.

Fuck.

What had I done?

Chapter 4

Ash

I needed a drink.

As I stood at the bar service and poured some scotch, I tried to block out the sound of cloth brushing against cloth as she came into the house. She was walking closer and my skin buzzed in reaction. My cock pulsed with need. I could still feel her kiss on my cheek.

I had to get out of here. Away from her.

"Toni, you should probably go," I said, turning to face her.

She stopped barely a foot away and her eyes met mine. She lifted her chin. "Why?"

"You don't want to know, and you don't need to know." I narrowed my eyes as she took a step toward me. I pressed my hands flat on the bar and tried to pretend that they weren't shaking.

"What's wrong? I thought we were going to try this friendship thing?" There was a bit of a challenge mixed in with the sympathy in her voice.

"Friendship." I could have bit the word in two. I backed up and she took another step toward me, not even flinching at my tone.

"You need to go."

Her eyes narrowed and I could tell she wasn't backing

down.

"I will," she said. "When you tell me why."

Fuck it.

I grabbed her arms and pulled her against me, nearly up onto her toes. "Because of this."

Her mouth was partly open, a shocked gasp escaping her as I fisted my hand in her hair. Before I could come to my senses, I slanted my lips over hers and plunged my tongue into her mouth. She tasted like sex and heat and hunger. The kiss was rough and desperate, a fire burning through me.

Finally, I caught ahold of myself and I tore my mouth from hers. My fingers tightened around her arms for a moment and I closed my eyes, fighting for air and control.

I opened my eyes and found her staring up at me. The words ripped out of me. "That's why. You don't need to be around me right now. I need something, and you aren't going to want to be the one to give it to me. I don't think you can give it to me."

"Is that right?"

I might as well have thrown down a gauntlet in front of her. Challenge glinted on her face and she lifted her chin, eyes glowing.

"You don't think I *can*? Just what is it that you want, Ash?"

"Toni." There was a clear warning in her name.

"Ash." She mocked the rough growl of my voice and the husky sound went straight through me. "Come on, tell me."

Instead of telling her, I caught her wrists and yanked them against my chest. Her eyes widened in surprise, then fluttered closed when I shoved my thigh between her legs. "You're pushing too far, Toni. Just go. Leave."

I leaned down and I bit her lower lip, harder than I should have.

Then I let her go.

Well, that had been the dumbest thing I could've done.

Turning away, I grabbed the scotch I'd poured and tossed it back. As I lowered the glass, something soft hit me in the back of the head.

I caught sight of something blue and wispy over my shoulder before it slid to the ground. I knew what it was. It smelled of her, but even if it hadn't I would have known. The slinky, close-fitting blue blouse that Toni had worn tonight. It had made her eyes glow.

I turned around, my heart pounding. She stood there, wearing a dark blue lace bra that cupped her lovely breasts to perfection. I could see the darker shadow of her nipples through her bra. They were hard, visible through the fabric, begging for my attention. Closing my hand into a fist, I told myself I wasn't going to give in.

I wanted more than she would want to give.

I wanted more than she *should* give.

And I couldn't give her what she deserved in return.

"You think I can't handle you?" She put her hands on her hips.

I sighed. "Actually, that's the problem. You can. But we've already been down that road, Toni. It doesn't end well."

"I know." She slid her hand down the slope of one breast, the smile on her mouth taking on a feline, feminine slant that was so mysterious and so damn hot, I felt my cock swell even more. I wanted her more than I wanted my next breath.

But what I wanted, what I needed...I couldn't ask it of her. I wouldn't.

"You aren't going to scare me off."

Her gaze slid down along my body and all the muscles in me tightened in response.

She smirked. "Although if we do this and you act like a dick in the morning, I just might cut yours off."

Instead of making me wince, the blunt delivery made me

want her even more.

Sucking in a deep breath, I tried to warn her. "Toni, you're pushing your luck."

"Am I?"

She reached behind herself, an action that thrust her small breasts up and out. My pulse kicked up, paused and then began to race hard and fast. My gaze remained locked on her breasts so I didn't realize she was dragging the zipper of her skirt down until she was wiggling her hips as she slid the material down to reveal a pair of tiny panties that matched her bra.

"If that was pushing my luck, then what am I doing now?" There was a teasing note in her voice as she closed the short distance between us.

Before my brain could fully process what she was doing, she rose up onto her toes and pressed her lips to mine. It was a quick, easy kiss. Followed by a hot, open-mouthed one that ended with her raking her teeth over my lip and I shuddered as she bit down.

"No strings. No promises. One night. Between friends. I think we both need it." She ran her fingertip across the spot she'd just bitten. "The only thing I expect is that you don't act like an ass when this is done. What do you say?"

Chapter 5

Toni

My words lingered between us.
What do you say?
His hands closed around my hips, palms hot against my skin. For the span of a few heartbeats, I thought maybe he'd push me away. Reject what I was offering. What I needed as much as he did, except for opposing reasons. He needed comfort and I needed to comfort him.

If he refused, I would leave, and I wouldn't try again.

He gently pushed me away, and for a few seconds, I couldn't think past the disappointment. Then his hands slid up my waist, his eyes darkening as I sucked in a desperate breath. His mouth closed over mine and I couldn't think at all.

I whimpered into his mouth and, after a moment, reluctantly tried to pull back. I needed to breathe. Had to. But he caught my chin, fingers biting into my skin. I felt his need to control...something, and knew that I could give him that.

With teeth, lips and tongue, he devoured my mouth, and I was sagging against the wall by the time his attention shifted elsewhere. A line of fire pulsed along my neck where he scraped his teeth across my skin and I shivered when he plucked at my nipples through my bra.

He did it again and again, the caress rough, edging on painful. I wedged my hands between us, shoving him back. He caught my wrists, and stared at me with glittering eyes.

"You backing out already?" he asked, his fingers flexing around my wrists.

"No." My voice was rough and raw, but steady. Backing out was the last thing I had on my mind. But I sure as hell wasn't going to make it easy for him...and I had a feeling that was exactly what he needed.

"Sure about that?"

"Bet your ass."

He grinned at me as he shifted both of my wrists into one hand and used the other to work at his tie. His eyes stayed on me as he replaced his one-handed grip with the tie. I couldn't keep track of the twists and loops but when he was done, I had enough movement that I could wiggle my wrists and there was blood flow, but there was no way I was getting out of that complicated set of knots. Not unless he wanted me to.

"Last chance, Toni," he said softly, leaning down until his lips were brushing against mine.

"I don't think I need it."

There was no warning for what came next. He simply moved, and then I was up over his shoulder. I had no leverage, and his shoulder dug into my belly. His hand on my practically naked ass steadied me as he turned and walked out of the dining room. I tried to turn my head to see, hoping there was none of the staff around, but my hair was in my way.

When he put me down a few minutes later, we were in his room.

Head spinning, I looked around. I'd been in here before, but it hadn't looked like this. Light shone in through the open windows and I couldn't stop the flinch. There were windows all around. Apparently, he'd had those thick curtains drawn when I'd been here before.

"Privacy glass," Ash said, his eyes locked on mine.

I shot him a look.

"Nobody can see it. Nobody but me will see what I'm going to do to you."

Do to me? Fuck.

He shrugged out of his suit coat and set it aside. Mesmerized, I watched as his fingers freed one button then moved to the next. With each inch of skin he bared, my heart pounded a little harder, a little faster. By the time he was done, I was just about certain my heart was going to jump out of my chest. He shrugged out of the shirt and I waited breathlessly for him to toss it off to the side, but instead, he took his time, folding it meticulously.

I groaned when he turned around and carried it over to the chair, but he didn't even look back.

My eyes dropped to his ass, his firm, tight ass, and his pants outlined that muscled curve to perfection. My fingers clenched, longing to sink into it, pull him to me. Damn, I needed him inside me. He turned and I saw the thick outline of his cock pressing against the zipper.

I bit my lip to keep from whimpering when he pressed his palm against the heavy ridge. The only thing that made me even the slightest been mollified was the knowledge of how I was affecting him.

But it didn't lessen my need for him. Only one thing would do that.

Jerking at the tie, I demanded, "Take this off."

"Afraid not." His lips quirked up. "Unless you want to call it off already."

"Yeah, right."

He moved forward at a quick pace, catching me off guard. I instinctively backed up and he grinned, the smile filled with something primal, almost savage. He grabbed my wrists and I resisted, staring at him in defiance. He won, but we were both panting as he forced my hands over my head. I glared at him as his came down.

Mine didn't.

My arms were stretched upward at an uncomfortable angle, and I couldn't bring them down. I tried, too. Craning my neck upward, I saw that he had hooked the tie over a hook hanging out from the wall, the kind of hook usually used for clothes.

Except this one was a heck of a lot stronger. It was supporting a fair amount of my weight. Granted, I didn't weigh much, but still, it was strong. And it kept me on my toes, literally, which also happened to be a position that pushed my breasts out. It was both embarrassing and erotic, and when Ash dragged his gaze down over me, the expression on his face left no doubt as to what he thought of this whole scenario.

He slid the back of his knuckles down the slope of my breast, over my nipples, down, down, down...my eyelids fluttered.

"You sure you're up for this?"

"Quit acting like I'm going to chicken out or that you're going to break me." I couldn't resist teasing him a bit. "Do your worst, Ash. I dare you."

Something dark and hot fired in his eyes.

I caught my breath when he grabbed the cups of my bra and yanked them down. It forced my breasts up and I whimpered when he lifted me, my back braced against the wall.

"Mine," he growled just before he sucked one nipple into his mouth. "You hear me, Toni? Mine."

That word, the possessiveness in his voice, should've pissed me off. Instead, it made me shiver with something that seemed a lot like agreement. I felt the edge of his teeth and moaned. How was it he could read my body better than any lover I'd ever had? He knew just the right line between pain and pleasure.

Even as he teased my sensitive flesh, he didn't waste any

time dealing with my panties, tearing them away like they were made of tissue. I couldn't even complain, not when his mouth was doing such wonderful things.

The rasp of his zipper was terribly loud and, a moment later, I felt the rub of his cock against my curls, but he didn't enter me. Not yet. I made a sound of disappointment.

"Did you really think it was going to be that easy, baby?" His voice was teasing and I knew we were just getting started.

Dazed from the overwhelming sensations, I shook my head, trying to clear it as my feet touched the ground. Then the whole room was spinning.

No. I was. He turned me around, the tie tightening on my wrists as he moved me.

"Wiggle your fingers," he ordered.

I blinked, confused.

"Can you move your fingers?" he asked.

I didn't bother trying to figure out why. I just wanted him to move things along. The need inside me was growing and if I didn't get some satisfaction, I knew I'd explode. As soon as my fingers moved, he fisted a hand in my hair and yanked my head back, sending needle-like tendrils of pain through my scalp, pain that merged with the heat inside me, fueling it.

"Are you wet yet?" he asked against my ear as he slid his free hand down my torso, my belly, between my legs. Without any warning, he pushed two fingers inside me. The sudden intrusion made me cry out and I tried to close my thighs, trap his hand until I adjusted.

He yanked harder on my hair and kicked my ankles apart, the movement forcing his fingers deeper inside me.

"You move when I say you move, or when I move you."

He pumped his fingers into me and I shuddered. I was wet, but he wasn't easing me into this. Another stroke and I moaned.

"Say you understand."

"I understand." Then, because every inch of me was desperate, on fire, I added, "Fuck me already, dammit! I'm dying here."

"Not yet. You don't want it enough."

I could almost hear the smile in the smug bastard's voice.

"How would you know?" I tried to push down on his hand, but I didn't have enough leverage.

He chuckled. "Because you're not begging me."

He kissed a path down my spine and I shuddered when I felt the edge of his teeth scrape over me, just above my butt. He fucked his fingers in and out of me, harder, deeper. I flinched when he slid the finger from his other hand between my cheeks.

"Have you ever had anal sex?"

I flushed, but answered honestly. "Sort of. My last boyfriend tried it."

"Did you like it?" His thumb ran down the seam of my ass.

"No. It hurt and he stopped." I didn't add that part of me had always wondered if that had been the real reason he'd broken up with me a few weeks later. "I don't think he knew what he was doing. I know I didn't."

Ash slid his thumb forward and I tensed as he gathered the moisture from my pussy and dragged it back to where he circled my anus before doing it again and again. "I know what I'm doing. And you'll like it, Toni. Even when it hurts, you'll like it." He pressed his lips against my shoulder even as his thumb teased me. "I'm going to make you feel so good."

Even though my stomach was churning with nerves, I didn't doubt he meant what he said...and that he could do it.

The fingers in my pussy kept up their steady rhythm even as his thumb began to apply pressure. I whimpered as he began to work his way past the tight ring of muscle. The muscles in my legs started to tremble as he finally penetrated my ass, pushing in and out in counterpoint to his fingers.

Relentless, he brought me teetering right to the brink before he stopped and I rocked against him, desperate. It wasn't enough. Hands bound and tied overhead, I could barely move. Without any conscious thought on my part, I did exactly what he said I would do.

I begged.

"Please, Ash. Please."

He surged upright, his hands leaving me suddenly empty. I would've protested, but then his arm went around my waist to steady me. The next moment, he was inside me. He pinned me between his body and the wall, taking me hard and fast. His cock swelled, thicker, harder, his thrusts bruising. I could hardly breathe as he drove the air from my lungs.

I didn't care about anything except the feel of him moving, taking.

Who needed oxygen, really?

That satisfaction lasted approximately ten minutes before I was cursing him again.

"You're a bastard, Ash. You know that, right?"

He'd stopped, just shy of a climax that I knew would've redefined the word.

He'd fucking stopped.

And then he'd picked me up and tossed me, facedown, on the bed. In a matter of only a couple minutes, he hogtied me. My hands at the base of my spine, my feet to my thighs, and he'd even taken the time to braid my long hair and twist the end into the restraints. I was completely and utterly helpless, every cell in my body vibrating with the need for release.

He bent over me, one hand on the back of my neck. The soothing circles he was making with his thumb felt like it should have been at odds with the rest of what he was doing, but it felt more like a reminder that I could trust him to eventually give me what I needed.

"Are you asking me to stop? You remember your safe word. All you have to do is say it and we'll be done."

I gritted my teeth. I knew he'd do it, knew he would stop if I said that simple word. He'd never force anyone to do something they didn't want to do. That, I knew, was the real question. What did I want?

I closed my eyes. I knew the answer. I'd always known the answer.

Him.

I wanted him.

"I won't say it."

He expelled a breath so faint that I almost didn't hear it. But there was no mistaking the twitch of the fingers on my neck and I suddenly realized that he'd been worried I was going to tell him to stop. Knowing how much he wanted me helped ease my anxiety and mentally prepare myself to accept whatever it was he was going to do next.

One cool, slick finger slid down the crevice between the cheeks of my ass. There was a faint, unfamiliar scent in the air, something I didn't recognize until Ash began to stroke the entrance to my ass, and the cool, slick wetness began to warm. Lube. I gasped when the warming sensation spread everywhere he touched.

Clinically, I knew what he was doing, and clinically, it should have been enough to cool the fire raging inside me.

It didn't.

Part of my brain reminded me what it had felt like before, how it had hurt, but another part reminded me that Ash would take care of me, that he'd make sure I felt good. That I could trust him with this part of me.

"I'm going to put my finger into your ass now."

I groaned and tried to shove my face into the bedspread, but I couldn't. Whatever he'd done with my hair had me completely and utterly trapped. My back and neck arched so that I couldn't hide my face. Then he was pushing inside me and I froze from the shock and the sensation. He pumped back and forth as my body tried to figure out if the intrusion hurt or not. He never gave me the time to reach a conclusion before adding a second finger. This time, I cried out at the burn as my muscles stretched. Fingers flexed on my hip as he held me in place, working the first two digits of his other hand in and out.

When I felt a third finger pressing against me, I tried to protest, "Ash, I don't..."

"Don't think, Toni," he said roughly. "Either say the word or don't. But don't think. Feel."

Suddenly, he brought his free hand down on the curve of my ass, lightly, and then harder, the sting and the burn mingling into an inferno. For an eternity, my world narrowed to the fingers pumping in and out of me, his palm hot against my skin. Pain and pleasure. Fire and flame.

Then he stopped.

Again.

While I gasped and shuddered, my brain and body trying to process the sudden loss, I felt the bed shift behind me. I tensed, understanding what was coming next. I tried to wiggle away, but he caught my hips.

"You know what you have to do if you want me to stop," he said.

He paused for a moment and I knew he was giving me my chance to back out. If I said it, he'd stop and I'd never get this chance again. But if I didn't say it now, he was going to follow through.

Several seconds passed and I didn't say a word. My heart thudded against my ribcage and I knew that, right now, my silence was consent.

I felt the head of his cock against my entrance and he fisted his hand in my braid. As he yanked my head back, he drove his hips forward, pushing past the ring of muscle.

His voice was harsh in my ear. "You told me to do my worst. You said you could handle it. Handle me. Let's see, shall we?"

With a snap of his hips, he was balls-deep inside me and a scream tore from my throat. I squeezed my eyes closed, tears slipping out as he held himself locked inside me. His cock was thick, pulsing with his own need, but he stayed still as my body struggled to accommodate him.

Just when I thought I'd adjusted to the sensations, he withdrew. I sucked in a shaky breath and tried to brace myself. I could do this. I could take it until he was finished. I could give him what he needed.

Then he sank back inside.

But it wasn't a deep, driving thrust, full of pain. It was slow and easy, drawing a whimper from me as the burn in my ass shifted to something different.

"You're going to come," he said, the word a deep, silken promise. He pulled my hair, the gesture rough, a sharp contrast to the almost gentle rolling motion of his hips. "You're going to come, and then I'm going to ride your hot little ass until I explode. You hear me?"

"Yes," I breathed the word. My hands closed into fists, then opened again. I'd never known I could feel this much.

He kept talking to me, promising pleasure, promising how good he was going to make me feel, how good I made him feel. The words blurred together until only the sound of his voice remained. Everything became a mix of heat and sensation, and pleasure rode the sharp edge of pain. I gasped out his name and struggled against the bonds, desperate for something, anything that would bring me closer to a climax that, only a few hours before, I would've said was impossible.

Then, without warning, it slammed into me and I screamed for the second time. Ash growled behind me as my muscles clenched, spasmed. So caught up in the sensations that rippled and shuddered through me, I was only dimly aware of his hips pummeling against me, his flesh slapping against mine. It should have hurt, and I had a feeling it would later.

But for now, it was the sweetest, most exquisite agony, the sort of pleasure that is painful in its own right simply because the body has no way to contain it all.

It was everything I'd been missing.

He'd kept his word.

Chapter 6

Ash

If I didn't let myself think too much, I probably could've been the most satisfied I'd ever been in my life.

I'd had good sex before. I'd had partners who aligned with my needs in ways I hadn't imagined possible.

But I'd never had anybody like Toni.

I never would've thought having someone who pushed and challenged me would be more satisfying than having a total Submissive, someone willing to automatically bend to my every whim.

It just went to show how much I knew.

Now, Toni was curled up against me, her hair damp from our shower, her skin smelling of my soap. It had taken every ounce of self-control I had not to take her again in the shower. For once, someone else's needs had come first. She'd been so tired and I knew she had to have been sore. She'd tried to hide it when I'd cleaned her, but I'd caught the little winces, the sharp intakes of breath. She'd practically been an anal virgin and I knew that, no matter how much I'd prepared her, I'd also been rough and she was going to feel it.

If I hadn't known how hard she'd come or seen the sleepy satisfaction on her face, I would've felt guilty for what I'd done. But I couldn't regret it, none of it. Not with the sound of that scream of pleasure still echoing in my ears. Not with my cock aching from how hard she'd clamped down on it when she'd come.

And definitely not with her tiny body curled against mine. She'd settled there as if she'd been made for it, her eyes closing almost immediately. Her breaths were soft and steady, and I tried to focus on them, let them lull me to sleep.

I tried not to think, but my brain didn't want to obey. Toni had helped me forget for a while, but I couldn't escape the thoughts forever.

Where was my sister?

I hadn't heard from the kidnappers in days. Too many days. I didn't let myself count them because if I did, I thought I might go insane.

But I knew it had been too long.

Had they already killed her?

But why? They'd asked for a ransom but hadn't given me a chance to pay it. And I would. I'd give them everything I owned as long as they gave her back.

Had something gone wrong?

Maybe she'd seen them and they'd decided it was too big a risk.

My gut clenched and I pressed my face into Toni's hair, needing the feel of her to ground me.

I didn't know what I'd do if something happened to my baby sister. For so long, she'd been my world. The beginning, middle and end. Even before our parents died, everything in my life revolved around keeping her safe and happy and now, without her in it...with the *thought* of a world without her in it, I felt like I'd been cut adrift. There was no focus and my world was just one giant, empty ocean.

I clutched Toni tighter. She made a small sound under her breath, but didn't pull away. Instead, she covered my hands with hers and held mine in place. Her touch grounded me, steadied me. Made it so I could breathe again.

I inhaled the scent of Toni's hair, focused on the feel of her body pressed to mine. But it wasn't the sensuality of her, the knowledge that, beneath my t-shirt, she was naked and that I could find comfort inside her. It was her presence, the fact that she held on with unwavering certainty to the belief that my sister would come home. It was knowing that she was here, that I hadn't driven her away.

With her in my arms, sleep came easier than I expected.

Dreams came even easier.

Isadora stood at the railing, staring out over the small private garden she'd designed and helped bring to life. She'd gotten down on her hands and knees and planted every single flower even though I'd told her she didn't have to. We had staff for that, had hired landscapers to take care of everything, including the garden. She'd laughed and told me it wasn't any fun if she couldn't do the work.

She glanced over at me and smiled, the affection in her olive green eyes making my chest hurt. She tossed her thick black curls and turned her face up to the sun.

"You're so serious, Ash. Why are you always so serious?"

"Why are you here?" I asked. Confused, I looked around. "How did you get home? Did the FBI find you?"

"Nope." With her usual impish smile, she lifted a finger to her lips. "Shhhh...it's a secret."

"Are you..." I couldn't bring myself to say it, to ask it. If I gave it voice, then it could be true, and that was a truth I couldn't live with. "Where are you, Iz? Tell me."

"I can't tell you because you don't know. This is a dream, silly." She turned to face me. "You don't think I'm really here, do you?"

"Then why..." I scowled.

"I'm just you, big brother. You never listen to yourself, but sometimes you listen to me. So your subconscious is pretending to me, hoping you'll listen to yourself better if you're me." She grinned.

"This is giving me a headache," I growled, frustrated.

"Everything gives you a headache, Ash." She shoved off the railing and took a step toward me. A few steps away, she flung herself into my arms, the way only Isadora would do. *"Lighten up. Live a little."* Her expression grew serious. *"Love somebody besides me."*

"Besides you my sister? Or besides you my subconscious?" I countered, not wanting to go where I knew she was heading.

She smacked me on the arm. "Don't be a smartass." She brought her hands up and cupped my face. *"Life is too short to never let yourself have one real thing for yourself. That's what Mom and Dad wanted for both of us. A happy life. Love. Don't shortchange yourself."*

She held me for a moment longer, then let me go, turning to the short stone wall again. She leaned over it...and leaned...and leaned.

And then she was falling.

I lunged for her despite the fact that I knew there was only a short drop into the garden. I reached for her, leaning over the wall myself.

Only there was no garden on the other side.

Just an empty, gaping void.

And she was gone.

I jerked upright.

Breath sawing in and out of my lungs, I looked around, trying to orient myself.

Toni was sitting too, staring at me, and I wondered if I'd called out my sister's name in my sleep.

The phone rang and I realized that had been what had

pulled me out of my nightmare as much as that void. I gave myself a mental shake as I snatched up my phone. A glance at the clock said it was still well before dawn.

"This better be good."

"And good morning to you too, Sunshine. I have news."

I blinked, trying to place the voice. Finally, my sleep-dazed brain started to work and I made the connection. "Agent Marcum?"

Across from me, Toni stiffened at the name.

Then the agent's words registered.

I have news.

"Isadora," I said, my voice stilted. The dream still loomed large in my head and all the fears I'd had in those last surreal moments came flooding back. *It's too late. I wasn't good enough, fast enough, strong enough. I hadn't been able to protect her.*

"Take a deep breath, big guy," Marcum said, her voice gentler than it had been a moment ago. "We have your sister."

"She's..."

The word lodged in my throat as the words clicked.

We have your sister.

Have, not found.

Sister, not body.

I didn't even remember leaving the bed.

One moment I was sitting upright with the sheets pooled around my waist. Then I was standing. Toni clambered out of the bed, staring up at me, her eyes wide, face pale. Without even thinking, I reached for her and she twined her fingers with mine.

I forced myself to ask the question, but found I couldn't finish it. "Is she...?"

"She's alive."

Marcum rattled off the name of a hospital, and I mumbled it back, hardly able to do much more than repeat the words I'd heard. Finally, Toni took the phone from me and told the FBI agent we'd be there soon.

After she hung up, she turned back to me and put her hand on my cheek. She pushed herself up on her toes and brushed her lips against my jaw. Her voice was gentle as she spoke, "Come on, Ash. Your sister needs you."

Chapter 7

Toni

The drive to the hospital was one of the most surreal experiences of my life. We took the Porsche and I knew that, for once, it had nothing to do with flash and all to do with speed.

We'd barely made it down the street before a New York City police officer pulled in front of us and turned on his flashers, clearing the way. Since I knew Ash hadn't made any calls, I assumed Agent Marcum had called in for an escort and made a mental note to thank her. Ash was already driving well over the speed limit and I knew he wouldn't have stopped for anything short of preventing an accident.

When we got to the emergency room of the hospital, I climbed out and stood on shaky legs. Adrenaline was coursing through my veins, but I knew I was going to crash soon, and hard. Before that, however, I was determined to be here for Ash and Isadora.

He came around the front of the car, hand extended even though he didn't look at me. Sliding my hand into his, I had to trot to keep up with him, but I wasn't about to ask him to slow down. If it had been one of my brothers in there, I'd have been running.

Agent Marcum, Lieutenant Green and a few other familiar faces were waiting just inside the emergency room doors.

"Where is she?" Ash demanded.

"You can't see her yet." Marcum stood between him and the rest of the waiting room.

"Step out of my way."

The words came out flat and I knew he was struggling to keep his temper in check.

"You can't go back there yet," Marcum said, her voice gentle but firm. "The doctors are treating her, and she needs a few moments of privacy to finish answering some questions."

"She needs *me*," he snapped.

"We've already let her know you're coming." Marcum didn't bat an eyelash or back down. "But there are a few things she'd prefer privacy for." She hesitated, and then added, "Most women do."

I saw the moment Ash realized exactly what Marcum meant. "She was...was she...?"

He staggered a little and I let go of his hand to wrap my arm around his waist, even though I knew if he went down, he'd take me with him.

"It's standard procedure, Ash," I told him, speaking quickly before Marcum had a chance to say anything. I didn't know what the situation was, but Ash needed a few minutes to process or he was going to snap. "When there's any kind of attack or kidnapping, there are always some questions that have to be asked. Trust me, no matter what happened, Isadora doesn't want you there for that."

His eyes met mine and I almost flinched at the lost look I saw there. The man who always had to be in control didn't know what to do.

I reached up and brushed his hair back. "Come on. Let's give them a few minutes to finish up and you can get your head together. Isadora is going to need you to be calm and strong for her."

For a moment, I thought he was going to argue, but then

he nodded his head. I breathed a sigh of relief. The last thing Isadora needed was her brother getting into a fight with the cops and the FBI.

He reached out and tucked some hair behind my ear. I'd pulled it back into a messy ponytail when I'd thrown on clothes and now it was falling out everywhere.

His eyes flickered behind me to Agent Marcum. "Ten minutes."

It took longer than ten minutes.

By the time the clock's minute hand had swept half around the clock face, Ash was getting edgy and irritable, more, even, than he had been lately. It had been all I could do to keep him from barging in anyway. As the half-hour mark started to tick past, I was about to get up and go ask if they could hurry. Before I could, the door swung open and Marcum appeared, a man in a white doctor's coat next to her.

Ash was on his feet in an instant. I was slower, much slower. I had to fight to keep from wincing as every muscle in me screeched in protest. Sitting for a half hour had left me stiff and remembering the events that had gotten me this way.

"You can see her now," the doctor began. When Ash reached for my hand, the doctor glanced at me. "It's best that only immediate family come."

"She's my fiancée," Ash said without batting an eyelash.

To my credit, I managed a tight smile even as I squeezed Ash's hand hard. But not as hard as his hand was squeezing mine. I was going to have bruises there too, but I didn't try to stop him. I could feel something very akin to panic radiating off him.

"She's also very close with the patient, Dr. Wyler," Marcum interjected.

"Very well." The doctor didn't looked pleased, but he stood aside and jerked his head at us before starting toward the ER doors. He stopped us just inside the hallway. "Before I take you to see your sister..."

Ash's grip on my hand tightened even more. I could see a thousand ugly scenarios playing out in his mind. Before he could give voice to one of them, I asked what I knew he couldn't. "Is Isadora all right, Dr. Wyler?"

"She will be." He focused on me after a quick look at Ash. "She's bruised, shaken, tired. She's also dehydrated and could use a few meals." He paused, and then looked at Marcum.

The agent nodded. "She managed to escape from her kidnappers. They didn't attempt to restrain her after the first couple of days, and it sounds like she played the complacent victim very well. They grew less watchful. She saw a chance and she took it."

"Iz..." Ash blinked. As if coming out of a fugue, he shook his head and rubbed at his eyes. "You're telling me that you didn't rescue her, that my sister escaped?"

"Yes." Admiration showed on her face. "Your sister is an amazingly strong woman." She paused and I watched something flicker on her face. "But by the time we got to the abandoned loft where they'd been holding her, they were gone." Her dark eyes were serious. "Your sister could very well still be in danger, Mr. Lang."

My belly went cold even as Ash's shoulders stiffened.

"We'll continue to look for who took her, search for answers, but she'll have to be careful."

"She will be." Ash nodded, his voice flat and hard.

"Very well." Marcum looked at the doctor. He nodded.

And then without another word, they took us into the

353

room where Isadora waited.

She looked terribly small on the bed. Logically, I knew it was just a trick of the mind. Isadora Lang wasn't a small woman. She stood a good eight inches or so taller than me and had curves I'd never dreamed of. But in that moment, as we hesitated in the doorway, she lay in the bed with her eyes closed and her shoulders hunched. She looked small.

One of us must have made some sound because her lashes flew open and she tensed in the bed. Before we could stay anything, she jerked up her hand. Ash and I both stared at the butter knife she held in it.

A butter knife.

And she gripped it with a fist so tight, her knuckles were nearly white. Then her eyes finally registered who we were and the knife fell from an open fist. She clapped her hands over her mouth and began to sob. Ash went to her immediately, but I stayed where I was, uncertain what to do or say.

"We'll leave you alone for a few minutes," Marcum said quietly.

I nodded, feeling out of place as I stood there. The door swung quietly shut behind me and I wondered if I should've gone with them.

Wrapping my arms around my middle, I shifted my weight from one foot to the other, trying to look anywhere but at the brother and sister. I couldn't, however, not hear her crying, or Ash murmuring to her in a low, gentle voice that seemed so out of character for him.

Slowly, the storm ebbed. When Isadora sniffed, I picked up the box of tissues from the table by the door and took them over to Ash. He smiled in thanks and pulled one out, turning it over to his sister.

"You're okay now." He leaned over and kissed her forehead.

She blew her nose. Then, slowly, haltingly, she shook her head. "No," she whispered. "No, I'm not. It's not over Ash."

He frowned, his forehead wrinkling. "It is. You're safe. You're home."

"I'm not safe!" Her voice had a shrill edge and her eyes glinted with something that looked a lot like the near-panic I'd seen on Ash's face earlier. "It's not over. This wasn't about me. It was about our parents. The guy who took me. He knew our parents!"

Chapter 8

Toni

"I want to go home, Ash, please." Isadora gazed at her brother with wide, desperate eyes.

From where I stood on the other side of the bed, I had a front row seat of the effect her words and tone had on him. She clutched at his hand and I knew Ash would move heaven and earth to make it happen.

"I'll get you out of here," he promised. He brushed a gentle hand over the one that gripped his arm and she loosened her fingers, allowing him to twine their fingers together. "If Dr. Wyler won't listen, I'll haul the lawyers in. They'll make him listen."

"You won't need lawyers." I managed a soft smile as he glanced over at me. "As long as she's stable enough to leave, they probably won't fight too much about letting her go home. Trying to keep an adult of sound mind held in a hospital takes some hoop jumping."

The door swung open and the poor doctor never stood a chance. Ash pounced like a feral dog on a stray rabbit. One long stride took him to the foot of the bed. Another to the door. The doctor's eyebrows shot up.

"Discharge my sister." It wasn't a request.

"Mr. Lang–" Dr. Wyler began.

"Discharge her," Ash repeated. "She doesn't want to be

here. She's been through hell. She can't sleep here. People keep coming in and out. Being here is stressing her out. I'm sure we can both agree that she'll rest better if she's under less stress. She'll do better at home."

I had to give the doctor credit. He took Ash's tirade like he handled irate, testosterone-charged alpha-prone family members every day of his life. Maybe he did, but I was willing to bet that Ash was still one of a kind. He smiled professionally at Ash and then nodded at Isadora. "Mr. Lang, you can rest assured that I have nothing but your sister's well-being on my mind. My patients are my primary concern, make no doubt."

He moved to stand at the foot of the bed. Isadora glanced at him and then away. Her face was red and I knew that, no matter how much she wanted to go home, she was embarrassed by Ash's outburst.

"How are you feeling, Isadora?"

Ash's eyebrows drew down low over his eyes, his expression stormy. Before he could say anything, I cut in front of him. "Ease up, Ash." I caught his arm and kept my voice low. "You want to take her home? Let's see if the doc thinks she stable enough first. You and he want the same thing, right? For her to be healthy."

He opened his mouth, then closed it with an audible snap. He nodded, but none of the tension in him eased. It wouldn't until she was home, I knew.

Behind me, Isadora finally spoke. Her voice was softer, more hesitant. She didn't sound like herself and it made my heart twist.

"I'm tired, Doctor...?"

"Dr. Wyler. We met before, but you've had a rough time. Aside from being tired?"

I moved to stand at Ash's side so I could see her. His hand closed around mine. The gesture startled me, but I didn't pull away. I needed it as much as he did. We both watched as Isadora twisted her fingers in the blanket.

"Scared. I'm just...scared, Dr. Wyler. I can't sleep here. I'm afraid every sound is..." Her voice trailed off.

"One of the men who took you." He nodded as he finished the thought. He consulted the iPad he held, going over her chart. He glanced over at me, hesitant, and then he looked back at Isadora. "May I discuss your personal health information with your guests or would you rather they step out?"

"No!" She practically shouted it. She shot Ash and me a desperate look. "They...look, my brother, well, it goes without saying he's family. Toni's my friend. They can stay."

He nodded. "Other than being dehydrated and some minor bruises and abrasions, you're in excellent health physically. The main thing that concerns me is your psychological well-being."

I could feel Ash tensing next to me. I squeezed his hand in warning. Isadora was busy staring at her lap again.

"You'll need to talk to somebody. Soon. If you don't, this fear..." He reached out and she flinched. He withdrew his hand. "You strike me as a woman who hates being afraid. Some people are shy, already withdrawn. Somehow, I don't think you were. If you don't learn how to deal with what's been done to you, it will be much harder for you to overcome this."

"I'll find someone to talk to." She managed a weak smile.

When he rose, he looked from her to Ash. "She should be fine to go home. I'll make arrangements, but she'll need IV fluids for at least another twelve hours. She should restrict her diet to a soft one for twenty-four hours, and then return to a normal one as tolerated. They didn't bother to give her much more than water a few times a day. Too much food too fast and it will do more harm than good."

"I can hire a nurse," Ash said immediately.

"I can do it," I interjected. All eyes turned to me, but I kept my eyes on Dr. Wyler. "And I can help with the psychological part of it too, if Isadora will let me. I'm just a couple of classes short of my Ph.D. And I've had enough medical classes that I can handle the basics she'll need."

He gave me a considering look and then nodded. He gestured for me to follow him out into the hall. "Let's go over a few things."

"Are you comfortable?"

Isadora sat tucked up in a fat chair in the library, blankets piled around her. There was a pitcher of tea within arm's reach as well as several books, snacks, anything she could possibly need. Doug and the rest of the staff had been hovering from pretty much the moment we stepped inside.

I was grateful.

My bedside manner when it came to physical issues wasn't the best. I wouldn't have thought about tucking her into a chair or grabbing a lot of blankets. For that matter, I wouldn't have thought about taking her into a big, warm room right in the middle of the house, either. I would have helped her to her bedroom and then offered to listen if she needed to talk. That's what I was training to do. But it was clear that was what Isadora needed.

She gave Doug a grateful smile as he topped off her glass. "I'm fine. Best I've felt in..." Her voice trailed off. After a moment, she murmured, "A while. It's been a while."

Ash looked like he wanted to hit something. I leaned over

and whispered, "Easy, baby. She doesn't need to see you get worked up." The endearment slipped out, but he didn't acknowledge it.

His jaw clenched, but he managed a terse nod.

When Isadora glanced over at us, I moved toward her and propped a hip on the sturdy arm chair. "They've got you set up in style here. I don't think I'm even needed."

"Yes, you are." She looked squeamishly at the IV in her left arm. A visiting nurse would be by the check on it and change out the bag in the morning, but until then, it was up to me to watch it.

"Just don't look at it." To emphasize my advice, I reached over and caught the sleeve of her robe, tugging it down. "Out of sight, out of mind."

Ash came up on her other side. "Do you want to rest?"

"No." Isadora licked her lips and looked over at the staff hovering around. "Actually, I want to talk to you. Alone. Can you...?"

Without waiting for Ash to say it, Doug hustled everybody out. I was on my feet, heading toward the door when she said my name. "You don't have to go, Toni."

I paused and looked back at her. "I don't think you need me in here for...whatever."

"I want you in here." She managed a weak smile and some of the old Isadora was in it. "You seem to be keeping Ash under control, although how you're managing it, I don't know."

"I don't know about that." I slid her a narrow look as I moved back into the room. The doors shut behind me. There was another fat, comfy chair angled not too far from Isadora and I sat there, hovering on the edge with my elbows on my knees.

"My kidnapping was never about the ransom." She made a face and clarified, "Well, it was about money, but they chose me for a reason. Because of our parents, Ash."

"You told me that at the hospital." He came over to her. A few feet away, he caught a heavy table and dragged it closer, sitting on it. Now he was close enough to touch her if he needed to, but he wasn't crowding her.

"I know. I just..." She darted a look at the door and then back at Ash and me. "I didn't tell the FBI everything, Ash. I don't trust them. I can't. Not after what I heard."

The terror trembled in her voice and her eyes widened. Her pulse fluttered visibly in her throat.

"What did you hear?" I leaned forward, drawing her attention toward me, away from the thundering look of rage on Ash's face. She needed to see encouragement, not anger.

"They..." Her voice cracked. "Toni, our parents died in a car accident. It was years ago, but I heard them talking about it. The kidnappers. And I don't think it was an accident. I think they planned it. I think they killed them. And this guy...the one in charge, he was going to kill me too. That was why I escaped, why I ran."

Chapter 9

Ash

"You didn't see anything that I can give to the cops? The FBI?"

Isadora flinched at my tone, and I knew I had to stop, take a deep breath. Her lower lip trembled and I wanted to pick her up and rock her the way I had when she'd been a child, when she'd cried after our parents had died, when the nightmares had woken her. But she wasn't a child anymore,

"I'm sorry," I said, pulling my chair closer to hers. I went to take her hand, then stopped. It was the one the IV was feeding into. She held out the other one and I took it, twining our fingers together. "I'm just worried. We have to find answers, or we're never going to be safe."

"I know." She yawned and knuckled at her eyes. "I want them, too." She caught her lower lip between her teeth, her gaze sliding to the door, to Toni, and then back to me. She appeared to be thinking hard. "The one guy, he..."

My heart lurched, jumped up into my throat. "What?" I forced myself to keep my voice down.

"I don't know, not exactly. He was always vague and he never really spoke much around me. But once, somebody asked him a question about why this was taking so long. He laughed and said a few days, a week, that wasn't long. He'd been waiting for years, and he'd keep on waiting if it got him what he wanted. Then he mentioned the wreck and..."

"It was an accident," I said, my voice wooden. "Dad lost control of the car."

"Maybe." Isadora smiled weakly. "Or maybe not. I mean, it was up in no-man's land, right? The car was destroyed. We couldn't have an open viewing. It's not like there was a lot of evidence. Maybe..." She sucked in a breath and then blurted out, "I've been thinking about this. A lot. I had to think, focus on something when I was there, or I'd go crazy. But maybe it wasn't a wreck. Maybe it was staged to look like one by somebody. Somebody so good that the cops didn't think to look deeper. If all the evidence was destroyed by the car exploding..."

"There's almost always evidence," Toni said from behind me.

I shot her a look, eyes narrowed.

She simply stared back for a long moment. Then she looked at Isadora. "The perfect crime is a crock, sweetheart. There's no perfect crime. There's always something, no matter how small, how insignificant. If this was in the middle of nowhere, it's possible the police department–"

"Sheriff's," I corrected. "A sheriff's department handled all of it."

"Okay. Then maybe the sheriff's department went on appearances. They aren't supposed to, but if your parents didn't seem to have any reason for somebody to kill them and nothing looked out of place, it seemed like an open and shut case."

"Our parents were rich." I laughed bitterly. "Wouldn't that have been reason enough?"

"Loaded or not, they'd only look at the people they saw as possibly benefiting." She chewed on her lower lip for a second. I could see the mental war waging. Finally, she said, "People like a partner. Or an...heir."

That caught me off-guard. It also shut me down flat, because I had absolutely no response for it.

A soft, sleepy sigh had me glancing at Isadora instead of trying to figure out what to say to Toni's comment. Her lashes were drifting down over her eyes.

A moment later, she jerked her head up, blinked and refocused. "Toni, if being loaded wasn't enough, what else..." She yawned again.

"Okay. That's enough." Toni stood. "Isadora, you need to get some sleep."

"But..." She looked over at me.

"Ash, come here a moment." Toni crossed her arms over her chest and stared at me. I stared back, mostly because that pose did amazing things for her breasts, but after a second, I rose.

She turned away and headed out into the hall. I looked back at Isadora to tell her I'd be right outside, but her head had already slumped. Her breathing was slow and even, her expression more relaxed than I'd seen since she'd first gotten back.

"That girl is exhausted," Toni said the second I looked at her.

"Are you reading my mind now?" I asked mildly. Leaning my shoulder against the door jam, I let my gaze slide back down to her chest.

Toni snapped her fingers and pointed to her face. "My face is here."

"I know." I grinned at her. "It's a nice one too. There are just other parts of you that are equally as distracting."

"You're insane." She shook her head and laughed softly as she glanced back in at Isadora. "She needs to rest. That was the whole point of bringing her home from the hospital, so she could rest. So...go."

She made a shooing motion at me.

"Go where?" I raised an eyebrow.

"To bed. Or work. Go running. It doesn't matter. Just give her some space so she feels like she can rest."

I reached out and hooked my hand in the front of her pants, drawing her closer. My stomach clenched when I heard her breathing hitch. "I have a better idea." I lowered my mouth to her ear and murmured, "How about I take you up to my room and bend you over the side of the bed and fuck you until neither of us can think straight?"

She swallowed hard. "I'm supposed to be watching Isadora."

"She's sleeping. She doesn't need watching right now." I reached down and cupped her, grinding the heel of my palm against her. "I, on the other hand, need you."

Her lashes fluttered and I rubbed her again, using my body to back her up until she was leaning against the wall with me pressing into her. It never ceased to amaze me how she could be so tiny, so much smaller than me, but I never felt like I could overwhelm her.

"Say yes, Toni." I added pressure when her breathing went ragged. Fuck, I needed her.

"Yes." She sighed. "Yes, you bastard. Yes." Then she pulled away and shot me a dark look. "In a minute."

I grabbed for her again, but she'd already ducked back through the door. Following her inside, I watched as she moved to the chair and fussed with it, easing the head back until Isadora was mostly reclined. My sister half-woke, muttering something that made Toni smile.

When she came back to me a few minutes later, she had an eyebrow cocked and challenge glinted in her eyes. I suddenly decided the bed wasn't what I wanted. It was too soft, and right now, I didn't need soft. I needed hard.

Which meant I wanted to keep her in place and I knew the perfect spot to do it.

I took her hand and led her down to my play room. I wasn't going to use toys today, but I did want the bench I had in there. It was exactly the right height and made for what I needed.

Less than two minutes later, Toni was squirming against the weight bench, her naked ass in the air, her breasts pressed flat against the padded leather, her hands bound underneath her.

"At some point," I said, stroking her hair away from her face. "I'm going to take you to Olympus and get us into one of the VIP rooms. They've got toys in there like you wouldn't believe. Even more than I have here."

"What, you mean like a hula hoop? A Barbie doll?" she quipped, jerking on the padded cuffs I'd used to restrain her wrists.

"No." I laughed. "No hula hoops. And the dolls I've heard about aren't really for kids." I ran my hand down her back and over the curve of her ass. "But they do have canes. I've never much been for caning or whipping, but I'd love to see your ass all red and hot for me."

She sucked in a slow breath and my stomach flipped as I realized it wasn't disgust or rejection.

"That idea excites you, doesn't it?" My voice was low, gravelly, as I moved behind her, undoing my pants as I went. I shoved them down and kicked them aside.

"Actually, I'm just wondering if you'll get past the talking stage – ah!"

She cried out as I shoved inside her. Her cunt was hot and wet, squeezing around me. Fisting a hand in her hair, I jerked her head around so I could see her face. "You have no idea how much I love that smart mouth of yours."

I traced her lips with my fingers. She opened her mouth and I pushed my first two fingers inside. She bit down and I felt it in my balls, like she was licking and biting on my cock instead of my fingers.

"If I shoved my cock in your mouth, would you suck and bite it like that?"

"Yes." She clamped down on me with the tight muscles of her pussy. "But not yet. You have to make me come first."

It was a challenge, a warning, a dare.

I should have pulled out and spanked her. She didn't give the orders. I did. If she'd been any other Sub, I would've punished her, then taken my pleasure. I would've left her gasping and wanting. Sent her home without letting her come.

Instead, I accepted the challenge and drove into her hard enough to make her wail.

And then I made her come.

While her pussy was still quivering, I pulled out and walked around to the front of the bench. Tangling one hand in her hair, I held her head steady as I pushed my glistening cock between her lips. Even with her eyes still glazed from her orgasm, she began to work her mouth around me. My hips rocked forward in a non-verbal warning. When her eyes met mine, I saw her consent and began to thrust into her mouth.

It was over too quickly, her mouth too hot, too skilled. I cried out her name as I emptied myself in her mouth and she swallowed every drop, continuing to work her tongue over me until I recovered enough to pull out.

Neither of us spoke as I untied her, rubbing her wrists and arms, then her legs. I'd need to clean up in here, but that would have to wait until later. We needed to sleep more. I hauled her up into my arms and started to walk, still naked, through the house.

She squirmed as soon as I opened the door. "Put me down! I need clothes."

"Everybody's already asleep. If anybody gets up, they'll see my ass and not yours as long as you're still." I pressed a kiss to her temple. "You're sleeping with me tonight."

She went still. "I am?"

"Yes."

Her body was stiff in my arms, her voice soft. "And are you going to turn asshole on me again?"

"No." I still wasn't sure how I felt about what happened, about what any of it meant, or even if I had a name for what I felt. But I did know I liked the feel of her in my arms. That I slept better with her next to me.

And that I didn't want her leaving.

Ever.

Chapter 10

Toni

A couple of things clued me into the fact that something wasn't quite right.

The sun was coming in at the wrong angle. The bed was far more comfortable – and bigger – than mine had ever been. And it was quiet. Blissfully, serenely quiet. Also, I felt rested, which was really wrong, because I never felt rested lately, not between working for Isadora, worrying about Isadora and school.

School!

Shit!

I practically flew out of bed and came to a halt when I saw the clock.

"Shit," I whispered. It was too late. I'd already missed my class.

One of the classes I needed to graduate and that I'd considered myself lucky to get into before this particular professor left on maternity leave – hence the reason for the odd scheduling. She was one of the hardest professors I'd ever had, but she was the best and I wanted to learn from the best.

Groaning, I tried to think as I headed for the shower. With hot clouds of steam and fragrant soap billowing around me, I tried to clear my head of the muddle of sleep.

See if I could find someone who had notes. Copy notes. Get assignments.

Make a sincere apology to the professor and hope she'd still let me stay in her class. I had a reason, of course. And a perfectly valid one at that, but I doubted my professor would see it that way. Only one of the ones whose finals I missed had let me make it up online. The other two had given me zeroes, making me glad I'd spent so much time pushing myself to get the best grades possible. I'd still passed.

But if I got kicked out of this class, I'd have to wait until the fall semester to take it again, and only if I managed to get in. I had to be careful or I was going to screw up everything.

Once I finished in the shower, I puttered around in Ash's closet for a few pitiful minutes, hoping to find something I could wear.

The discreet knock I heard just as I was pulling on a burgundy button down shirt had me flushing. I had no doubt it was one of the staff, and even less doubt that they knew what had happened between Ash and me.

I didn't know the woman's name, but she smiled at me as she held out a stack of clothes. "Here you go, Miss Gallagher."

"Ah...thanks." Recognizing my jeans and panties from yesterday, I took them gratefully. They smelled like they'd come fresh from the laundry, and I flushed at the thought of how they'd gotten there.

My shirt was in the pile, too but I liked the feel of the burgundy silk so after I put on my bra, I put Ash's shirt back on, tying it into a knot at my waist. After glancing around, I concluded that I'd left my sandals downstairs last night.

Now I had to find them and check on Isadora before trying to fix the mess I'd made of my class.

She wasn't hard to find.

I just followed the sound of laughter to the kitchen, puzzled by how easy and light she sounded after last night.

When I saw the lean man sitting next to her in the cozy little nook, I realized I should have guessed the reason. Messy bronze hair, dancing hazel eyes...I knew who this was.

Both of them looked at me. The shadows were still in her eyes, but Isadora didn't look quiet as frail as she had yesterday. I didn't need a doctor to tell me why.

Focusing on the man, I held out a hand. "Colton, I presume?"

"You got it. And I bet you're Toni."

We shook and I took the seat opposite Isadora. My belly grumbled demandingly at the smells drifting through the air, and Isadora gave me an understanding smile. "I hear you. They're making omelets. I convinced them that was on the soft diet."

"They'll be fine." I checked the IV bag. "The nurse has been out."

"Yep." She gave me a guileless smile. "I told them that you were taking a shower since you'd been up all night taking care of me."

Flicking at a damp strand of hair, I shrugged. "I did shower."

She grinned as she leaned against Colton, her expression telling me that she suspected the real reason why I'd been in the shower. She didn't say anything though. As I watched, her entire body relaxed as soon as she touched him. It was like she could breathe easier, think easier...just be, all because he was there. It made something in me sigh with envy.

"When did you get over here?" I asked.

He rubbed at his neck, eyes squinting. "Three? Isadora woke up and called me. I came right over. I would've come to the hospital..." There was a tightening around his mouth as he said it.

Isadora interrupted, her voice soft. "Don't be mad, baby."

"I'm not mad." He kissed her temple. "I just think your

brother is a dick. He could have called me."

"Ash can be..." She hesitated.

"A dick," I offered.

She started to laugh. "Well, yeah. Sometimes." Then she glanced at the shirt I was wearing. "That's a nice shirt."

Shit.

"Ah..." I flamed red.

Fortunately, I was saved from an explanation by the timely arrival of food. We spent the next few minutes filling our empty bellies and then Colton stood up. I could read the reluctance in every line of his body.

"I have to go, sweetheart." Isadora's face fell, and my heart twisted. He bent over, gently kissing her as he brushed curls away from her face. "The assholes at the plant will fire me if I don't show up. I'll come back tonight, Dory. I promise."

"Okay." She gave him a game smile.

He caught her hand, kissed her fingers, and then he was gone.

I waited until he was out the door before I spoke, "He seems like a good guy."

"He is." Isadora was still looking at the doorway, as if waiting for him to come back. After a long moment, she turned back to me. "He's definitely not a dick."

"Ash has his moments." I wasn't sure why I felt the need to defend him when I'd been the one who'd said it in the first place.

"I assumed you thought so or you wouldn't be wearing his shirt." She hesitated before asking, "So when did that happen?"

"Hmmm." Lips pursed, I reached for the bread basket. I wasn't sure I wanted to have this conversation, but I did feel the need to stay at least a little while longer to make sure Isadora was okay. "Well, we were both pretty stressed, you know, when you disappeared and..."

"So you two were just...relieving stress."

I looked up at her. She had a sunny, open face, but she managed to pack a lot of innuendo into those few words and the look in her eyes was telling.

"Yes...no." I sighed. "It's complicated."

"You had sex with my brother." She shrugged. "That's not complicated. He's a good-looking guy. The complicated part is that you have a thing for him."

Shit. Was it that obvious?

"You'd rather I didn't." I nodded slowly. "Of course. I understand–"

"It's not that." Isadora smiled a little sadly. "If I thought it would save you the heartache, I'd lie to you, but I know you're the sort of person who likes honesty, so here it is. Ash doesn't do commitment. I think you do."

Well, that was honest. Trying not to let any emotion show on my face, I said, "Why do I get the feeling there's a story here?"

"Because there is." Not looking at me, she reached for her cup of tea and sipped. "It's short, and not very sweet, and it's probably a lot of why he's such a dick. He was seeing this girl when our parents died. Lily. Sweet girl. I liked her a lot. She was...well, I thought she was perfect for him. She knew when to push, when to back off, when he needed to take a break. When I needed a break. She helped him get through what happened to Mom and Dad. They were going to get married."

My heart froze. I must have made some sort of sound or moved – something – because Isadora looked up at me, her gaze solemn.

"About two years after Mom and Dad died, they were going to go on a romantic weekend to the Poconos. He told me he was going to officially propose, give her Mom's engagement ring. Then, the weekend came and he went to go pick her up, but she was gone."

Gone? "I don't understand."

"Neither did we." Her voice was quiet. "He looked for her, came back home to see if she was here. Called up there. But she was gone. She never came back for the stuff she'd kept here. A couple days later, her roommate said she came home from work and Lily's stuff was gone. It was like she'd fallen off the face of the earth. Neither of us saw her again. Ever."

I stared at her. "That's..."

We finished the sentence together. "Weird."

"It is." She nodded, the expression on her face sad. "Ash used to be a little silly, you know. He used to laugh more. He used to play. But after that, he shut down. She'd been the one person he'd thought he could count on, that he could trust. And she left him without an explanation. He hasn't let himself get close to anyone else since then."

I understood what she was saying. Really.

But I had a feeling I was already in too deep. "Thank you."

I pushed back from the table and rose. I needed to go. Now more than ever, because I had to think. Before I took more than a couple steps, however, I stopped, curiosity getting the best of me. "Hey, what was her name? Her full name?"

"Lily. Lily Ann Holmes." Isadora smiled a little. "Don't try to track her down on Facebook or anything. I already tried years ago. She's a ghost."

The familiar words sent a strange little shiver up my spine. I tried to brush it aside as I turned back towards Isadora. "I almost forgot. I need to look at your IV. After all, Mr. Lang did assign Dr. Toni to your case." I tried to reach for a chipper tone of voice and failed, coming off tired and resigned.

"You should have slugged him instead of...well, you know."

"I did that once. It didn't have a lot of effect." I didn't

realize what I'd said until after the words slipped out.

"You..." She started to laugh.

If I could have pulled it off, I would have laughed with her. Instead, I made a ridiculous attempt to prolong the examination of her perfectly normal-looking IV insertion sight. "It was my understanding that the nurse will discontinue it when she comes back out at noon. Did she confirm that with you earlier?"

"Yes, Dr. Toni." She caught my free hand with hers and said, "Now quit stalling."

"Stalling?" I wasn't stalling. Stalling meant I had intentions of talking about it once I was ready. I didn't plan on talking to her about this at all.

"If you don't tell me the story, I'll ask Ash," she threatened.

My eyes narrowed. "You know, you look all sweet and innocent..."

"It's an act." She gave me a serene smile.

"I've figured that out," I said wryly. "Doesn't mean I'm going to fall for that look. I'm the queen at this. I have four brothers. You only have the one."

"They can't be any worse than Ash." She made a face.

"Bet me. Four, remember? And I've met your brother. You haven't met any of mine."

"True." She pursed her lips. "But, still, if you don't tell me, I'll ask Ash. You want me to get *his* version? Or yours?"

I sighed. "You've got a point."

Doug promised he'd personally stay with her. There were any number of people within the house and Ash had put his security detail on full force as well.

Still, I felt like a heel leaving her.

But I knew she'd never let me stay, not once I mentioned missing my class.

Case in point, she waggled her fingers at me from her chair and gestured theatrically towards the door. "Go. Learn. Shrink."

I gave her a smile and headed for the door. I was going to have to scramble now to make it to the professor's office before she left for the day.

Or not...

One of the cars was waiting at the curb. "Doug thought you could use a lift," the driver said, smiling at me.

"Yes. Yes, I could." Instead of hot-footing it to the subway, I sank into the leathery softness of the seat and closed my eyes, thinking about my conversation with Isadora.

I'd told her everything that had happened since she'd been kidnapped. All of it. When I'd gotten to the part about him having me arrested, she'd been furious. Then she said she didn't know why I hadn't just torn off out of there and told Ash to kiss my ass. She'd laughed when I told her I hit him instead. Her expression had sobered as I explained about Vic.

When I finished, I realized she would feel guilty about what had happened to Vic and me for a long time. That, of course, made me feel guilty. I shouldn't have said anything.

I pinched the bridge of my nose. Maybe if I hadn't been so shaken by what she'd said about Ash's girlfriend.

She's a ghost.

Frowning, I pulled out my phone. The little Wifi signal lit up and I glanced at the driver. "Does the car have Wifi?"

"It does indeed." He smiled at me from the rearview mirror. "Mr. Lang conducts a lot of business to and from his office."

"Can I use it?"

"Of course. Get ready and I'll give you the password."

It only took a minute and I was cruising through search results on various women named Lily Ann Holmes. Except they weren't her. None of them seemed the right age. None except for a few on those goofy yearbook sites. I clicked one that was local, and found somebody who might be a fit. The age was closer. She was a year younger than Ash was now. And pretty. Granted, the hair was way, way out of style, but pretty nonetheless. And she had wise, young-old eyes. The kind of eyes that would fit the woman Isadora had described.

What had made her that way, I wondered. What had made Lily the sort of person who stayed with a man who was raising his little sister? And what had happened to make her leave that same man, just as they were planning to spend their lives together? Which one had been the real Lily?

Then I wondered about Ash. Wondered the one question I couldn't stop asking.

Did he still love her?

Either the hormones had made my professor soft, or she could tell the whole Isadora thing had really torn me up. She gave me my syllabus, as well as the names of the other students until I heard one I knew. Then she made me promise to not miss another class, since there were so few during the short session, and we were done.

I was on the subway by three, and by four, I was back at the Lang household. When I walked inside, I saw that Isadora had pulled out boxes and scrapbooks. Judging by the looks of things, she'd been going through them all day.

"What are you doing?" I asked as I dropped down next to

her. The IV was gone and she looked a lot better. Her color was back and other than the weight she'd lost during her captivity, she almost looked normal.

Then she glanced up at me, and I saw that her glib, easy humor was gone.

What had happened to her had changed her. I hoped Ash was prepared for it. If it was hard for me to see her like this, I could only imagine what it would be like for him.

"I didn't see them. They kept me masked or in the dark." Her voice was soft, but there was no hesitation. She sounded certain, and far stronger than I would have expected. "But I saw pictures. One of the agents...the lady? Marcum? Agent Marcum showed me the picture that was taken off the security camera here. That man, something about him bugs me."

"What do you mean?" I skimmed the pictures she'd spread around. It hit me almost as soon as I asked the question. "Son of a bitch. You recognized him, didn't you?"

"I don't know. But there's something about his eyes. Something weird..." Shaking her head, she flipped another picture over. "None of these are helping."

"What are you looking for?"

"I don't know!" The sharp sound of her voice echoed through the room. She stopped and sighed, rubbing her hands over her face. "I'm sorry, Toni."

"You don't need to be sorry." I reached out a hand, covering hers. "You went through more hell than I can imagine. If you were totally steady, I'd be worried."

"Steady." She laughed weakly and pushed a hand through her hair. Her curls were looking a bit more wild than usual. "You know, I used to wish something crazy would happen to me. Then I met Colton and he's wonderful. I love him and he drives me...um. Well..."

She blushed.

I smiled. "That's good."

"Yeah. It's beyond good. But there was still this part of me...everything is so...normal. Ash has protected me from everything. My entire life. Ever since Mom and Dad died. And before that, they protected me." She twisted her hair up behind her head, then let it fall again. "I wanted a life. Excitement. Then, one day, I'm outside, taking a walk and bam – the world goes dark. I wake up, and it's still dark. I'm blindfolded and..."

Her voice hitched.

I leaned over and wrapped an arm around her neck, hugging her. I'd always been the baby in the family, but I felt protective of Isadora, almost like she was family. "You're going to be okay, you know. You're stronger than anybody knows, even you."

She hiccupped. "I don't feel strong."

"You are." I gave her another minute and then nudged her back. Part of what I'd been learning over the years was how to know when to give comfort and when to be tough. "Come on. You need to focus and get to work. You don't want Ash coming in here and seeing you like this. He'll go in hyper-worry mode, won't he?"

She sniffled, and then, with a watery chuckle, she straightened.

"You're right." She swiped at her eyes and shook her head. "Man, you know him a little too well. How did you get him figured so fast?"

"Eh. This part of him is easy to understand. He's a brother." I snorted. "I got too many of them. But we girls never want to lose face around them, do we?"

Chapter 11

Ash

She was home. She was safe.

She was home. She was safe.

I'd woken up three times during the night to tell myself that and finally, I could believe it.

But only if I went to check on her.

I did that twice, and would have done it a third time, but as I was walking down the hallway sometime around three, I heard low, hushed voices in the foyer.

Adrenaline surged and I ran the rest of the way, only to stop when I saw Isadora leaning against a tall, lean man. Colton.

She was shaking, her shoulders trembling as she clung to him.

Slowly, I backed away and spent the next few minutes in the hallway, letting my breathing returned to normal.

Isadora must have called him. It occurred to me that maybe I should have done that earlier. It seemed like she really needed him here since she'd called him in the middle of the night, but I just hadn't thought of it.

Under my breath, I muttered, "That's because you're a self-centered asshole."

Tired and irritated with myself, I returned to my room and

stretched out in the bed next to Toni. I turned toward her and pulled her to me. She was soft and warm, and the feel of her had my cock stirring. I wanted to pull her onto her knees and drive inside her. Wanted to slide inside her and take her slow, drawing out our pleasure.

She was sound asleep, but I knew I could have her awake and moaning in a matter of minutes.

And because I wanted it so much, I didn't let myself.

I was walking a thin line with her and I knew it. I recalled her comment about me going back to being an asshole again in the morning, and I told myself I wouldn't. I didn't plan to. But I had to find a way to balance this obsessive need for her with everything else.

I didn't have time for a woman in my life. Especially not somebody like her. Somebody who'd take a man over – and he'd be grateful for it.

But I couldn't imagine letting her go, either.

The thought of her not being there...

Mine.

She already felt like mine.

Shit.

I had to find a way to make all of this work.

Isadora was home.

She was safe.

Toni was still here.

I could make it all work. I just had to find the right balance.

"You're really going into work?"

It was just barely past seven in the morning when I met up

with Isadora in the library where she'd slept. She looked like she'd slept well, too. Colton sat at her side, but I barely spared him a glance. He was glaring daggers at me. I couldn't really blame him, but I wasn't going to apologize either. She was my sister.

Speaking of...she said my name, drawing my attention back to her.

"Just for a few hours," I said. I stroked a hand over her curls. "Toni's still here. She'll stay with you and keep you company."

Isadora made a face at me. "I'm not a little puppy who needs somebody to watch me. Besides, she has a life. I can't expect her to drop everything. The nurse is coming later, though, and the staff is here."

I opened my mouth to argue with her. I told the hospital I'd have a doctor on hand. Granted, Toni wasn't a medical doctor, but she had more training than the rest of my staff.

"Ash. She can't quit her life to make you feel better," Isadora said flatly, already knowing what I was thinking. "If you insist that I be watched over twenty-four seven, then *you* do it."

She gave me a sweet smile, and I gave her the glare that could silence an entire boardroom. It had never worked on her, and this time was no exception.

I scowled at her. "Fine. I won't expect her to put her life on hold."

"Thank you." She took a sip from her coffee cup before reaching over and stroking a hand down Colton's arm.

The gesture made my stomach clench, but not just in my usual protective big-brother way. The way they were together, it sent a twinge of jealousy through me and my thoughts automatically flashed to the tiny redhead still asleep in my bed.

"Colton can stay a little longer, and the nurse you hired will be here, like you said. Plus the staff, and security. I'm hardly alone."

"Sounds like you've got all of that under control," I said softly. But she didn't. There were shadows in the back of her eyes. It wasn't a surprise, not really. All I had thought about was getting her back. Now I needed to figure out how to make it all better for her. "So what's the problem?"

"Problem?" Isadora gave me a bright smile that didn't quite reach her eyes. "There isn't one. I just..." She stopped then and sighed, looking away. "Never mind. Go to work, Ash."

I'd upset her. Colton reached over, and ran his hand up and down her back. She leaned against him, snuggling in close as her features relaxed.

I'd known my little sister her whole life. I'd been there when the nurses had brought her in from the nursery so my mother could nurse her the first time. I'd been the one who'd held her at our parents' funeral.

But it was the guy sitting next to her who managed to make her feel better. I'd just upset her somehow. Lately, I always managed to do that, no matter how hard I tried not to. "Iz..."

"I'm fine." She patted Colton's thigh and gave me a tired smile. "I'm going to order up a massive breakfast for Colton and me, and we're going to talk. I'll be fine. You can go."

There wasn't much point in pushing her. Besides, it would be better to leave before Toni woke up.

I needed to regain perspective, and, strange as it sounded, work was a good place to do that.

There was definitely some necessity involved, no doubt. Running the massive companies my parents had merged under the Phenecie-Lang umbrella wasn't a job that could be done part time. Sometimes it was a struggle to get it done in the standard hours I allowed myself. Over the years, I tried to keep it to a forty-hour work week because of Isadora, but that wasn't always an option for a CEO.

My admin had done a good job keeping everything together during the crisis, but I could only stay away for so long.

It was a welcome respite, though, coming into the staggering skyscraper that housed the headquarters of the family empire.

The longer I'd been in the house, the more I'd wanted to stay.

Spend the morning talking to Isadora. Be there when Toni woke up. I almost pulled her on top of me the moment I'd awoken, wanting to keep her close. I actually woke up smiling because she'd cuddled up into my arms while we'd slept, and had one fist resting on my chest, right over my heart. It had felt good there, felt right.

She felt good. She felt right. Like she belonged.

But thoughts like that would only get me in trouble.

Thoughts like that were part of why I'd come into work.

I needed distance, needed to rebuild my walls, and remind myself why the only person I could let matter was my sister.

I'd been in love once. I'd loved Lily as much as I'd loved my family. She'd been my world. After my parents died, she'd been the rock that had kept me from falling apart. She'd helped me deal with Isadora, helped me learn how to become a father to a little girl. And then she disappeared.

Yet another loss I hadn't been able to control.

Sometimes Isadora demanded to know why I was such a control freak. She had no idea just how deep my need for control went, but I knew where it started. I didn't need any armchair psychoanalysis to figure it out.

Losing my folks, being thrust into the role of running the company, taking care of my sister. Lily.

She'd left me.

I'd never known why, either. I'd gone to get her for our

romantic weekend. I'd had my mom's ring ready. But when I'd gotten to her apartment, instead of finding her packed and waiting for me, she'd just been gone.

Whether there had been another man or what, I'd never found any answers.

All I'd ever gotten was a letter from her, tear-stained and full of apologies. Nothing had gone how she'd planned, it had said, but she hadn't really loved me and she hadn't been able to lie anymore.

I could still recall that sickening sensation as I realized she'd left. That she hadn't just changed her mind about getting married, but that she'd never wanted to be with me in the first place.

I'd never told Isadora about the letter. Better she have good memories of Lily and the grief of not knowing the truth. The truth that it had been my fault, that I'd been the one who'd taken Lily away from her because Lily hadn't wanted me.

I wasn't going through that again. I wasn't putting myself at the mercy of somebody else like that anymore.

A small voice at the back of my head whispered that Toni wasn't Lily. I knew that voice too well. It had spoken to me a lot in the weeks after Lily had left, telling me to look for her.

The voice knew shit.

What I did know was that while losing Lily had gutted me, if I let myself get lost in Toni, it would destroy me.

Inside the offices of Phenecie-Lang, I was greeted with courtesy and polite smiles. There were a few of the ass-kissers as well, but I was long used to ignoring them. Everybody else, I nodded at or spoke to as deemed necessary.

Nobody actually seemed overjoyed to see me though. They never did.

The only person who was ever actually happy to see me was my sister.

And Toni...

"Shut up," I muttered to that little voice again.

One of the suits in the elevator bank gave me an odd look. He thought I didn't notice and I let him think that. I preferred that nobody was aware that I was having a mental breakdown. I hit the button for my private elevator and slid inside before I gave them any more free entertainment.

Yeah, Toni was happy to see me. Probably the same reason I enjoyed seeing her. We were good in bed. Fuck that. We were great in bed. What I needed to do was find a way to have that, but still keep my distance.

I went straight to the top. This floor was mine, and mine alone. Along with my office and the office for my administrative assistant, there was a small, state of the art gym, a conference room, a kitchenette, a small but formal dining room, and a bedroom. Sometimes I ended up working far later than I wanted to.

Most of my time was spent in the office, though.

Melody was already striding toward me when I stepped off the elevator. She'd kept everything running smoothly in my absence, and I made a mental note to give her a raise.

She held a stack of files in her hand and didn't even bother with a greeting. "I have contracts that you need to sign, contracts you need to review, and contracts that can wait. There's also other material that needs your attention, some of it quite urgent."

"I can stay a few hours this morning, but that's it. What I can't get done, I'll take home with me to finish up."

"Of course. Are things getting better?" She didn't ask anything too personal, but she'd known more than anyone else, which wasn't saying much.

I'd been able to keep the kidnapping out of the news. Hopefully, it would stay that way, otherwise, my PR team would have some dancing to do to make sure the shareholders and everybody else knew that the company and its holdings were secure. Even the most 'family-friendly' businesses still put the almighty dollar ahead of family.

"Yes." I managed a faint smile. "I'll still be in and out for some time, but I'll probably be able to spend a bit more time here than I have the past few days."

"I'll help as much as I can. Here." She held out the files to me and I accepted. "Be warned, some of these are going to take a couple of hours...each."

"Wonderful." I blew out a breath and took the paperwork into my office, shutting the door behind me.

Those few hours went by quicker than I would have thought possible. As much as I worried for my sister, a part of me relished getting back to work. Now that she was safe, I could actually focus on my job for a little while.

Even though some of it could feel like obligation at times, I loved my job. Even the contracts, as dull as some might consider them to be, appealed to me. It was a puzzle, a huge puzzle, and it all added up to money earned and jobs for all the people who depended on the Phenecie-Lang Corporation.

And right now, the contracts were a much needed break, something new my brain could puzzle over instead of everything that had been eating at me for time untold. I could think about this instead of Isadora or Toni.

Money and the making of it was one love I could count on in my life. It was safe.

Money wouldn't screw me over. If things went bad, it was because I messed up, the market wasn't right, I'd taken a bad risk or somebody else was just better. That was just the game. But it wasn't the money itself.

Money was safe.

As I went to open a new contract, there was a knock at the door. "Come in," I called out.

Melody came in. "I'm sorry to interrupt." She gave me a rueful smile. "You said you had a few hours. That was just over three hours ago. Should you be going?"

I looked at the clock and blew out a breath.

It had indeed been well over the time I had planned to stay. "Yeah, it's well past time to quit." I didn't want to leave my sister alone for too long.

"Of course." She strode forward, carrying a solid stack of files in her hand. "This is the material that needs to be reviewed and copies of the contracts that weren't urgent. I assume you focused on everything that needed to be signed off on immediately?"

"Yes." I scrawled my name on one final thing and handed it off. We traded off and she handed me the bag I'd left on the floor near my desk.

"Are there any questions on anything, or are there any details you need taken care of, Mr. Lang?"

"Yes." I gave her a quick smile. "Have you taken care of that raise I told you about?"

She laughed. "No. A raise for myself has to come from somebody other than me."

"Okay. Email me and remind me. I'll get it taken care of. As well as a bonus." I gave her a serious smile. "Trust me, you earned it."

It was late afternoon before I got home.

I'd planned to go straight there, but I called to check on

Isadora, and when Doug had assured me she was fine, I decided to stop and get her a present. It was an old habit, one from when we'd first lost our parents.

When she'd have a bad day, I'd buy her something.

It never changed anything, or fixed anything, but it made me feel better, and sometimes it made her smile. Foolish, maybe, and materialistic, but old habits died hard.

I found what I was looking for at Tiffany's. While they were wrapping it up, I saw something else. It was a diamond collar.

It looked like something a queen would wear. No, an empress.

An image flashed through my mind. Those glittering diamonds rising in a thick, exotic fashion up a slender neck and draping down in chains to trail over shoulders and collarbone. I could see it on Toni, her hair spread out on my pillow, diamonds glittering.

I pushed the image aside, and when the sales associate asked me if I would like to see it, I shook my head.

Toni and I were involved in a sexual relationship. Nothing more. And that, that wasn't something that went with 'nothing more.'

That was something a man gave a lover.

When I walked in, I heard the murmur of low voices coming from the living room. Immediately, my body hardened. The lower, huskier one...Toni.

I almost turned and walked right back out.

I couldn't do this.

I shouldn't be doing this.

I shouldn't be near her or around her until I had better control of myself.

I went to the living room, swinging the blue bag with a little more emphasis than needed.

Toni's eyes went right to it. The wistful look that passed through her eyes made me think of that collar again. It made me think about turning around and leaving again...to go back and buy it.

Her eyes met mine for just a moment, and then she looked over at Isadora. "Looks like your brother is back to himself. He bought you a present."

A cutting remark leaped to my lips, but I bit it back. I told her I wouldn't be an asshole again, but I had to keep distance between us. At the same time, I refused to put that hurt or anger in her eyes again. Never again.

"Hey, when something works, why change it?" I smiled at her.

That was when I noticed how tense she was. The muscles in her shoulders relaxed slightly.

I wanted to do something, say something. I wanted to make it better. Instead, I looked over at Isadora and held up the bag. "So, do you want it?"

She rolled her eyes. "Of course I do. Gimme."

I laughed and carried it over to her, putting it in her hands. As she tore into it, I looked around, studying the files and scrapbooks. "What are you two up to?"

"Why don't you sit down?" Isadora smiled and patted the space between her and Toni.

"Let me get a drink first." While I was up, I put in a call to the kitchen for some food. I shot them both a smile, making sure to include Toni in it. "I'm starving. Skipped lunch."

Toni was studying me, her eyes slightly narrowed. I tipped my bourbon at her.

"Would you care for a glass?"

She shook her head. "No, thanks. I'm more in the mood for a good, cheap beer."

"I can get good beer here," I offered. "I'm not much for cheap."

"I never would have noticed." She arched her brows and slanted a look at the space between her and Isadora. "You ready to sit?"

"I think I'll take this side." The space between her and my sister was big enough and I'd have a better view of what they were doing.

But it was next to Toni.

Distance, I reminded myself. The key was distance. As long as I managed to keep that thought in mind, I might do it okay.

Chapter 12

Toni

"Is everything okay?"

I moved up behind Ash as I spoke.

True to his newest form, he moved away, but he was so casual about it, flashing me an easy smile. I couldn't even fault him for it. He wasn't being cold about it. No return to asshole mode. Instead, he went to the big display of flowers that sat on the table in the middle of the library and drew out a single, long-stemmed rose, turning to hand it to me.

I took it, but I wasn't charmed by the gesture.

I was irritated.

"As good as I can expect things to be, I guess. Did Marcum or the police call with any news while I was gone?"

"Not that I'm aware of." I shrugged, twirling the stem of the rose between my fingers as I studied him. "But then again, I did leave for a bit to go talk to my professor about missing her class." I didn't add that it was because I overslept after spending the night with him.

His lids flickered, but he nodded. "Isadora reminded me that it's not like you can put your life on hold. You did enough of that last week. I appreciate everything you've done to help."

"Of course." I took a step toward him. It wasn't a good idea, but I couldn't seem to stop myself.

He looked down into the thick, pewter stein he held. He'd

indeed found me a good beer – another one of his attempts to keep me at bay throughout the evening.

"I'm running low," he mused. Without looking at me, he started toward the door.

Fuck it.

"Ash?" I turned away so he couldn't see my face if he turned.

"Hmm?"

I didn't glance back at him, but I could tell from the reflection in the sparkling glass of the windows that he had paused in the doorway.

"Tell me about Lily."

He was looking at me now. I could feel the weight of his stare as strongly as if he was actually touching me. His hands on my shoulders, dragging down my arms, grabbing hands, holding me in place.

Five long seconds ticked by. I counted them off in my head as I studied the flawless petals of the rose I held.

"What did you say?" His voice was flat.

"I want to know about Lily." Spinning suddenly, I lifted my chin and met his gaze.

His eyes had gone blank, and he stared at me in pure shock.

It only lasted a minute. Then he was striding toward me. His hands shot out and he grabbed my upper arms, hauling me to him. "Who told you...?" As quickly as he grabbed me, he let go and I nearly stumbled. "Isadora."

"Yeah. We had some girl time earlier. She told me about Lily, said you hadn't bothered to get involved with anybody since. She also told me I was wasting my time with you. You might want to get in my pants, but that it would never be anything else."

"I never promised otherwise."

The coolly delivered words hit me like a slap, but I didn't

let myself react. Instead, I just nodded. After all, it wasn't totally unexpected. I would've been stupid to actually think otherwise.

"So what's with the iceman routine today?"

"I wasn't aware I was doing any...routine."

"Oh, please." Scoffing, I took a step back. "You're acting like I've gone and picked up a communicable disease." I paused, putting more distance between us. Then with a cold smile, I added, "That means contagious."

"I know what it means," he snapped. "And here I thought I was being courteous. You didn't want me to be a dick. Would you rather I be an ass?"

"This isn't any better!" I glared at him from several feet away. "Right now, you're treating me like a stranger. I don't think I deserve to pay because some chick hurt you a long time ago."

"You're not paying, Toni." His tone had taken on that flat note I hated. "That would imply you meant the same to me as Lily." He paused, as if letting me digest what he was saying. "You don't."

I stiffened, but my expression stayed the same.

"We're great in bed, and you're fun to be around, but we barely know each other. If it wasn't for what happened with Isadora, we wouldn't even be having this conversation. Lily, though...we were going to get married. She was my world."

It was harder this time, not letting myself react.

We're great in bed. You're fun.

Translation: you're a good fuck, but that's all you're good for.

I was an idiot.

Swallowing the knot in my throat, I said quietly, "Well, it's nice to know that I've provided an adequate service for you."

Ash's eyes flashed. "Toni, that's not what I meant."

"Isn't it?" I looked at him as I struggled to keep my voice even. "I thought we'd become, I don't know, friends. I thought I was helping you, offering you..." I shook my head. "It doesn't matter. I can see it clearly now. I've been your distraction while Isadora was missing. Now that she's back, you don't need to be...distracted." He started toward me. Jerking up my hands, I said, "Stay back."

"Look, you need to calm down."

He did not just say that.

"Don't tell me what I need to do!" Baring my teeth at him, I jabbed a finger in his direction. Still, I managed to keep my voice down so no one else would hear. "You don't *know* me, remember? You don't know *what* I need." I raked him over with a derisive look and added, "Unless we're talking about sex, right? Because that's all you know. How to fuck someone. Well, you're done fucking me."

"You're overreacting," he snapped.

"Like I said, you know sex, but nothing else." I gave him a look of mock pity. Holding up a hand, I ticked off a finger as I listed some of the others. "There are certain things you don't say to a woman, and that's one of them. It ranks right up there with *Are you on your period or something, you're not wearing that, are you* and my favorite...*it's not you, it's me*." With a saccharine smile, I said, "And, for the record? When you don't see me around again? Rest assured, Ash. It's *you*, not me."

"What..." he sputtered. "Are you quitting? That's real professional, Toni." He crossed his arms over his chest and glared at me.

The look I gave him was pure contempt. "Of course not, *Mr. Lang*. I don't have to quit to never see you again. Isadora lets me set my own hours, and from here on out, I'll be quite certain to set them so I'm not anywhere near this place during the hours when you're here. I'm done putting up with this shit."

Jutting my chin up, I refused to let him see how much

he'd hurt me, how much I'd been thinking about whatever it was we'd had.

Without another word, I turned to the door.

He said my name, but I didn't look back. There really wasn't a point.

A woman on the New York subway got used to a lot of things. I knew I had.

Bracing my feet and locking my knees in place so the guy next to me who's trying to encroach on my space with his legs spread, and his thigh shoving up against mine...yeah. Used to that.

The guy across from me who was staring at my tits, and pretending otherwise when I met his eyes and stared him down. Used to that, but so fed up with it.

The flirtations that went straight into annoyed insults when I didn't respond.

The flirtations that turned into hurt masks when I made it clear I wasn't interested.

And then there were the creepers.

Tonight it was an unknown creeper, *and* the guy across from me. He wouldn't stop staring at my tits, and when I finally managed to catch his eye and glare at him, all he did was lick his lips and lean back in the chair so he could stroke his penis through his pants.

"Hey!"

The deep, sharp bark of a voice came from the man a few seats down from mine. I shot him a startled look, but the crotch lizard across from me didn't even look away. At least not until a giant of a man crossed the aisle and bent down, shoving his face into the other guy's space.

"You keep that up, and I'll rip your dick off and feed it to you."

The guy's demeanor suddenly changed. He shriveled and he wouldn't look at me or anybody else. The hand on his crotch moved to lay limply against his leg.

The tall guy turned and met my eyes. "You cool?"

"Yeah." The unexpected display of gallantry made me smile. I needed that tonight. "Thank you. Thank you very much."

Dark eyes set against equally dark skin crinkled a little as he smiled. "Ain't nobody should have to put up with that shit, ma'am." He nodded his head at me and sat back down.

When he got off at my stop a few minutes later, I glanced at him cautiously. He nodded at the crotch freak. "He still watching you. I'm just gonna make sure you get out of here okay, if you don't mind. Or you can call the police."

He said it with a deep southern drawl and the sound made me smile.

Po-lice.

"Thanks. My brothers don't live far from my apartment, so I'll call them once I hit street level."

From the corner of my eye, I saw the creeper shifting on his feet. Then he darted back onto the train. It rolled forward a few seconds later.

Strangely, I still felt eyes on me.

The sensation continued as we moved up the steps. "This isn't your normal stop, is it?"

"Nope. Still have a few more to go." He shrugged it off. "You got brothers? How many?"

"Four. One lives out of state, but the other three?" I laughed. "If it wasn't for all the buildings, I could throw a rock and hit their homes, two of them at least." Slipping him a look, I asked, "Why are you doing this? Is it a southern gentlemen type of thing?"

"Naw. Maybe it's a big brother thing. I got two little sisters myself. Guess I like to think that somebody would step in if they were getting that kind of treatment." He glanced around as we came to an intersection. "You wanna make that call to one of your brothers now?"

I nodded and pulled up Deacon's number. He answered on the third ring, and I kept it casual, asked if maybe he was in the area. He was, a block up at a pub with some friends.

Smiling at my unnamed escort, I waved and then moved with the crowd to join my brother.

And still, I had that odd feeling of being watched.

The sight of my building ahead was a sweet one.

I was more than ready to get off the street, even with Deacon walking along next to me. He hadn't entirely bought my excuse of me just feeling kind of blue at the end of a rough day, so I ended up telling him I'd gotten spooked by somebody on the subway.

I'd gone with the insubstantial creeper I'd felt watching me but hadn't seen, rather than the freak, though.

Knowing Deacon, he'd want to go back and try to hunt the jerk down. I didn't want to deal with that.

If I saw that pervert again, I'd take a picture of him and post the asshole on Facebook. Then he'd have my brothers *and* their friends hunting for him. If he thought my stranger savior had been scary, he'd probably end up shitting his pants when he saw my brothers.

"You need to get some rest." Deacon bumped shoulders with me as I unlocked my front door. "You haven't had an easy past couple days."

"I know." I gave him a tired smile. "That's why I'm not asking you to come up for a beer or anything."

"You're an ungrateful sister," he teased.

"Yep." Grabbing him in a quick hug, I squeezed tight. "And to further prove that, I'm leaving you here. Go on. Lemme alone. I'm tired."

Deacon shook his head and gestured to the door. "Get your ass inside and I will."

"Save me from protective older brothers." Rolling my eyes, I headed to the door, keys in hand. Once I was inside, he turned and headed off. I took the time to grab my mail, and then I trudged up the stairs. Now that I didn't have to pretend, my smile faded and my mood turned bleak.

I never promised otherwise.

Ash's voice seemed to mock me with every step I took.

We're great in bed. You're fun.

I was such an idiot.

That would imply you meant the same to me as Lily meant.

I hadn't been looking for a happily ever after or anything. Not really. But I hadn't really been thinking I was just a handy fuck, either. And that's all I'd turned out to be. The knowledge made me feel stupid and childish, because if I'd been thinking, I would have realized this sooner.

I was so disgusted with myself. How could I have done this? And why with him

But if I was going to have a meltdown, I was doing it in the comfort of my own apartment.

Grasping my keys, I jammed the one for the lock and wrenched it to the side. Then the deadbolt. Shoving my way in, I slammed the door and dealt with the locks before spinning and falling back against the door.

"I. Am. An. Idiot," I said quietly. "An *idiot*. How could I do this? And with *Ashford Lang*?"

He was one of the biggest assholes I knew.

But what had I done?

I'd gone and fallen for him.

Tears burned my eyes and I slid to the floor, my hands pressed to my eyes.

This wasn't real. It couldn't be real. I fought the war with tears and won, mostly out of pride. I'd already done something stupid. I wasn't going to compound it further by letting myself cry over a guy who'd already made it clear that I hadn't ever been his friend. All I'd been to him was a piece of ass.

"Not anymore," I said. I pressed my fingers to my eyes. "Not anymore."

I drew a deep breath. Then another. When I finally thought I was steady enough, I got my feet under me and started to push myself up.

Something slid under my hand. Out of reflex, I picked it up, and for the first few seconds, I didn't really comprehend what I was reading.

It just didn't make any sense.

That primal part of my brain understood before the rest of me did.

There was a grainy picture taped to the letter.

It was...me.

Ash and me.

Under the picture was a few short lines.

It won't take anything to slip in his place one night and slice your pretty neck. Talk to the police or even think about it, and that's what will happen.

The letter with its ugly threat fell from my numb fingers.

I suddenly remembered how I felt like I was being watched earlier.

I probably had been.

Who had been watching me? And for how long?

And the most important question…why?

Blindfold Vol. V

Chapter 1

Ash

"Toni took off in a hurry."

I didn't bother looking up at the voice from the doorway. I could practically hear the reproach in my little sister's voice, although her tone was calm and easy. "It's late. She's been putting in a lot of time here, as you pointed out."

"That is true, but is that why she left?"

The direct question was a lot harder to avoid, and Isadora knew I didn't make a habit of lying to her. Others maybe, but not her. Shifting my gaze upward, I met her eyes. Green, like mine, but a different shade, more like our mother's than our father's.

I didn't say a word, but she must have seen something on my face because she scowled.

"I guess not."

She came into the library and went straight for the bottle

of bourbon I'd left out. I frowned as I watched her study the bottle. Then, with a thoughtful expression, she poured some of it into a glass for herself.

"Iz, you don't like bourbon."

"I don't like a lot of things, big brother." She shrugged and turned to look at me. "I need something stronger than a Cosmo at the moment. Now, are you going to tell me what happened between you and Toni?"

I was careful not to lie. "What makes you think anything happened?"

"I saw her face as she was walking out." She lifted the glass to her lips and sipped. Her nose wrinkled and she shuddered. "Damn. That's strong."

If she hadn't been working on getting me to talk about something I didn't want to talk about, I might've thought her expression was funny.

Isadora wasn't giving up. "Plus, I can see your face right now. Something happened."

I gave her a smile that I knew didn't come close to looking genuine. "Everything's fine, sweetie. Okay, it's just—"

Her voice sharpened. "Don't lie to me."

I stared at her. Isadora didn't talk like that to anyone, and definitely not to me. Not ever.

She took another drink, a longer one, deeper one. "I'm going to assume she mentioned Lily."

"Fuck, Iz." I tossed back the rest of my bourbon and slammed the cut crystal glass down so hard, it was a miracle it didn't shatter. I couldn't even look at my sister now. "Why did you tell Toni about Lily? Were you *trying* to hurt her?"

"No, Ash. I'm trying to protect her. Toni's the kind of person who has relationships. You don't. You just do sex." There was a fierce protectiveness in her voice that made my chest hurt. "I don't want you hurting her!"

"I didn't want to hurt her, either!" The shout was so

vicious, we both flinched. I turned away, disgusted with myself more than angry at my sister. "She thinks I was just using her for sex."

"Well, you were."

"No, I wasn't," I fired back. The last look I'd seen in Toni's eyes had left me feeling hollowed out and empty. The feeling hadn't faded with the passing hours or the amount of alcohol I'd consumed. I really didn't want to be discussing this with my sister either, yet I couldn't seem to stop. "I wasn't, Iz. Not really. It just happened." I sighed and ran my hand over my jaw. I needed a shave. "Anyway, it's not like I've got time for a relationship."

"You never have time, Ash."

She'd come up to stand next to me without me realizing it. As she slid her arm around my waist, I closed my eyes. I'd been a jackass, to her and Toni. I didn't want comforted. I didn't deserve to be comforted.

"You spend all your time working or here with me. On the rare occasion you do go out..." She let the sentence trail off.

I was surprised to find myself blushing when she pointedly looked away. Shit. I hadn't realized I'd been that obvious about it. I could only hope she didn't know exactly where I'd gone. That was definitely not a conversation to be having with my little sister.

She continued, "When you do go out, well, it is all about sex. You can't deny that. But maybe the thing with Toni was different. It's not like you ever made a habit of sleeping with anybody I brought around the house before."

"It was a mistake." I'd come to that conclusion in the time since Toni left. It had been a mistake to ever go near her. I'd have to find a way to rectify it. For her sake, and for Isadora's.

"Why? Because you actually let yourself care?"

Damn her. "I–"

"If you tell me that you don't, I just might punch you." She jabbed me in the chest. "I don't want to hear that bullshit. I know you. I see how you are with her. You watch her, Ash."

"She's a beautiful woman." Feeling defensive, I struggled with a reason to make her just stop talking.

"You've known a lot of beautiful women," Isadora countered. "You watch her for other reasons."

"No..." Then I stopped. Catching her hand, I squeezed it once before releasing it. Before she could reach for me again, I walked over to the window. I'd laid the rose I'd given Toni on the windowsill. She hadn't taken it with her. I should have just thrown it out, but I hadn't been able to do it. Now, I picked it up and studied the delicate velvet petals.

"I do watch her," I admitted quietly. "I do care. But it doesn't matter. I don't have time for a relationship, Isadora. I just don't."

"And I already pointed out that you never have time." She gestured to everything around us. "What if Dad had decided he didn't have time? Or Mom? What's the point of everything you do if you never have time to share it with somebody? What's the point of *anything* if you end up all alone? I know some people want it, but, Ash, can you really tell me that's what you want?"

I didn't answer. I couldn't answer. After a few minutes, she must've gotten tired of waiting, because she left.

I dropped down onto the nearest chair and stared at the abandoned rose.

What's the point...?
I didn't know.

I fell asleep.

I didn't know how long I was out, but I startled awake when I heard the alarm being disarmed.

That put me on my feet.

The sound of the door opening took me out into the hall.

What I saw next had me clenching my jaw.

Isadora.

Dressed in a nightgown and robe. Wrapped in Colton's arms. He looked like he'd just gotten off work and he had his face tucked against her neck, while she clung to him.

They looked...right.

They looked complete together, even if Isadora's shoulders were rising and falling erratically, as though she was holding back a sob.

"I can't sleep, baby," she whispered against his chest.

I withdrew farther back into the shadows of the library, keenly aware that I was intruding on a private moment. Still, I heard them.

"I keep having nightmares. It's like I wake up and I'm back there, all over again..."

"It's okay, Dory," Colton said, his voice low, harder to hear. "I'm here. I have you and I'm not letting you go."

I turned away. Quiet as I could, I went back to the couch and sat down. I leaned back and closed my eyes. I hadn't known she was having nightmares. How had I not known? I was glad she had somebody to talk to, to turn to in the night.

The knowledge made me feel more alone than ever.

Toni's face was the last thing I saw before I slid back into sleep.

Morning dawned too bright and too early. Lying there in my bed, I tried to shut it out, along with the voice of my sister from last night.

But her words circled through my mind over and over in an endless loop.

What's the point?

She was like a ghost, trapped inside my skull.

If you end up all alone...what's the point?

I could picture her with Colton, him helping her shoulder the burden of everything that had happened to her. There'd been a time when she would have turned to me, her older brother. For as long as she had been alive, I had been there for her, even before our parents died. It was strange to realize I wasn't the one she turned to anymore.

Realistically, I knew I couldn't expect to be the only one in her life. Isadora was funny and bright and sweet. She loved people. People loved her.

Unlike me. I had wealth and power, and that attracted people. But that wasn't the same thing as having people like me. Care about me.

I lived a very solitary existence, and it was becoming more solitary all the time. First, we lost our parents. Then I lost Lily. Once I'd stopped trusting everybody except my sister, it had been inevitable that I'd have no one but her.

Then Toni came along and shaken my world.

Pushing her away had been instinctive, and I'd done it from the beginning. I could see that now. She was funny and determined, and she didn't shy away from anything. She was everything I didn't have.

So, of course, I'd pushed her away. Tried to keep her at arm's length like I did with my staff.

Other than Isadora, there was nobody I really talked to, and even my relationship with her wasn't as close as it had been. It had taken seeing her with Colton last night to realize we were drifting apart. Or we already had.

What's the point...if you end up all alone?

Twelve hours ago, this was the last place I'd expected to end up.

Twelve hours ago, I had convinced myself I was doing the right thing, establishing a safe distance between Toni and myself. I'd thought we could have a purely sexual relationship. I just needed to find the right way to propose my brilliant plan.

I could have my cake and eat it too.

Six hours ago, I'd had myself convinced it was best that she knew the kind of person I was.

Now I was just hoping she'd let me through the door.

I couldn't quite remember how I'd gotten through the security door that first night. Maybe somebody had taken pity on a drunk bum. Or maybe somebody equally as drunk had been going through and I'd just followed.

I had no idea, and that actually bothered me. Toni should be completely safe, and it was clear that she wasn't here.

Except right now. There was nobody around who looked interested in opening that door, and the memories I had from before were so blurred by booze and memories of being naked with Toni, I had no room in my skull for something as mundane as how I'd gotten inside.

The only memory I clearly recall was of those minutes when I'd woken to find myself in her bed. Even those memories were somewhat muddled by the miserable hangover I'd had. It likely would have been much worse if it hadn't been for her pouring water and ibuprofen down my throat the night before.

Sometimes there'd be a faint flicker of something more. The brush of her mouth on mine. Her body pressed against me. Her voice sharp as she ordered me to drink water, and then soft as she cried out my name.

That was all I had though.

Dread gripped me as I lifted my finger to jab at the doorbell.

It was very likely she wouldn't let me in. But I had to try.

Before I had a chance, the front door opened and a cute black girl just an inch or so taller than Toni stood there. She cocked her head to the side and studied me, lips pursed. With an intense scrutiny, she looked me over from head to toe and then propped her shoulder against the door.

"Well, hello. Can I help you?" She seemed amused to see me standing there.

"Ah...hello. I'm here to see Toni. Toni Gallagher."

Dark eyes glinting, she said, "There's only one Toni in the building. She know you're coming?"

I thought about trying to charm my way past her, but the look in her eyes told me it wouldn't work. I went with the truth. "No. And I'll be honest, if she did, she probably wouldn't let me up." I fudged the next bit. Sort of. "We've been seeing each other and we had a pretty bad fight. I want to make it up to her." I gave her a sheepish smile rather than a charming one. "I don't suppose you'd help me out?"

"If you're trying to make it up to her, where's the candy? Roses? Something sparkly?" She glanced at my decidedly empty hands.

"Toni isn't the kind to be impressed with it." Also, I hadn't thought of it.

"Huh." She grunted out the noise, then shrugged. "That's true enough. So, what if I say no?"

Sliding my hands in my back pockets, I looked away. "Then you say no. And I start pushing on that buzzer and play the waiting game."

I felt like a bug under a microscope, the way she watched me, but whatever she saw must have satisfied her.

"Good for you," she announced with a decisive nod. She stood aside and held out the door. Just before I would have crossed the threshold, she grabbed my arm. "Don't make me regret this."

I gave her a short nod, hoping neither of us would regret it.

As far as things went with Toni, I had more than enough to regret already.

Chapter 2

Toni

Bent over the coffee I just poured, I tried to will the caffeine into my body so I wouldn't have to expend the energy to drink it.

I hadn't slept worth shit. At best guess, I'd gotten maybe two hours altogether, and that had been in stops and starts throughout the entire night.

A bleary-eyed glance at the clock told me I had to leave in an hour. I'd stayed up late attempting to read the section from the syllabus that they'd covered yesterday in class, but I knew I hadn't processed any of it. I was supposed to meet one of my classmates on campus to get notes, but even the thought of having to look over things made my head hurt. The whole idea of school was making my head hurt. I was down to the last few classes I needed, and I just wanted to...quit.

The thought made me wanted to cry.

I couldn't quit. I didn't want to *not* be a psychologist anymore, but life was kicking me so hard and fast lately, I felt like I was going to break.

First, I'd lost the job that was supposed to have gotten me through school, then everything had happened with Isadora and Ash...

My throat knotted up as his face drifted through my mind. "Quit it," I said out loud, my voice rough. "You'll get over him."

I would, too. I wouldn't waste my heart on a man who'd never love me. But I wasn't dumb enough to think it wouldn't hurt a little first.

Before I'd even had time to start that process though, I'd found that damn letter. That *fucking* letter.

They wanted to make sure I knew they could get to me or my family.

They wanted to scare me.

They'd succeeded.

Whoever the hell *they* were.

I felt sick inside.

What was I supposed to do? Part of me wanted to go to the cops, no matter what the mysterious 'they' had threatened. Yet another part of me still didn't trust them after what they'd done to me and my family. I'd lost my scholarship and so many other things thanks to them. Sure, it had been Vic getting in trouble that had started the whole mess, but they hadn't helped.

I didn't want to trust them now, but I didn't know who I could trust, either.

My hand shook as I lifted my coffee to my lips. It scalded my tongue as I took a sip, but I didn't care. I needed the heat almost as much as I needed the caffeine. I felt frozen inside, frozen in a way I knew no heat or sweater could penetrate.

My mug had barely clicked down on the counter when I heard a knock at the front door. Immediately, I tensed, my limbs locking into place for one terrifying moment. Then, suddenly, I shoved backward, surprising myself when I actually moved so hard I fell against the opposite counter.

I groaned at the impact, banging into the sharp surface with enough force to form a bruise. Straightening, I rubbed at my hip as I stared at the door.

Now I was really shaken. Nobody was able to get in my

building without being buzzed in, and I hadn't done it. Maybe someone else had, but that didn't explain why they were knocking at my door. It might've been an innocent mistake, but I wasn't going to take any chances, not with my nerves shot and my stomach churning.

I started toward the door, pausing to grab my Louisville Slugger from its place behind the front door. I held it in my right hand, comforted by the familiar feel of it. I'd played baseball off and on most of my life, and I could still swing hard enough to do serious damage.

"Who is it?" I demanded, satisfied that my voice wasn't shaking.

The rest of me sure as hell was.

Relief went through me in a rush when I heard a familiar voice answer.

"It's me. I heard you yell. Are you okay?"

Ash.

My relief mixed with irritation.

Now my heart was racing all over again, and my hands felt damp and sweaty. The honest part of me knew that had nothing to do with being irritated and that irritated me even more. But I didn't care about the honest part of me.

A sudden rush of longing swept over me, then faded as quickly as it had come. I seized onto the anger before it could go too, because anger was a lot better than the hurt that still echoed inside me.

For the first time since I'd read those chilling words, I felt warm. A side effect of what I was feeling, I knew. That emotion could warm me better than two cups of coffee, and it also managed to chase away the rest of the fear and clear my head of the last of the cobwebs.

Still gripping the bat, I dealt with the locks left-handed and wrenched the door open. "I'm fine."

Ash's eyes slid from my face to the bat. "And still mad at

me, apparently."

Curling my lip at him, I said, "Yeah, well, I don't plan on getting another assault charge because of you. No man is worth it." I tossed the bat back into its place. "Especially not you."

His mouth tightened.

"Don't let the door hit you in the ass on your way back out."

"I'm not leaving just yet."

Over my shoulder, I shot him a dark look. "Oh, yes. You are. I'll get the bat if I have to."

"Toni..."

Spinning on my heel to glare at him, I shouted, "No! You're not doing this again! I put up with your mood swings and your bullshit when you were dealing with Isadora's disappearance, but I'm done! You don't get to push me away any time you like! I'm tired of dealing with your whiny, bullshit insecurities!"

Ash stiffened, a flush creeping up his neck.

I waited, heart racing, my breath locked inside my lungs.

He'd explode or he'd leave. One or the other, I knew it.

But...he didn't.

"You're right."

"Oh, don't give me..." I stopped halfway through my rant as my brain processed what I'd heard. "Wait, what?"

He turned away. "You're right."

Moving to the window, he looked outside. My apartment was up on the second floor and he looked down onto the street, seeing a much different view than he was used to.

His voice was quiet as he continued, "You should know that Isadora tore me a new asshole last night. Once you were gone, I...I couldn't sleep. I closed my eyes and I saw you. All I see is you."

He turned back to face me and I saw the shadows under his eyes. Waspishly, I glared at him, arms crossed over my chest. "Poor Ash."

"Your sympathy warms my heart," he said dryly.

I huffed out a breath and pushed my hair back from my face. As I did, his gaze slid down to my chest. In that moment, I was acutely aware of how the tops of my breasts looked pressing against the low-cut top of my chemise, how the pajama bottoms I wore rode low, just below my hip bones. Judging by the look in his eyes, he was just as aware of the exposed skin as I was.

My arms went over my stomach again. "Yeah, well, I didn't exactly sleep that well myself. If you want real sympathy, find a sycophant. Somebody is bound to give you some real pity."

"I deserved the sleepless night." He took a few steps in my direction, his eyes locking with mine.

I barely even noticed he *had* moved until that four feet between us narrowed down two feet, then one, then it was all but gone.

"I deserve pretty much every cutting insult you have under your belt, Toni."

"Is that an invitation?" I gave him a tight smile. My entire body was humming, just from him being so close. I knew I should take a step back, but I couldn't get my legs to obey.

"Not really." He reached up, trailing one finger down my cheek.

The light contact made me shiver.

"After I say what I came to say, if you want to throw me out, I'll go. But I need to say this."

I struggled to keep the edge to my voice. "I'd rather just throw you out now. I'm not really in the mood to hear anything you have to say."

"Toni, please."

It shouldn't have mattered to me. What I'd wanted, needed, none of it had ever mattered that much to him before.

Why should what he wanted matter to *me* now?

Sometimes, one of you just has to be willing to bend. To compromise. And the one who does it is often the strongest one in the relationship.

My mother had told me that once, after she and dad had argued over her interviewing for a job. She'd wanted it. Dad hadn't wanted her to leave the family business.

I didn't even remember the specifics of it, but when I'd asked her later why she hadn't just gone after it anyway. I'd been maybe seventeen, eighteen, and the feminist in me had balked at my father's behavior. And then she'd given me that advice.

I'd taken those words to heart in all aspects of my life, but it was no good if I only did it when it wasn't that hard.

Ash and I didn't have a relationship, but I could still listen to what he had to say.

Besides, if I were really honest, I'd have to admit I didn't want to be alone just yet. If I was, I'd have nothing to think about except the note, and I needed a few minutes of not thinking about it.

All night, I'd thought about calling one of my brothers. I'd thought about going back home, even. Back to the house where I'd grown up with my parents.

In a way, that house would always be home. But I hadn't let myself do it. I wasn't alone now. As angry and hurt as I was, it was nice to have somebody here, even if it was *him*.

"Fine," I said finally. "Say what you have to say."

"Do you mind if I sit?"

Mind? Out loud, I said, "Sure. Make yourself at home." I threw open my arms, sarcastic warmth filling my voice. "At least until you say whatever it is you have to say. Then you can get the hell out."

The caution in his eyes scraped against my nerves like nails on a chalkboard and I turned on my heel. I needed coffee to deal with this. Alcohol would have been better, but it was too early and I wasn't that desperate. Yet.

More than a little spiteful, I almost didn't pour him any, but at the last moment, my mother's upbringing kicked in, and I fixed him a cup as well. After I'd doctored mine with cream and sugar, I carried both back with me into the small space I used for a living room.

It wasn't much, but it was mine.

Curling up in my favorite chair, I stared at him over the rim of my mug. "So, what's this big, important thing you need to talk with me about?"

His eyes still focused on the coffee I'd given him, he sighed softly. For a few moments, he didn't speak at all. Finally, he shifted his attention to me, his bottle green eyes seeming even brighter against the dark shadows that lay under them. "I already told you that Isadora gave me a rather strong talking to last night."

"Talking to?" I snorted at the phrase.

To my surprise, he gave me a sad smile. "You can thank my mom for that. She learned it from my grandmother. Gram was...well, not exactly what you would probably expect."

He paused and took a sip of coffee.

When he continued, I had to admit, it surprised me even more. The personal talk wasn't like him.

"My grandfather met her in Mississippi. It was pretty much love at first sight. She was..." He puffed up his cheeks before blowing out a quick, hard breath. "Let's just say he surprised everybody, and shocked society when he brought back the beautiful girl from Biloxi, Mississippi. She didn't give a damn what anybody thought of her, and her favorite thing to do was shock the hell out of everybody." He smiled, a fond one. "You probably would have liked her."

"And you're telling me this why?" I asked levelly. "You don't do relationships, and me liking her would only matter if you and I were involved. You made it clear last night that all we have – *had* – was a sexual relationship." I gave him a hard look. "Please note the past tense."

His eyes darted away and a shadow crossed his face. "That's exactly what I wanted to talk to you about."

"Past tenses?" I asked, saccharine dripping from the words.

He ignored me. "I'm glad Isadora told you about Lily."

"Oh, yeah. I could tell. It was so obvious by the sweet way you talked to me." I stirred my coffee, watching the liquid swirl in my favorite mug.

"Yeah, one of the other things I'm sorry for." His voice was soft. "But if I hadn't done that, then we wouldn't have argued, and Isadora wouldn't have torn into me. And I wouldn't have figured some things out."

He put his coffee down and rose.

My heart skipped a beat, then another as he went to his knees in front of me. The look in his eyes was intense, and I felt like he'd cut me open, laid me bare, with that stare alone. I felt more vulnerable and exposed now than I ever had.

I didn't like it.

When he reached out and covered my hand with his, I flinched.

He didn't move his hand though, or stop talking.

"She asked me a question – just a simple one, but I couldn't answer her. I still can't." His thumb rasped across my skin.

Between the intensity of his voice, his eyes and the rub of his thumb across my inner wrist, my thoughts were in shambles.

"She asked me what the point was."

Confused, I shook my head.

"She asked if there was a point to anything. To *everything*. She told me that if I was going to push everybody away, keep everybody out, then what was the point to anything I did?" He lifted one shoulder in a half-shrug. "I'm alone. The only person in my life is my sister, and we're growing apart. She doesn't need me the way she once did. She has Colton, and something tells me she might be looking for a new place, making a home somewhere else for the two of them. Then it'll just be me in that big house. What do I have in my life, Toni? There's...nothing."

Seriously? He came here to whine? "Yeah, I can see how you have so much nothing. You have a giant, beautiful house, and cars that would make my brothers weep. You belong to an exclusive sex club where beautiful women line up to submit to you." I curled my lip at him. "That's a whole lot of nothing, all right."

But my voice shook. My heart was aching despite myself, while another part of me warned me not to let myself get sucked in again.

"Things don't make a person happy, Toni." He lifted my hand and pressed a kiss to my palm.

Jerking my hand away, I glared at him. "Yeah, I know that. Now you're starting to get it and you're considering trying something else to fill the void? Yay. Goodie for you. Go find a girl who cares."

Not one who's already in love with you and tired of hurting.

I shoved him back and stood, moving into the kitchen to get some space between us. I needed to be away from him. My heart couldn't take it. Tears burned my eyes and I could feel myself coming apart.

He came in behind me, his steps slow. Not hesitant, but slow, like he was giving me time to move away.

I wrapped my arms around myself and ducked my head. I wanted him to go, to leave and never come back.

And my heart broke even more at the thought of never

seeing him again.

"I'm not *considering* anything, Toni. I'm realizing. I don't have a life. I have an existence, and it's all I've had for a long time. Maybe since even before my parents died. And I'm tired of it. From the moment I saw you, I felt more alive than I had in years. I want *that*. I want *you*."

"*Want* is easy," I whispered. My voice shook and I squeezed my eyes closed. I could feel it in my chest, the most dangerous thing I could feel.

Hope.

I couldn't hope.

Even though I knew he was close behind me, when he touched my shoulders, I jerked. I spun around, anger and panic sending my heart racing. My eyes were wide, hands shaking. Too much. It was too much. The letter, now him showing up here like this...I couldn't take it.

Sucking in a breath, I started to babble out some sort of lame excuse to cover up my reaction, but it was too late. His eyes narrowed on my face and whatever else he might've wanted to say vanished.

"What's going on?"

Shit. He didn't need to know any of this. "Nothing."

He shook his head. "You're lying. When you answered the door, you looked like you were going to take my head off with that bat. I thought you were just pissed at me, but you didn't know I was coming. And now that I think about it, you looked more scared than mad. Something's going on. What is it?"

I lifted my chin. Hell, no. "You don't need to worry about it."

"Toni." His voice held a low warning.

"Ash." I mocked him as I found my footing again. "Just a reminder, I'm fun and good in bed. That's it. There's nothing between us, so it's not like you have any business demanding to know jackshit about me."

Turning away, I crossed my arms across my stomach so Ash wouldn't see them shaking. My gaze fell on the letter. I stared at it, unable to look away.

And that was where I messed up.

Because when Ash came around, he saw where I was looking, took one long step forward and picked up the letter. I tried to stop him, but couldn't grab it in time.

Defeated, I slumped back against the counter and waited.

I didn't have to wait long.

His eyes cut to mine seconds later. "When in the hell did you get this?"

I glared at him, not appreciating his tone. His face softened and he put the letter down. I watched how he did it, gingerly, handling it no more than he needed to, and then he came to me.

I shoved my hands up to create a barrier between us. "I don't want you touching me."

But my voice wobbled and tears burned my eyes. My hands dropped.

He took it as an invitation, but I didn't have the strength to protest. "Toni, it's going to be all right." He brushed my hair back from my face. The way he said it, it was as if he had no doubt in the world.

"You can't know that."

"Yes, I can." His voice was firm, his gaze intense. "Because I'm going to make sure of it. I won't let anything happen, not to you or your family."

I believed him, but when he slid his hand down to cup my face, I pulled back. I wasn't ready to let him comfort me. Touch me.

His face spasmed, but he nodded. "I'm sorry, Toni. I've been an ass to you, and I'd undo it all if I could. I can't, and I know that. I'm sorry." The words all came out in a rush.

Shivering, I moved over to my chair and sat down. When

Ash came over with a blanket, I stared at him, and then slowly nodded. He wrapped it around my shoulders. I wasn't completely freaking out, but I was in shock. I knew the symptoms.

After tucking the blanket around me, he stroked a hand awkwardly up and down my arm. I closed my eyes and some of the tension drained away.

Again, he said, "I'm sorry, Toni."

I shook my head. "I can't keep doing this hot and cold thing, Ash." Tears pricked my eyes, but I fought them. It was a win, but a narrow one.

"I know." He paused, and then added, "About that letter..."

I looked up at him.

His expression was serious. "We have to go to the FBI."

Chapter 3

Toni

Marcum's eyes skimmed the letter for what seemed like the hundredth time even though we hadn't been in her office more than ten minutes. She wasn't handling it as carefully now that it was in plastic. She wore latex gloves too which, aside from me thinking it was overkill, told me how seriously she was taking things.

I still felt like shit though. My gut was a mess. It had been since Ash had called her from a coffee shop near my apartment, telling her we needed to speak with her, but he had reason to think one or both of us were being followed. She'd told us to stay put and somebody would be there to get us.

Look for the ugliest bastard you ever saw. He's the one I'm sending after you. He's going to tell you that he's in the mood for curry. That's how you know he's the right guy. Got that?

If things hadn't been so serious, I might've laughed.

Twenty minutes after she disconnected, a big, hulking brute of a guy with strangely long arms, a sloped forehead and a shuffling sort of gait came through the door. He'd ordered coffee, then turned and ambled our way. He had the pale skin of a man who never went outside unless he had to. Then, as he'd gotten closer, I'd seen the scar that bisected his face.

Yeah. He was pretty damn ugly. But if he was our rescue,

he was the best thing I'd ever seen.

After he'd dropped into the seat across from mine, he glanced around casually. "These coffee places, all the same, you know? You two hungry?"

Ash glanced over at me.

I'd been too busy trying not to freak out, being surrounded by so many people, any one of whom could've been the person who'd written the letter.

The big guy had smiled. "I'm in the mood for some curry. You guys wanna join me?" Then he tipped the coffee cup at us. "After we finish this, of course."

When Marcum's eyes returned to the top of the page to start reading again, I finally lost my patience.

"For crying out loud, that letter isn't that complicated." Shooting to my feet, I repeated it back to her, word for word, and then listed off how many words had been on the document. "Why do you need to keep reading and re-reading?"

"Because I obviously don't have a memory like yours," Marcum said dryly.

I glared at her.

"That was kind of impressive," she said, smiling a little.

"Thanks," I snapped. "I take requests. Want to hear the St. Crispin's Day speech?"

"I'll pass."

"Too bad. I'm really good at it." I could feel myself relaxing a bit as we bantered. Which, I now realized, had been her intention.

Ash's eyes slid back to me and he cocked his eyebrow. "You know the St. Crispin's Day speech?"

"Yeah. I can also quote the movie *Independence Day* to you in its entirety." Along with a few others. I'm a lot of fun at parties."

"I imagine you would be, but not for that phenomenal memory." He reached out and took my hand, lifting it to his lips. "It's going to be okay, Toni."

The warmth of his mouth on the back of my hand only made me more aware of how cold I was again. I started to shiver and he frowned. When I tried to tug my hand away, he moved in and pulled me up against him, his big body warming mine in a way no jacket, no cup of coffee, no blanket ever could. For a few moments, I let myself be comforted.

When I took a step back and glanced over at Marcum, it was to find she'd finally placed the letter back on the battered desk.

"This is...problematic," she said.

"Really?" I interjected, cutting off just as she was going to say something else.

She lifted her eyebrows.

I glared at her, not feeling at all chastised.

She continued, unconcerned, "Problematic, but not particularly surprising. We've been..." She hesitated a moment, her eyes moving back and forth between Ash and me in a deliberate manner. "Aware of the relationship between the two of you for a while. It stands to reason that others would be as well."

"Others?" Ash asked quietly.

"Surely you've suspected that you have somebody following you, or at the very least, watching you."

She wasn't even looking at me as she said it, her attention focused entirely on Ash now. A muscle pulsed in his jaw. He gave a short, quick nod, a vast ocean of violence somehow contained in that simple motion.

"We've been watching as well, but whoever's doing it is good. We haven't been able to actually see anybody. Equally concerning is the fact that if we haven't seen them..." She grimaced. "We have to consider that somebody might have seen us. That's why I had one of our more skilled undercover agents bring you in."

"You're talking about..."

Marcum grinned at me. "Solokov. He's one of our best. A piece of work, isn't he?"

"What do we need to do?" Ash demanded, impatience clear in his voice.

Marcum sighed and looked down at the letter again. "There's any number of answers to that, Mr. Lang. We already have fingerprints from both of you, so we can run for prints immediately. We'll have to figure out the best way to get the video feed from the security cameras in your building without alerting anybody that we're looking at it–"

"I own the building," Ash interrupted calmly.

What the fuck? I stared at him. He owned my building?

He didn't even glance at me.

Marcum leaned back in the chair, her dark eyes speculative. "You own her apartment building."

"It was a Phenecie-Lang investment back in the eighties, along with hundreds of other properties." He shrugged.

I actually felt a bit of relief at the explanation. At least he hadn't bought it after we'd met. That would've made things even more awkward between us than they already were.

"Technically, I should say my family's company owns it. It amounts to the same thing."

Marcum shook her head, chuckling. "Well, that would definitely simplify things if you could find a subtle way to get us the video feed without making anybody aware of why it's being taken or who needs it."

"I'll get my top security man on it. He's former NSA. If he can't do subtle, I don't know who can. What else?"

I sat there, listening to them talk on and on while my head spun.

This was so far beyond me at this point, I didn't know what to do or think. Give me a study on the long-term psychological effects of bullying or how to counsel a victim of domestic abuse. Hell, I could even work with Isadora and her post traumatic stress issues. I wasn't prepared to deal with being a victim of stalking.

Maybe I had my own control issues to address.

"Toni."

I jerked my head, feeling like I'd been in some weird sort of fugue.

Marcum was looking at me and I had a feeling she'd said my name more than once. Probably once times five. At least. "What?"

"You know you can't go back home."

No. Actually, I hadn't figured that part out yet and I swore, feeling like an idiot. "Fine," I muttered. "I'll go back to my parents. I've got clothes and stuff there–"

"That's not a good plan," Ash said. "They know where your parents live."

Narrowing my eyes, I glared at him. "Yeah. Thanks for that reminder."

"Toni, you need to think now." He leaned forward and covered my hands with his.

I pulled my hands away as the reality hit me hard and fast. They knew where my *parents* lived. My brothers...my nieces, my nephews.

Oh, shit.

My breath started to come in hard, fast pants and I clambered up out of the seat, unable to stay still. Before I could give in to the fear inside me and take off, Ash caught my arms.

"Breathe."

"I am breathing!" I tried to shout it, but I couldn't get enough air in.

His voice was calm. "No. You're panting and you're freaking out. Take a deep breath."

"Let me go!" I tried to wrench away and couldn't.

"Sure. But you need to calm down first. I'll let you go

after you take..."

He let out a grunt of pain as I drove my fist into the meaty part of his chest. I wanted to hit him again, but I forced myself to focus on breathing. He'd been right. I really needed to breathe.

"For the record, I don't like being manhandled. Or told to calm down."

"I'll keep it in mind." He rubbed at his shoulder, but I could see a hint of something in his eyes. A hint of something that said he was holding back a comment about manhandling me.

I looked down at my hand as it gave a throb, grateful for a reason to look away from him.

"Are you ready to listen now?"

Moving over to the window, I braced my hands on the broad window sill. Then I forced myself to breathe in – really breathe. With each slow, steady inhale and exhale, the fog cleared from my head. "Yeah."

"You can't go home. You know that." He wasn't being patronizing, but he was talking succinctly.

"I also know that my family's in danger. My family, my brothers...Ash, I've got a two year-old niece. Her mom stays at home to take care of her. Who's going to watch over *them*?"

"I am."

At his calm pronouncement, I turned to look at him.

Marcum was shaking her head, but he held up a hand. "Look, I can hire private security, and I know the best. I'll get teams watching everybody until we get this wrapped up."

Shivering, I hugged myself, arms crossed over my middle. "And what if it takes years, Ash?"

"Then that's how long they'll watch." He came to me, cupping my cheek in his hand. "You're in this because of us. Because of me. I told you, I'm not going to let anything happen to you or your family."

Slowly, I nodded. "Okay. Okay." I could do this. I looked over at Marcum. "I can probably go to a hotel for a while. Will that–?"

"No hotels."

I turned toward Ash.

His eyes gleamed as he met my gaze. "You're coming home with me."

I raised an eyebrow. "Is that a fact?"

Chapter 4

Ash

"You'll be comfortable in here."

Out in the hall, I leaned back against the wall while I listened to my sister chattering on with Toni. Their voices dropped to a lower murmur, and while I knew they probably weren't talking *about* me, I had little doubt I was the reason for the lower voices.

"Are you sure you're okay with all of this? If you want, I can get you into a hotel. I'll make sure there's security and everything." Isadora's voice was low.

I ground my teeth together. Her offer made me want to storm into the room and tell her she was grounded. Granted, I didn't exactly have any right to ground her any more. I hadn't had that option for years, unfortunately.

To be fair, I couldn't really demand Toni stay here if she didn't want to, but if she tried to leave, there was going to be one hell of a fight. I didn't want her leaving. I wanted her here. Here where I could protect her and make sure she was safe.

If I was being honest though, I actually wanted her upstairs in my bedroom, but she was taking one of the many guest bedrooms. Not even a minute after she'd declined dessert, she'd asked Isadora where Doug had put her things. She hadn't even looked at me when she'd asked it. And my traitor of a sister had said that Doug had put Toni's things in the biggest guest room...which hadn't been where I'd told him to put them.

She didn't want to share my bed. Right now, she didn't want to even be near me. And I couldn't say that I blamed her.

Isadora stepped out into the hallway and slid me a look before heading off. Unfortunately, whatever she was trying to tell me, I couldn't figure it out. I wasn't going to ask her to explain though. Colton had arrived earlier and was down in the kitchen at the moment, eating a late meal. No doubt the two of them were going to spend a nice, cozy evening together.

Envy was a bitch.

How did this come so easy to Isadora?

Shoving off the wall, I ducked into the bedroom without knocking. The pale ivory walls, the vivid green accents and furniture made Toni's hair look brighter than usual as she stood by the bed, taking clothes out of the hastily packed suitcase. She glanced up and paused expectantly.

When I didn't say anything right away, she sighed. "I'm tired, you know. I didn't sleep much last night. I'm planning on soaking in that huge tub and then collapsing on these very expensive sheets."

"Are we going to finish the conversation we were having in your apartment?" I asked bluntly.

"No." She met my gaze levelly. There was no pretense in her eyes, no attempt to hide what she was feeling. She looked battered, bruised and, like she'd said, tired. "I get that you want to talk, Ash, but I don't want to. Maybe you've decided you want to try something new, but it's not about what you want."

The truth of her words hit me hard. "Toni, I..."

"Please." She shook her head, turning back to the task of unpacking her clothes. Doug told her the staff would handle it, but she'd refused, saying she'd rather do it. "Don't. I can't think about this right now."

A strange hollow ache took up residence in my chest, and I heard Isadora's voice all over again. *What's the point?* Good question. Had there been a point to any of this? I'd tried and I lost her anyway.

I heard her move and looked up.

She'd moved away from the suitcase and, as our gazes connected, she pushed a heavy lock of hair behind her ear. The dense, dark red drew my eye, but I wasn't remembering how it felt to fist it around my hands as I drove into her. Instead, I found myself thinking about how alone she'd looked that morning, how much I'd wanted to hold her.

Then I remember how Isadora had leaned against Colton, how I'd seen her relax against him, knowing he'd take care of her. As her older brother, I had to hate him on principle, but I couldn't deny that he loved my sister. I'd seen it so clearly as he wrapped his arms around her, giving her his strength.

I wanted it with Toni, wanted it more than I'd ever wanted anything in my life. I wanted her to trust me, and not only with her body. I wanted her to trust me with her heart.

And I'd probably fucked up any chance I ever had of that.

My voice was quiet. "I get it. I've fucked up over and over with you. I'm an ass, and I have been for a long time. You're the first person who's ever..." The sentence trailed off and I took two steps towards the door, then paused without looking back at her. "I want to try to be...better."

She didn't say a word as I left.

Two hours in the gym didn't help burn off the tension, and a half hour in the hot tub didn't help. Ten minutes under an icy cold shower did nothing except make me curse and shiver.

In the end, I went with an old-fashioned remedy and turned the water up to hot before turning my back to the spray and sliding my hand down my chest, my belly, and lower. Toni had been haunting me worse than usual. I'd pounded out more than five miles on the treadmill, but instead of running away from her memory, it had felt like chasing. Every pound I'd lifted, it had been like I was pulling her *to* me.

Now, instead of fighting, I let them come, all the thoughts and memories of the one person I wanted…and couldn't…have.

Her smoky blue eyes. The silk of her hair wrapped around my hands. Her lips gliding down my chest. Her mouth closing around me. That impossibly hot, wet suction. Except I knew it wasn't her mouth on me. My fist tightened and I closed my eyes, trying to focus on the fantasy.

It didn't take long. Several strokes later, my breathing shuddered and I groaned as my dick jerked in my hand. The climax was empty, but it eased the dull ache in my balls.

Nothing helped much later, though, as I lay in my bed.

My empty bed.

What's the point…?

Hell if I knew.

The sound of the bright, happy voices coming from the breakfast room was enough to make me want to back up to my bedroom and shove my head under a pillow. Either that or find a bottle and hide in a corner somewhere. If I got good and drunk, maybe the weekend would pass in a blur, and I'd have a reason to go back to work Monday morning.

I'd told Toni I realized that my life was empty. I'd told her that I wanted to be better. But I didn't know how. How to be better. How to give my life meaning.

I felt like I was nineteen again, suddenly thrust into a role I didn't know how to play. Because I loved Isadora, I'd learned how to be what she needed, who she needed, but I knew I'd been a poor substitute for what she'd lost. For what we'd both lost. I'd grown poorer still through the years and now I wanted to change all of that. For my sister, for myself. For Toni.

I just didn't know how the hell to do it, and I hated not knowing.

All I knew how to do was make things worse.

Like yesterday.

When we'd finally gotten back to the house, it had been later than I'd planned because Toni had insisted we go by her place so she could get some clothes. We'd argued for nearly ten minutes while still at the FBI office, and we'd kept arguing the entire ride to her apartment. I told her I could buy her whatever she needed and she'd sneered for a minute before laughing a bitter, pitying laugh.

Money isn't the answer to everything, you know.

She was right. I knew she was. And I supposed that was one of the reasons I didn't get it. She was only going back for clothes, toiletries, stuff I could easily replace. It was just stuff.

It had taken Isadora to make me realize the problem.

Toni had needed the comfort of her own things around her.

And I'd wanted *me* to be enough. Although there was no reason for me to even think she'd feel that way. I'd never done anything but betray and hurt her.

As I entered the breakfast room, their conversation paused. Swinging a look over at them, I said sardonically, "Don't let me interrupt the party."

"Oh, don't be such a grump." Isadora grinned at me and crunched a piece of bacon. Normally, I would have joined them at the table, but I didn't know if I could handle sitting with Toni *and* the almost too sweet cuteness that was my sister and Colton. He was staying here for a few days, apparently.

When I'd come down for a drink around midnight the night before, it had been to find Colton and my sister going over the classifieds online. Because of the angle of the computer, I'd been able to see the screen even though I'd paused in the doorway. They'd been looking at apartments.

I'd been so fixed on what they'd been looking at that I hadn't realized the two of them had been having a minor argument of sorts. As I listened, I realized that they'd been disagreeing because he'd wanted to factor in his income. That had made me like him a little more. In true Isadora fashion, she'd been insisting she pay for it alone. Aside from the annual income she received from her share of the company, she also had a hefty enough trust that she could live wherever she wanted. Most guys would like that.

From the shadows, I'd watched them come to a compromise. And I learned more about the young man than I'd known before, both about him personally and the kind of person he was. He'd always wanted to be a teacher, but hadn't had the money for school. As they talked, Isadora had come up with a plan. She'd handle things while he went back to school, and then they'd go back over their finances once he started teaching. *Look at this way,* she'd said, *if you had the money and I wanted to go to school but couldn't, wouldn't you take care of it?*

Colton had kissed her even before she'd finished with her statement. *I guess I can be a kept man for a while.*

She'd laughed. *Oh, baby...I'm keeping you* forever.

Forever.

The word echoed in my head and made my chest tighten.

Looking over at Toni, I found her watching me over the rim of her coffee cup.

I never used to think *forever*.

I never used to think about a lot of things.

But now, all those things crashed together in my head, and they were all tangled up with her, this frustrating, amazing woman with the turbulent blue eyes.

I tried to smile at her, to show her that I wasn't angry with her, but the muscles in my face didn't want to cooperate.

She looked down at her plate, her expression blank.

"There's plenty of food left if you're hungry," Isadora's voice was easy-going, but I knew she'd seen the exchange. There was something sharp in her eyes.

The kidnapping had matured my sister in ways I wasn't entirely sure I liked, but there was nothing to be done for it. Nobody could go back. Things couldn't be undone. I knew only too well the truth of that.

I also knew that if I turned and walked out of the kitchen, they'd all know it was because I was still running. And I couldn't keep doing that, especially not after my discussion with Toni yesterday.

Still, I wasn't in any mood to eat. "I'm not too hungry."

Toni's shoulders drooped slightly and my heart gave a wild thump.

When I took a step toward the table, her eyes slid up to mine and I managed a smile this time. I sat in the seat next to hers. "But I will sit down while I drink my coffee." Giving her a sideways glance, I asked quietly, "How did you sleep?"

"Lousy." She shrugged and went back to picking at her food. "The room's lovely and all, but...it's not mine."

Isadora and Colton were quiet now and I knew they were listening. Toni must've known it too, but she didn't look up from her plate.

"I kept thinking about my family," she continued. "My

parents are worried. My brothers are mad. And it's not like I can explain anything yet, can I?"

I was reaching for her hand before I even realized what I was doing. I didn't stop myself, though. She jumped when I touched her, but didn't pull away. She did, however, look up.

Twining our fingers together, I held her gaze with mine. "I'm sorry."

I felt stupid saying it, but I didn't really know what else to say.

"So." Isadora broke the silence and drew my attention away from Toni. "I already have our weekend activities planned."

I blinked at her. She what? "And what's that?" I asked.

A laughing smile on her face, Isadora propped her elbow on the table and cradled her chin in her palm. "Going through paperwork and pictures. Trying to see if we can't find something to jog my memory or a picture or something. Figuring out who the hell is doing all this, remember?"

I nodded my agreement as Toni shifted on the seat next to me and leaned forward, a frown on her face as she looked at my sister. For a moment, all I could think was that she'd managed to move closer to me. I felt the warmth of her thigh against mine, and the scent of her flooded me. A fist closed around my throat and my cock pulsed, suddenly hard and uncomfortable.

"What exactly are you looking for, Isadora?" Toni's voice was gentle, but firm. "Do you really think you're going to find something or are you just hoping?"

Isadora's eyes slid away.

I understood. In the face of Toni's unwavering confidence, the newly found assurance that Isadora seemed to be relying on just didn't seem as steady. But she didn't back down like I'd thought she would. Lifting her chin, my sister met Toni's gaze again.

"I'm not sure, but there's something to find. I'm sure of it, and I'll know it when I see it."

"Are you sure?" And then Toni's voice trembled slightly. "I'm kind of relying on you for this, Iz."

My fingers tightened around Toni's and she jerked as if she'd forgotten I was there. Still, she didn't pull away, and I counted that a win.

"There's something connecting him to my parents, Toni. I know there is." She reached for her coffee and folded her hands around the mug, staring grimly into the liquid. "Now I just have to find it."

I felt a tug of pride in my gut at the steadfast surety in her voice. It was like she didn't have a doubt. In that moment, I think she was more certain than I was. Usually, I was the one who knew what I was doing, the one who had a plan. I was the one in control.

Except, at the moment, I didn't have a clue what the hell I was doing.

Chapter 5

Toni

We'd been at it for two hours and it wasn't getting any easier. I'd been trying not to feel self-conscious with Ash sitting across from me, looking through his own stack of photos and scrapbooks. Every once in a while, I felt his eyes on me, and it took everything I had not to look at him.

It had taken even more strength not to hunt him down last night.

I'd felt more alone in that big, beautiful bed than I'd thought possible. I didn't want to be alone there.

Fuck it. I didn't want to be without him, period.

It would have been easier if he'd gone all asshole on me again, but he'd been polite, had smiled at me. Even now, he was being civil.

I didn't want him to be *civil*.

I wanted him to...

Stop. I yanked my attention away from all the drama in my head and focused on what I was supposed to be doing. The newspaper articles in front of me were starting to blur together so I shuffled them off to the side. There was no use looking at them if I couldn't pay close enough attention.

I reached for a leather-bound baby book. Isadora's name was elegantly inscribed in the leather, making it clear this baby book had been custom made for her. When I opened it, I saw that the pictures and decorations were done by hand, and I smiled at the notes written in the margins or on the lines provided.

Isadora lifted her head today.

Isadora laughed.

Isadora seems to be recognizing her brother. She smiles when she sees Ash.

Next to the last one, there was a picture of a pre-teen Ash holding baby Isadora. She was looking up at him as if he was the most amazing thing she'd ever seen while he grinned down at her with a look that could only be described as brotherly pride.

"You were an adorable baby, Isadora," I said.

"I'll have you know that I'm still adorable." Isadora shot me a grin. She put down her book when she saw what I was looking at and came to stand behind me. Her face softened as she looked over my shoulder. "My mother was big on keeping these."

Seeing the smile on her face and how she'd relaxed, I turned the page and watched as she reached out to touch another one of the pictures. This one was of the whole family. Then, as she touched another one, her eyes strayed to different images on the page. Her gaze slid away for a moment, and then moved back. I watched as her hand closed into a fist as she sucked in a slow breath and then blew it out hard.

I tensed. Something was up.

"Dory?" Colton was at her side. "What is it?"

I reached over and touched her hand. "Isadora?"

"That's him," she whispered.

Ash's head jerked up and he crossed the distance to his sister in a few quick steps. Next to me Isadora swayed, her face gray, lips bloodless. She started to sway even as Ash reached over to take the book from my lap.

Dammit!

I shot up and grabbed Isadora's arm. "Calm down, sweetie. You need to breathe, okay? You're going to be fine." As I lowered her into the chair, I continued to talk, keeping my voice low and steady. "You're safe, okay? You're safe." I crouched down in front of her, using my hands to ease her head down. "You with me?"

"Yeah." Her voice was reed-thin.

Letting go of her head, I gave her a warning. "Don't look up just yet. Take a few more breaths and move slow, okay?"

"Yeah." Her body shuddered until Colton came up behind her and put his hands on her shoulders. After a minute or two, she finally looked up at me, her eyes dark and haunted.

"You're safe, Isadora," I repeated.

"I know."

The smile she gave me wasn't entirely convincing, but I suspected she was trying to convince herself more than anything else. She flicked a look around the room before letting her gaze fall back to the book Ash now held at his side.

"What was it?" I asked, drawing her attention back to me.

"A picture. There's a picture," she whispered. "The man in it...I saw him there, Toni. The place where they held me. I saw him."

She surprised all of us when she held out a steady hand and asked Ash to pass the book over. I sat back down beside her as she flipped through it, Ash pacing back and forth in front of us like a caged tiger. Colton rubbed a hand up and down Isadora's back as she flipped through the pages. All of us seemed to be holding our breath as we waited.

When she came to the page just before the one where she'd seen whoever it was, she paused, her hands flexing wide before clenching into fists. I heard the deep breath she took in, releasing it slowly before she turned that final page.

"Him," she said. "It was him. He was there."

I looked.

Colton looked.

Ash looked – and then he looked again.

Then he swore a long, loud line of expletives that had all of us staring at him, open-mouthed.

Isadora got to her feet and Colton's arm flew around her waist to brace her. "Ash, who is he?"

He turned away and, in a movement of sudden fury, swept his hands across the top of the elegant bar service, sending crystal and glass flying. Isadora let out a startled yelp and Colton pulled her more tightly against him. No one thought Ash would hurt his sister, but her fainting wasn't out of the question.

"His name is Daniel Trask." Ash's voice was lifeless. "He was...he used to be Dad's business partner."

"Dad had a business partner?" Isadora looked mystified.

"For a while, yeah." Ash turned to look at his sister, ignoring Colton and me entirely. "You weren't even in school when it happened. He was arrested, went to jail for embezzling millions from the company. Mom and Dad tried to keep it as quiet as possible."

Isadora sucked in a breath. If Colton hadn't been there to steady her and ease her back to the couch, she probably would have collapsed onto the floor. He wrapped his arm around her and she curled against him as we continued to listen to Ash.

"The money was never recovered. Somebody on the inside must have tipped him off. When they caught him, he was home, packing. He had his passport and tickets for some island down in the Caribbean. They barely got there in time to arrest him."

"Where is he now?" I asked.

He finally looked at me. "Who knows?" He shrugged, but there was nothing casual about it. "He was released from prison a few years after Mom and Dad died."

"You said his name's Daniel Trask?" I asked.

"Yeah."

"Okay. That's a start." I grabbed my laptop from my bag. "Any idea if he stayed in New York? In the US?"

"No. He left." Ash walked over to the window and looked outside.

I didn't need to see his face to know his thoughts had drifted off somewhere. Colton had wrapped his arms around Isadora and was talking to her softly. Every now and then, she'd nod. I turned my attention from the three of them and to my computer.

As I'd hoped, Vic was logged into Facebook and I asked him if he was still any good at tracking people down. For a while, he'd earned money on the side doing skip tracing – basically, finding people. Specifically, criminals. He hadn't been a bounty hunter or anything, but Vic had always excelled at making money the easy way, and he'd once told me that most of the time, criminals were the stupidest people in the world, hence, easy money.

He replied with a quick, *Hell, yeah.*

I sent him the name and what I knew about the man. Then I added, *Please don't ask.*

He wasn't happy with my addendum, as evidenced by his lengthy internet silence, but finally, he answered with, *I know you, Toni. This isn't about a dinged fender or looking for some old flame. If you don't promise to let the cops know about anything I find, I'll take matters into my own hands...and I'm not above going to Mom*

I promised. I wasn't about to go all vigilante. And I sure as hell didn't want Vic telling Mom. Four brothers, I could handle. Billionaire CEO who enjoys bdsm, no problem. My mom? Hell no.

As soon as I promised, Vic agreed, and in less than fifteen minutes, I had answers and some updated pictures.

Vic, you're a wizard. Thank you.

The room was quiet, but I still felt like I was interrupting when I spoke.

"He went to Monaco." Skimming the information Vic sent me – and was still sending – I relayed the pertinent facts. I could feel eyes on me. "Made a lot of money in construction over there. Then, no surprise there, legal troubles. One of the companies he was invested in was shut down. Corners were cut and workers got hurt. Two died. The government came after them. One thing after another. He's broke now. Or close enough. And..."

I stopped, my heart starting to race as I saw that last bit that Vic had sent me.

"And what?" Ash asked sharply. "Where are you getting all of this anyway?"

I closed the Facebook window and cleared my browsing history as Ash came striding toward me. Ash didn't need to know that I'd involved my brother.

"You have your ways and I have mine," I told him.

For good measure, I closed the top of my laptop, but he grabbed it anyway. Scowling, he flipped it open, but it was set to lock, and I kept it password protected.

"And *what*?" Isadora demanded.

"He's back in the US right now." I looked over at her as I said it. "He flew in last week."

"How do you know all of that?" Ash demanded again.

"I know somebody who's really good at finding people." I held out my hand for my laptop. He ignored me, tapping at a few keys. His scowl deepened when none of the combinations worked.

"You'll never guess my password, so stop trying."

He shoved the laptop into my hand, his gaze furious.

"This guy's threatening my family now too, Ash." Moving to sit next to Isadora, I typed in my password and brought up a search, using his full name and the city Trask had listed as his current residence.

It brought up a fairly limited search and there was one image attached to a news article from four months ago. Clicking on it, I skimmed the post, only barely glancing at the image, but when I started to scroll down, Isadora stopped me.

"Wait," she said, her voice strangled.

Her voice was harsh, her cheeks pale save for a flag of red riding high on her cheekbones.

"That's him," she whispered.

I looked down to see her pointing at the man standing behind the man I assumed to be Daniel Trask. He was staring grimly at something off to the side of the camera, while the man behind him stared directly into the lens, like he wanted to punch the man holding it.

Isadora's next sentence caught my attention. "That's the man who grabbed me."

Chapter 6

Ash

"We have to go to the cops. Call Marcum."

Toni's words sounded oddly loud and I instinctively glanced at Isadora. Colton was holding her, but she was still shaking. A surge of protectiveness went through me.

And then I saw Isadora look over at Toni and nod in agreement.

Hell no. "We're not going to the cops."

As Toni swung her head around to stare at me, I continued, "We're not calling Marcum. Not yet. Not right now."

Isadora didn't say anything, but Colton's mouth drew into a tight frown, his shoulders rigid. I didn't care about what he thought though. This didn't involve him. Toni narrowed her eyes, and I braced myself for the explosion that was coming. It didn't matter. This was my family in danger. My *only* family. I was going to protect Isadora no matter what it took.

Or who it pissed off.

"And why aren't we calling the cops?" Toni asked, her voice deceptively quiet.

"I already mentioned that Trask had somebody working with him on the inside. I don't know if it was inside Phenecie-Lang...or if there was somebody dirty on the force or with the FBI." Crossing my arms over my chest, I stared down at Toni, refusing to let myself be distracted by her. "Plain and simple, I don't know who I can trust, and until I do, I'm not risking my sister."

"She's not the only one in danger here," Toni said, fury vibrating in every word. "I deserve to have a say in what happens."

"This is a family matter," I snapped. "It doesn't concern you."

"Ash..."

I heard Isadora start to speak, but then Colton was murmuring something and they were walking out of the room. I didn't have a chance to process any of that though, because Toni was coming at me.

"I had a letter shoved under my door!" Her voice rose and her eyes flashed as she jabbed a finger at me. "A letter that threatened my family, Ash! That sure as hell concerns me!"

"And they kidnapped my sister! They might have been involved in the death of my parents!"

"So because you were involved first that means you get to be in control? The danger to my family is less important? Or do they just not matter?" Her voice cracked. "Fuck you, Ash. I have a right to have a say in what happens to my family!"

"My parents might be dead because of a dirty cop!" I wanted to grab her and shake her. Didn't she get it? What if something happened to Isadora? To her? I could keep security on her family until we had a better idea of what was going on. Her and Isadora, I had to keep close. "I don't want anything else happening!"

"Yeah." She curled her lip in a sneer. "To you. To your sister. But fuck the rest of the world. You're a real prince, Ash."

"That's not what I said." I caught her arm when she turned away, but she jerked back.

"Maybe not, but that's kind of your usual go-to attitude."

She raked me with a dismissive look. "I'm sure you've got it in your head that you'll just keep security on my family while you try to work this out, but what happens when they decide they'll go after one of my dad's employees since they can't get to him? Or Trask sends someone to the school where my sister-in-law teaches? I'm guessing these clowns don't much care about collateral damage."

She was coming up with scenarios I couldn't even try to find answers to, and I could see her fury growing, the distance between us spreading all over again.

But I couldn't do it.

"Toni, if we call the cops, and one of them is dirty, then everybody is in danger," I said.

"News flash, asshole," she snapped back at me. "Everybody already is in danger."

Chapter 7

Toni

I was done. Done with this world where I'd never belonged. Done with this man who didn't care about the hell he was putting me and my family through.

I turned and walked out of the room. I heard footsteps behind me, but I ignored them.

"Toni."

"Go away," I said shortly.

He didn't.

I made it up the first flight of stairs, but on the landing, he caught my arm. I whirled around and slapped him without a second thought.

"I told you to stop manhandling me, you bastard!" I growled at him.

I raised my hand to slap him again, but he caught my wrist. In a blur of movement, he shoved me against the wall, and pinned my captured wrist over my head.

Heat and rage merged together, then exploded as he slammed his mouth down on mine. His tongue shoved between my lips, and I bit down as I struggled against his grip. He growled and let go of my hand to shove his between my thighs. I'd worn jeans. I was both grateful and miserable of that fact just then.

As he rubbed against me, his tongue curled around mine

and teased, taunted. I should've pushed him away, but my hands clung to him. He shifted against me, grabbing my hips and lifting me. My legs automatically went around his waist, pressing him in just the right spot against me. He rolled his hips and the friction bordered on pain.

Fuck.

If he stopped, I was going to kill him.

When he pulled his head away, I grabbed him and yanked his mouth back to mine.

He bit my lower lip and it made me whimper.

His hand pushed my top up and roughly yanked at my bra until he had my breast freed. As he worried my nipple into a tight little point, I arched my back, pushing my breast against his fingers. The need inside me was a burning, a sharp, painful desire that I knew was going to break me...

Fuck.

"You're not doing this to me again." I pushed against his chest as I untangled my legs from around his waist. As Ash took a step backwards, I managed to get my feet underneath me.

"Doing *what*? Look, we can talk about–"

"Doing *what*? Are you fucking serious?" I shoved him again, just because I had to get rid of some of the anger, some of the hurt. And he was the closest outlet. To my complete and utter horror, my voice hitched, then cracked. "You try to act like I'm not just another piece of ass..."

"You're not," he insisted. "I came after you because..."

He started toward me, but I slapped at his hands.

"No." Shaking my head, I backed away from him, feeling sick inside. "You came after me because you wanted to fuck, because that's what you do when you get pissed."

"Toni..." His voice trailed away as his gaze landed on my face.

Something he saw there must have spoken volumes

because he lapsed into silence.

"You might've thought you meant it, but only because you enjoy sticking your dick inside me. It's lust and that's easy enough to satisfy anywhere. You should know." I wasn't going to listen to my hormones or my heart anymore. It hurt too much. I had to think of my family. "You seriously think I should be okay with letting you call all the shots on this."

His eyes flicked away.

Clenching my hand into a fist so I didn't reach for him, I shook my head. I understand where you're coming from. You love your sister, but that doesn't mean you've cornered the market on that emotion. I love my brothers, my parents. You think you'd do anything to protect her? Multiply that by four for my brothers, then make it six because I've got my mom and dad. Now add in Deacon and Franky's families. Children, Ash. My nieces and nephews. You think because she's all you got that you love her *more*? Or maybe because you're loaded that your decisions somehow trump mine?" I squared my shoulders. "Guess what? I don't care about your money. I don't care if you can buy and sell this block three times over. Respect and decency, compassion, all that means more to me than how much money you've got. And you don't respect me." The truth of that statement made my chest hurt.

"That's not true," he said, shaking his head.

"It is. Otherwise you'd already understand this simple fact: I'd die for any of my family, twice over, and they'd do the same for me, but you want me to sit back and twiddle my thumbs while you decide what's best." I couldn't even meet his eyes. It hurt too much. "You think you get to make all the calls, because your sister is all that matters."

The misery inside welled outside of my control now and my voice broke. My eyes were burning and I fought not to cry. Not in front of him. This time when he reached out, I moved away so violently, I almost fell.

"Don't you touch me, dammit! I already told you, you're not doing this to me anymore!"

Slowly, his hand fell to his side.

I needed to get out of here.

"Please, just leave me alone."

For a moment, he looked like he was going to try and say something else, but in the end, all he did was nod. He shoved his hands into his pockets as I turned away.

I couldn't fall apart.

Not yet.

Not with my families' lives at stake. My heart could wait.

Chapter 8

Toni

I could still feel his eyes on my back as I closed myself inside the guest room they'd given me last night. My suitcase still lay open, propped on a stand I'd found in the closet. I hadn't put everything away. On some level, I must have had an idea that this wasn't going to work out.

"How many times are you going to let him hurt you like this?" I whispered.

To be fair, I hadn't exactly intentionally set out to let him get to me like this at all today. But something about him just brought it out in me.

Further proof that I needed to get out of here.

"You know better than this," I said, sighing. The sound came out wet and broken, the tears I was fighting edging closer and closer. I didn't have time for tears. I had to pack. Call a cab. Get out of here without Ash trying to stop me. I didn't know if he still would, but I had to do it while this hurt was still looming large in my mind. If I waited too long, I might forget how bad the ache was, or get needy and desperate. And stupid.

Everybody had a right to be an idiot once in their lives, I supposed. My brothers had all done it. Vic more than once. And if I started counting relationships in there...Deacon and Franky might've married great women and hadn't dated much before them, but Kory and Vic more than made up for it.

Considering how the past two weeks had gone, I was going to write this off as *my* idiot time. Between the finals I'd missed and papers I'd turned in late, not to mention the fiasco of missing my class earlier this week, I was sure pretty much everyone who knew me would agree I'd been an idiot.

It didn't take more than ten minutes to re-pack what little I'd gotten out, and just as I was closing my suitcase, somebody knocked.

I ignored it.

I had no desire to talk to Ash again although he'd probably just barge in anyway. I should've just locked it. A moment later, the door opened and I clenched my jaw as ugly words boiled up my throat. I spun to yell at him, except it was Isadora who slid inside.

She looked at me, then at the suitcase. "You're leaving," she said, her voice calm.

"Damn straight." My voice was husky, but level. Looking into her concerned eyes, I made up my mind. "I'm also quitting. If you need me to work two weeks for official notice, I will. But I'd rather not. I'm sorry."

Her lips pursed, and she sighed. "This hasn't exactly been the easiest way to start out a new job, has it?"

"Oh, the job was wonderful." I hurried to reassure her. I didn't want her thinking any of this was her fault. "I really enjoyed working with you. It's just..." I let my voice trail off.

"I know." She moved deeper into the room, tugging her pale ivory shawl more closely around her shoulders. "Do you hate him?"

"What...no." I wished I could though. Turning away from her, I levered my suitcase off the bed. "I'd like to, but no. And it's not all...I'm down to the wire with my classes and I'm barely able to concentrate. I missed an important class a couple days ago because I was so tired, I slept through my alarm. And

I missed another class yesterday."

Looking defeated, she settled down in the chair. "You've worked so hard. I can't let you put any of that at risk. But is now the best time to leave? It's not safe. You know that."

"I'll go to a hotel." I shrugged. I hadn't really thought further ahead than getting away from Ash. "I'll order in pizza and watch movies. When it's time for class..." I frowned. "There's campus security. Or I'll talk to my brothers. Vic'll come with me. I'll be okay."

"Toni, please." She had a pleading tone in her voice.

I shook my head and hoped she couldn't see the tears in my eyes. "I–I can't. I can't be around him, Iz. It's just too hard."

Chapter 9

Ash

The door closed softly behind my sister, but the sound echoed in my head.

I was still sitting on the stairs, looking at absolutely nothing when somebody came out. My head jerked up and my heart leaped.

I was half-way to my feet when I realized it wasn't Toni. Isadora bore down on me with a look of complete and utter disgust on her face. The sight of something so foreign on her face caught me off guard, and I found myself backing up a half step before I realized what I was doing.

"You're an idiot. And an asshole!"

I almost looked around, sure that my baby sister couldn't be talking to me like that. Her voice was harsh, almost unrecognizable, and I suddenly realized that her eyes were glittering with tears.

Shit.

"What are you doing?" she demanded.

"Iz..."

"You know what, just don't." She held up her hand. "Do you know what she's doing in there? She's leaving, Ash. *Leaving*. She's putting herself in danger because she can't even stand to be around you."

"Like hell she is!" The words popped out of me before I

could stop them. I started to step past Isadora.

"You can't stop her," she said as she grabbed my arm.

"If I have to tie her to a fucking chair—"

"Like they did to me?" Isadora said, her voice flat.

I went still, shock freezing me. "No..." I had to clear my throat. "Iz, no. Not like that. I just...I want her safe. I need her safe."

"And she wants her family safe. You can't control everything, Ash. But because you can't seem to get that through your thick head, we're going to lose Toni." She glanced back toward Toni's closed door. "Look, I know you never got over Lily leaving you like she did. But Toni isn't Lily. Nobody is."

"Iz, don't." I shook my head. I didn't want to think about Lily.

"Look, I know she broke your heart, and that you hate not knowing what happened to her. I tried to find her for you, tried to find out why she'd..."

"She didn't love me."

Isadora shook her head. "You don't know that. I found out that her things were moved out of her apartment by a moving company. No one's seen her since..."

"She wrote me a letter."

My sister's eyes widened, then narrowed. "She what?"

I sighed and ran my hand through my hair. "A couple weeks after she left, I got a letter in the mail. No postmark, nothing I could use to try to find her. But after I read what she wrote, I didn't want to find her." I worked to keep my voice flat, emotionless. "She said that she couldn't lie to me anymore, that she didn't love me. She never had. She was just using me."

Isadora was silent for a moment, and then her expression hardened.

"So what?"

I blinked.

She continued, "You've judged every woman you've met based on Lily and what she did, and it's unfair. You're going to lose the best thing that's ever happened to you because some woman broke your heart years ago? You're not just an asshole. You're a stupid asshole." She took a step towards me and poked me hard in the chest. "If you lose Toni because of Lily, you deserve to spend the rest of your life alone and miserable."

Before I could recover, the door opened and Toni stood there. I sucked in a breath at the sight of the suitcase in her hand. Her gaze flicked past me to settle on Isadora and she nodded at my sister while ignoring me completely.

"I've got a cab on the way. I'll call when I get settled."

Isadora's mouth wobbled before firming into a smile. "Okay."

Toni started toward the steps and my head spun, desperate for something, anything, to keep her from going.

"Don't go," I said, the words coming out through stiff lips.

She didn't even pause.

"Toni, wait."

She kept right on walking.

Getting desperate, I moved toward the railing as she started down. "Dammit! Toni, please."

I didn't remember exactly when the shroud of ice had settled around my heart, but I did remember when I decided to never allow myself love anybody again.

It had been one month to the day after I'd planned on proposing. I'd been trapped inside the office buildings of Phenecie-Lang while a miserable snowstorm had raged outside. Isadora had been safe at home with the staff and I'd been alone. As I'd stared out into the blowing wind, I'd decided that Lily leaving had been a good thing. Love, after all, made a person vulnerable. Better to protect myself. Isadora would be the only person I'd let myself love.

Now, with each step Toni took away from me, I could feel my heart breaking despite myself. It didn't matter that I tried to push her away or that I'd never said the words out loud.

I could almost hear the ice in my chest cracking, thawed by a warmth that had nothing to do with temperature. It was her. All her.

I couldn't go back to that again.

"I love you."

She hesitated for a fraction of a second, and I grabbed at the chance.

"Please, Toni, I've fucked this up so many times and I know that. But please. Please, baby. Please don't leave me. I love you."

Chapter 10

Toni

I could feel hysterical laughter bubbling up in my throat, and fought to keep it back.

Was he fucking kidding me?

I love you.

I told myself to keep going. That was all I had to do. Keep walking. Down the steps. Out the door. Out of his life forever. Dazed, I took another step, then two more.

"I love you, Toni."

He said it a third time. My hand tightened convulsively on the handle of my suitcase, and I sank down on the stairs, setting my suitcase on the one below me. My legs simply wouldn't hold me anymore.

I closed my eyes. *Don't listen to him. Don't listen.*

Not a single stair in the whole Lang house would dare squeak, not a single floorboard either, but I still knew exactly when he came up to stand behind me.

"Don't do this," I whispered. I told him before that I didn't beg, but I was begging him now. Begging him not to hurt me again. "Every time I try to pull myself free, you do or say something that sucks me right back in. You keep hurting me or twisting me up and I'm tired of it. I'm so tired." My voice cracked on the last word.

I sucked in a breath as he put his hand on my back. As he

began to move it in soothing circles, I struggled not to lean into his touch, to take the comfort he was offering. I knew all too well that his comfort came with a price.

"I'm so sorry, baby," he murmured. "I'm not a nice guy, Toni, but you're the only person who makes me want to be better. Please, stay. We can talk this out. You were right. I shouldn't be the only one making the decisions."

Hesitantly, I looked up at him. Was it possible that he really understood the deeper issue here?

"We'll call the FBI," he promised.

"It's already done."

At the sound of another voice, both Ash and I looked up. Or, rather, down. Colton was at the bottom of the stairs, his eyes hooded and expression grim as he looked up at us.

Ash tensed.

Sensing the explosion, Colton took a couple steps up to bring him closer to us. "Toni was right. Your family's not the only one involved." He ran his tongue across his teeth before he added, "I didn't get a letter, but there was a picture of my dad shoved under the windshield wiper of the truck I drive for the plant sometimes." He looked past us to where I knew Isadora was standing at the top of the stairs. "You don't trust the cops, Ash, and I get that. I don't always trust them either. But if we go running around like a bunch of kids playing junior detective, somebody will get hurt. I want my family safe. And even if you don't like me, that includes your sister."

Isadora came down the stairs, not looking at Ash or me as she stepped around us. As she wrapped her arms around Colton, I waited. My insides felt strangely hollow, like everything had been scooped out of me.

"You're right," Ash said finally. "You're all right."

He might've said more, but the doorbell rang and we all stiffened. A moment later, Doug came to tell us that Agent Marcum was waiting for us in the main sitting room.

Ash helped me to my feet and put his hand on the small of my back as we walked down the stairs. I didn't pull away, but I didn't encourage him either. My head was still spinning from everything he'd said. I needed time to process, but I knew I didn't have it. The FBI was waiting and I needed to focus on that. Once Agent Marcum was done, I could worry about everything else.

It was a long and frustrating two hours before she finally left.

After Agent Marcum departed, Isadora and Colton quickly made themselves scarce. As they walked out, Doug came in.

He glanced at Ash, but directed his question to me. "Should I call another cab, Miss Gallagher? I sent the other away because you were busy with Agent Marcum."

Woodenly, I stared at the floor. It was the smart thing to do, and I was supposed to be smart. Walk away. Don't look back.

"No, thank you," I said without looking at Ash. I needed to see this through, to see if he meant anything he said.

Once the two of us were alone, however, I had to fight the urge not to change my mind. The tension between us was thick, uncomfortable, but I didn't want to be the one to break it. I wanted to know if he was willing to step forward, to take responsibility, without me feeling like I was talking him into it.

I shifted my gaze from the floor to my hands, studying my fingernails without really seeing them.

"Are you going to look at me?" he asked finally.

"I know what you look like." Despite my words, I turned my head. I knew it'd be childish of me not to, and what I said had been juvenile enough. I needed to be a grown up about this. I wasn't five and I wasn't being scolded by my mother for putting itching powder in Vic's shoes or tying all of Franky's socks into knots.

Not that I'd done any of that.

Ash looked awful. It was as though he'd aged decades in the past couple hours. His face was hollow, eyes dull. Somehow, in the hours that had passed between his declaration on the steps and now, the light that had been inside him seemed to have died out.

I felt the same way myself. Empty. "What do you want, Ash? Why are we still doing this?" I asked. The sound of my own voice made me flinch, but I kept going, saying all of the things I'd reminded myself of over the last couple hours. All the reasons why this wouldn't work. "Nothing's going to change. You want to control, to dominate, and not just in the bedroom. You told me that in a Dominant / Submissive relationship, there has to be trust, and that's the problem. You expect trust when it comes to sex, but you won't give it anywhere else. And that's fine if all you want is sex, but I'm not wired that way. Part of it's my fault for thinking we could have that in the bedroom, and at least be friends outside of it. But even that doesn't work with you. You don't respect me."

His jaw tightened and I knew I was hurting him. I could see it, and I hated myself for it, but I wasn't going to lose myself to him.

My voice hitched as I continued, "You don't love me, Ash. You want to possess me. And, sooner or later, it will break me. And I'll hate myself. I'll hate you."

"I don't want to..." He looked down, rubbing at the back of his neck. Shoulders slumped and head bowed, he looked defeated. "You're right. I'm a control freak. And I don't trust anyone. You know about Lily..."

"No," I snapped, irritated. Shaking my head, I got to my feet and started to pace. "I don't want to hear about how your ex vanished and that's why you can't–"

"She sent me a letter," he interrupted. "I never told Isadora because I wanted her to remember Lily as a good person, someone who loved us both." He turned slightly so he wasn't facing me. "But she hadn't loved both of us. She'd never loved me. It'd all been a lie."

My heart broke, but not only for the man standing in front of me. It broke for the young man who'd given up everything for his sister, who'd thought he'd found a ray of happiness in all of the grief. And then found out that it'd been a lie.

"I never wanted to be hurt like that again, so I closed down," he said quietly. "I threw myself into my work, into raising Isadora. I told myself that she was the only person I could love because I knew she'd never betray me. She was the only person I could trust. And for years, she's been the only person I've ever wanted to let close." He turned back towards me, eyes intent. "Until I met you."

I swallowed hard. I wanted to believe him. I was tired of fighting with him, of being hurt by him.

"I tried so hard to not...I thought if I reduced what I felt for you to just sex, it'd go away. But it didn't. I couldn't stop thinking about you, wanting you. Yes, I want to control, to dominate you. I want to possess you because it's the only way I know how..." He swallowed hard. "I'm desperately in love with you, Toni."

The baldly stated words made my heart clutch and I wrapped my arms around my middle. He came towards me and I wanted to run. I wanted to run as fast and far as I could and never look back. What I felt for him was too big, too scary, and I'd meant what I said. He had the power to break me, and if he did, I'd hate myself. And him.

When he reached me, he went to his knees in front of me and I stared down at him. He put his hands on my hips and gently coaxed me down to sit on the chair. We were the same height now and it took all my self-control not to look away. He slid his fingers into my hair, cupping my head in his hands. "You're the only woman I'll go to my knees for. I'll beg, if that's what it takes. Just tell me. Please, Toni. Just tell me what to do."

Fuck.

I was still a novice to all this Dominant / Submissive thing, but I knew Ash, and I knew what it cost him to say those words, to ask me to tell him what to do. His fingers moved to cradle the back of my head and I fought a groan when he began to massage my scalp. Reflexively, I let my head slump forward, resting high on his chest.

"If you don't love me, if you don't want me, just tell me, please," he said into my ear. "And I'll get up right now, and leave you alone. Doug can arrange for your safety, and I won't bother you again. But you have to tell me that you don't care about me."

Damn him.

"I can't," I whispered.

He tilted my head back until I met his searching gaze.

"You can't?" The vulnerable hope in his voice was my undoing.

I shook my head. "No. Because it wouldn't be true."

The feel of his mouth on mine sent a shock through me and I shivered. His hands slid down my back and my arms moved to circle his neck. When he tugged me down onto his lap, I went slowly, although I couldn't say reluctantly.

He paused as he slid his lips down the line of my neck. "Do you want me to stop?" His breath was hot against my already over-heated skin.

My body definitely didn't want him to stop. Ever. But my brain was still looking out for my heart.

I pushed myself away from him and stood. It was easier to do this if he wasn't touching me. "You need to understand something," I said. "I'm done with the back and forth shit. I'm not expecting an overnight change, but if I don't see you trying to do better, if you aren't respecting me and my opinions, I'm gone, Ash. I'm not going to give you a warning, and I'm not going to let you in the next time you come around. It'll be over. For good."

He nodded his understanding. "I will do better. And when I start to be a domineering asshole – outside of the bedroom..." He canted a grin at me. "Then I want you to call me on it. I'll listen."

"Will you?" I wanted to believe him.

He stood in front of me, his expression serious. "I will." He leaned down and pressed his lips to mine. This time, the kiss was deeper and...different. Hotter, sweeter, more intimate. It was almost like he was kissing me for the first time.

When he lifted his head, I was shaking, my body swirling with myriad emotions. My knees were weak, but his hands were on my hips, holding me up, giving me strength.

He pressed his mouth to my ear. "I want you naked."

The words were soft, more like a question than an order. With a start, I realized he was waiting for permission.

"Since when do you wait for anything?" I asked him.

"Since I'm trying to prove to you that I can be different."

My stomach clenched. He was serious.

"I never said I wanted anything different in the bedroom."

His eyes darkened and, for a moment, he didn't do anything at all. Then he moved with a speed that left me breathless. He scooped me up into his arms and headed straight for the stairs. I had a feeling that if the sitting room had a door, he wouldn't have even bothered taking me upstairs.

He went into the first door he came to and kicked the door closed behind him. I looked around, surprised that we weren't in a bedroom, but what must've been some sort of small sitting room or reading room. He carried me over to a fat, over-stuffed love seat, and put me down on the heavily padded top before fumbling with my jeans.

Precariously perched there, I swayed a little as he dealt

with my shoes, and then tugged me down so he could get me out of my jeans.

"One of these days," he said against my lips. "I'm going to make love to you slow and easy."

I could have told him that I didn't want slow and easy, but then he was lifting me onto the top of the love seat again. A moment later, he buried himself inside me, and I cried out his name. His fingers bit into the soft skin of my ass as his cock stretched me wide. I whimpered at the conflicting sensations of pain and pleasure. It happened so fast, my body wasn't prepared, no matter how much I wanted it.

He rested his forehead against mine as he held himself still inside me. "I love you, baby. Please, don't leave me."

I strained against him, gasping when I felt his body rub against my clitoris. He shoved his hand under my shirt, cupping my breast through the material of my bra. He teased first one nipple, and then the other into hard, demanding points. I writhed against him, desperate for him to move.

"I love you," he said again, the words fiercer this time. With his free hand, he yanked on my hair, forcing my head back so that we were staring at each other. Staring into his eyes, I realized he was serious. He meant it.

I let go of his shoulders and reached up to cup his face. Drawing him down, I brushed my lips against his. Only then did he begin to move, harsh, demanding strokes that drove deep inside me. I squeezed my eyes closed and pressed my face against his neck. Every thrust sent a shudder through me as he reached places inside me that no one else had ever been. And it wasn't just physical I forced myself to admit. I could feel the difference. He wanted my pleasure, but not for him. He wanted it for me.

As if sensing some of what I had inside me, the demanding pace of his strokes slowed and Ash eased his grip on my hair.

I kissed his neck, tasting the faint tang of salt. My lips brushed over his skin as I spoke, "I love you."

His entire body went rigid.

And then he surged upright against me, hard and fast three times. He said my name as we came, clutching me against him. As he pulsed inside me, I came too. I clung to him, riding out my orgasm as I listened to him whispering over and over again.

"I love you. Please, don't leave me."

I loved him too, but the words in my head weren't me asking him not to leave me, so I didn't say them out loud. That didn't stop them from repeating in my mind though.

I love you. Please, don't hurt me.

Chapter 11

Ash

Isadora wisely kept up a running banter in the room. She almost sounded like her old self, but I could tell the difference. And I hated it. It made it that much more important that we find Trask and stop him. Personally, I wanted to be the one to find him. Find him and beat him to death with his own spine, but that wasn't looking very likely.

Marcum had called with an update while Toni and I had still been...occupied upstairs. We'd moved from the reading room to my bedroom and I'd finally been able to take my time with her.

It still hadn't been enough time. I knew as soon as I'd brought her to climax again and again, felt her writhing in pleasure beneath me, that all the time in the world wouldn't be enough.

And then Isadora had been at my door, saying Marcum was on the phone and trying not to sound smug.

It had been only three hours since she'd left, and I hadn't been expecting a call any time before next week, especially after she'd told us to be patient. But then she'd called and sounded excited, said her partner had something. She'd be in touch.

I didn't know what that meant. He had something? What

was it? What were they going to do about it? Would it lead them to Trask?

"You're brooding."

Toni's soft voice, spoken directly into my ear, went straight to my cock. I had to fight the urge to turn to her and pull her closer. Kiss her. Lose myself in her. This wasn't the time or the place, but I had too much tension built up inside me and I could think of only one way to burn it off.

Hell, I would've wanted her even if I hadn't been tense.

I still kept seeing her walking down the stairs with her suitcase in hand.

Nothing would erase that memory from my mind, but maybe if I had her wrapped around my cock for a good two or three hours a day for a couple weeks, a month, a year, the impact of what almost happened would lessen.

"Not going to talk to me?" Toni teased quietly.

"Too busy brooding." I tried to smile, but didn't do a very good job of it. Shooting a look at the clock, I muttered, "Why didn't she just tell us what the hell she had?"

Toni squeezed my hand. "If you keep staring at the clock, it's going to make time go very, very slow."

I brought her hand to my lips and kissed it before letting go. I leaned towards the table, glaring at my laptop as it sat open in front of me. Toni had sent me everything she'd gotten from her brother, but I didn't know why I bothered staring at it. I wouldn't find anything.

Trask had left the country after he'd gotten out of jail. If he wanted revenge, why hadn't he gotten it then? Had he only come back now because he was broke? Had he kidnapped Isadora to get money?

"He gets arrested fifteen years ago." I was barely aware I was speaking out loud. "Gets out of jail ten years ago and moves. Comes back just as Isadora gets taken." I ran my hand through my hair. I was overdue for a cut. "There's a record of him coming into the country, but nothing since."

"Your mumbling is going to drive me crazy." Toni ran her hand along my arm, and, for a moment, I let myself enjoy her touch, but then I focused back on the keyboard, trying to jog my brain into working.

Why couldn't we find him?

It hit me.

They hadn't been able to find the money he'd taken either.

"Son of a bitch." I did a search of Trask's name, and pulled up everything I could find about the trial. I'd been a teenager when it first happened, but there was something I just remembered. "He had a partner. Or, at least, everyone had assumed he did. Reuben Stefanos. They never found him. Search warrants are still active."

But what if there'd been no Reuben Stefanos? What if the name had been an alias Trask had used to hide his funds?

And what if he was using part of that alias now to stay under the radar?

The first combination – Reuben Trask – was a bust. I tried Stefan Trask next. Nothing. Stefanos Reubens. Stefan Reuben. Jackpot.

And then I started to read.

"Son of a bitch," I breathed.

"What is it?" Toni asked.

I glanced over at Isadora. I didn't want to say it, not with her here. It would break her. Her eyes narrowed as she came over to where Toni and I were sitting.

"What is it, Ash?"

I wanted to tell her not to look, but I knew my sister. That'd just make her more determined to see it.

"When Daniel Trask was arrested, the FBI thought he had a partner named Reuben Stefanos, but nothing was ever found. I was just thinking that maybe Trask was using versions of those names as an alias." I explained it as quickly as possible so she wouldn't be completely shocked when she saw it. "He was. Stefan Reuben."

"And you know it's Trask because..." Her voice trailed off as she got close enough to see what was on my screen. "Son of a bitch."

"Will someone tell me what's going on?" Colton came to stand behind her.

"It's a fucking picture of Daniel Trask." Isadora's voice was shaking as she read the caption next to the picture. "'Stefan Reuben enjoys local BBQ with wife, Caitlin Holmes, and stepdaughter...Lily."

I read it and I was looking at the picture, but I still didn't believe it. Not even hearing Isadora say it. But there was no doubt. The picture was on the grainy side, but it was clear enough for me to identify the man as Daniel Trask.

And the teenage girl next to him as my ex.

"She was..." Isadora sank down next to me. Her face was pale, her eyes wide. "Do you think...no...I mean..."

"I told you what her letter said."

Toni wrapped her arms around my waist and rested her chin on my shoulder as I spoke. I put my hand over hers and squeezed, letting her know I appreciated the comfort.

"You think Trask had Lily dating you?" Isadora asked. "That she was spying or something?"

"I don't know," I answered honestly. I didn't know. But I sure as hell had my suspicions.

"Who's Lily?" Colton's voice was low.

In a hurried, hushed tone, I heard Isadora give her boyfriend a quick summary. Colton uttered a low oath, and I thought I might end up liking him after all.

"Do you think Lily went to Monaco?" Toni asked softly. "After she...left."

"Where's her mom now?" Isadora asked suddenly.

"What?" I looked over at her.

"Lily's mom. Caitlin Holmes." Isadora leaned closer to me and gestured at the screen. "She told us she didn't have family. Was she just keeping us from her mom because her mom didn't know what Trask was doing?"

I scrolled further down, and sucked in a breath. "She died." I felt Toni stiffen behind me. "Caitlin Holmes died two months before I met Lily. Suicide."

"Can you find the exact date Trask was released from prison?" Toni asked.

I threw a curious look over my shoulder.

"I have a hunch," she said.

It took me a couple of minutes, but when I found it, I swore again. "He got out the same day Lily disappeared."

Toni nodded grimly. "That's what I thought."

We all turned to look at her.

"Share." The word was terse, but I squeezed her hand to make sure she understood it wasn't because of her.

"I'm just guessing here," she said. "But I think at some point, Trask told his family who he really was, and when Caitlin committed suicide, he convinced Lily that your family was somehow at fault. He used that to convince Lily to spy on you guys."

My heart squeezed in my chest. I didn't want to believe what I was hearing, but on some level, it made sense.

"I think she ended up caring about you," Toni continued. "And when Trask got out of jail, he wanted her to help him with something." Her eyes slid to Isadora and then back to me. "Maybe a kidnapping."

"Shit," Isadora breathed.

"I think she refused, and that's why she left." Toni let the statement sit for a few seconds before she added, "She wrote that letter and then she...vanished."

Silence fell for nearly a full minute.

"You don't think she simply moved away, do you?"

Colton asked the question I knew everyone was thinking.

I answered it, "Trask killed her for not doing what he wanted."

"Fuck." Isadora sank back against Colton.

"Yeah," Toni agreed. "That about sums it up."

I couldn't have agreed more.

"We don't have any proof," Colton said. "But this is probably something Marcum might want to know."

"I don't want to distract her." I turned back to my computer. "Not until we know for sure that we have something."

Eyes turned to me and it was Isadora who asked the question. "How do we do that?"

I pulled up two more browser windows and put searches into all three. Isadora and Toni each leaned in from either side, so I didn't have to explain. They saw it only a few seconds after I did.

An apartment registered to a Lily Trask.

Fuck me.

"I'm going over there," I said abruptly as I stood.

I hadn't gotten more than two steps when Isadora was right there. "No!" She caught my arm and shook me. "You are *not*! Didn't we decide we were going to be smarter than that?"

"*We* are." I turned to face her, catching her hands and lifting them to my lips to kiss them gently. "I want you to stay here with Colton and Toni. The security system's been upgraded since they got in before. I have double the security and everyone is working in pairs." I glanced up at Colton and he nodded at me, knowing what I was going to say next. "And I know Colton's not going to let either of you out of his sight. But I have to go over there."

"And do what?" She stared at me, terror in her eyes. "You won't find anything that can help you figure out what happened to Lily."

"I'm not looking for Lily." I hugged Isadora without looking at Toni. "You have to understand, sweetie. It's not about her. It's about you. It's about Toni. These sons-of-bitches have done enough. But if they did hurt Lily too..." I didn't want to go there. "Look, I just want to know if they are there, okay? If I see anybody or anything, I'll back off and call the cops."

"I don't want you going over there alone." She pressed her face against my chest.

"He won't." Toni was already on her feet, and pulling on a battered jacket. "Let's go."

"Wait...no." I shook my head as Isadora took a step back. "You're staying here."

Toni shrugged. "I will if you will."

"No." I almost had to force the word out through gritted teeth.

"It's not up for debate." She twisted her hair into some sort of quick knot, securing it with a band she pulled from her pocket, staring at me all the while.

"No. This could be dangerous." When all she did was cock her head at me, I had to keep my jaw clenched and count to ten before I responded with one of my usual asshole comments. "It's not all that likely, but what if they're there? Trask and whoever he's working with are smart. The cops never even found this place."

"That you know of," Toni pointed out. "And for all you know, this isn't anything. But, on the off chance it is? You're right. They are dangerous. That's why you're not going alone."

"That's why you're not going at all!" I barely managed to keep myself from shouting it.

She gave me a sweet smile that I knew was anything but sweet. "Ash, I'm calling you out. You're being an ass. I've already told you that I can take care of myself. More, I've proven that. You've seen it." She gave me a half-smile. "How does your nose feel, by the way?"

Red crept up the back of my neck. "This is different. This isn't about you getting in a free shot on someone who isn't expecting it."

"No. You're right," she agreed, to my surprise. "It's about you going after people who, for all you know could have murdered somebody. And I'm not going to let you go tearing off after them." She looked up at me, her expression frank. "I know you. You're going to get hot under the collar if you see them. You're going to think about what they did to Isadora and you're going to lose your temper. If I'm there at least you'll stay in the car."

"No," I growled, my stomach twisting at the thought of Toni being anywhere near danger. "This isn't up for discussion."

"Right again." Her eyes narrowed and the look on her face hardened. "It's not. You and I both know that if you physically wanted to hold me back from going, you could do it. But make no mistake, if you leave here without me? I won't be here when you get back."

The impact of her words hit me, and I took a step back. I drew in a slow breath and tried to keep from feeling the sudden stab of panic that went through me.

But she didn't give me time to fully process her words before she continued, "I promise, if I leave, you will never see me again, and if you try to come after me, I will call the cops. I'm not joking, Ash. If you walk out that door without me, we're done. For good."

To her credit, Toni didn't sit in the car with a smug smile on her face. She actually looked nervous as we started down the road, and it took everything I had not to offer to turn the car around and drive her back. She clutched her phone like a talisman, and I knew that, at the first sign of trouble, she'd be calling Agent Marcum.

I wasn't expecting trouble. I wasn't expecting anything, really. Just because there was an apartment listed under the name Lily Trask didn't mean anything. It didn't mean that Daniel Trask was using his former step-daughter's name.

And it definitely didn't mean that we were wrong about Lily being dead, and that she was using her step-father's last name.

This entire thing was stupid. I knew it, but I couldn't seem to stop myself. I had to know the truth.

Please don't let Toni pay for me being stupid and stubborn. I don't know who that thought was directed to, but I felt helpless and just sending that simple thought out there felt like it was better than nothing.

"This isn't too far from where I grew up," Toni said as I swung a left.

We were only about a half mile from our destination. It was a residential area for the most part, the buildings a mix of older homes and those had been set up into multi-family apartment homes. I slanted a quick look at Toni as I came to a stop at a traffic light.

"My parents' house is two blocks north," she said, gesturing. She gave me a proud smile. "A genuine house. We keep telling them they should put it on the market for a cool million and move somewhere. Retire somewhere with a beach."

Aside from wanting the distraction, I wanted to know more about her, so I went with it. "If they're interested, give them my number. I'm always looking for real estate."

Toni laughed softly. "My dad's told us more than once that the only way he'll leave that house for good is when they take him out in a body bag. It's been in the family for over a century. It'll probably stay in the family even longer than that." She reached over and stroked her fingers down the back of my hand. "How brave are you?"

"Is this a trick question?" I asked warily.

"Well, I already know you're stupid. I mean, we're here, right?"

From the corner of my eye, I could see her staring out the front of the windshield, a smile on her lips.

"But that's not what I mean. How brave are you?"

I frowned as I started forward again. "I've honestly never thought about it."

"You might want to think about it. If you really want this thing between us to work, you need to." She twined our fingers together, and I knew she was only half-teasing. "My parents are going to want to meet you...and my brothers have already told mom and dad about...what happened. Or, at least, the part that they know about. And since that includes me going to jail..." Her voice trailed off.

But I didn't need her to continue. I could only imagine what her parents thought of me.

A picture of my mother's face popped into my mind. *"Whatever you do, Ash,"* she'd once told me. *"Try hard not to make an enemy of the parents of the woman you fall in love with. Treat her right and they will treat you right. Treat her wrong..."* She'd laughed softly then, and had looked over at my father.

Even though all four of my grandparents had died when I'd been young, I knew that there'd been animosity of some kind between my father and my maternal grandfather. I didn't know what, but my mom's statement had always made me wonder what had happened.

Now, my insides were twisting enough to make me want to puke. Suddenly, finding a kidnapper and possible killer didn't seem quite as nerve-wracking. "So," I asked, striving for a normal tone of voice. "Are they big on holding grudges?"

"It depends," Toni said as she glanced over at me, her eyes dancing. "If you impress my mom, you've got a chance because she has my dad wrapped around her finger. But if you screw up with her? It won't be pretty."

"Great," I muttered, nosing into an empty spot just down the street from where we needed to be. It wasn't exactly a legal parking spot, but I wasn't worried about getting a ticket since we weren't getting out of the car.

I didn't have time to brood about Toni's parents, though. There could be answers here. Answers to what happened to Isadora. To Lily. To my parents.

"Which one is it?" Toni asked, squeezing my hand.

"Bottom left." I pointed with my free hand.

"So I guess we just sit here until..." Her voice trailed off and her hand tightened on mine until it was painful. "Ash."

I followed her gaze.

My heart gave a hard, painful slam as I saw a light flickering through a gap in the windows. A shadow passed in front of it, paused. The curtain swayed slightly, and then the shadow moved away. For several long minutes, neither Toni nor I moved or spoke. We just watched.

Then Toni tugged on my arm. "Ash. Look."

He was clad in a long, dull gray jacket, striding up the sidewalk casually. Nothing about him would draw attention. Not really. But as he looked right, then left, his movements almost deliberately lazy, his gaze zeroed in on me. His eyes slid past the black sedan we'd come in. It was a little too high dollar for this area, but it was the most sedate vehicle I owned. The dark tint kept him from seeing through the window, but I had a feeling he still knew who was inside.

Shit.

"It's him?" Toni asked softly.

"Yeah."

I watched as he glanced around once more, and then headed up the steps.

Toni let out a breath as she turned to me. "What do we do now?"

Chapter 12

Toni

I knew what I wanted to do, but I asked anyway. I couldn't expect him to take my thoughts and desires into consideration if I didn't do the same for him. So, I blew out a soft, steady breath, and counted to twenty while waiting for an answer. When none came, I offered my opinion. "I think this would be a good time to call the cops."

Ash made a face, tapping his fist against the steering wheel, but he didn't discount it outright, so I gave him silence as he thought. He didn't speak for the next few minutes as the activity behind the window we were watching grew more agitated. Shadows moved and merged, making it impossible for us to know what was going on beyond the fact that it didn't seem to be good.

Ash said something under his breath, his soft words lost as my phone began to ring. It was Vic's ringtone, and I gave Ash an apologetic glance. "It's my brother." I didn't bother to specify which one until I answered, "Hey, Vic, make it fast. I'm kinda busy."

"Ah...yeeeahhhhh..." He drew the words out. "That's actually what I wanted to talk to you about."

The tone of his voice made a shiver go up my spine. "Spit it out, Victor."

"It's just...well, you wouldn't by any chance be doing

some...investigating of your own?" He hesitated, and then continued, "Because that might not be the best idea at the moment." Off in the background, I heard my brother talking to somebody in a hurried tone. When he came back on the phone, his voice was stronger. And more concerned. "I'm serious now, Toni. You need to go. Shit is about to go down in all kinds of different ways."

Adrenaline surged through me, followed quickly by a chill. "Trouble..."

"Yeah. Go!"

I shot a look over at Ash. He was still staring at the building, but I had a feeling he could hear the conversation clearly enough. Judging by his clenched jaw and the tense set of his shoulders, however, he wasn't planning on going anywhere.

Shit.

I'd known this was a bad idea.

I looked over at the building too. The activity behind the window had gone still. But there was a sudden tension that hadn't been there before. Now that I thought about it, things had been oddly quiet before. Throat strangely dry, I looked up the street, and then down, noticing things I'd missed earlier.

The plain car parked a few spaces up from ours. Nothing fancy, but still a bit out of place.

The couple that looked almost too casual at the bodega. They were together, except they weren't. No touching and no lingering looks. They smiled and leaned toward each other, and others might have been fooled, but to me, it looked fake, forced. And they kept watching things besides each other.

Something was off.

Something was really off.

Just as that thought came into my head, I heard a noise. Tires, squealing as they rounded the street.

Then, another sound. Sirens.

I tensed.

A black SUV slammed to a stop next to my side of the car, and Ash wrapped his arm around me, hauling me back against him. The driver was focused in the opposite direction, but the man in the back seat was looking at me.

And his gun was pointing in my direction.

Shit.

Vic's voice shouted at me from the phone I still held clutched in my hand.

"I'm here," I said without lifting the phone to my ear. Vic's shouting ceased. "Somebody's got a gun pointed at us."

Vic's furious cussing reached my ears much better than his tinny response from a few seconds ago.

"It's going to be okay." Ash's voice was low and steady in my ear.

My heart was racing. The body's fight or flight response, I told myself. I knew which one I wanted to go with. Flight. Flight sounded really good. But I didn't have anywhere to go.

"Uh-huh." I kept my eyes on the man with the gun. He was no more than ten feet away. Would be hard to miss us at this range.

"Son of a bitch..."

Behind me, Ash tensed.

The men and women I'd already guessed to be undercover cops were running, some towards us, some towards the apartment building.

"Get down," Ash said.

"What?"

He didn't explain, just pushed me down and covered me with his body.

A bang nearly deafened me, and I heard Ash swear again. He shifted and I felt something hard scrape against my cheek.

"Are you hurt?"

His voice sounded strange, muffled, and for a moment, I

was afraid he'd been injured. Then I realized it was only that my ears were still ringing. I nodded.

"I'm fine." I pushed back against him.

"Wait." He kept his hand on my back as he lifted himself up slowly. "Fuck," he muttered.

I sat up, confirming I wasn't in any danger when Ash didn't immediately protest. As soon as my head cleared the window – or what had been the passenger's side window – I saw what Ash was staring at.

Another gun being pointed at me, at us. Except I was pretty sure that the woman holding it was a cop, and a familiar one at that. She didn't look like she was about to shoot us, but she didn't look entirely friendly either.

"Stay where you are," she said.

"Like hell..." Ash started to move, but stopped when I reached over and put a hand on his arm.

"I think it's okay, Ash." I was surprised at how steady my voice sounded.

Behind the cop, I saw two men being pulled out of the SUV. The driver was swearing, but the man who'd had the gun – the one who'd shot at Ash and me – looked almost bored. I cut my eyes toward the apartment building again and saw Trask being led out in handcuffs.

"All right, rich boy, let's get you and the lady out of the car nice and slow."

We did as she ordered, but as I stepped onto the sidewalk, my eyes narrowed, as much at how familiar she seemed as the way she was talking to us. It was something about the way she cocked her head, the set of her chin...

"Son of a bitch."

A man's voice caught my ear and I looked toward it.

"Vic?"

The cop scowled. Without looking back, she said, "Gallagher, I told you I'd handle this." Pointing at me and Ash, she said, "You two, my car. Now."

Suddenly, it hit me. Holding. The people. The smells. The hooker–

"It was you!" I shouted.

Her eyes darted away from mine. "I don't know what you're talking about."

Vic's hand clamped over my arm before I could press the matter. "Come on, Sis. You should sit down. *Now*."

I glanced behind me to make sure Ash was following. I wasn't surprised to see that he was right there, his eyes finding mine. He wasn't going to leave me.

Chapter 13

Toni

"Give me a reason." Marcum glared at me.

"Ah...well, I can tell you that I didn't think we'd see anybody." I shrugged.

My head was pounding with all that had happened.

Finding out that my troublemaking brother who used to get in trouble with the cops so often was now one of their informants...and with the FBI.

The 'hooker' who'd been in the holding cell with me hadn't been a hooker. She'd been undercover on Vice at the time and had chosen to stay in the cell as soon as she recognized me. Because she knew Vic.

The FBI was pissed at Ash and me for nearly getting ourselves killed by being where we weren't supposed to be. Marcum had told us to wait, but we'd taken matters into our own hands. We hadn't called her with what we'd found. If we had, we might not have been shot at. We might not have left the house at all because Marcum might have told us that my brother had helped her find the dirty cop. And that the dirty cop had given her the name Lily Trask.

My head was swimming, and all I wanted to do was go home.

Or maybe not home. Maybe somewhere I could just have Ash hold me.

Except I had a bad feeling I wouldn't be heading home, or anywhere with Ash, anytime soon. In the past two hours, I'd been questioned by the cops, by the FBI then more cops. Now the FBI was taking its turn again.

I hadn't seen Ash yet, but I wasn't surprised.

My experience with cops might have been limited to what happened with Vic and then my addiction to crime shows, but one thing I knew to be accurate was that they were pretty big on not letting the people they were questioning have time to talk. Once they'd let the EMTs look us over, Ash and I had been separated. He hadn't been happy about it, either.

He'd actually argued the point for several minutes before I'd gotten him to listen to me. I'd known he could've called in some favors, but I hadn't wanted special treatment simply because Ash had money and friends in high places. Not even when it would benefit me.

Marcum must've been with Ash the last time the FBI had questioned me, because I'd spoken to an agent whose name I couldn't remember. Now, she was sitting across from me, and the expression on her face said there was a good chance Ash had done something to piss her off even more.

Placing my hands on the surface of the desk, I blew out a slow breath and then said in a soft voice, "Agent Marcum, look. I'm not trying to bullshit you and I'm not trying to stonewall you, either. Ash and I weren't expecting to find anything."

"Then why did you go?" she demanded. "And how the hell did you find Trask?"

I kept it simple. "We figured it out."

"You figured it out." Marcum crossed her arms. "You want to expound on that?"

Not particularly.

I didn't say that though. I was tired, not stupid. So, for the third time in two hours, I gave her the story, telling her about how Isadora figured out that there was a connection to her parents, how we'd gone through old photos and albums looking for clues.

And how we'd found one.

Then about Lily, and how Ash had started putting things together. Including the possibility that Trask and his associates were at the apartment building. When I finished, I fell silent and waited for more questions. It didn't matter what she asked or how she asked it, my story wouldn't change.

"Why didn't you call me with it? I told you I was looking into it, that I had a lead. Do you have issues trusting law enforcement?"

"Well...yeah." Shrugging, I crossed my legs and started to swing my foot. "But that's not the point. We didn't want to give you a false lead. Ash didn't think..."

A part of me insisted I be quiet now, but holding something back never went over well with cops. Marcum wouldn't be any different.

"Ash didn't think we should say anything until we were sure. And, well, you obviously know there was a dirty cop, so..."

"So he didn't want to risk it," she finished my sentence.

I nodded.

"But he trusted me." She gave me a questioning look. "Why?"

"That's personal."

"Nothing's personal if it involves an investigation of mine." Marcum shook her head. "You two interfered with a federal investigation. I could throw both of you in jail. So...just give me a reason, Toni. Or in this case...*don't* give me one."

"He called because of me," I said after another few seconds of internal debate. "Ash wanted to wait a few days, try to see if he couldn't figure more out on his own, but I was too angry. They'd involved my family." Tears burned my eyes now, and it took more effort than I liked to keep them back. I was so tired. "I told him if he wouldn't do something, then I'd do it."

Marcum's ran her tongue across the inside of her teeth as she cocked her head, leaning closer as though that would give her a better view. "So he called. Just like that. Because you threatened to if he didn't?"

"Not exactly." I drew in another breath and curled my hands into fists. "He saw me with my suitcase. I told him I'd leave too. That I'd never come back. That's why he agreed."

The door swung open before she could ask anything else. A tall, thin black man with a silver-edged mustache peered in at us before beckoning to her. She nodded at me and then I was left alone.

Exhausted, I lowered my head to my arms.

I wanted this done. Even if they arrested me, as long as I had a flat surface so I could sleep, I'd be happy.

"For the record," Marcum said, her voice flat. "I don't want us crossing paths like this again. Ever."

My head still spinning, I nodded at her. She gave a short nod in reply, and then leveled a glare over my shoulder. Turning to look at the object of her disdain, I didn't notice her leaving. Then I just didn't care because it was Ash.

I practically collapsed into his arms, relief and something much deeper flowing through me.

He cupped my face in his hands, studying my face. "Are you hurt? You're not hurt?" he demanded, craning my chin to the right, then the left.

"I'm fine," I told him. "You were there when the EMTs checked me out."

I kissed him, rising on my toes to reach his lips.

He kissed me back, sliding his hands down my shoulders, then my arms and wrists and fingers. I broke the kiss as his fingers explored. There was little eroticism to the touch, and I knew he was searching for injuries I hadn't told him about.

I leaned into him. "Take me home."

"I will. Just..." He held me more tightly, clutching me to his chest. "I'm sorry, Toni. Dammit, I'm sorry. I was stupid. I don't know what I was thinking. I'm so sorry. I put you at risk..."

"Just take me home."

He nodded and kissed me again. Then again, each more frantic than the last.

After the fourth one, I tore away from him and caught his hand. "Home," I said, squeezing him.

It wasn't until we got there that I realized I hadn't really specified what I'd meant by home. But I was okay with his choice, so long as it meant I got to fall asleep in his arms. Preferably sooner rather than later.

But as soon as we walked in, Isadora was there with Colton, flinging herself at her brother while a blank-faced uniformed officer stood behind them, watching the reunion.

"You're all right!" She hugged Ash, then me, and then Ash again. "I was so scared. The news said there'd been a gunshot reported, but nothing else."

"It's okay," he said, pushing her curls back from her face. "They got Trask and the men who were working with him. You're safe."

She sniffled, and then turned away as she started to cry. Colton came up to her and wrapped her in his arms, guiding her away as he spoke softly to her.

Envy curled through me. And then Ash came up to stand

behind me, his hands on my shoulders. He slid them down, then around my waist to pull me back up against him. I went willingly, craving his warmth and strength.

"It's over," I said quietly.

"Yeah. It is."

A breath shuddered out of me.

In the circle of his arms, I turned to face Ash.

Cradling his cheek, I rose on my toes and pressed my lips to his. He responded by parting his lips and sliding his tongue across the seam of my mouth. The sensation sent a ripple through me as I opened my mouth, my arms sliding around his neck. And then, a moment later, I was gasping because Ash was picking me up, his hands cupping my ass. I wrapped my legs around his waist, groaning as his denim-clad cock rubbed against my core.

I didn't even remember him carrying me from the foyer to his bedroom, but suddenly, we were at his door. He paused there to press me back against the wall. He yanked my t-shirt up, shoving it up until it was twisted under my arms. He yanked the cups of my bra down and lifted my breasts out. While he teased one nipple into taut firmness with his thumb and forefinger, he used teeth and tongue on the other, until I was whimpering and rocking against him.

Then he was moving again, taking me the couple extra feet into his room, where, for one unimaginable second, he stopped touching me. It was only for a moment, though.

"I need you." He cupped my face as he stared down into my face. "I need you so much."

Desire coiled tight in my belly. "Then take me."

He growled as he claimed my mouth, his fingers tearing at the button of my jeans. I pulled at his shirt, just as desperate to feel him as he was me. This wasn't going to be slow, and I was just fine with that.

I needed him.

He groaned as my nails raked down his chest. As he broke the kiss, he spun me around. He pushed my pants down to my knees as his other hand put pressure between my shoulder blades, bending me toward the bed.

A moment later, he drove inside me, hard and fast. I wailed, pain and pleasure spiking through me. I wasn't wet, wasn't ready, but I wanted him, wanted more. My hands twisted in the raw silk of his comforter, seeking purchase as I pushed back against him.

He withdrew and surged deep again, the friction rough enough to make me whimper. His body curled over mine as he thrust into me, each stroke rubbing against that spot inside me as his hands slid up under my t-shirt. His fingers rolled and tugged on my nipples, sending jolts of pleasure that helped slick his way.

"I love you, Toni," he said, his voice raw and molten.

The sound made something break open inside me, something that fed my need until it was nearly unbearable. I lifted my hips as best as I could, taking his cock as he rode me with quick, short digs.

It was hot, and raw, and he came almost immediately after I did, our bodies left shaking and trembling as we slumped onto the bed. He twisted us around into a relatively more comfortable position and tucked me against his chest. He pressed his lips against my temple.

Neither one of us spoke, but I didn't need him to say anything right now. We had issues we'd need to deal with, decisions to make. But that could wait. For now, I just wanted to fall asleep in the arms of the man I loved.

After the shitstorm the last few weeks of my life had been, I felt like I deserved it.

Chapter 14

Ash

TWO MONTHS LATER

"Are you okay?"

Toni took my hand as we sat in the courthouse.

Daniel Trask had just been sentenced to life in prison for kidnapping Isadora as well as the first-degree murders of our parents. And the second-degree murder of his step-daughter, Lily. They'd found her remains buried in the community garden next to the apartment. Forensics put her death at around the same time she'd originally disappeared. When Trask took his plea deal, he confessed to having killed her shortly after she'd refused to help him extort money from me.

My gut churned just thinking about it.

Our mysterious ghost had been one of Trask's accessories...and apparently the smartest one of the bunch. Less than an hour after his arrest, he'd rolled on Trask and everyone else involved, singing like the proverbial canary. He was doing a shorter sentence thanks to his cooperation. It wasn't good enough, not for me, but it meant that Trask had taken a plea deal and saved my sister the pain of having to testify. It had taken two months to put it together, and it had been hellish to listen to the allocution, but it was finally over.

"Ash?" Toni squeezed my hand again.

"I'm...processing." I rubbed my thumb over the back of

her hand.

A man turned toward us, nodding when he caught my gaze. Jefferson Sinclair had handled the case personally, never passing us off to assistants or refusing to take our calls. And I knew it wasn't just because of our name or our money. Sinclair was one of the good guys. I liked him and had to admit, if I'd been a criminal, the man would have made me leery, because he was an absolute shark.

Toni leaned into me, her head resting on my shoulder. "Let's get out of here," she said softly. "All of us."

I caught Isadora's eye, and she nodded. She was leaning on Colton, and I could tell how much this had taken out of her. My eyes met his and we exchanged an understanding look. My respect for him had just kept growing over the past couple months. He'd been there for Isadora, night and day, whatever she needed. I was still an overprotective big brother who scowled at the thought of them sleeping together, but I'd seen in him what Isadora had seen.

If any man was worthy of my sister, it was him.

As we stood up, I automatically patted the pocket of my suit jacket. Isadora saw me and managed a smile. We'd talked before coming to court today. I hadn't wanted to do this until this was over.

"It feels kind of empty, doesn't it?" Isadora said as we started toward the door. "I guess I wanted to face him, yell at him or something."

"Even that wouldn't have done any good," Toni said, coming in between us and hooking her arms through both of ours. "The idea of closure is all well and good, but now you all have to figure out how to accept not just that it's over, but the things you thought were the truth weren't. That takes a little more time."

I nodded. Toni and I'd had this talk before. One thing I'd discovered about dating a psychologist: I'd never get away with not talking about my feelings again.

Isadora was quiet. I suspected she and Toni had been talking too. I hadn't asked though. I trusted Toni not only with my life and my heart, I trusted her with the most precious thing I had. My sister.

My heart gave a wild thump. In the last couple months, I'd come far from the man I was. I knew I had a long way to go yet, but I was hoping Toni would help navigate me through it.

Whether it was by mutual unspoken agreement, or just getting out of the somber setting of the courtroom, when we emerged from the car several minutes later, we all seemed to breathe a little easier and move a little lighter.

Isadora was laughing up at Colton, and Toni took my hand, swinging them back and forth, giving me that brilliant smile of hers that made my heart clench tight.

It was hard to believe that I'd once thought I didn't want her in my life. Now I couldn't imagine it without her.

The maître d' saw Isadora before me, and smiled broadly at the sight of her. News of her kidnapping had gone public after the fact, and for a few days, she'd been a minor celebrity. She'd handled it with her natural grace, and had then quietly retired from the spotlight. She and Colton were still trying to find a place, but they hadn't wanted to move until everything was settled. She was also looking at going back to school. She wanted to be a victim's advocate. When I'd found her poring over college catalogs, she told me that this had been a wake-up call for her, that she wanted her life to mean something.

Everything was changing.

I was thinking about change all throughout the meal, and about the next one – or what I hoped would be the next one.

When the server brought out champagne, and then left us alone, Isadora linked her hand with Colton's and leaned against him. Her poker face was shit, and she couldn't keep her eyes from sparkling or her lips from curving into a smile.

Toni looked between us, eyes narrowing. "What's going on?"

When I slid out of the seat, her eyes widened.

"Son of a bitch."

Looking from the ring I held in my hand to her face, I said, "That wasn't exactly the reaction I was hoping for."

Isadora started to giggle and I shot her a dark look before focusing back on Toni.

"I've been waiting on this until today was done. I wanted to close that chapter before starting a new one."

Her lips parted, eyes wide.

"A new one that will be all about us. Together. Will you marry me?"

Thick lashes fell down, shielding her eyes. Then she launched herself at me.

I had to close my fist around the ring to keep from dropping it as I caught her and wrapped my arms around her, hugging her tight. "Is that a yes?"

"That's a *hell yes*."

Chapter 15

Toni

The house was quiet around us.

I hadn't officially moved in, but I'd been staying here more and more over the last couple months. Isadora had been staying here less and less. She'd confided in me that she was trying to get Ash used to her absence a little at a time.

Tonight she was staying with Colton, so when Ash and I slipped inside the house, Ash turned to me and pressed me back against the door even as it was still closing. His mouth came down over mine, but when he tried to tug open the buttons on my blouse, I caught his hands.

"I'm not sure Doug's heart can handle this."

"He's not here." Ash bit my lower lip. "I gave everybody the day off. And then told them all to get the hell out."

He licked the spot where he'd bitten me before he slid his mouth down along my jawline and began to move lower, his hand returning to the buttons of my shirt and freeing each one.

This time, I didn't try to stop him.

When he had my blouse completely open, I started to move to help him, but he stopped me. Keeping his eyes on my face, he stripped me completely naked as I stood there. By the time he was done, I wore nothing but the ring he'd slid onto my finger just a few hours ago.

A ring I still couldn't believe I was wearing.

His lips danced across the flat plane of my belly, and then down until he was flicking his tongue through my curls. When he found my clit, I whimpered and cupped the back of his head.

"I can't stand up too long if you do that."

"Don't worry." He shot me a dark, hungry look. "If you fall, I'll catch you."

I groaned and dropped my head back against the door, giving over control to him. Ash stiffened his tongue and began to thrust it inside me. A few seconds later, I was crying out his name. He gripped my hips, holding me in place until I came, and then he scooped me up into his arms and carried me into the nearby living room.

When he stretched me out by the fireplace, I gasped. Something buttery soft was against my skin and I looked down at the blanket spread out beneath me. I looked around. There was a bucket of wine chilling. Roses.

As I pushed up onto my elbows and watched, Ash picked up something from the edge of the blanket. He pushed a button, and I gasped as a fire roared to life.

"Wow. Way to go, Casanova. Firelight, wine and roses. You're going to get me thinking I'll get this all the time once we're married."

Ash went to his knees and crawled to me.

"And now you're on your knees for me." I grinned at him.

"I told you once before, you're the only woman I'll ever go to my knees for." He hovered over me on all fours, leaning down to brush his lips against mine. "I love you."

"I love you, too." Curling my arms around his neck, I tugged him down closer.

He came, but only for a moment, giving me another quick, teasing kiss.

When he pulled away, he went up on his knees and stripped away his shirt. Eyes on his chest, I didn't notice the cloth he'd pulled from his pocket until he brought it up in front of him.

"I asked you this once before." His voice was soft. "And I'm hoping that, now, the answer can be different. Do you trust me?"

My chest tightened as I caught my breath. I knew what he was asking, what it meant. We'd been dealing with communication and with trust, both in and out of the bedroom. I'd given him control in ways I'd never done before, had sex in ways I'd never dreamed.

But I hadn't let him blindfold me.

My eyes met his. "I trust you."

His entire face lit up and my heart skipped a beat. He leaned down over me and fastened the blindfold in place. My pulse fluttered. I held my breath, wondering what he had in mind.

I heard a pop.

"Open your mouth," he said softly.

I did and he pressed something to my lips – a wineglass.

"A toast, Toni. To the rest of our lives."

I sipped the wine and the sweet red rolled down my throat.

"Like?"

I nodded.

"Let me know when you want more."

"I get to ask for things tonight?" We were still working out the rules when it came to how this dynamic worked.

He cupped my face and lifted my mouth until I felt his lips brush against mine. "You can ask me for anything any night."

Another deep kiss and I felt like I was going to melt. He eased me back onto the blanket. A moment later, I gasped when something velvety soft stroked down the outer curve of my breast.

Then came the scent.

The rose.

He stroked the petals along my breast, down across my belly, across the curls.

"Spread your legs," he said.

I did, whimpering in need.

He teased me lightly, giving me only the barest hint of a touch with the petals before stroking my leg from the crease of my thigh all the way down to my ankle before switching over and doing the same to my opposite leg, but going from bottom to top this time.

I found myself lifting my hips when it drew close again.

Ash chuckled softly and cupped me between the thighs. "Want more?"

"What do you think?"

He slid a finger inside me. I would have clamped my thighs around his hand if he hadn't pressed down on my right knee and stopped me.

"I think you're lovely."

He twisted his wrist and curled his fingers inside me. My back arched and I cried out. Then he stroked his thumb over my clit, and I came hard and fast.

By the time I came down, he was naked and I could feel his body hovering over mine.

"Now," Ash breathed against my lips.

I didn't have the air to answer, but it didn't matter. It wasn't like I was going to argue. Grabbing onto his shoulders, I arched up to meet him. We came together, bodies sliding together with a perfection that made me moan. My nails dug into his back as I rocked against him. It was as if every cell in my body was on fire, every nerve blazing. I'd never been so aware of him as I was at that moment.

He twisted his hand in my hair and pulled my head back. He kissed me, his hunger matching mine.

"Tell me you love me," he said against my lips.

I didn't say it. I whimpered it.

He slammed into me harder and I was shaking from the force of the climax building inside, as he demanded it from me again.

"Tell me you love me."

My hand found its way into his hair and I fisted it, pulling it until he growled. I held him in place until I could put my mouth against his ear.

"You're mine."

He rolled with us, pulling me on top of him. My spine arched and I cried out at the new angle of penetration. I couldn't take it anymore. I reached up and tore off the blindfold, looking down at him.

He stared up at me, eyes dark with desire. As I watched, he reached over and dipped his fingers into the wine. He pinched my right nipple, fingers wet with the rich, red liquid, and then did the same with the left. I shivered as he sat up, holding me in place on his lap. The shift put pressure on my clit and my eyelids fluttered. When his mouth closed over my nipple, I gasped. He sucked hard, sending jolts of pleasure through me.

"Delicious," he murmured before turning his attention to the other one.

He urged me into motion, and as I rocked down, he thrust up, meeting me with every perfect stroke. Staring into each other's eyes, we rode each other straight into climax.

It was breathless, beautiful and perfect, and I knew that it was more than pure physicality. I loved him.

I trusted him.

I collapsed onto his chest as all the strength went out of me and his arms wrapped around me. We lay there together for several minutes, catching our breath, until I finally rolled off him. I didn't go far, snuggling down against his side as I rested my head on his chest.

I wasn't sure how much time passed before I finally broke the silence. "You know, I think this room could do with a makeover."

Ash snorted, his laugh more relaxed than I'd ever heard him. "I just went out of my way to fuck you blind, and you're thinking about redecorating?"

I rolled onto my stomach and shoved up onto my elbows, grinning at him. "Well, yeah. I mean, it's my professional opinion that this room is totally depressing."

Ash raised his head and kissed my chin. "Dr. Lang, if you want to redecorate, then knock yourself out."

"I love you," I murmured.

He pulled me down against his chest again. "I love you too."

I closed my eyes as he pulled me close, his arms tight around me. The fire behind us crackled and popped, warming our bare bodies enough that, for the moment, we could just lay there and enjoy the feel of skin on skin.

Fabric brushed against my fingers and I opened my eyes to see that my hand had found the blindfold I'd tossed aside. I smiled as I rubbed the soft fabric between my fingers.

I'd always thought I needed to be in control, have a plan. Now I knew the truth though.

Sometimes, letting go was the best thing I could do.

Blindfold Epilogue

Toni

I stared down at the ring on my left hand. It'd been there for nearly a year, but there were days I could still hardly believe it. This was one of them. I doubted it'd be the last, especially since it was about to be joined by another one in less than an hour.

I turned towards the full-length mirror for the first time since Isadora had finished putting the final touches on me. For nearly a full ten seconds, I stared, not recognizing myself. My soon-to-be sister-in-law had pinned up my long hair in a mass of curls that had taken most of the morning, and then she'd insisted on doing my make-up as well. All of that, plus the simple but elegant dress made me look far different than I did every day.

"Beautiful."

I looked at my mother in the mirror. Her eyes were darker than mine, but the shape was the same, and I knew I'd have those same faint wrinkles around my eyes when I was her age. If I also had half the love she did, I'd consider myself lucky. I was already lucky. I had my family. I had Isadora.

I had Ash.

Things happened so fast between us that, even after his proposal, I'd been concerned about our relationship. We'd gotten together under such insane circumstances, and our relationship was anything but traditional. I'd worried that, once things had settled down, we'd find that all of the passion between us had gone.

I was wrong.

If anything, I loved Ash more now than I had before.

"Could I have a minute with Toni?"

I heard the door close as my four bridesmaids left. Isadora was my maid of honor. My sisters-in-law, Yvette and Beth, were also attendants, as was Rachelle, my brother Vic's former ex-girlfriend. Well, maybe not his ex for much longer. At least, I hoped that'd be changing soon. They had a son together, but Vic hadn't been very reliable the first few years after his son had been born, so their relationship had been rocky at best.

Over the last year, however, Ash wasn't the only one who'd been making strides in his personal life. Vic had started working with our father, and was working even harder on making things right with Rachelle. He'd told me not more than a month ago that he didn't just want to be in his son's life. He wanted Rachelle back too.

I hoped it worked. My brother wasn't perfect, but he deserved happiness. Plus, I liked Rachelle better than most of the other women he'd dated over the years.

"I'm so proud of you." My mom's voice was strong, but I knew her well enough to tell her emotions were at the surface. "Your father and I both are."

I turned towards her and she caught both of my hands in hers.

"You've always known what you wanted," she continued, her eyes glowing with the light of motherly love. "And you've worked so hard to get it. Fought tooth and nail against everything that's come against you. You've grown into a woman even more beautiful and amazing than we ever could have hoped."

She pulled me into her arms, and I looked up, blinking hard, in an effort to keep myself from crying. My make-up was waterproof, but I didn't want my eyes to be red when I walked out there.

I managed to hold on, even if just barely, so when Isadora knocked to tell us that it was time for my mother to head into the sanctuary, I didn't need to do more than take a slow breath before I was ready.

And I was ready, I realized with a start.

The nervous flutters in my stomach had shifted at some point. Now they were twists and coils of a different kind.

Excitement.

Desire.

I wasn't just ready. I was eager. Eager for Ash, but not only physically. I was eager to start my life with him. It was true that we'd all been working on moving forward since the trial ended, and we'd had a series of milestones since then, but this was the one. The one that really made me feel like our life was truly beginning.

When Isadora stuck her head back in, I smiled and followed her out. I could hear the music Ash and I had selected, and the thought of him waiting at the end of that aisle made my pulse skip a beat. I caught a glimpse of my niece and nephew as they went from their mom at my end of the aisle to their dad who was waiting near Ash.

"Ready?" My dad stepped up next to me and held out his arm, his face the very definition of pride.

"Definitely." I nodded as I threaded my arm through his, and we waited our turn.

I tried to concentrate, to remember every detail, but the day jumped in fits and starts, some parts lost in the background, others stark and clear.

The feel of Ash's hand as his fingers wrapped around mine was an imprint, never to be forgotten.

The traditional words faded into background noise.

Our self-written vows stood out, and I knew I'd remember his as well as my own.

"From the first moment I met you, Toni, you defied my expectations. And you've continued to do that, every minute, every hour. I know that I don't deserve you, but I promise to spend the rest of my life loving and protecting you. I trust you with my life and my heart. You're my world, my everything. I love you, Toni. And I can't wait to spend the rest of my life with you."

Then it was my turn.

"The first time I saw you, I couldn't believe how good-looking you were. Or how arrogant." I paused, giving the audience a moment to quit chuckling. "But I quickly learned that there was more to you than your looks. Or your arrogance. I saw a man who loved his sister more than anything, who was intelligent and passionate. And I fell in love with that man. You amaze me, and I know you'll continue to amaze me in the years to come. I trust you with my love and with my heart. I love you, Ash."

Other words buzzed by, but then I heard the important ones.

"...husband and wife. You may kiss the bride."

Ash stared down at me for a long second and then cupped my chin. I expected a harsh kiss, something fierce and passionate, especially since we hadn't had sex in two weeks – surprisingly, at his insistence – but his lips were gentle as they came down on mine. He took his time, his tongue sliding into my mouth, slowly exploring every inch. Searching. Seeking. Discovering. As if it was our first kiss.

And then it was over and we were walking back down the aisle, hand-in-hand.

The receiving line was a blur, a series of hugs and well-wishes that I was grateful for, even though what I really wanted was to take my husband to the nearest private space I could find and feel him inside me.

As soon as the limo door closed behind us, I knew that I hadn't been the only one thinking that way. I barely had time to register Ash moving before he was kneeling in front of me, mouth and hands hot on my skin. He kissed me with the near-desperate hunger that had been missing from our wedding kiss. His teeth scraped over my bottom lip, and I moaned into his mouth as he pushed the skirt of my gown up far enough to get his hands underneath.

"Need you," he growled as his mouth moved down my jaw and throat, nipping and sucking until I knew I was going to have marks.

I shot a glance towards the front of the limo, but the driver had already put up the partition window, giving us complete and total privacy. I took a second to hope that the intercom was off too, and then Ash's hands were sliding up the outside of my thighs and I didn't care anymore.

He hooked his fingers under the waistband of the sheer white lace panties I was wearing and pulled them off. He tucked them into his pocket and I gasped as his head disappeared under my skirt. I bit my bottom lip as I arched off the seat, his tongue licking and probing every inch of me until I was writhing against his mouth.

A year ago, I would've denied I could ever make the mewling, whimpering sounds that were coming from me, but my time with Ash had taught me that he could make me do a lot of things I'd never dreamed of.

Case in point, having my new husband going down on me in the back of a limo while we were on our way to our reception. Not exactly something I would've expected of myself before Ash.

I was panting, on the brink of orgasm, when he raised his head. I made a noise of protest, my body a humming, needy mess. I reached towards him and heard his zipper even as he leaned into me. His mouth came down on mine, and he thrust into me. He swallowed my cry, his tongue sliding into my mouth even as he rocked against me. I could feel his tension as he fought for control, and I intentionally tightened around him.

"Fuck, Toni," he groaned as he pulled his mouth from mine. His eyes were dark as he looked at me. "I'm going to punish you for that."

I smiled at him and wrapped my arms around his neck. "Make me come, and you can punish me all you want."

He started to pull back and, for a moment, I was afraid I'd gone too far, that my punishment was going to be to spend the entire reception with my body throbbing in need. Then he snapped his hips forward and I nearly screamed. *Nearly* only because he clapped a hand across my mouth in time to stifle the sound.

"Don't want Lewis to get the wrong impression of what's going on back here."

One hand over my mouth, the other slid behind my back to hold me in place as he drove into me with hard, rough strokes that had me trembling after two, and coming after two more. His hips jerked as my muscles convulsed around him, his fingers flexing against my face. Three more hard thrusts sent sparks of painful pleasure through me, drawing out my orgasm, and then he buried himself deep, coming with a primal moan that made my stomach flutter.

His hand dropped away from my mouth as he kissed me gently. We stayed together for a moment longer, letting our bodies calm and cool. I hissed as he pulled out of me and a look of concern crossed his face.

"Did I hurt you, baby?" He brushed his fingers across my cheek.

I smiled as I shook my head. "Only in a good way." I reached up and wrapped my fingers around his. "I'll be feeling you inside me through the whole reception." I drew his hand to my mouth and kissed his fingertips. "I guess that'll have to be enough to get me through until we make our escape."

He sucked in a breath as I scraped my teeth across the top of his middle finger. "You really want me to punish you, don't you?"

I gave him a mischievous smile and darted out my tongue, touching it against the pad of his finger.

He rocked back on his heels, watching me for a few seconds before he moved up to the seat next to me. He turned our hands so that our fingers laced between each other, but he didn't speak.

Based on the thoughtful expression on his face, I had a feeling he was trying to decide on my punishment. My stomach twisted in a good way. In the time we'd been together, Ash had shown me that, even if uncomfortable at first, in the end, I would enjoy being punished. He never hurt me, never made it so that it was something I dreaded, no matter how it started.

He slid his hand into the pocket of his jacket and pulled out my panties. I started to reach for them, but when his fingers curled more tightly around them, I dropped my hand and waited.

"I don't think you deserve to have these back." One corner of his mouth tipped up in a partial smile. "That's your punishment." He put my panties back into his pocket. "You're going to spend the rest of the night without them. Every time we dance, every hug, every greeting. When I take off that garter." His eyes flicked down to my leg. "You'll know that I could slide my fingers inside you, right there in front of everyone." He leaned over and brushed his lips against my cheek. "And if you're good, maybe I'll do just that."

Fuck.

Ashford Lang was pure evil.

We'd been at our reception for nearly two hours, and the entire time, he'd been tormenting me. Whether it was his hand sliding down my back just enough that his fingers were brushing the top of my ass while we shared our first dance, or trying to eat while he kept leaning over to whisper all of the wicked things he wanted to do to me, he appeared to be thoroughly enjoying my discomfort.

Now, the meal was done. We'd cut the cake and stuck to our promises not to shove anything into each others' faces. We'd had our first dance, and then I'd danced with my father and each of my brothers while Ash took turns dancing with my mother and Isadora. I'd thrown my bouquet, and intentionally aimed it at Isadora, earning a good-natured glare from Ash.

He'd been true to his promise when he'd taken off my garter. Keeping my dress discreetly at my knee, he'd reached higher, ignoring the whistles and cat-calls, as well as not-so-subtle threats from my brothers. He'd used one hand to work down the garter, while his other went higher between my legs, lightly brushing his fingertips across my sensitive skin. It had been all I could do not to moan right there.

Much to my brother's embarrassment, Vic caught the garter, and I was pretty sure that Ash had thrown it at him intentionally. When I'd seen the sideways look Vic had thrown Rachelle's way, though, I made a mental note to thank Ash for it.

Now, we were at the part of the night where we were supposed to go around and greet people. We hit my extended family first, aunts and uncles, cousins and second cousins. Both of my parents had come from relatively large families, so there were a lot of them.

Because Ash and Isadora didn't really have any family, we'd forgone the traditional sides of the church, encouraging people to sit wherever they wanted. Most of Ash's invites had gone to the staff, Phenicie-Lang employees and other business contacts. There were a few exceptions, such as Agent Marcum and Jefferson Sinclair, who we'd both wanted to invite.

Standing with Isadora and Colton right now were another pair Ash and I had invited for our personal connection.

Dominic Snow was CEO of Winter Enterprises, the company that had been responsible for sending me to Isadora. Specifically, it had been Robson Findlay who'd done it, and he was here too, but Dominic and his gorgeous wife, Aleena, were connected to us in other ways too.

Over a year ago, Dominic had started a charity called In From the Cold that worked on finding and rescuing victims of human trafficking. At first, he'd specifically focused on babies who'd been sold on the black market – like he'd been – but the charity had expanded to include other aspects of human trafficking as well. Aleena worked with him as his personal assistant, which is how they'd met, and it had been she who'd come to see Isadora after the kidnapping had gone public.

Isadora had already decided she wanted to become a victim's advocate, but Aleena's visit had solidified things for her. Now, in addition to her college courses, she volunteered at In From the Cold.

But it hadn't only been my new sister-in-law Aleena had spoken to.

Ash threw Phenicie-Lang behind the charity while I'd taken a job as an on-staff therapist. It wasn't the easiest job in the world, and there were days I came home from work devastated by the horrors people had recounted. But Ash was always there, ready to give me whatever I needed.

"Congratulations!" Aleena gave me a hug to go along

with her warm smile. Dominic offered his own greeting, but only shook my hand. He wasn't the sort of person who touched casually.

Well, except his wife. He always seemed to be touching her. Holding her hand. His hand on the small of her back. Arm around her shoulders. I knew they'd gone through a lot to be together, and the similarities of their relationship to Ash's and mine went deeper than even that.

While Aleena and I had only known each other for a year, there were aspects of our friendship that made us much closer than we would've been without them. Mainly, she and I were both still relative novices in the world our husbands had brought us into. She and I shared things that neither of us could share with other friends. Things others wouldn't understand.

Like the way pain could turn to pleasure, enhance intensity. How surrendering control could be freeing. The way punishment could be a good thing. How being submissive didn't have to mean humiliation. How a lover could be rough, fierce, but then gentle when it was all over.

Though neither of us ever considered sharing, the four of us would often see each other at Olympus, sit together during the entertainment. A couple of times, we'd gone so far as to engage in some slight exhibitionism, being a bit more open about touching, but we'd never let it get to a place where things would be awkward between us. I was grateful for that because, as close as Isadora and I were, the things Ash and I did...not something one shared with one's sibling.

"You look amazing," Aleena said. She stepped back into Dominic's waiting arm, and he wrapped it around her waist, his hand resting on her hip.

I knew the two of them had gotten a lot of shit when they'd first started out together. Partly because she was his assistant, but there'd been some people who'd been mortified, not by his being her employer, but by the difference in their social status...and their race. Now, the novelty seemed to have worn off and most people barely even gave them a second glance anymore. And the ones they did get were almost always admiration. They were a gorgeous couple.

Almost as gorgeous as their daughter.

"Did you bring Carly?" I asked.

Aleena shook her head. "She's got a new tooth coming in, poor thing."

"Speaking of, I'm going to go call Leann and see how things are going." Dominic kissed the top of Aleena's head before heading towards the lobby.

Aleena shook her head as she watched him go, love shining on her face. "I swear, her teething bothers him more than it does her." She turned back to me. "If he does this with every kid, he's going to drive himself nuts."

"Every kid?" I raised my eyebrows. "Are you...?"

She flushed prettily. "No. Not yet. But we're trying for a second."

"That's wonderful!" I pulled her into another hug, and then handed her off to Isadora who offered her own congratulations.

As I stepped back to Ash's side, something occurred to me. I tried to keep it off my face, but I knew I hadn't succeeded because Ash leaned down to speak quietly.

"Are you okay?"

I nodded. I could feel the flush creeping up my neck and hoped most people would think it was from being overheated. I was hot, but that wasn't what was making me blush. I turned and put my lips against his ear.

"I was just thinking how that might...complicate things."

He gave me a puzzled look and I knew I was going to have to say it.

"Being pregnant. And what they do...what we do..."

His eyes widened, and he glanced down. "You're not...?"

I shook my head. "No, but I want kids, and you said you do too."

"I do." His lips twitched, and I knew he was trying not to laugh. "I guess we'll have to ask them when the time comes. Or buy a really good lock."

I glared at him and he broke, chuckling. It was a low, warm sound, one of his genuine laughs that I always loved to hear. He pulled me into a hug and kissed the tip of my nose.

"Don't worry about it," he said. "We'll figure it out when we need to. Together."

Together. I put my head on his shoulder. I liked the sound of that.

We'd been debating over our honeymoon for months. Ash wanted it to be a surprise. I wanted to have some say in where we went. The one thing we agreed on, however, was that neither of us wanted to spend our wedding night traveling, even first class. We didn't want to be exhausted when we arrived wherever it was we were going.

So Ash decided that we needed a wedding present to ourselves, in addition to our honeymoon. He already had a private jet that he used for work, but he wanted something better for our trip. Better turned out to be a slightly bigger airplane...with a bedroom in the back. It wasn't very big, mostly taken up by the bed, but that was what we wanted it for anyway.

"I don't think I'll ever get used to this," I said as I followed Ash into the plane.

"Being my wife?" he teased.

I rolled my eyes. "Being rich. I know you want me to think of it as 'our' money, but being able to personalize a plane with a queen-sized bed just so we can travel in a bit more style is crazy." I glanced over at him and grinned. "And where is it we're going again?"

We'd come to a compromise about the surprise thing. I'd given him a list of the top places I wanted to go someday, and he would make the final arrangements. That didn't keep me from trying to figure it out though. I especially liked to use it when we were in the playroom. It'd triggered some of Ash's more...interesting punishments.

"Cute." He gave me a sideways look. "You're just lucky I was already planning on telling you our itinerary, or I'd be taking it out on your ass."

I almost told him to do it anyway, but I wanted to know our destination even more than I wanted to continue flirting. "So which is it? France? Italy? England? One of the other places?"

He nodded a greeting at the flight crew, and led me back to a pair of side-by-side seats. We settled in and buckled up as the crew moved around, getting us ready.

"Yes."

I blinked at him, then realized he was answering my question. "Which one? I gave you a list of ten places so I'd be surprised no matter which one you picked."

As the plane began to rumble down the runway, Ash reached over and took my hand, a pleased expression on his face. "All of them."

I stared at him. I couldn't have understood him correctly. Ten different places all over the world, and not just in Europe either. The Bahamas. Alaska. Brazil. I shook my head.

"Another good thing about owning a private plane with a bedroom," he said. "Makes scheduling a ten-destination honeymoon much easier."

"But...we don't...I mean...work..." I was aware I was stammering, but I couldn't stop myself.

"Relax," he said. "I've got it covered. Besides, we're not doing long periods of time in each place. And we're mostly going to be sleeping while we travel." His eyes darkened as his fingers tightened around my hand. "Sleeping and...other things."

Heat spread through me as I listened to him talk about everything he had planned. As we waited for the all-clear from the captain that we could move back to the bedroom, Ash told me each stop, what specific sites he wanted us to see. And when he finished, he looked over at me, a strange, vulnerable look on his face.

"Is all this okay?"

A surge of love went through me, and I knew that question was more than four simple words. He was asking about control, if this was one of those decisions I wanted a say in.

But he was also worried that I wouldn't like his surprise. Not just because of the control issue, but because Ash was actually a lot more vulnerable than people knew, especially when it came to relationships.

"It's perfect." I raised our hands and kissed his knuckles.

"You're perfect." He bent his head and pressed his lips to my forehead.

I was pretty sure I dozed off at some point after that, because the next thing I knew, I was being carried. I hovered there, half-in, half-out. Ash set me on the bed and I felt the soft cotton of expensive sheets beneath my hands. Then my dress was sliding off and I was left completely bare.

Before I could even get chilled, Ash's body was sliding over mine. He settled between my legs and I felt him nudge against me, hard and ready. He propped himself up on his elbows as he looked down at me.

Our eyes locked and he slid inside me, skin against skin. No matter how many times he did this, how often my body stretched to accommodate him, it felt like the first time.

Exquisite.

He moved with slow, steady strokes, each one pushing me to my limit, pressing his body exactly where I needed it to give me the right friction in the right place.

"I'm going to make you come," he murmured. "And this is going to be just the beginning. I plan on making the most of our flight, and only some of that time sleeping."

I whimpered as he rolled his hips, the head of his cock pressing against my g-spot. I ran my fingers through his hair as I arched against him, trying to pull him deeper, more tightly against me.

"I'm going to take you from behind, have you ride me. Tie you up, spank you. Make you beg for more, beg me to stop." He kissed me hard. "You're mine."

"Yours," I agreed. And I was. Heart, body, mind and soul, I was his. And he was mine. He had a ring on his finger to prove it.

Half a dozen more strokes and the pressure inside me exploded. I cried out. He moved slowly, coaxing out every last drop of pleasure. But still, I wasn't satisfied. I'd never be satisfied, no matter how much of him I had. I wanted more. And so, I knew, did he.

He was still hard as he pulled out of me. The expression in his eyes was heated as he sat back on his heels and looked down at me.

Shit. I knew that look.

"Hands behind your knees." His voice took on that authoritative note that made things low inside me twist and turn.

I reached down and hooked my hands behind my knees.

"Lift your legs."

I did. I'd never been ashamed of my body, but a year ago, spreading myself open like this would've embarrassed me. Now, the heat flooding me wasn't from shame, but desire. I didn't know what was coming next, but I knew I was going to like it.

"Pull your knees to your chest." Ash wrapped his hand around his cock, giving it a few slow strokes. "I'm going to fuck your ass now."

I took a shuddering breath. We'd had anal sex a couple times over the past year, but never from this position. He'd told me before that it'd be more intense this way. And based on how he was looking at me, I didn't think he was planning on taking it easy. Not this time.

When a slick finger probed at my ass, I breathed out, relishing the slight burn as the digit pushed past the ring of muscle.

"Relax, baby," he said as he moved his finger in and out. "This is all the stretching you're going to get."

I whimpered, but didn't protest. I knew if I used the safe word we'd established, he'd stop, but I didn't want him to stop. I'd never used it before, and I wasn't about to start now. I trusted him.

I wanted him.

I wanted this.

After just a few moments, he pulled his finger out and something much larger took its place. He eased himself inside, each inch making me gasp and writhe. My head fell back, my eyes closed, but I kept my grip on my legs, holding myself open for him.

Tears leaked out from under my eyelids, and then I felt his thumb brushing over my clit, turning pain into pleasure. He kept up the steady circles until he was fully buried inside my ass.

"Open your eyes."

I forced my eyes open, breath coming in desperate pants. My body was on fire, pain and pleasure fighting. My muscles were shaking, my fingers barely able to hold on to my legs.

"I want you to come again." Ash put his hands on the back of my thighs, holding my legs in place. "Touch yourself."

Obediently, one hand went between my legs. I was still slick from my previous climax, and my fingers rubbed across my throbbing clit. Ash drew back, and then pushed forward, harder and faster than before. I moaned, but my fingers didn't stop, my eyes didn't close. Too much sensation was coursing through me, but as Ash began to drive into me, my fingers never stop moving.

Time lost all meaning, my world narrowing down to our two bodies. To the feel of him stretching me, splitting me in two. The feel of my fingers working the swollen bundle of nerves. The look of need and love in his eyes as he looked down at me.

The sound of my name as he ordered me to come.

The world went white, and I cried out, uncaring that the flight crew could hear me. All I cared about was Ash following me over the edge, his breath hot on my neck as his body slumped down on mine.

When I woke up, hours later, Ash was wrapped around me. Though I had no memory of it, I knew he'd cleaned me up before climbing into bed with me. I knew because he'd done it before. His responsibility as the Dominant in our sexual relationship, he'd shared, was to look out for me even after the sex was done.

I wondered how far into the flight we were, then realized it didn't matter. Ash had taken care of it. I didn't need to do anything. I could let it go.

I snuggled back more tightly against him and felt his cock start to harden against my ass. I smiled. All I had to worry about was how sore I was going to be by the time we finally got home.

I reached behind me, sliding my hand between us until my fingers wrapped around his thickening shaft.

"Mmm..." He made a sleepy sound as he nuzzled the back of my neck. "Ready for another go?"

I gave him a squeeze and heard him suck in a breath. "Definitely ready," I said. "Now I just want to know if you brought the blindfold."

THE END

Acknowledgement

First, we would like to thank all of our readers. Without you, our books would not exist. We truly appreciate each and every one of you.

A big "thanks" goes out to all the Facebook fans, street team, beta readers, and advanced reviewers. You are a HUGE part of the success of the series.

We have to thank our PA, Shannon Hunt. Without you our lives would be a complete and utter mess. Also a big thank you goes out to our editor Lynette and our wonderful cover designer, Sinisa. You make our ideas and writing look so good.

About The Authors

MS Parker

M. S. Parker is a USA Today Bestselling author and the author of the Erotic Romance series, Club Privè and Chasing Perfection.

Living in Southern California, she enjoys sitting by the pool with her laptop writing on her next spicy romance.

Growing up all she wanted to be was a dancer, actor or author. So far only the latter has come true but M. S. Parker hasn't retired her dancing shoes just yet. She is still waiting for the call for her to appear on Dancing With The Stars.

When M. S. isn't writing, she can usually be found reading– oops, scratch that! She is always writing.

Cassie Wild

Cassie Wild loves romance. Every since she was eight years old she's been reading every romance novel she could get her hands on, always dreaming of writing her own romance novels.

When MS Parker approached her in the spring about co-authoring the Serving HIM series, it didn't take Cassie many seconds to say a big yes, and the rest is history.

Printed in Great Britain
by Amazon